# A Compelling Draw from the First Page

"*Blood Dragon Rising*, Book 1 in the Dragon Shadows series, weaves a love story, a fantasy, and an epic adventure into the story of Lisette de Lille, whose marriage to a staid nobleman proves anything but dull.

Just because it's set in the Caribbean and involves pirates doesn't mean that *Blood Dragon Rising*'s audience should be limited to swashbuckling audiences alone. Nor does it represent historical fiction as it follows noblewoman Lisette's much-changed life as she becomes a pirate.

This elusive flavor is just what spices *Blood Dragon Rising* so nicely, keeping it from being a set genre read by expanding the potential of its attraction to a wide range of readers.

G.S. Carline employs especially haunting imagery to capture Lisette's environment and the influences that lead her astray (or, more likely, into the person she really was meant to be). These descriptions of her world and the dragon that haunts it prove a compelling draw from the first page, luring readers to learn more about Lisette's life, powers, and destiny.

Lisette's forceful personality, perceptions, and interactions with a host of women lend an especially vivid, female-driven force to the story which is uncommon in tales of pirates and Caribbean experiences.

From immortal souls and ladies of the house to pirate ships and dragons, G.S Carline creates a

satisfyingly moving story that proves ever-changing, unpredictable, and hard to put down.

It's rare to recommend a Caribbean pirate story to such a wide audience, but libraries will find that it captures the attention of fantasy readers, mystery fans, and pirate queen enthusiasts alike. *Blood Dragon Rising* deserves a prominent place in collections strong in novels that center on a diverse set of female characters whose lives, experiences, and strengths take center stage." *–D. Donovan, Senior Reviewer, Midwest Book Reviews*

"*Blood Dragon Rising* is a fantasy adventure novel about a kidnapped woman who learns to become a pirate and uncovers the truth about mysterious blood dragons, all while seeking vengeance against those who have wronged her. Lush descriptions and compelling dialogue enhance the narrative, but where the writing really shines is in fast-paced action-adventure sequences. Carline has created an incredibly likable character to root for, and it's exciting to see Lisette's defiance in the face of cruelty and the way she redefines herself and her goals throughout the novel. *Blood Dragon Rising* benefits from many genuinely surprising twists that keep the narrative fresh." *–BookLife by Publisher's Weekly*

# Blood Dragon Rising

*Dragon Shadows, Book 1*

By G.S. Carline

Cover art by Joe Felipe of Market Me
(http://www.marketme.us)

BLOOD DRAGON RISING
Copyright © 2022 G.S. Carline
All rights reserved

ISBN-13 978-1-943654-24-6

 Published in the USA by Dancing Corgi
Press

This book is dedicated to my childhood.

# A Brief Note

I love writing fiction because I believe that in fiction is where we find eternal truths. That being said, the Caribbean islands I am about to transport you to, do not exist. I wanted to tell a pirate story and I wanted it to have a Caribbean feel. What I did not want was Caribbean reality. I don't want everyone getting fussy about what year it is and who was ruling Europe and attempting to establish themselves in Jamaica or Tortuga or whatever island that really exists. It means a lot of research on my end just for insignificant details that detract from the story of a young noblewoman who is transformed into a pirate—and more.

So, my story takes place in a small group of make-believe islands, an archipelago if you will, somewhere to the east of Tobago and Trinidad, called Los Peces Pequeña (The Little Fishes). Back in Europe, there are always kings who send nobles to conquer islands because everybody wants to rule the world. And there is magic wherever you look.

BLOOD DRAGON RISING

*Heated blood,*
*Blackened heart,*
*Love and mercy*
*Torn apart.*

DRAGON SHADOWS, BOOK 1

# 1

Lisette stood on her balcony, trying to draw in breath. This evening's gala required her to wear a corset and although it pushed her breasts into two fine mounds, the reward seemed hardly worth the pain. Such was the price for turning twenty.

The sun had sunk below the horizon, but light still fought the darkness, giving the sky an ashen, brooding quality. The island breeze was too warm, and she pushed at the damp curls along her neck. She gazed outward to sea, willing her body to breathe despite its entrapment.

The silver waning crescent of moon flickered as a shadow swept across it. The shadow rotated toward her, revealing familiar eyes that pierced the darkness. Familiar and fearsome.

The first time she saw him she was six years old, and he was plunging his talons through Uncle Luc's chest, tossing her uncle to the ground, and setting him ablaze. Afterward, he'd circled back to her. His large paw pushed her until her back hit the wall.

Her heart pounded violently as the claws extended, brushing their cool hardness against her cheek. The leathery pad of his paw held her tightly. She'd raised her hand to her neck, spreading her fingers for protection. His breath smelled of ashes.

For fifteen years he'd come to her, always near her birthday when the moon was in transition from waning crescent to waxing. The full moon never saw his shape. The new moon hid it too well.

As always, she raised her hand to her neck for protection, mesmerized by the dragon descending before her. She pressed herself against the cold stone wall. There was no room for her in her corset for her furious heartbeat to pound, except to push the beating into her neck and her temples.

The beast's crimson feathers covered a large lithe body, with a line of golden spikes down his back to his tail, which he whipped about like an annoyed cat. His head was almost delicate in structure, with the large liquid eyes and wide nostrils of a high-bred horse. The ridge above his eyes drew a line to two arched horns between his pointed ears.

A combination of many animals, he'd been artfully assembled for a fearsome appearance. And he still smelled of ashes.

Lisette slid to the ground, thinking of escape. The only thing escaping was her consciousness and she struggled to keep from fainting. She sat motionless. Time seemed to stop as he approached. He was terrifying—and beautiful.

His talons extended, encircling her waist, pressing

their needle-sharpness against the corset. Her eyes met his, seeking answers in the silver crescents. His lips curled as he inhaled, causing her to exhale. Their breaths took a steady rhythm, his inhale drawing in her life, hers choking on his smoke and ashes. No words passed between them, but she knew his intentions.

He wanted her dead.

Consigned to her fate, she lifted her chin in defiance. He could kill her, but he would not break her. She would meet her end with one final show of courage.

At the last possible moment, he extended a massive pair of wings in a slow, lifting motion. He gave her a final fierce glare and huffed an ashy breath of smoke before disappearing into the night.

Someone was knocking at the door. Mama entered, sounding impatient. "Lisette, are you ready? Come along."

Lisette tried to shout, but her dry throat could only whisper, "Out here." She closed her eyes, squeezing tears down her cheeks.

The rustle of stiff petticoats covered in silk made its way to the balcony, accompanied by clicking heels.

"What are you doing?" her mother asked. "You are ruining your gown."

Lisette looked up, pushing the words from her mouth. "I saw the dragon."

Her mother helped her to stand and brushed at her gown in silence. The older woman's face paled, though her voice remained steady. "Don't be silly, Lisette. Dragons do not exist, except as a figment of your imagination."

"But Mama—"

"Now, come inside." The tall, regal woman took her daughter's elbow and steered her away from the balcony and back into the chamber.

"But the dragon—"

"Lisette!" Mama's voice turned sharp and commanding. "There. Is. No. Dragon. You will get over this childish hysteria and forget all this madness. Now."

Lisette was still trying to calm her trembling body and she wished desperately to get out of her frock and its vise so she could have a proper cry. Even more, she wished her mother believed her just once. It was not the first visit from this beast, nor their first argument about whether he existed. Mama could not be moved.

"Yes, ma'am." Lisette unfolded the fan strapped to her wrist and waved at her flaming cheeks, drying her tears as well.

"Honestly I do not know what is wrong with you." Mama continued to fuss with Lisette's hemline. "It will be a relief to get you from this house and let Eric deal with your fantasies."

Lisette nodded, still remembering the feel of the talons around her waist.

"There, that's better," Mama said at last. "But why must you scowl so?"

Lisette opened her mouth for one more protest about the dragon but decided against it. "I am joyful, Mama. Eric is a fine catch. I'm sure I shall have a fine life."

"A fine life?" Her mother cocked her head, hands clasped in front of her. "Lisette, you are to be married to a handsome man, to bear him handsome children, and one day to rule this island for France. You act as though it's an enormous bore."

Lisette lowered her head. "Did you love Father when you married him?"

Mama waved the question from the air. "No one in the aristocracy weds for love. Marriage is duty to the Crown. We make unions to strengthen our political ties."

"Don't we fall in love at all?"

"Dalliances are permitted, of course." Mama looked down, shrugging. "Some even have grand passions. But to disrupt the marital state is akin to treason."

Lisette eased herself into a chair and attempted a tired sigh. Her corset rendered it a small huff. "If we are only marrying for political reasons, why must we be virgins?"

The older woman shook her head. "Politics is all about men and power. Either they have a little and want more or they have much, and they still want more. A woman is an object to be possessed and her husband must be the first buyer."

Lisette stared at her mother. "And you wonder that I am not excited."

"We do what we must, for king and country." Mama lifted her chin and glanced at her daughter. "I am assuming you do not need instruction regarding the marital bed."

Lisette shook her head. "Genevieve told me all I need to know."

"Thank the gods for ladies' maids. It's a rather coarse subject to discuss with one's daughter." Her mother stood tall, hands folded at her waist, her left eyebrow arched in judgment. "Try to be happy, dear. Yes, you will have to bed a man you don't love, but at least he is handsome, and you will be the mistress of your own home. In time, you will have children—if you need to love something, you can give them your heart."

"Yes. Children." Lisette attempted a smile, even though she could not imagine anything she wanted less. "Splendid."

Mama glared at her. "Let me be clear. You need heirs. We don't want the Medina family—"

"Yes, yes, the greedy Spanish loyalists will try to

nab Île des Oiseaux for themselves." Lisette rolled her eyes. "Political intrigue bores me so."

Her mother's jaw tightened. "Lisette…"

"Of course, I will not disappoint you." She bowed her head to keep her face from betraying her feelings. "Or Le Roi."

"Good. I shall meet you downstairs." Mama turned and stalked to the door, swishing her gown and waving her right hand impatiently. "Hurry along."

Lisette watched her mother step through the doorway into the hall. The Duchess Juliette de Lille was exquisite, tall and shapely, her skin a delicate shade of the palest blush, like the luster on a pearl. Her caramel hair perched in an upsweep of braids and curls, with a measured amount of tendrils hanging to accentuate her long neck. The swish of her gown was as musical as water running over stone, and every head in every room turned to watch her glide in.

Lisette glanced down at her herself—several inches shorter than her mother, her curves had less room to maneuver in her dresses, and she was constantly battling the Caribbean sun to keep her olive skin from darkening. As for her hair, it was thick, auburn and unruly, like her father's, giving her the look of being constantly in motion. All she had to do to earn Mama's clucking tongue was walk into a room too quickly.

And her eyes…almond-shaped, green with gold flecks, and completely unlike the eyes of anyone in her family.

She sighed and looked in the mirror. Her front teeth were much too large, in her own opinion, and had to be restrained by her lips in order to keep from leaping out as the first thing anyone noticed about her. *No one else in my family has such a mouth full of teeth, why did I get everything that no one else wanted?*

After a few attempts at a ladylike smile, she gave

up and frowned instead, an expression that suited her at the moment. "I suppose my new life can't be any worse than my old one."

A polite knock on the door took her attention. Three raps and the creak of the hinges, it could only be one person.

"Daughter, are you dressed?" her father asked.

Claude de Lille was not a tall man but managed to look that way. His chest was broad and legs solid, giving him the appearance of a fighter. Much like Lisette, his thick auburn hair sat in a curly tangle though for a duke, his face was constantly bright-eyed and smiling.

"Good evening, Papa, I am almost ready." She ran her hands down her golden gown, her fingers lingering on the raised brocade. The dragon crossed her mind then evaporated. Although he was not as dismissive as her mother, the duke was always uncomfortable when she mentioned the subject.

*Better let the dragon alone tonight.*

The duke strode to her and put his hand on her arm, leaning in for a kiss on the cheek. "You look beautiful."

"Thank you," she replied, smiling.

He stretched out his other hand, which held a folded silk scarf. "I've a present for you. Happy birthday."

Lisette took the square from him. It was light in her palm as she unfolded it. She gasped at its contents.

"It's magnificent," she said, pulling out a large emerald on a slim gold chain and holding it high to watch it sparkle. The jewel was deep blue-green with fire in its depths. Its delicate setting glowed a rich golden hue and wrapped about the emerald like a vine. She turned it around, marveling at the goldsmith who fashioned the gold strands that embraced the jewel. On the back, she noticed engraving. Holding it to the light she saw odd lines—a backwards "J" with two dots under it, followed by what looked like a "u" with long tails. "Is this the jeweler's mark? What strange symbols."

"Long ago, on one of my campaigns in Turkey. I was—gifted this. I knew it was just the thing to give to my daughter." He took the necklace from her. "Let me put it on you."

She watched in the mirror as her father stood behind her, clasping the necklace. He fumbled a bit with the delicacy of the catch, smiling at her when he was successful. She regarded the jewel now nestled into the curve above her cleavage, where it glistened with the light. Her eyes caught the green of the emerald and the gold of the dress.

"I was told the symbols mean good luck and fair sailing." He smiled, but she caught the hint of a tear in his eyes. "It suits you."

She turned to him and kissed his cheek. "I shall treasure it always. Sometimes I wish I didn't have to marry and leave you."

"I shall miss you, my Lizzie. But the wedding is months away. Let's think about that later—tonight is for celebration." He took her by the hand and led her to the door. "I must go greet Count d'Auguste. Jules will escort you into the room."

Lisette nodded and walked with him. "Yes, Papa."

The air was cooler as they descended, but there was still a steamy quality to the evening. She dabbed at the moistness around her cheekbones, catching one last tear as she did. The betrothal to Eric would be announced tonight. The wedding would be in a few short months. It was all happening whether she wanted it or not.

She allowed herself a small, resigned sigh. No one cared what she wanted—not even her. Slow, steady breaths brought the scent of night-blooming jasmine, calming her as she walked down the stairs and prepared to start her new life.

She had no idea how new her life would become.

Julian de Lille waited for Lisette at the bottom of the staircase. He was two years younger and already a head taller than his sister, but she still considered herself his defender.

He offered his hand, a mischievous smile on his face. "Ready to make it official?"

"Do not say anything," Lisette warned.

"Me? Say anything?" He wrapped his arm around hers, elbow to elbow. "Why, I would not dare to say that you are marrying a dolt of epic proportions."

"Eric is not a dolt," she managed through clenched teeth.

"Sister, please. Eric is an inbred, from a family of inbreds."

She glowered at him, although she could not think

of an argument. "Eric may not be smart, but he appears to be a good man."

"Beauty follows opportunity, not honor." Jules turned toward the great hall, leading her forward. As they crossed the threshold, his elbow jabbed her in the rib. He winced when he hit the bones of her corset instead. "Ow, your wings are tight tonight, Poussin."

*Little chicken.* She hated that nickname and his spreading grin showed her how much he enjoyed the tease. Her internal fire banked high, reddening her cheeks. She wished to knock him sideways and brawl the way they had done throughout their childhood. Instead, all she could do was grit her teeth and smile in return.

"Beware, little brother," she warned. "You know I always get my revenge."

By the time the pair entered the gala, there was already a large gathering. A trio of musicians provided lively music and most everyone was dancing a grand gavotte, with others helping themselves to the victuals. The room was warm with bodies, swirling with the smell of roasting meats and sweat and flowers.

Candles lit the space, aided by the large open fireplace, making it appear that flames danced from the stone walls. Mirrors everywhere reflected the light and strands of crystal beads hung from the fixtures. A long table of food and drink sat along one wall, leaving the rest of the space for dancing.

Her father was in the corner talking with Eric's parents, the Count and Countess d'Auguste. Jules often compared them to a tall, elegant pair of matched carriage horses, "although not quite as smart." He was not wrong. Lisette recognized the grin her father wore— it was the expression he reserved for when he wished to be somewhere else.

Scanning the room, she saw her mother walking

toward the food, thoroughly engrossed in conversation with a large man—a duke, Lisette recalled. It was difficult to remember the title of every nobleman and woman on these islands, especially when she didn't care.

As she stood in the arched doorway a small, wizened body rushed toward her. The Baroness Elena de Thibault held out her arms to her niece. She wore an ornately beaded maroon silk gown, her greying hair piled high with jeweled combs. The baroness always presented herself impeccably, trying to draw attention away from her face, which, despite her best tricks, showed a history of many sorrows.

Jules stepped back to allow his aunt access to Lisette. He bowed, grinned, and disappeared.

"You look beautiful." Lisette gestured to her aunt's gown, taking an exaggerated interest in it.

She brightened. "Isn't it lovely? I had to beg Luc's mother for hours to pay for it, but it was worth every minute." Her aunt persisted in squeezing gold from her late husband's mother and too much was never enough.

"Honestly, Tatie," Lisette scolded in gentle tones. "If you are in need, come live with us."

"Thank you, dear, but no." Patting her niece's hand, Elena gave her a condescending smile. "I'm afraid your mother does not share my exacting nature when it comes to the finer things. I prefer silk embroidery, not common linen, and definitely diamonds and pearls. My sister has done her best, but even the fine brocade of your gown is cheapened by a mere emerald."

Lisette's hand rose to her necklace but stopped. She would not let Tatie Elena have this moment. Instead, she smiled. "Thank you, it was a birthday gift from my father. I rather enjoy its simplicity."

Her aunt did not notice her mockery. "Do not worry, Lizzie. Fortune sometimes shows up where you least expect it."

Lisette looked away to keep from rolling her eyes. A servant with a tray of goblets caught her attention. "Very well, Tatie. Have yourself some cake and wine, and a good turn around the dance floor."

Her aunt clutched her, fingernails pressing into her flesh and eyes filling with tears. "Lizzie, always remember that I do love you."

"And I you." She kissed her aunt's cheek and turned to the servant.

He stepped up and offered a goblet. It was late season mead, sweet and light, one of Lisette's favorites. She had to be careful not to let it dull her senses. Her heart still quivered from the encounter on the balcony. It would not do for her tongue to loosen and talk of dragons spill forth.

As she took a sip, she spied Eric. He nodded at her and strode across the room. He was a handsome man, tall and broad as a Viking, with golden curls and eyes the color of a bright sky.

Dragons left her mind, pushed aside by Jules' insults. It was true that Eric was not as quick-witted as most, but he was dutiful, and they would have beautiful children. She prayed they would have his looks and her wits.

As he approached, he extended his hand. She slipped her fingers into his palm, curtsying.

"Lisette." He withdrew his hand as he bowed, letting his vision wander past her. "Congratulations on your birthday."

"Thank you. Have you had food or drink? The mead is excellent this year."

Eric looked stiff and wore a most ridiculous grin. "No, I haven't. I fear the music has been so lively, I joined in the dance and could not stop myself."

A striking brunette strolled toward the couple from

out of the crowd. The indigo shine of her gown accentuated her curves, and her gold jewelry gleamed. Her movements matched the music, although she was not dancing. Dark eyes sparkled and red lips curled in a sly smile.

Lady Mercedes de Medina.

"Lisette." Mercedes opened her arms to embrace her. "¡Feliz cumpleaños!"

Lisette's skin prickled with Mercedes' touch. It was like hugging a serpent. She tried to make her step backward appear that she was taking stock of Mercedes' beauty and not retreating in revulsion.

Mercedes always protested that she did not speak French, although Lisette doubted her. Polite as always, Lisette responded in Spanish. "Gracias. You look lovely this evening."

"Ah, not so much as you. Turning twenty agrees with you. What a stunning gown. Your seamstress certainly works with your assets. And that emerald." She fondled the jewel at the edge of Lisette's cleavage. It was all Lisette could do to refrain from shuddering. "Breathtaking."

Mercedes was two years her junior, the daughter of the Count and Countess de Medina, a Spanish family who had recently moved to Île des Oiseaux. The three castles had always been occupied by French nobility, but when Count Thibault died, Spain's king had maneuvered a position on the island and installed his own nobility in the now-vacant castle. The Medina family were welcomed cautiously.

Lisette held her chin a little higher. "Are you having a good time?"

"Oh, yes." Mercedes laid her hand on Eric's arm. "Eric and I have been dancing."

Lisette glanced at Eric, whose blush was advancing up his neck to his ears and cheeks. The way Mercedes purred over her soon-to-be-fiancé would be an insult in most courts. Still, tonight called for manners and not honesty.

"How lovely." Lisette's mouth smiled, even as her eyes did not.

Eric cleared his throat. "Lisette, would you honor me with a dance?"

"Delighted." She shivered as a cold hand took her goblet.

"Let me hold this while you join your fiancé," Mercedes said, as if directing a toddler.

Lisette returned a wan smile and took Eric's arm to join the dancers. After a formal bow and curtsy, they merged with the group, pacing back and forth, shoulder to shoulder, around one another. All the time, Lisette considered his blush, and the looks he and Mercedes had exchanged.

*Perhaps he's started his dalliances before getting married.* "Eric, are you...happy? I mean, how do you feel about our marriage?"

He had taken her hand and at her question, his feet stopped moving, causing her to step into him. Pushing her back, he found his place in the dance again. "Apologies."

Lisette stared at him. A feeling of dread overwhelmed her. She didn't want to do this at all, but there was no way out. "We are about to join houses, and our lives."

"Yes, I am looking forward to it." They turned about another time and he added, "Forgive me. No one has asked me how I feel about, well, anything."

"Nor I." She gave a small shrug. "But we do what we must for our families, yes? King and country."

He looked past her, the redness returning to his cheeks. "Yes, of course. Our families."

They finished the dance and walked to the buffet. Lisette reached for another cup of mead. Long, cool fingers on her arm intercepted her motion, as Mercedes handed her a goblet.

"Here is your cup. I thought you might like something to refresh you after your dance."

"Thank you." Warm from the exertion, Lisette took a long drink of her wine. It tasted a little sweeter than earlier.

"Why don't we go outside and cool ourselves?" Eric's hand was at her back, ushering her toward the balcony.

"Yes, it will be nice to have a quiet moment." She took another sip and walked outside with her soon-to-be-betrothed, leaning on his arm. Her steps wobbled and her vision blurred. She stopped and turned back, toward the great room. "I should have some food. This wine does not agree with me."

Eric glanced over her shoulder. "I'm certain Mercedes would prepare a plate for you."

Tatie Elena stood at the arched entrance to the balcony. She was turning people away, a lace square at her eyes. Lisette nodded and tried to veer toward her aunt, to ask why she was crying, but Eric steered her further outside. They were alone.

*Perhaps he has something to discuss with me. Too bad the wine is making my head so fuzzy.*

They walked to a stone bench and Eric helped her to sit. "Lisette, I need you to understand something."

His voice was low, and his words ran together. Staring up at him, she tried to focus. "Forgive me, understand what?"

"I'm the one who is sorry, Lisette. I didn't intend to do this."

Her tongue grew heavier as she spoke. "Marry me? Oh, yes, it's been hard—"

16

"Eric, isn't it done yet?" Mercedes had appeared, her hands empty.

Eric whined. "Mercedes, do we have to?"

"There is no other way. If she stays, you will have to marry her. You cannot refuse your parents."

Lisette held her head, to stop its spinning. What were they saying? Behind her, the bushes rustled with hidden movements, followed by heavy boots on the stone. She tried to see who it was, but they were blurry in the darkness.

The shadowy figure spoke in a harsh whisper. "Is this the one?"

"Yes." Mercedes sounded aloof, businesslike. "Do you have the gold?"

"Five hundred pieces." Coins tinkled.

"Eric..." Lisette's voice was thick and muddy. "What are you doing?"

"Lisette, it's in our best interest to align ourselves with Spain. Mercedes explained it all to me. Spain controls the trade route. If you and I marry, we'll ruin our island's chance for wealth and political influence."

Even as groggy as she was with whatever Mercedes had put in her drink, Lisette rolled her eyes at her betrothed's stupidity.

"You swear she's a virgin?" the gruff voice said.

Mercedes's wicked laugh was the last thing she heard before everything went black.

Lisette's stomach woke her, pitching and rolling like she'd eaten a bad meal. She pushed herself into a sitting position while her arms complained, and her head throbbed. Her throat was on fire, and she wished desperately to quench it.

Pressing fingertips to her temples did not quiet the drumming, nor did it clear the mushiness in her brain. Her head was too heavy to hold up, so she leaned over as much as her corset would allow, resting elbows on knees.

"Where is Genevieve?" she moaned. "Genevieve!"

She looked up to call for her maid again and saw strange shadows in the darkened space. This was not her bedroom. It wasn't any room in the castle. The smell at last hit her, of wood and rum and mildew and rust and seawater. At first, she feared she might be sick and heave whatever was in her stomach. Then she feared she wouldn't.

It wasn't only her body lurching to and fro. The floor was moving to the same rhythm.

With some effort, she sat up and peered into the dimness. The small room had a round window on one wall. There were barrels stacked everywhere. She had made enough ocean voyages to recognize this as a hold. Staggering to her feet, she fell against the porthole and looked out. All she could see was dark water, peaking and ebbing in windswept curls. To the right, hints of gold and orange lit the crests of the waves. This meant either sunrise or sunset, depending upon which direction the ship was heading.

Aching and nauseated, she leaned against a box and rubbed her head, trying to piece together what happened. Snippets returned of the previous evening— or was it longer ago?

In slow, muddy bursts, she retraced her memory. Eric and Mercedes and bad wine—and now, a ship. At last, she realized—she'd been kidnapped.

"This is unacceptable," she muttered. "I shall have someone's head. When my father finds me and pays my ransom, I shall have his guards hang every dog on this ship and I shall laugh to see them swinging in the breeze."

She plopped down again, exhausted by her hoarse and haughty rant. Mama and Papa were no doubt frantic—well, at least Papa was. What had Mercedes and Eric told them? And Tatie Elena, who clearly knew and yet let it happen. Lisette could barely fathom her mother's sister as a co-conspirator. Jules' face appeared in her mind, taunting.

*He'll never let me forget my mistake. That is, if I ever get to see my family again.*

Fear gripped her heart and she allowed herself a

few tears before righteous anger took over. She pushed herself to her feet, tottered to the door and banged on it a few times.

"Open this door," she croaked, before doubling over in a coughing fit. With nothing to soothe her dry throat, she collapsed to the floor until her spasms stopped.

With no one to listen to her demands, there was nothing to do except cry again, a little harder this time. At last, she quieted and looked up. The light was growing in the room. Sunrise. She brushed at her face and considered what she would do if she couldn't go home. Somehow, she needed to gather her strength and her wiles.

The last words on the balcony came back to her. "You swear she's a virgin?"

*I've been sold into slavery.*

She hoped this was a crew who traded at other ports. If they weren't, she would become their plaything, lucky to live through the experience and likely tossed overboard when they grew tired. If they planned to sell her, at least she would be safe until they anchored at a proper harbor. The captain would not risk spoiling the goods.

*Or am I a service? I wonder how much these brigands will charge Papa for my return. Will Eric still marry me?*

She was willing to enter a loveless marriage to Eric and bear his children, even if she wasn't thrilled about it. Not her ideal life, but it was her duty. Apparently, Eric disliked the notion so badly, he was willing to sell her to pirates.

Marriage would not happen now, and Eric would be lucky to escape with his life if she ever saw him again. That snake Mercedes—what punishment would be enough?

*If they were here right now, I would kill them both. Even Tatie Elena—how could she have betrayed the family?*

She stared at her once-pretty golden gown, pooling around her legs. It was filthy now, with several tears in it. She pulled at the material, trying to smooth it. Rubbing her stiff neck, she discovered her emerald was missing. Having her father's gift stripped from her made it all real.

"Papa, where are you?" She collapsed, sobbing in the morning shadows.

Her sides hurt, mostly from the corset. Standing, she reached up, under the front of her gown, fumbling with the yards of fabric until she found a ribbon. She tugged on it until it came untied, pushed the back of the gown out of the way to find the loosened ribbon and pulled at the lacings. Yards of fat petticoats hampered her progress, so she stepped out of them to give herself more room to maneuver. It took a long time, but at last she was able to put her hands down the front of her bodice and work the corset out.

She threw it into the corner, rid of one tormentor.

Her throat was drier and more wretched. A slurp of rum from one of these barrels would no doubt feel like swallowing fire, but her body's desperation grew. She studied the barrels, looking for an easy access. They all had plugged sides, but she had no way to pull a plug, nor a cup to drink from.

Sitting beside a barrel, she leaned against it. "Probably burn my insides," she croaked, "but at least it'd calm my nerves."

She looked at the locked door and wondered if they planned to keep her in this hold for the entire trip. Which would be worse? Starving to death in her own misery and filth, or tossed to the crew, forced to endure whatever humilities they desired?

*I am the Lady Lisette de Lille, not some worthless village trollop. If they insist on defiling me, I shall insist on dying with honor. But today I shall live, and I shall not show weakness.*

The light shifted across the floor as the sun moved in the sky. It was high overhead when a key rattled in the lock. Lisette stood and prepared for the door to open.

A lanky man in a filthy muslin shirt and wool pants stood in the doorway, his head cocked like a bird. One of his eyes stared vacantly to the side, while the other eye focused on her.

"Mistress," he said with a bow, his Spanish coarse with an accent she didn't recognize. "Cap'n Rocco invites you to dine wif 'im."

Rules and convention had been ingrained, causing her to hesitate. A lady would starve to death instead of dining with a pirate. Survival, however, took precedence over duty. And staying alive required food.

Lisette stretched tall into a regal stance, running her thick dry tongue across her lips. "Lead the way," she managed without coughing.

He gestured down a dark aisle and walked forward. She followed, her bare feet cold on the rough wood floor. The sailor kept slowing, glancing over his shoulder.

"I won't run off," she told him. "How long have we been asea?"

"A week."

She frowned. *A week? That didn't sound possible— I couldn't have been unconscious that long.*

Whether it was a week or a day, it didn't matter. She was on a ship, far from home. Her parents had no idea where to look for her. Eric would have plenty of time to dab his eyes, feign grief, and—what—announce his engagement to Mercedes? She allowed herself one tear of self-pity.

At last, they came to the cabin. The sailor knocked and opened the door, stepping out of the way. Lisette held her spine rigid, lifted her chin, and walked into the captain's quarters. The door shut behind her and she glanced back.

The sailor was gone.

All Lisette could see was a silhouette at the far window. The back of his head was covered in dark curly hair, broad shoulders filled his shirt, and she detected the outline of knee-high boots with a faint blousing of trousers atop.

He said nothing, nor did he even glance in her direction, so she looked around. It was a typical captain's cabin. There were windows on three of the four sides. The wall with no windows was covered in maps, with a rack of swords and daggers in the middle. In front of her was a table containing a roast bird of some kind, surrounded by potatoes and apples.

Beyond the table, against the stern wall was a bed. It was highly improper for an unmarried noblewoman to be alone with a man and a bed, but she was only interested in the food and drink. The captain was still absorbed in whatever he was watching outside. Her stomach grumbled for sustenance as her mouth struggled for moisture.

The sailor who led her aft had spoken Spanish, so she greeted her captor in that language. "Buenas tardes, Capitán. How thoughtful of you to invite me to dine."

He raised his hand, keeping his back to her, and responded in French. His voice was low and silky, with a Spanish accent. "S'il vout plait. Eat."

She sat at the table, looking everywhere for a pitcher of drink. Finding none, she picked up an apple and sank her teeth into its flesh. It wasn't ale, but the juice soothed her throat.

There was a knife at her plate, which she used to carve a piece of what looked like it might be chicken. Or maybe duck. Possibly seagull. She didn't care, it smelled heavenly. Peeling a strip from what she'd cut, she tried a small bite. It tasted moist and flavorful, perhaps more delicious due to her hunger. She shoved the rest in her mouth and cut another slice.

The potatoes were hot, but she juggled one onto her plate, and cut it open to cool. She considered the knife in her hands. The captain's back was still turned. The knife could easily be slipped into the folds of her skirt— or his ribs.

She considered her odds. Kill the captain, sneak aboard one of the small boats, if she could, lower it, if she could, and row it—where? She knew they'd been heading south for the past few hours, but had they always been going south, and for how long?

And what would happen to her if the captain was dead, and she couldn't get off the ship? As the captain, he was the only one holding the crew back from having their own ideas about her. She shuddered—the crew's ideas might see her raped and dead.

Would she be able to kill him? She imagined trying to run the knife into his body. There would be but one chance. If she hesitated, it would be worse than if she never tried.

Eat now, she told herself. Escape later.

As she reached for the potato, she looked up to see the captain standing over her. She froze as she met his eyes. They were deep blue and set in a sharp, tanned face. Dark curls framed his shaven cheeks and a short goatee encircled full lips. His muslin shirt was open, revealing a curious amulet tied around his neck with a dark cord. A golden hand with folded fingers and a heart in the palm—protection against the Evil Eye. The heart was inlaid with a red stone.

She had expected an older man, grizzled, and scarred from battle. While mature, he was muscled and good-looking. And stupid and cruel, she reminded herself. And beneath her. A pirate.

She met his glare with her own regal sneer. "Thank you, Captain. I was quite hungry."

He picked up the pitcher and poured its contents into two goblets. "Rum?"

"Yes, please." As she extended her hand, he moved the goblet away. She stood and reached again, and he continued to step away, keeping it just out of her grasp. The entire time, his eyes never left hers.

Pining for drink, she continued to follow him, staying a cautious distance away. As he gazed at her she could feel heat rise in her chest, the blush spreading up her neck to her cheeks. No man had ever dared to stare at her thus, not even Eric. The corners of his eyes crinkled, no doubt at her embarrassment, though he did not smile.

At last, she stood by the window with him. The harsh midday sun exposed everything without shadows. Still staring, he handed her the rum. She took the goblet and moved back before taking a small sip. It burned but it also quenched.

He stretched his arm in a wide gesture. "Mademoiselle, welcome to the ship *L'Implacable.*"

"The Merciless." Lisette nodded. "A fitting name for a pirate ship."

"I do apologize for this inconvenience. I am not a purveyor of young women, as a rule. But I am in the business of gathering gold and favors. The man who is purchasing your, ah, attributes, owes me both."

"May I ask, Captain, if this man requested me specifically or any virgin?"

His lips curled in a devilish grin. "Odd that you should inquire. He did ask for you by name."

This was not good. "Does he happen to be a Spaniard?"

"Have I been part of a happy rendezvous?"

She scowled. "No. My betrayers sympathize with Spain. Apparently, they have many friends who can do them...favors."

Her free hand knotted into a fist as she grasped the depths of Mercedes' plan, and the ease with which that horrid girl convinced dear, stupid Eric.

"Wicked beasts. I shall kill them." She blinked, startled by her own voice as much as her words.

The captain took a deep drink. All the time, his eyes traveled from the hem of her tattered gown to the top of her disheveled head. Lisette was aware of the thin silk chemise under her gown and remembered the layers of undergarments she had shed in the hold. She blushed again.

"I was going to charge a thousand gold pieces for you, but I think I will ask for more. I was told not to expect too much, but you are much more silk purse than sow's ear."

"Would not my father offer you more?"

"No doubt he might. But there are advantages

beyond gold to be had."

"I don't understand."

"I believe you do." He smiled. "A ransom to your father keeps Île des Oiseaux under French rule. A sale to the Spaniard ensures the island will soon become Spain's."

"And you are loyal to El Rey?"

He chuckled, smoothing his beard. "I am hunted by him. The scourge of his seas, consuming his ships, stripping them of gold and bounty, murdering their captains and crew."

Lisette frowned. "Then why do you want another Spanish-ruled island?"

"I am the shark hunting his meal. More islands mean more ships to bring them goods. More ships for me to feast upon."

She took a hefty swig, liking the burn in her chest and the numbness that crawled into her head. The entire world had decided it was better for her to be sold to a Spanish pig and the island to belong to Spain. No one was interested in what she thought about it.

An idea took shape, one of desperation. "Aren't you afraid I will not give your client his money's worth?"

He laughed. "What, fight him? This gentleman likes his virgins with a little resistance. It makes the taking more exciting. The last time I met with him, he still wore scratches on his face as a badge of honor."

She took another, bigger gulp. "And if he finds out I am not a virgin?"

"He would be most disappointed." Captain Rocco had stopped smiling. "I was assured."

"By people who could not have known differently." Her heart raced as she willed herself not to blush.

"How do I know you are not lying to me?" He stepped into her, gripping her arms, and backing her until she was against the wall. He was so near, his body heat clung to both of them. He reeked of rum and sweat.

She opened her mouth, trying to invent a story of her deflowering. The act itself could be easily described. Genevieve told her of the love and tenderness of her wedding night. Mama considered it no more romantic than rutting livestock. But with whom would she have performed the deed? She had been too proud to dally with a villager, or a stable hand, and Eric had been too proper to even steal a kiss.

"I-I-I…" The more she tried to collect herself, the higher the flame in her face and the heat in her body. "Captain, I am not accustomed to describing my intimacies with strangers."

He pierced her eyes with his, as if he might dig the truth from her. She was so close he could have bitten her. Or kissed her. Her body was trapped against his, their hearts beating at the same pace. His breath came and went in rhythm with her own.

At last, he pushed her from his grasp. "Gods damn it all. This is what I get for believing a Spanish wench."

He threw his goblet against the wall and strode across the floor. The metal clanged against the wood, flinging the rum in a dark stain. Smacking his hand upon the table, he turned toward Lisette.

Cold fear ran through her body as he stomped back to her.

He grabbed her again, roughly, and wrapped his arm around her waist, burying his fingers in the folds of her skirt. His body was taut, eyes narrowed, and his breath came in angry huffs. He pulled a small blade from his belt, and she said a prayer for her soul. She dared not look away, fearing that the moment she flinched, she should get a dagger in her ribs.

Sharp metal slipped between the ribbons that held the bodice in place. Notch by notch, the dagger moved up her spine. Each time, the edge of the blade threatened to turn toward flesh. Inch by inch, a sharp pressure bore into her, turned, ripped ribbon, turned again. Each turn was a tease. With every stroke, the captain lingered, as if deciding whether to slice ribbon or girl.

She awaited the sting, her eyes spilling tears.

With a final cut, the dress puddled around her feet, leaving her in a fine silk chemise, wishing she had not discarded her petticoats and corset. He tossed the dagger and removed his vest and belt.

*So he is going to take me for himself. The captain always gets first servings.* This would not be like Genevieve's story of love. The beasts in the field were the best she could hope for. *When he finds out I am still a virgin, he's going to kill me.*

His large, rough hands grabbed her waist. She pushed away from his chest, but he held firm as a stone wall.

She swept the back of her hand across his face. "Let go of me."

He dropped her to the floor, his eyes wide, and she backed away. She saw pure wrath and regretted her action for a moment. But no one handled her body like that. Not even if they did have a dagger.

Rocco took a step forward but a noise at the door made him stop. "Who knocks?"

The door eased, opening a sliver. "Chunk here, Cap'n. Time to relieve the watch."

"Aye." Rocco grabbed a sword. As he strode to the door, he turned to glare at Lisette, voice menacing. "I will finish with you later."

The door slammed and Lisette collapsed, breath heaving, body curled in a ball. Heavy footsteps passed the door, and more were stomping overhead,

30

accompanied by clanging metal, and shouting. Orders to the crew, no doubt. She rested there, too shaken to move.

"What was I thinking?" she whispered, shedding tears as she squeezed her eyes shut. "He was willing to keep me captive until we arrived at the pig's—I could have escaped. Now he will rape me, then he will kill me for lying."

She propped herself upright and brushed a stray curl from her cheek. Her choices seemed simple. Admit her lie, and hope he believed her. Fight his advances and probably die. Or submit to his desires and perhaps live, depending upon his whim.

She considered what her wedding night with Eric would have been like. There would be no lying or fighting, but there was no love. Not much different than with Rocco—submission to a man's desires, never considering what she wanted.

*For king and country, or for my own survival? In the end, does it matter who I lie with?*

Perhaps giving herself to Rocco would not be so bad if he could help her with her goal of returning to her home. There had to be a way to appeal to him, an offer that would guarantee more than simply the promise of more ships to loot. A plan sprouted, fuzzy and incomplete. If she could fill it in, offer it to the captain, it might give her what she needed in order to get what she wanted.

As Lisette formulated her scheme, she heard a different kind of noise on deck. The crew's shouts became louder and more excited. Rising, she looked out of the windows. The dark form of a tall ship appeared off the starboard side. The glinting sun's rays revealed its flag.

Spanish.

She considered what might happen if Spaniards captured this ship. They might return her to Île des Oiseaux, especially if she offered her father's gold. The ship drew closer, the waiting oppressive. Footsteps overhead increased in speed.

No doubt the cannons would be roaring soon.

Lisette rubbed her neck. Her entire body felt stiff, as if fear and dread locked her bones in place. She looked down at her silk undergarment, so revealing. If Rocco lost the battle and the Spaniards boarded, this would not do. She picked up her gown. It had been in tatters, anyway, but now the entire back was torn apart.

Tossing it aside, she looked around for other options. She found some in a chest at the end of the bed. Inside were shirts, breeches, and a belt.

The captain was easily three times her size, but she slipped into a pair of breeches and cinched them tight with the belt. The shirt engulfed her. She rolled up the sleeves and knotted the hem. The result was a far cry from her noblewoman's wardrobe, but she was in no position to be picky.

After the third time of pushing the hair from her face, she pulled it back into a long braid. She was tying a ribbon from her gown around the end when the roar of cannons shook the cabin and took her legs out from under her. She regained her footing and ran to the window.

Smoke rose from the galleon, splinters still hitting the waves. Rocco had initiated the attack. Lisette held on to a bedpost while the floor underneath swung to starboard. They were coming about to fire again.

The Spanish ship swiveled, smoke puffed from their cannons, and she braced for impact. The explosion nearly knocked her down again, and chunks of wood rained outside. The roar of the cannons was Rocco's answer.

The ships argued this way for some time, one belching at the other, the walls and floor shuddering with each hit. She kept watch as well as she could at the window. *L'Implacable* cut through the smoke and maneuvered ever closer to the other ship, and she got a good look at its figurehead, a large, dark warbird in mid-scream.

"*El Águila Negro,*" she said to no one. *The Black Eagle* was legendary as a warship. Even she had heard her father talk about its exploits against the French and the English.

The sounds of screams caught her attention. Over them, Rocco roared the order. "No prisoners!"

She strained to get a better look. Men on ropes were swinging across in both directions. It would appear each side was going to try to clear the other's decks. There was stomping and shrieking, the clang of metal and moan of death. Waiting for the end was nightmarish, and she wondered how long this battle would last.

The cabin door burst open, and she turned. A Spaniard entered, sword drawn and dark stains on the blade. He was tall and handsome, and fit his uniform well.

"Where's the treasure?" he asked.

"I don't know," Lisette said. "But I am a noblewoman and have been taken hostage from my family on Île des Oiseaux. They would gladly pay gold for my return."

The man smiled. "You don't look noble to me. More like a pirate's wench."

She stretched herself to her haughtiest bearing. "My name is Lady Lisette de Lille, daughter of the Duke and Duchess de Lille, regent of Île des Oiseaux. I was kidnapped by my father's enemies and sold to this pirate."

"My apologies." He bowed and walked to her. "I'd be happy to escort you to our ship and return you."

She nodded. "Thank—"

He grabbed her around the waist with one hand, and, tossing his sword, tore at her shirt. She screamed and pushed at him, as his hand clamped down on her breast, while his tongue slopped up her neck. Winding her fingers into the hair on his temples, she wrenched them violently, causing him to yelp and loosen his grip.

She ran toward the door, falling to her knees as he tackled her. He seized the belt she'd tied around her waist, and yanked on the oversized breeches, trying to remove them. She continued to inch forward, kicking at him to let her go, screaming the entire time.

As he pulled her to him, her hand hit something metal on the floor. Captain Rocco's dagger—she grabbed it and plunged it into his shoulder.

"I said let go of me!" she shrieked.

In an instant, his weight fell away, and hands lifted her. She looked up into the face of Captain Rocco. He quickly set her upright.

"Are you hurt?" he asked.

She shook her head. Behind him, the Spaniard sprawled on the floor. Dead or unconscious, she did not know. Rocco released her, and she adjusted her clothes.

"Keep this door bolted," he said and turned to the Spaniard, but the man had risen from the floor.

He rushed at Rocco, pushing him against the table. Rocco punched him in the stomach. Staggering back, the Spaniard glanced down and picked up his sword.

"So, you want to waste my time here?" Rocco asked, drawing his own blade.

Lisette had never witnessed an actual sword fight. Her own training had been done with Jules and kept a secret from Mama. Even the most vigorous matches she'd seen had the look of a dance. This was ruthless, no fancy footwork or graceful thrusts. The men battled around the table, over the bed and back toward the door, jabbing and taking wild swings, each aiming for the other's torso.

She tried to find a safe corner, but it was nearly impossible. As she backed around the table, attempting to avoid them, she became aware of the dagger in her hand. She had not let go when she stabbed the Spanish pig.

The Spaniard had trapped Rocco against the wall. Rocco stepped aside, tripping on the edge of her discarded gown. His leg slid out from under him and slammed him to the floor. The Spaniard raised his sword to bring it down on the captain's vitals.

Without hesitation, Lisette leapt behind the stranger and pushed the dagger into his back. It slid easily between bones through the meat to the softness inside. She kicked the back of his knees and shoved him down beside Rocco. He fell, his weight pulling the dagger out, leaving the hilt in her grip. Blood covered the blade, up to her hand. She froze, staring at the body, blood staining the Spaniard's coat and pooling on the floor.

He groaned and attempted to stand. Rocco jumped to his feet and put an end to the man's complaints with a slash of his longsword. He ran toward the door, turning at the last moment.

"Thank you. Now, bolt the door behind me."

Lisette continued to stare at the dead man. Blood formed a ribbon of red around his waist and gathered under his arm. His last breath had stopped the fountain. She was glad his face was turned away, where his eyes could not see her. His sword lay just beyond his right hand.

Trembling, she looked down at the dagger, her heart pounding viciously. The blood on the blade turned her stomach while adrenaline pumped her with excitement. Her head felt light and her eyesight blurry. Above, the sounds of swords and guns and guttural screams seeped into the room, but inside these four walls, there was an absence of noise as if silence swallowed even a whisper.

Rocco told her to bolt the door, stay inside, but that seemed impossible. The sounds of the battle frightened and intrigued her. If she stayed one more moment, she would start screaming and never stop. She reached across the dead man to take his sword, feeling its heft.

*This is not my fight. I have no experience. Well,*

*practically none. Julian taught me to fence, but we didn't actually battle. Not like this.*

Still, she could not stay here without going mad. Desperation took her out the door and up the steps. If she could get away from the dead man and breathe fresh air, she might feel better.

On deck, however, there were more dead men and less fresh air. Her eyes watered from the stench of smoke and gunpowder and men and death. Most of the fighting was on *El Águila Negro*, but there were still a few Spanish sailors trying to claim the helm of Rocco's ship.

A burly man in a uniform caught her attention. He was hacking at the rope that held the mainsail. His attempt to disable the ship alarmed her—what if she was stuck in the middle of the ocean with these brigands?

"Stop that!" She stomped her foot.

The man turned his head, spit the word, "wench," and went back to sawing at the ropes.

"I am not a wench. I am a lady." She swept the long blade through his midsection, squealing as she did. He crumpled, and she squealed again.

This alerted another Spaniard, who ran to engage her, his eyes wide. "You're a girl."

"Lady." She slashed at him.

He held his own sword up in defense and parried. His skills were lacking, but he was keen on killing her, which kept her blocking his swings and unable to advance. He had backed her to the helm and around the wheel when Lisette tried a different tactic. She gave him a sly, coquettish smile and lowered her sword a little.

"My, how strong you are," she told him.

He smiled back, no doubt anticipating a very personal surrender. Stepping into him, she pushed his blade away and brought her knee up between his legs. He doubled in pain, and she struck upward, catching him square in the chest. The tip of her sword hit bone, deflecting before sinking into his body.

He fell and she found she was no longer shocked by putting her blade through flesh. Her pulse racing, she looked around for more uniforms to puncture.

Captain Rocco stood, mid-deck, bodies piled around. Men were screaming on the galleon where Rocco's crew slashed their way to any and all treasure. His men who had remained on *L'Implacable* set to work clearing the decks of the bodies, uniformed and pirate. The captain glanced up and pressed his way through the carnage to the wheel, where she stood.

Lisette met him, sword in hand and glaring in defiance. He leaned into her, stinking of gunpowder, and sweat. His fingers caressed her shoulder and traveled down her arm. She winced and glanced down, noting a line of bright red running to her hand, and dripping from her little finger. He wrapped his hand around the hilt of her sword. She let him take it.

"Pretty good with a strange blade." His voice was low. "You seem to have a scratch."

She looked back up at him. "It seems that way."

"Let's go back to the cabin and clean it up." He picked up her long shirttail and wiped at her face. "And dry those tears."

She brought her hand up to her cheeks and felt the wetness, now aware of the catch in her breath. How long she had been crying, she did not know.

He towered over her, and she swayed, her head spinning from the fight and her body still pulsing with agitation. If the captain took her now, she wouldn't fight him—or maybe she would. Maybe she'd mount him in a frenzy and enjoy it. Maybe she'd kill him. She no longer knew what she was capable of.

All she could do was turn and walk down the steps, back to Rocco's cabin, where they would be alone.

Behind her, the Spanish crew continued to scream.

Lisette walked straight into the room, to the pitcher on the table. With no goblet nearby, she picked it up and drank. It was warm and biting. She took several burning gulps, each sting slapping her further out of her hysterical shaking and into a calmer disposition.

"Your goblet's over there." The captain gestured toward the window, not far from the man she'd stabbed.

In the late afternoon air, the smell of death commanded her attention. She turned away from the body, holding her hand against her nose. "Couldn't he be removed?"

Rocco opened the door and whistled. Within moments, one of the crew dragged the dead man away. A small lad of no more than thirteen, wiry and unkempt, followed with a bucket and rag. He sloshed the dirty water around the wood floor, until he had replaced the dried bloodstains with a wet spot of questionable cleanliness.

As fast as he had arrived, the boy scooted from the cabin, making eye contact with no one. Lisette recalled the housekeeper at the castle—she would have never accepted this half-hearted mopping. She stepped around the puddle and fetched the cups, pouring both of them a full drink.

"Congratulations, Captain. I hope that ship had plenty of riches."

"Doesn't matter. It was a Spanish ship. I burn them all, rich or poor." He nodded toward the table. "Sit down. Take off the shirt."

She frowned and pulled the shirt around her tightly. "I shall not."

"You're injured. Take off the shirt so I can patch you back together."

She looked down at the torn sleeve. The cut was not large, but it was deep. She eased herself out of her top. Her gut still tightening, she held the shirt in front of her as she sat next to him and looked at her arm. The blood had eased its flow, and the paths it had taken downward were crusty.

The captain ripped the shirt from her, doused it in rum, and pressed her wound. She yelped and pulled her arm away, but his hand was firm.

"Sit still." His voice had the same bark as when he gave orders on deck. He gestured to her filled goblet. "Drink that."

His commands made her want to slap him for insolence. She glared at him, huffed, and held her arm out for treatment. "Thank you…I guess."

"You saved my life." He continued to focus on her arm. "And threw in with us on deck. Why?"

"I don't know." She gazed toward the wet spot on the floor, where the dead man once sprawled. "I told him who I was…offered him gold. He tried to rape me instead."

"Not the most gracious response, I admit. But what about the men on deck?"

She shook her head and took a sip of her drink. "I realized no Spanish ship would take me home, not for all the gold I could offer. When I saw those men trying to destroy the only ship who might be able to deliver me, I—" She turned to look at him. "I want to go home."

Rocco frowned. "I'm afraid that's not possible. Besides, what is back there now? The island will belong to Spain, if not now then soon."

"I understand that, but I am worried about my family. A lot can happen in a week."

"What do you mean?"

She stared at him. "The sailor that brought me here said it's been a week since we left my home. I'm not sure I believed him, but—"

"One-Eye told you a week?" Rocco leaned back and roared in hearty laughter. "One-Eye don't know time!"

Lisette felt the warmth blooming in her chest, up her neck. "How long has it been?"

"A day. Or will be, with the setting of the sun."

She pounded the table with her free hand. "Gods damn it."

"If it's any consolation, it will take us little more than a week to get to the buyer."

She considered her original plan, to convince the captain that this viscount wouldn't want her. It wouldn't work. The captain was wrapping her arm now. He didn't seem to mind if he was delivering a virgin or not. She watched the muslin strip winding around her pale skin, layers neat, lined up. Or maybe he did mind.

"The buyer expects a virgin. No doubt he will kill

me when he discovers my lie."

Rocco frowned. "Pity, but I shall still have my gold."

"He will surely think you cheated him on purpose." She needed another, better plan. "Won't that ruin your reputation?"

"Not really. I'm a pirate."

"No retribution? No revenge?"

He shrugged. "He's not a big man. Viscount. They're always little men who rail against being little men. His brother rules the island—he is a count, so there's always a little jealousy."

"What if you sold me to him, and I escaped…" She tipped her goblet, but there was no more rum, which was just as well. Her brain felt fuzzy, and her body was entirely too relaxed.

He grinned. "I very much doubt that would happen."

"But IF I escaped…" She frowned. "And returned to your ship…you could take me home, and my father would give you a reward. Double the money I make for you."

"Or he could hang me. I am a pirate."

"Not if I tell him you helped me."

Rocco scowled. "After kidnapping you, selling you to the viscount, making you fight your way back to the ship, I hardly think you will tell him that."

He had a point. She spoke quickly. "What about a ransom instead of a reward? The end result is the same—more gold for you."

He paced, rubbing a worn, silver band on his finger. "That won't work. First of all, I know the viscount. You'll not escape. I imagine he'll kill you when he finds out you're not even a virgin."

The rum took control of her mind, pulled down her

defenses. "It's possible that I lied. In truth, I've never…"

His fist slammed the table. "I'm not sure what makes me maddest—that you lied to me or that I almost ruined my property."

"Apologies, Captain, but can you blame me for wanting to escape?" Lisette talked faster, to keep him from killing her. "At the castle, someone gave me something to make me sleep. What was it? I could slip it in the viscount's drink."

"No." He stared at her, his expression one of both hate and pain. "You will go to Barragan. Whether you live or die—it will be out of my hands."

His voice sounded like her death sentence. Lisette's eyes burned with tears, her chest tightened with the desire to weep, but she straightened her shoulders and threw her goblet at him. He ducked and tossed his goblet to join hers before striding toward her.

"I am telling you. I am a virgin." She lifted her chin but could not stop her body from shivering. "And a noblewoman."

"Nobility counts for nothing on this ship." He grabbed at her, and she shuffled back, falling against the table. "Get into my bed."

"Absolutely not." She scrambled for an exit, while his hands reached for her belt. It untied too easily, and the oversized breeches fell to her ankles.

He leaned in, his beard brushing her face, his lips teasing her ear. "There is no place for you to go. Get into my bed or I throw you outside to the crew."

Her neck craned away from him, and she brought her hands up to push, hit, slap him away from her. He caught both wrists and shoved her against the wall, trapping her against his body. The thin silk of her chemise accentuated the curve of his muscles, down to the swelling that pressed from his breeches.

"Very well," she whispered, defeated. Her stomach churned with dread, but she held herself as tall as her short frame could stretch. It was the moment he had promised, to deal with her. She would not bow to him.

Turning, she strolled up to the platform, taking her time and gathering all the haughtiness her nobility could muster. "Crude, but I suppose this bed is sufficient. And where will you be staying, Captain?"

His expression flashed from a cold glare to confusion to anger. "Wherever I please, Girl. Do not forget that."

She kept her backbone straight and her face cool and dismissive. "As you like," she said, before slipping under the covers.

He walked to the bed and stared down at her. Tearing the sheet away, he kept his eyes on her face, while his hand stroked her shoulder, down the side of her body. At her breast, his fingers traced the curve and she held her breath, glaring at him.

His face clouded over, and he laid his hand upon her neck, his fingers pressing. Her breath came harder, more labored. Fear took her. She opened her mouth to beg for her life, put her hands at his arm to press it away. He bent down, his breath warm on her ear and she closed her eyes.

"I will save you, Girl, for now. But do not forget I am a pirate. I owe you nothing."

A bell rang on the deck somewhere, and the captain tossed the covers over her. Boots tromped across the cabin, and the door slammed. When she next opened her eyes, she was alone.

Lisette lay, curled into a ball, limp with fatigue. *I was supposed to be a lady in a castle, not the property of a pirate. And now, I have killed three men. A murderess, without a priest to confess to. Is committing murder more sinful than lying in a pirate's bed?*

Frightened and awaiting his return, she fell into a restless sleep.

A loud thud woke her. She sat up and grasped the covers. There was a hint of light on the horizon, sun's rays pushing back the night. The door swung a little, and she heard a soft groan. The closest thing to a weapon available was the candle next to the bed. Not perfect, but better than nothing. Clutching it with one hand, she held the covers with the other, aware of her thin chemise.

Captain Rocco burst in, banging the door shut behind him. He shuffled toward her, yawning, wearing only a pair of thin cotton drawers.

Lisette held onto the candle as he lurched to the opposite side of the bed. She had never seen such a nearly naked man before. He was muscular, tanned, and had tattoos across his shoulders. She had nothing to compare it to, but his drawers hid nothing, and the outline was substantial.

A small gasp escaped her.

"Shh. Hush, Virgin." Rocco put a finger to his lips. He climbed into bed and stretched out, pulling at the covers.

This was it, then, when he would take her. She wished he would do it and end her apprehension. Virginity wasn't worth this fear.

It took all her courage to keep her voice steady. "Just, get it over with."

"Sleep, Girl. Word of honor, I shall stay on my side of the bed." He turned his back to her, and she watched his body relax before her own eyes closed.

The room was much lighter the next time she woke, although the sky outside was fogged. The air was cool and filled with the scent of the sea, a commingling of green, vibrant life and stagnant death. As she rose into consciousness, her arms were around something warm and cozy. It was the captain's back.

A brief notion of ladylike behavior flashed across her mind, and Lisette froze. Easing herself away, shivering at the cold sheets, she closed her eyes again.

An arm across her midsection opened them some moments later. She looked over at Rocco, still asleep, seeking warmth as she had. He wrapped his body around hers and buried his face into her hair. Staring at the ceiling, feeling the ship's roll, she was aware of his arm, draped under her breasts, and curled around her ribs. A heavy leg leaned onto hers, his hair scratchy. Her side pressed into his torso, and she could feel the outline of his entire body, in detail, along her skin.

Again, she held her breath, thinking of all her mother's instructions on what ladies do and do not do. This was definitely on the do not do list.

Warm lips nuzzled her neck, aided by a moist and tickling tongue. They kissed and suckled their way upward, where they teased at her earlobe.

*Unacceptable!* She pushed him away. This might be inevitable, but she would not surrender easily.

"Tempest," Rocco whispered, and rolled back to his side of the bed.

*Tempest?*

He was still asleep, caressing her while he dreamed of another. Oddly, this made her relax a little.

Her mother's voice was in her brain, scolding her, telling her this was wrong, and she should die protecting her honor. She looked over at the windows, watching the light dance on the horizon. It was good to be alive, even if this pirate ultimately took her by force. Honor wasn't worth dying for.

He moaned for Tempest again, and Lisette felt the love in his voice, along with heartbreak. She didn't believe in romance. An arranged marriage had always been planned for her. Now she reconsidered. People fell in love. Sometimes they were nobility, sometimes they were peasants.

Sometimes they were pirates.

Rocco took a long breath and sank deeper into sleep. Lisette turned to stare at the ceiling and listen to the water lapping against the ship, while she imagined torturing Mercedes, and rewarding herself with a night of pleasure with her beloved, whoever he might be.

The sun was high, the fog gone when she next opened her eyes. For a moment, she forgot where she was and what had happened. When she did remember, she hoped yesterday was a dream.

One quick look around proved her wrong. Here she was, in a strange bed, in a room that tilted to and fro. She took a physical inventory. All limbs were still here, in working order. Nothing particularly sore, apart from a few general aches. She let her fingers wander to her legs and lifted the covers to examine everything. No pain, no blood, and no memory of being invaded.

As she lifted the covers, something fell to the floor. She looked down and found a pile of clothes. Someone had left them, possibly Captain Rocco. Was that his first name or his last, or his only one? Maybe pirates didn't require more than a single name.

Lisette rose and picked the clothes from the floor—a plain cotton slip and brown frock. She put them on while she wondered where Rocco procured them. Did he entertain women often? There was hard bread, cheese, and dried fruit on the table. A pitcher held some kind of drink. Her stomach growled at the sight of food. Sitting at the table, she cut a chunk of bread from the loaf.

She had almost finished her meal when the door opened, and Rocco strode in. He took no notice of her, pouring himself drink and sitting at the opposite end. After filling a plate, he finally spoke.

"We will not be in port for six more days." His eyes were on his meal as he spoke. "You will stay in the cabin at all times. I'll have my cabin boy provide you with water and soap to freshen yourself each day. When you require the latrine, I will have someone escort you."

She gestured toward the windows and the open sea. "Afraid I might escape?"

A guttural noise, nearly a growl, punctuated his look of annoyance. "I like to keep my goods intact. My parcel should arrive looking her best."

The blood rushed to her face. His tone was that of a merchant selling a cow and not a very fancy cow at that.

"Where is my silk dress?" She leaned away and pointed to her clothes. "These are not exactly finery. By the way, what woman gave these up so willingly?"

"All of them." He smirked and cut another large chunk of bread.

The early morning of close bodies ran on in her mind, and his exploring mouth lingered on her skin. Stabbing a piece of cheese with her knife, she pursed her lips, tried to remain silent, and failed.

"By the way, who is Tempest?"

The glare he shot at her sucked the air from her lungs. Rocco pressed his thumb along the ridge of his dagger. His jaw tightened, but she glimpsed pain in his eyes. They sat in the silence, hearing only the creaking of the wood.

"Survive Barragan and escape, and I will return you to your island. In the meantime, you will stay here in my cabin, without complaint." He rose and went to the door, pausing long enough to snarl, "Do not ask about Tempest again."

Lisette could only watch the sunlight cross the sea for a brief period. She considered taking a nap, but instead explored the captain's cabinets. Most of them were filled with weaponry, maps, and a compass. One drawer held a collection of trinkets. The shells, beads, and ribbons surprised her, until she picked up a scrap of parchment with the words "Always, Tempest" written on it.

This woman obviously meant something to Rocco.

Shutting the drawer, Lisette turned to another, taller cabinet across from the bed. It was filled with bottles, but the shelving appeared shallow for the space. She moved the bottles aside and tapped at the back. The wood gave slightly, so she pushed at it. A panel opened, revealing a cache of bound papers, topped by a small wooden box.

She picked up one of the manuscripts and opened

it. There were pages and pages of stars, charted, with notes about each one in a crisp script. After studying a few pages, she put them aside and picked up another. More navigational notes, basically an advanced instruction book on how to sail a big ship through bigger waters.

There was also a chart of the moon's phases, made to be overlaid on a calendar. Someone had drawn a circle around the new moon and its waxing and waning. Inside the circle, they had written "Dragon Eyes." A dragon's shadow darkened her thoughts and she shuddered.

Turning her attention to the box, she found a vial, wrapped in a small square of paper. A poem had been written in a flowery script.

*Heated blood,*
*Blackened heart,*
*Love and mercy,*
*Torn apart.*

The vial was empty, save for a dark brown crust on the bottom. Under the vial were letters. She opened one. It was written in Spanish, in a delicate hand.

*My dearest Tristan,*

*I am counting the days until your return. Our little home is as you left it, except there is a new count, Juan de Medina. He is a large, ill-mannered Spaniard, and I am uncomfortable around him. His avarice extends past food and drink, to women, and to excess of all manner.*

*I miss your arms around me at night, the warmth of your breath in the hollow of my neck. I miss our bodies entwined in love, and the late nights of talk and laughter. The crones in town keep asking me how it is we do not have children yet. I tell them we have not yet been blessed, but their tongues are wagging behind my back. I pray they do not discover our sheepskin secret!*

*Let the days grow shorter and bring you to me quicker.*

*All my love, Tempest*


It was hard to picture Rocco having a first name, let alone, "Tristan." Lisette put the other manuscripts back on the shelf, closed the panel, and rearranged the bottles, hoping the captain would not see the dust had been disturbed.

*Who am I kidding? He'll realize it immediately.* She found a rag in one of the drawers and dusted all of the shelves, the cabinets, and the furniture. *I can tell him I kept myself busy.*

The sun was deepening into its late afternoon shades of crimson and amber when she sat on a bench by the window and opened another letter. She checked the dates. The first one she read was almost twenty years ago—was the captain that old? Each letter went back further into time. She read the story of a woman who was resigned to her husband's fate but yearned for him. Some were day-to-day minutia, but some were personal. Yes, Tempest assured him, she would always love him.

The cabin boy from the previous evening appeared at the door as if blown in by a harsh wind. Lisette leapt from the seat and hid the letters behind her skirt. The boy ignored her and set about clearing the table of its morning contents, so she wandered to the bed and slipped them under the mattress.

"What is your name?" she asked.

"Me name is Willie." His voice had a croak to it, as if it couldn't decide whether it would ring high or low. "But Cap'n calls me Poussin."

"Little chicken, eh? I know a boy named Julian

who calls me Poussin." She helped him stack the plates. "I don't care for the name. Do you?"

"Pardon, m'lady, but we ain't got time for being friendly. You be leaving us shortly." He juggled the dishes in one hand as he opened the door with the other. "I'll be bringing th'evening meal next."

As soon as he left, she rushed to the letters and put them back in their hiding place. Rocco might join her for dinner. He couldn't find anything amiss.

True to his word, Poussin returned bearing another roasted bird of some sort. This time there were no potatoes but there were other root vegetables on the platter. He bobbled a bit with the food in one hand and the plates in the other, so she came forward and helped him set things on the table.

"Ya don't have ta—" he began.

"I enjoy helping." She placed two knives beside two plates. "You're not much younger than my brother, and I miss him."

She worried about her entire family. The further away they sailed, the more days that passed, the more anxious she grew.

"Poussin, do you have a family or a home?"

He jumped away from her as if she'd poked him. "No, m'lady. And you don't ask me no more questions."

His response was startling, but he dashed from the cabin before she could say anything else. As she sat at the table, her foot kicked something. She picked it up— it was a large feather unlike any she'd ever seen. She laid it across her hand.

The shaft was transparent and hard as an iron blade with a needle-sharp point. It nestled in her palm, running fully from the tip of her middle finger to her wrist. The plumes growing from the shaft were long and silky, flowing over thumb and pinky finger. The feather was dark red. It reminded her of the stain from the Spaniard.

She spent a few minutes playing with her discovery, stroking its softness, until footsteps neared the door. Instinct told her to hide what she'd found. Rushing to plop into a chair, she stuck the feather in her skirt's pocket.

The captain entered, carrying a pitcher and two goblets. Pouring two large draughts, he handed one to her and sat. They ate without conversation. All the while, she stared at him, trying to reconcile the educated man with the steadfast lover and the ruthless murderer. As for Rocco, he never glanced at her, not even under her steady glare. At the end of his meal, he rose, gave her a slight bow, and left.

She waited for him to come back, wondering what tonight would hold. Eventually, the door opened, and Poussin entered. He carried a piece of fabric, which he laid on the table.

"A gift from the cap'n. He says he'll see you in the morn." Turning quick, he scurried out and shut the door behind him before she had a chance to say a word.

She picked up the material. It was a fine silk chemise, sheer ivory, trimmed in lace. She undid her clothes and tried it on. It was a bit long but fit her curves nicely. Maybe too nicely. The bodice barely contained her breasts, the lace struggling to span her cleavage.

As she moved around the cabin, blowing out candles, she caught her reflection in the windows. A memory overtook her, of being a little girl and riding in a closed carriage through darkened streets. Women stood outside the taverns, leaning against the stone walls, and sassing the men who walked by. Their clothes were bright and gaudy, exposing a little too much ankle and an impossible amount of décolletage.

She went to the washbasin, splashed a bit of water on her face, and looked again. Cleaner skin made no difference.

*I look like those women. Wanton. Loose.* There was a hardness around her eyes now that matched a charred quality in her heart. It had not been long since she was kidnapped and yet, how quickly she had changed.

"It doesn't take much time," she told her reflection, "for your life to be ripped away from you."

She snuffed out the last candle and slipped under the covers. Poussin said the captain would not return until the morning, and she wondered whether that meant before or after she awoke. Perhaps he would come in with the dawn again, having Tempest on his mind. She glanced at the wall across from the bed, where so many blades hung, and considered taking one to sleep with. If Rocco tried to ravage her again, he might wake up to a knife in his ribs.

But then what? There would be no escape from the crew, once they discovered what she'd done. Fighting Rocco might save her virginity, but at the cost of her life.

As a noblewoman, chastity was one of those attributes that lifted her from the village maids. Manners were crucial, bloodlines were a gift from God, beauty was Heaven's extravagance, and purity was paramount.

In her short time away from home, Lisette could see it was all useless. Courage and cunning were the only things worth cultivating, the only things necessary to surviving this world. Manners were a façade, useful for the manipulation of others. Bloodlines were random and undeserved. Beauty was dependent upon another's eye.

Virginity was a curse.

For seven days and nights, the captain took his meals in the cabin, held brief, terse conversations initiated by Lisette, and left before sunset. Each morning, he staggered in with the dawn. His routine did not change—of falling into bed and almost instantly to sleep.

Lisette made certain she was awake and clothed when he entered, watching the sunrise on the water. She would greet him with a nod and be ignored in turn.

After she finished Tempest's love letters, Lisette turned to Rocco's notes on navigation by the stars. She found she enjoyed the rules and logic by which the stars were plotted, recognized, and followed.

"Who taught you to sail, Captain?" she asked one evening as she sliced into a roasted potato.

"Sailors."

She tried not to let his brusque answer affect her attitude. "A pirate ship?"

"No."

"A French ship?" she snipped. "A merchant's vessel? A rowboat?"

"Spanish." He rolled his eyes. "We sailed for the King's armada."

"The same Spaniards you loot and pillage?"

He shrugged. "Spain and I have parted company."

"So you have said. I am fascinated by the idea of navigating by the stars. Do you always recognize the stars over each sea?"

"Yes." He rose and walked to the window. Pointing a little upward, he said, "Each ocean has its stars for each season. You see that brightest star?"

She walked over to the window and gazed in the direction of his hand. "Yes."

"If we were headed for Tortuga, it's what I'd use as my guidepost, to make certain my bearings were correct. And that trio of stars?" He pointed to the far left. "That's the path to Tobago."

He stood close, strong and calm in the moment. It nearly made her forget he was at heart a ruthless man, except for the love he had for a woman named Tempest. She turned to meet his gaze—so near, a single move would join their lips. With no warning, his expression hardened.

"Tonight, you will be delivered to Antonio Barragan. I will send Poussin in with your gown. There is no lady-in-waiting, so my little chick will have to do."

He turned and left the cabin, and a shadow fell on her heart.

Poussin soon entered, carrying too much fabric for him. He tripped on its many layers, struggling until he reached the bed and could lay the dress down.

"Here is your gown. Cap'n says...I am to help you." His face burned scarlet, all the way to his ears.

Lisette picked up the dress and studied its construction. "Help me spread it out here on the floor. Then turn your back to me."

They got the skirt unfurled so she could find the center. The young boy turned away, hiding his face in his hands. She slipped out of her frock, leaving only her chemise. Tiptoeing over the indigo swirl into the middle of the fabric, she pulled the waist over her hips, slipped her arms into the sleeves, and held the bodice up to her chest.

*That corset in the storage room would make this look a lot better, but one must make do.*

"All right, you may turn around."

As he looked up, she turned her back to him. "Know how to lace a dress?"

"Never laced a dress, but I laced plenty of jerkins back home." Cold, bony fingers took the ribbons and wove them in and out.

"Be sure they are tight." She blew out her breath and held it, trying to get the bodice as snug as possible. "How long have you been with Captain Rocco?"

"Don't know. Ain't got the time to count time."

"Do you know who Tempest is?"

The fingers stopped their work. "That name ain't spoken here."

"So I gathered, from the captain. But we are not with him, at this moment."

Poussin was not agreeable. "Don't matter. I ain't talkin'."

She frowned and tried the trick she always used on her brother. "You might as well tell me, Poussin. If you don't, I'll tell the captain you did."

He relented, pouting. "She was Cap'n's wife, long ago. He was in the Spanish Navy. Come home from a trip an' she was gone. Word was, some local count took her, like you'd steal someone's prize mare. By the time he hunted 'er down, she was dead. Cap'n raged into the castle, an' tried to kill the count. Count called him a traitor. Tried to put him in his dungeon, but he escaped." The boy finished his duty and she turned around. He shook his head. "That's when the Cap'n's heart blackened. Stole this ship from the Spanish fleet and run up the skull 'n' crossbones. He's been piratin' ever since."

It made so much sense. The ruthless man was not heartless. Simply broken and hurt and angry. Poussin handed her a hairbrush.

"Cap'n says to do somethin' wif your hair." The young boy opened the cabin door. "He'll be back for you later."

"Thank you for your help," she said. "I am most—"

His exit, slamming the door, cut her off.

"—grateful."

Brushing her hair and braiding it, Lisette pictured Genevieve's warm fussing over the curls and combs, and nearly cried. Soon she would go into a stranger's home and would be expected to fight for her honor. The stranger expected her to lose.

She had other plans.

Searching the drawers, she found a small leather sheath with straps. After, she checked the wall for a dagger that would fit the leather. There were several, but only one slid in and out of the sheath as though they were a pair.

Lisette raised her skirt and tied the sheath to her upper right thigh. Feeling about the gown for a seam on the right side, she found one and carefully opened it. She did the same for the chemise. From the skirt, she stuck the dagger through the openings she had created and laid it into the sheath. She practiced a few times, reaching through the skirt, finding the dagger. It pulled it out easily.

Now she felt a little safer.

She picked up her discarded frock, folded it, and placed it on the bed. The feather in her pocket made a crease. Taking it out, she wiggled it down the front of her bodice.

"Come along, feather. You might bring me good luck."

The cabin door opened, and Rocco appeared. He scrutinized Lisette, from top to bottom. "I suppose, since he asked for you by name, your appearance isn't important. Still, I like to think my goods are of exceptional quality."

"Do I meet with your approval?"

He studied her again, moving closer. When he was looming over her, he pinched her cheeks, giving each one a little slap. "You're a little pale."

She stepped back, tripping on the hem of her dress, and scowling. "You could have just told me."

As he turned away, a resolute sadness crossed his face. He pushed his shoulders back and cleared his throat. "Anything else?"

"Have you any shoes?" She lifted her skirt, displaying bare toes.

"Of course." Walking to the door, he whistled, and muttered a command.

Moments later, Poussin ran in, carrying a pair of satin slippers. Rocco motioned to a chair and knelt beside it. She took her seat, and he gently guided each foot into a shoe. They were a little large but he laced them tightly so they would at least stay on. When he was done, he stood and offered his hand.

She accepted it and allowed his well-muscled arm to lift her upright. They left the cabin and stepped onto the deck. It was the first time she'd seen it since the battle two weeks ago. The moon was halfway to fullness, the masts outlined in the dim light. A black flag waved from the top, painted with a pair of crude white skeletal hands under a skull. The air had cooled, and a breeze fluttered across her shoulders. It would have been a beautiful night to stroll around, and Rocco's arm was strong and comforting.

It was a pity that she was a captive on a pirate ship, and that Rocco was her captor.

Most of the men had been on the island for the day. A single longboat waited to be lowered. The shoreline was dim in the half-moonlight and lights from buildings winked in complicity. The captain paused at one of the boats and nodded to a crewman, who grabbed Lisette and hoisted her in as if she was a sack of flour. The captain swung in beside her. Soon they were on the water, the large sailor rowing them toward shore.

"Take this." Rocco handed her a vial. "Put it in his drink and he will sleep within moments."

She smiled and stuffed it down her bodice, while her stomach churned a sour lump. Glancing at the captain, and the shore, she prayed that she didn't become ill. She pressed her hands against her skirt, touching the hilt of the dagger for solace.

This had to be Isla de la Soledad. The de Lille family traded with their merchants, and it was the closest island in the direction they had been heading. She had hoped to visit one day.

Not like this, however.

Once ashore, the captain escorted her through the streets of a loud, shabby corner of town. Raucous music rang through the large inn, its porch and boardwalk splintered and sagging in the early evening light. The scent of frangipani almost masked the odors coming from the open windows, but she could still detect a heavy tang of rum and old ale in the air. Rocco's hand at her elbow gave her the bravado to stroll as if she belonged there.

Women with kohl-rubbed eyes and painted lips called to the pair as they went by, offering a night of pure delight. One young man got in on the action, proposing a "taste of a real man" according to him, although a steely glance from Rocco silenced his boasts.

They arrived at an inn furthest from the main street, but close to a small cove. Even in the dimness, this place looked to be the worst building of them all. Gray, dilapidated, it leaned toward the water as if it might topple. Lisette made careful note of her surroundings for when she made her escape. Rocco steered her toward a shoddy stairway careening up the back of the structure.

She stopped. "I thought this was a wealthy man."

"Oh, he is." Rocco continued to herd her up the steps to a door at the top. "He likes to come here to indulge in his fantasies away from prying eyes with higher morals."

Her heartbeat skipped, and she drew back, grasping Rocco's arm. His body cradled her for a breath before stiffening and setting her on her own. He held his hand at the door to knock, whispering in her ear, "Good luck."

The softness of his lips lingered.

The door opened on the third rap, and there stood a small, preening man with ink-black hair and a pencil-thin mustache. He was a velvet dandy, decorated in brass buttons and golden braids, with pale hosiery emphasizing his thin legs. His face was skeletal, his complexion waxy and pocked.

"Antonio." Rocco held his hand out.

The man shook it and lowered his arm, but Rocco's remained.

"That's a fine greeting, but I require my gold." Rocco's exacting statement sounded more demanding in Spanish.

"First, let us look at the package." Antonio said.

Rocco led Lisette into the room, giving her a small jerk to get her through the doorway. "You know, Antonio, when I agreed to this sale, I had no idea who this girl was. She is not just a virgin for your playtime. She is a pawn in your political games. I think fifteen hundred sounds more reasonable."

Antonio frowned. "We had a deal, Rocco."

"You had a deal with a girl. What does she understand about bargaining?" Rocco paused, a sinister gleam in his eye. "Perhaps your brother the count could settle this for us."

"There's no need to get Xavier involved." The Spaniard's face flushed, and his eyes bugged, before a sly grin spread across his pallid skin. "How about twelve?"

"Thirteen and I say my goodbyes."

The little man went to a drawer and pulled out a pouch. It jingled as he counted the coins.

"Thirteen hundred." He handed it to Rocco while staring at Lisette like a starving man's dinner.

Rocco confirmed his payment, bowed, and left without glancing in her direction. As he disappeared, her courage wavered, and she took one half-step to chase after him, beg him to take her from this place. Holding back, she steeled herself for what was to happen.

The viscount closed the door and bolted it. He turned to Lisette, running his tongue across his thin lips. "Mercedes has told me much about you."

Her pulse sounded in her ears. "Odd, she has not mentioned you."

"That's all right." He gripped her wrist. "By tomorrow we shall be well acquainted with each other."

She wriggled loose from him. "No introductions? No drink? Should we not enjoy the evening, nobility to nobility?"

"Not particularly. I don't buy my toys for the conversation." He shoved into her, backing her against a wall, pressing her with his stomach. He was a slight man, but he was strong, and his jacket hid an overfed, overdrunk belly.

She slipped down and around him, going for the door. It dawned on her that she was foolish to think she might drug this man, or even talk her way out of this mess.

"Mercedes said you were a smart one." He lunged for her, but she jumped over the bed, picked up a water pitcher and threw it at him. It bounced off his shoulder and he shouted a curse.

"Odd, she did not say the same about you." She tried again. "Sire, can we not have a drink and talk for a while?"

"You goddamned wench." He flung himself at her, over the bed, grabbing her dress. "I'd like you to last for at least a week, but if you are going to insult and injure me, we'll have only the night."

Lisette's heart was racing, her body shaking, and her jaw clenched. She lunged down and bit his knuckle. He screamed and released her. She ran to the door and lifted the bolt, fingers fumbling.

The door was half open when a strong, bony hand shoved it closed, and gripped her upper arm. A stinging half-slap, half-punch to the face knocked her backward. Two hands shoved her shoulders onto the bed and lifted her skirt up her legs.

She shook the stars out of her brain and pushed at his chest. He pried her legs apart and seized the hair between her thighs so hard, her eyes spurted with tears.

"You will have me, Wench, then you will suck me, then you will have whatever else I decide to ream you with." He pulled a small blade from his belt and held it between her breasts. "Now lie still."

Her left hand grasped and pushed his chest to keep him away while her right dug through the layers of skirt, looking for the tear in the side. He extracted an erect but slender piece of manhood from under his jacket.

At last, she pulled the dagger from its home. Angling it upward, she snatched his jacket and yanked herself up, poking her dagger against his rib cage. A hard thump and a pinging sound stopped her.

The two combatants looked at her chest. His blade was deep within the fabric of her bodice. He jerked the knife back. It was missing a good inch, broken off. No blood from any wound spread across her bodice, no jagged edge embedded in her torso. His face registered confusion, mirroring her own.

Taking her opportunity, she twisted her blade into him, feeling the crunch of bone and squish of flesh.

*"What?"* The word was a gurgle and a screech as he reeled backward, pulling her with him to the floor. Lisette landed on top of him, driving the dagger in even further. Struggling to her feet, she tugged the knife from him and stood. He was coughing blood. She turned toward the door to unbolt it and flee, but his hand caught her by the ankle.

"Help, I've been stabbed by this thief." His attempt at a scream was a low moan.

"Shh, shut up and you will live." She kicked his hand from her foot.

"Help." Even in his weakened state, he continued to try to yell. His hand was now on his wound, pressing against it to stop the flow.

She considered her options. Open the door and run for it, hoping no one will hear him and come to his aid. Or silence him. In the end, he made the decision easy.

"You French whore." He spat bloodied words. "I'll kill your entire family. But first I'll tell them what a *putain* you are."

One swift slice of her blade, and his throat wore a ruby smile. "You should have had that drink, *puerco*."

She went to the door and stopped. Turning around, she opened the drawer where he had stored his pouch of gold. There were many more coins in it, so she took it. Underneath was another pouch, made of velvet. Her hands shook as she poured the contents onto the bed.

Jewels. Loose stones without settings, rings, and

necklaces. One necklace she recognized.

"My emerald." Mercedes must have somehow delivered it to this worm. She seized the closest thing to her hand, a small mirror, and threw it at the wall. It banged against the wood, glass exploding in a hundred tiny slivers. "Mercedes is a dead *puta*."

Breaking a mirror was supposed to give one seven years of bad luck, but her life couldn't be worse than what it was now. She fastened her emerald about her neck and pocketed the two pouches before pulling the feather from its hiding place.

Locked within the long, silky plumes, glinted the tip of Antonio's knife. She picked it out and tossed it. Holding the feather up to the light, she stroked it. The tendrils gave way and let her finger comb through.

"What are you?"

The sound of her own voice jolted her back to the predicament at hand. Returning the feather to its hiding spot, she unbolted the lock and listened for voices or footsteps. There were none, so she slipped out, closed the door, and ran down the stairs. The half-moon had eased its way toward the center of the sky, bathing the cove in a silver sheen.

She hurried back toward the town, gripping the pouch to keep the coins from jingling. With this much gold, she'd be able to get a room for the night and passage on the next ship home. She smiled. Rocco could have been a rich man if he'd worked with her. She remembered wrapping her hand around his arm, and his warm morning kisses on her neck. A small part of her heart sank, knowing she'd never see him again.

As she walked into the better-lit part of town, she missed his presence by her side. Fewer citizens strolled at this hour, but every head turned to look at her. She glanced down and saw a dark stain splashed across the skirt. The blood of the rich and powerful, now dead,

Antonio.

There would be too many questions if she stayed here.

She could see *L'Implacable* at the edge of the harbor and imagined there would still be boats to bring the crew back after their shore leave. The bag of gold would have to serve as her ticket back onto Rocco's ship.

*I guess Rocco will be a rich man, after all.*

Veering toward the path they had taken from the pier, she strode with determination, trying not to run. One last building stood between her and the shore, a graying structure with darkened windows. If she could get past that, she'd make it to a boat and row back to the ship.

A figure stepped out of the shadows and grabbed her arm. It was a man, short and square in build, with a devilish grin on his face.

"Hey, girlie, what yer doin' out this late?" He jingled his pockets. "I got a few coin 'ere if yer want to swallow my sword."

"Absolutely not." She yanked her arm, but he held a firm grip.

"Here, what's that all over yer dress?" he brayed. "Looks like blood. Maybe we should tell the poli."

She stepped into him and pushed her dagger at his throat. "Maybe we shouldn't."

The stranger let go of her and backed away, his hands in the air. "Apologies, mistress."

He turned and ran, calling out for help. Lisette gathered her skirt and raced down the beach, to where they'd come ashore, her heart beating in terror. If anyone found Barragan, they would certainly hang her first and ask questions later. He may have been a horrible man, and she might be a lady, but a dead viscount would not be good for the citizens of Isla de la

Soledad.

Once on the beach, she stopped running and stared. There were no boats.

Peering through the darkness, Lisette could still see the outline of Rocco's ship under the half-moon. A steady, swooshing noise sounded like oars, so she trained her eyes and ears on the direction it came from. Eventually, she made out the shape of a small boat, rowing toward *L'Implacable*.

She waded into the bay, thankful the waves were small and undulating. It didn't take long for her skirt to soak up the water, clinging to her legs and dragging her downward. She would never be able to swim to the dinghy with this weight pulling at her, so she stood, waist-high in water band took out her blade. A couple of strokes and she was down to her chemise again. She tied the pouches around her neck, and dove into the sea.

The water was cold and dark, and she hoped there was nothing on the hunt tonight for tender, splashing fishes. Her entire being was exhausted from fighting and killing a man, and nearly getting caught, but fear and anger drove aching arms to stretch and battered legs to kick.

Before she knew it, she was close to the dinghy. The crew did not appear to be in any hurry to get back to the ship. Judging from their songs and laughter, they were a little better from drinking. A rope hung from the back of the boat. Lisette grabbed it and found the rest of the trip to be much easier. While they rowed, she listened.

"Why's the cap'n disappear some nights?" This was a young voice.

The crew grew silent.

One rough voice broke the hush. "Cap'n has his ways, and we don't talk about it. Gives us the lion's share o' the plunder, stays close to a few ports, lets us have our fun."

"I ain't kickin' a fuss." The young voice apologized. "I was only wondering. Before this, I was on the *Chien Fou.*"

Another voice, further forward, asked, "What about the *Chien Fou?*"

There was a round of shushing and someone repeating, "What? What?"

The original young voice burst above the rest. "I was on a ship with a blood dragon."

Scuffling, fighting bodies rocked the boat back and forth. Lisette's arms burned, trying to hold on as the rope tugged side to side in response. Several men converged on another, and there was the sound of fists hitting flesh.

The rough voice spoke again. "You keep your mouth shut, boy. Don't ever say those words again." There was no more talk, only oars pushing through the water.

The boat sidled up to the ship. Lisette watched the men tie off the boat and climb the ladder as quickly as monkeys. She knew she did not have the strength to hang onto the rope while the boat was lifted. With one desperate heave, she pulled her body from the water and flopped inside. The boat was up quickly, and she was out of it and on deck, surprising the sailors who manned the ropes.

"The captain said..." one of them croaked.

"Yeah, but he never..." another offered.

"Should we?" a third suggested.

Her drawn dagger silenced them. Sopping in her ivory chemise, she stalked toward the captain's cabin, her face burning in embarrassment. Behind her, snippets of conjecture floated in the breeze, the crew wondering if they should stop her. She kept going, checking behind several times as her humiliation turned to anger. When she got to the cabin, she threw the door open and stomped inside.

A banquet of meats, fruits, and vegetables all glistened with the glow of candlelight. On the captain's bed, a woman with long black hair was kneeling, naked, rocking back and forth. Underneath her was Rocco, obviously enjoying himself, at least until Lisette's entrance. The couple stopped and looked at her as she slammed the door, the woman grasping at the covers to hide herself.

"Do not mind me, I can wait. Take your time." She sat and grabbed food sloppily with her hands, tearing bread, stabbing at the meat with a knife. Her hands shook with each move.

The dark-haired woman whimpered about an audience, and Rocco entreated her to finish what they had started.

"And keep it quiet up there," Lisette growled, her voice as shaky as her hands. "I'm trying to eat."

She was on a second helping of potatoes and lamb when the woman with dark hair walked past, dressed. Rocco whistled at the door, gave some quiet commands to a crewman, and sent the stranger out. Filling a plate and goblet, he sat across from Lisette.

"Why are you back here?"

She grabbed the pitcher and poured herself some rum. "I escaped."

"I admit, I'm surprised. How did you get Barragan to drink the potion?"

"I didn't." She scowled. "We fought. I won."

He leaned back in his seat. "And now I am in awe. I suppose you left him bruised and battered?"

"I left him dead." She fought sudden, angry tears.

For a moment, he stared back, silent. At last, he said, "Pity I wasn't there. He had more coin in his pouch for me to plunder."

"Pity."

"But my first question still stands. Why are you back here?"

"I had enough blood on my dress to arouse suspicions. One man tried to detain me and call for the police." She took a long drink. "I didn't know where else to go."

"I see." He nodded. "And now you expect me to deliver you to your family?"

"No. I only ask it." She sighed and untied the strings around her neck, holding out the pouch filled with coin. "Is this enough for my passage?"

"Perhaps." Rocco took the bag and poured its contents onto the table before holding his hand out again. "And the other bag?"

She threw the pouch of jewels at him. He stared at her, letting his eyes drift down her neck to the emerald. She put her hand around the stone. "This. Is. Mine. A gift from my father. The deceitful wench Mercedes took it from me, and you will only take it if I am dead."

Rocco picked up the pouch and looked inside, moving the contents about with his fingers. "This will do nicely. Of course, my obligation to deliver you is done. Perhaps I take this and throw you to the sharks."

"I swam with them tonight. They're not interested." She pushed her plate away and drained her goblet. Her body ached and her heart was leaden. "I want to go home."

Rocco stopped eating and his ice-blue eyes stared through her. She had seen this expression before, on the first day when he cut off her gown. Her skin prickled at his coldness. He walked to his trunk, while she sat upright and wrapped her hand around her dagger.

"Put that down, Girl." Returning to her, he held out a jacket. "And put this on. You have an alarming propensity for losing gowns. And you look a bit cold."

She looked down at her chemise, still damp and clinging, and showing every curve, every pimple. Wrapping herself in the coat, she was immediately soothed.

Rocco still glared. He stomped to the cabinet where the secret papers were hidden and took out a bottle of liquor.

"You want to go home." He turned away, regarding the bottle. "Many would like to go home who can't." Shaking his head, he scowled again. "Why is this bottle so clean? If you've been snooping about, I—"

"No, Captain, I am bored, stuck in the cabin all day. I spend part of it cleaning, for something to do. If I had paper and a pen, I might write instead."

His eyes narrowed and searched hers. Lisette kept her face calm. It was true, she was bored. And she did tidy things up. Whatever else she might have done, she forced from her mind.

"I'll get you paper. Stay away from these cabinets."

"Take me home and you won't have to worry about your precious cabinets."

He strode toward her, his hand raised to strike. She tilted her chin up at him, her anger building again. Her pursed lips dared him to follow through. He turned away, a look of disgust on his face. Bottle in hand, he left the cabin, slamming the door.

She retrieved her clothes from a hook on the wall. Peeling the silk chemise from her body, she put on the cotton slip and walked over to the washing bowl. She held the chemise up and examined it. The swim had washed the blood from it, so she rinsed the salt water out, and hung it over a chair, hoping it would be wearable again when it dried.

The moon was slipping from the sky, and exhaustion caught her. She stashed her feather in the pocket of the frock and laid it by the bed for the morning. Blowing out the last candle she climbed into the covers. Tired but wakeful, she looked out at the view. A bright star hung outside the window, the one the captain had shown her. It would lead her to Tortuga if she could steer a ship. She recalled the captain's papers about navigation and tried to recite a few rules. By the fifth one, her eyes fluttered shut.

Incessant pounding awoke her with a start. Lisette sat up to see Rocco in the doorway. He shoved the door closed, and staggered toward the bed, one hand swinging a lantern. Obviously, he had finished the entire bottle of whatever he had carried off with him. She wasn't certain how long she had slept, but there was no light at the horizon.

Her father was a jovial drunk. Uncle Luc hit people. She braced herself to find out what kind of man Rocco was when he'd had too much.

He stomped to the bed and stood over it. His eyes, even in the dim light, appeared glazed with the same frustration and rage as when he left. He yanked the covers from her, his eyes searching the bed in frantic sweeps.

"You weren't supposed to come back," he said. "You were supposed to go away."

He seized her by the wrist and jerked her from the bed. She fell but found her feet as he dragged her to the lantern, shrinking from him as he tugged.

"I can't have you here. I don't want you." His words ran together in a slur.

"Believe me, Captain, I would prefer not to be here, either."

"All these years." He stumbled away, mumbling. "This was a bad idea. I should have finished it."

"I don't understand—"

He turned, pointing and yelling. "I don't want you here!"

She stepped back, leaving some distance in case his hand swung at her face. "I don't want to be here. Take me home and you never have to see me again."

"If only I could," he whispered. She opened her mouth, but he held up his hand to silence her. "We are not going to Île des Oiseaux. I'll not change our route for you."

"What…" She was not certain she wanted an answer. "What are you going to do with me?"

He shook his head, still facing the sea, the moonlight glinting off the water. "I cannot bear it. At the next port, I will give you enough gold to meet your needs. You can get a ship home from there."

"But my father would pay ransom for me."

"You believe he would, but I know he would not." He faced her. "In the short time you've been gone, the island has fallen to Spain. No one could tell me where your parents are, but they most assuredly are not in their castle, flush with coin."

"What?" she gasped. "Where could they be? I need to be home now!"

"It does not matter. You cannot help them."

"How do you know?" She scowled. "Stupid pirate, what do you care about family, anyway?"

Without warning, his hands were on her shoulders, pushing her against the wall. The wood drove into her back, but there was no time for the pain, as she was preoccupied with his hand, now wrapped around her throat. He was not squeezing, yet. She could still breathe. The tightness in his fingers walked a line. A little less would be a caress. A little more would be death.

"I know more than you would in a lifetime." His face was inches from hers, breathing drink and rage. "I lost my mind, my life, my everything when my wife was murdered."

She restrained herself from gripping his arm and kept her eyes on his. Even in the darkness, they glowed red. Her heart climbed into her ears and beat a furious rhythm. The dryness of her mouth made it impossible to speak.

"You were supposed to die tonight, too." His hand tightened. "Why are you still alive?"

Her eyes widened. Why did he hate her so? One thing was certain. She needed a good answer if she wanted to live.

"You are a ruthless man." Lisette forced the words, filtered through the squeeze of his palm on her throat. "I confess I fear you, have feared you each day since I was brought here. Even so, for all of your coldness, you have not harmed me, so you are not entirely evil."

His fingers moved up her neck, stopping to stroke the pulse along her jaw. Their eyes remained on each other, locked in study. His grip tightened, and she imagined her statement about not being harmed would not be true for long.

As his hand pressed down, she raised hers, to his face. Trembling fingertips traced his forehead, curving around to stroke his cheek. Fighting the tears that would render her hysterical, she said the only thing that came to mind.

"I do not know why you despise me, but I am sorry. Sorry for your loss, and sorry that I discounted it. I know you still mourn her."

Rocco's free hand grasped hers, squeezing her fingers hard. She winced as the bones rubbed together. His face contorted as if in great pain, and he clutched her hand to his chest, his breath ragged. The squeeze became a caress. He brought her palm to his mouth, where his lips lingered against her skin, his goatee prickling.

After a moment, he bowed his head and laid it atop her breasts, moving his hands, now gentle, away from her throat and to her back. She encircled his head in her arms and kissed the top before laying her cheek against it. His hair was soft.

"No one ever said that." His words were muffled.

"No one but me was sorry for my loss."

He lifted her as easily as a bottle of rum, and placed her on the bed in a soft, if somewhat swaying motion. Lying beside her, he wrapped her in his arms. "Thank you."

Lisette rested her head on his chest, wondering if he had truly calmed or if there would be another storm of anger. They remained that way for what seemed a long time, long enough for her to relax and believe the roaring was over.

"Captain," she whispered. "When do we arrive at the next port?"

He didn't answer for a moment, and she assumed he was asleep. Instead, his hand stroked her hair. "Two weeks."

Two weeks. His gentle touch reminded her of home and family, two things that were gone from her life now. Mercedes and Eric would be married soon if they were not already wed. The news of her family distressed her—if her father was as stubborn about his land and title as he was about everything else, there was little hope for them.

She turned her face into his shirt and sobbed. He responded by pulling her closer, continuing to stroke her hair. His lips pressed her forehead, and he made shushing noises. This horrid man who threatened to end her life, who plainly wanted her dead, was now comforting her. The strength of his arms around her, his gentle lips on her face, softened the last steel of her heart.

"Do not despair," he whispered. "You may find them yet."

The first light was creeping into the cabin when she became aware of a hand, gentle and languid, stroking her thigh. Cool air around her legs announced her slip had worked its way up as she slept and was now tangled around her waist, leaving her exposed. She reached for the covers, but a whisper in her ear stopped her.

"Tempest."

Her open and yearning heart now winced at the name. She could not be in love with Rocco, not because he was her captor, but because his love would not be returned. She was not Tempest.

Despite her sadness, she enjoyed the sensation of his fingertips working their way up and around her inner leg. For the moment, she could put prim, noble Lisette aside and be his Tempest. As he continued to caress and massage, his hand climbed higher, until he lifted her slip to expose more of her body.

Within moments, his palm cupped her breast as his kisses roamed up her neck to her cheek. She had never felt such physical delight and could not resist arching her back and letting out a sighing moan. Once again, she felt his love for Tempest in each soft press of his lips on her skin. She remembered Genevieve's words about her wedding night and her body's desire to join with her husband's. Maybe she was ready for this.

Rocco rolled back to his side of the bed, mumbling. The words he sighed were, "I love you, Tempest."

She watched the covers rise and fall with his breath, noticing how the light gave him a hazy glow. Captor or not, her body yearned for his touch. Twice she reached out, to stroke his hair, run her hand down his arm, make him realize she was here, and could be his.

Each time, she pulled back. He loved Tempest. Lisette did not exist in his dreams.

She woke up alone. Stretching out, she did her usual check. Once again, she found that Rocco had left her unharmed and intact, but she was now shocked to discover her own disappointment.

Rising, she slipped into her dress, and washed her face in the bowl. There was no food set out, and she was hungry. She remembered Rocco's words.

*Two weeks to the next port.*

Before looking for food, she was curious about her lucky feather. She pulled it from the pocket of her shift and set it on the table. It looked no different than before, long red plumes on a steely shaft. She took a small dagger from the wall and stroked the feather with it. The plumes puffed in resistance.

Intrigued, she plunged the blade into the center. Her arm vibrated with contact as the knife bounced from the plumes, its tip shattered. She picked up the feather. It remained undamaged.

"You are more than lucky." She held it aloft, spinning it in wonder. "You are magical."

Lisette placed it in her pocket and felt the familiar growl in her stomach. The sun was well above the horizon. Poussin usually delivered breakfast before now. She paced for a few moments, wondering what to do. This wasn't like the castle, where she could ring the kitchen for service. She wasn't supposed to leave the cabin, but she wasn't supposed to starve.

"I honestly don't understand why I'm expected to stay in here like some kind of prisoner." She opened the door and marched to the deck.

Sunlight spilled across her face, fresh and bright, although the breeze was cool. She walked toward the front of the ship and looked up. The sails reminded her of the family cook in her apron, taut and fat. The crew were all busy, pulling on ropes here and there, climbing up and down, even scrubbing the deck.

Lisette stood watching, a strange desire rising in her to join in. Her heart lightened in exhilaration, enjoying the rush as the ship cut through the water, feeling wind and salt spray and seeing nothing but the sea all around.

"What are you doing?" Rocco barked from the helm.

Lisette turned, startled. The crew had stopped their work and were standing, staring at her. She felt a blush creep into her face and walked back toward him.

"I was hungry."

"I shall have Poussin bring you food." His voice was a scold. "You cannot be up here, distracting my men."

She frowned. "Captain, these men have seen women before. I want to learn to sail a ship. Can I not roll up my sleeves and work?"

"Absolutely not. I'll not have my men babysitting a landlubber. You want to learn something? Go find a weak-kneed sluggard at the next port to bring you aboard." Rocco stood at the wheel, tall and glaring. "Now, get below deck."

Lisette opened her mouth to argue. She caught a glimpse of the men, their eyes shifting from the captain to her and back again.

"Yes, Captain." She curtsied and left, returning to the cabin and boredom.

Poussin came in shortly after, carrying a tray bursting with sustenance. She helped him set the plates on the table.

"Poussin, I was wondering…" She pulled the feather from her pocket. "What could you tell me about this feather?"

Any tan the young boy's face had disappeared, his eyes popping and mouth gaping. "Where'd you get that?"

"I found it on the floor. Is it yours?"

He backed toward the door, crossing himself over and over. "Throw it out. Throw it out and never mention it, nevermore. It's bad luck."

"Bad luck? But it has already saved my life once." She held it up by the shaft and he held his hands up in self-defense.

"Be careful with that! Do not prick yourself on the tip."

"Poussin, is it possible this came from—" She walked toward him, but he dashed from the room and slammed the door. Twirling the feather in her thumb and forefinger, she watched the plumes spin, red and bright. "—a blood dragon? The next time that boy comes in, you and I are going to get some answers."

The aroma of dried meat put her curiosity aside, and she sat, stuffing the feather into her pocket. As she poured rum into her cup, she was reminded of her lavish meals at home. Her parents had been deposed—where were they now? How could she find them? Rocco would not help her. He wouldn't even return her to Île des Oiseaux. She would need to book passage on a ship.

And if her parents were not on their home island, she'd need to travel further. This meant having enough coin to pay her way. Or having enough skill to earn her way. An idea swirled around her mind, a desperate and frightening notion, one that would be easy for Rocco to reject, unless she convinced him. She poured another cup as she worked out her plan.

By the time Rocco entered, she had been drinking and planning for almost an hour. As usual, he said nothing, but plopped down and reached for the pitcher, a scowl on his face. "Wasn't this full?"

"Maybe. Here, have some food." She handed him a roll. "Captain, I realize the awkwardness of my request, to learn how to sail. I also realize that you have no obligation to help me in the least."

He shot her a wicked glare. "I can't decide whether I want to dump you at the next port or dump you off the plank right now."

Her heart shrank a bit. "Might I suggest something else? How many ports will you stop at this year?"

"Six or so."

"What…if…" She slowed her words, to avoid slurring them. "…you sold a virgin at every port?"

"Every port?" He frowned. "What are you thinking?"

"I am thinking, you could sell me."

"Are you drunk?"

"I am a…LADY." She lifted her chin. "Possibly, I have consumed too much."

"That's what I—"

"But it's still a good idea." Lisette talked faster, to keep him from stopping her. "It will be easy. You sell me, I escape, come back to the ship, and we do it again at the next port."

"It's ludicrous." He waved the idea off. "Even as a pirate, I have to deliver on some promises. No one will believe me by the third port."

"True," She had to think through her rum fog, a difficult task. "But what if *you* do not sell me? What if one of your crew poses as my brother or father? *They* sell me, and no one is the wiser."

"And how do you think you'll get away from these men?"

An image of Viscount Barragan, gurgling in his own blood, flashed across her mind. "Well, I do hope I don't have to kill them all. But I still have that vial you gave me."

"That was not quite successful last time." Rocco shook his head. "I cannot be leaving a trail of dead nobles behind me."

"They can't all be pigs. Besides, it would still be good for you—you'd have gotten your payment already. If I can't escape, you sail without me, but with extra coin for yourself, yes?"

"Look, Girl. I've done plenty of pirating. I know how to deal in stolen property. This is not a venture I've ever tried."

"Then you do not know it won't work."

He stared at her, through narrowed eyes and furrowed brows. "Why are you doing this?"

"I'll need gold to find my family. Not to mention, I need vengeance." She stood, swayed, and grabbed the table for support. "You want gold, and Spain's ruin. With gold, I could avenge what my fiancé and that snake Mercedes de Medina did to me and my family."

He silenced her with a raised finger. "Lady de Medina? The daughter of the Count de Medina?"

"Yes, I thought you knew. She was the one who sold me to you—she and Eric d'Auguste."

"I didn't know." He shook his head. "Names are usually not exchanged in this kind of arrangement."

Lisette drained her cup, regarded the pitcher, and

decided against a refill. "When they betrayed me, I swore I'd get even. Now that they've chased my family to who knows where, my grudge has deepened. I intend to make them pay."

Crossing his arms, Rocco tilted his head back and grinned. "Why shouldn't I sell you and keep all the money?"

"Why shouldn't you? Because if you cross me once, then I never do it again." She wagged her finger at him. "The Medina family is Spanish. You want to destroy the Spanish. I want to destroy Medina. We are sharing the same goal."

He sat, running his finger around the rim of his goblet and looking at her. "I'll consider it."

"Thank you, Captain." She sighed. It would be risky, but if she did it once, she could do it again. Hopefully it would not involve murder this time. "Of course, if I knew how to sail, I could be earning my keep on this ship."

Rocco stood and walked to the window. "Come here."

She followed, attempting to appear sober, cautiously remaining out of his strike zone. He held both hands out. She moved closer, taking small steps, at last extending her own hands to meet his. Reaching forward, he grabbed her wrists, squeezing hard, and pulling her to him. Turning her hands over, he thrust pale white palms toward her face.

"See these hands? They've never done a ducat's worth of work." He ran his fingers roughly up and down her palms, causing her to wince and pull away. "They are going to stay that way, at least until I sell you off."

She folded her arms, a blush of anger flooding her neck up to her cheeks. "As you wish."

"I don't believe your plan will work. But either way, I will be up one bag of gold." He strode to the table and picked up a hunk of dried meat before leaving.

Relieved and optimistic, she spent the day studying the maps on the wall and trying to figure out, based on where they had been and the direction they were sailing, what port she'd be sold at.

Her little island home was the northernmost hub of Los Peces Pequeña. From what she could tell, they were headed due south, which would take them to Isla de Pimienta. Her family had connections with the Spanish duke there. Even if Rocco betrayed her, perhaps the duke could be persuaded to help her find her family.

*I could be on my way home soon.*

The sun was low on the ocean curls when footsteps approached the cabin. Certain it was Poussin, Lisette stood next to the door as it was opened, and food was carried in. She closed the door behind him and bolted it. He was hers to interrogate.

Except it wasn't Poussin.

Captain Rocco put the food on the table and turned around. "What in the devil are you doing?"

Her skin could not have blushed more crimson. "I, uh…I am lonely. Can you blame me, Captain? You do not like to converse while you eat, so I try to enlist Poussin to talk to me."

"By bolting the door?"

"He does not like to talk."

"Talk about what?"

*Think fast, Lizzie.* "Anything. Nothing. Where we are headed. Where we have been. News. Rumors."

Rocco poured a goblet and sat, motioning for her to join him. "Poussin doesn't want to serve your meals or help you in any way."

"Why?"

"He says it's work beneath his duties, but I know the real reason." Rocco kept slicing meat, focused on his food. "He's afraid of you."

"How silly. Why would he be afraid of me?"

"Why, indeed?" He faced her, his blue eyes cold. "I'll not have you rooting your snout into what's mine."

"I am only passing the time."

"Is my late wife part of passing the time?"

"For a woman, yes. I'm sorry, I know you don't wish to speak of her, but I felt I needed to know enough of the story to know what to avoid. I believed asking someone else was preferable to asking you to relive your tragedy."

"Well, it's not."

"I understand. Never again." She prayed Poussin had held his tongue about the feather, patting her dress, and feeling the hard shaft under the cloth.

Rocco reached into his belt and withdrew something soft and brown, holding it out for her. They were leather gloves with no fingers. "I have reconsidered my earlier stance. Put them on your hands. They will protect you from callouses while you work."

She tried them on and although they were a bit large, she could wear them.

"You will start tomorrow." He nodded toward her. "Keep your dagger with you. I have ordered the men to work with you without meddling, but they are men at sea. My crew are good seadogs, not gentlemen."

"Thank you, Captain. I promise to work hard."

He stood, making a harrumphing noise. "I promise to work you hard. Perhaps I can make you too tired to snoop."

Reaching the door, he grabbed a broad-brimmed hat from a hook on the wall, and tossed it on the table, before striding out. Lisette retrieved the hat and ran to the mirror. It was a man's hat, to be sure, but it would keep the sun off her face. She smiled at her reflection.

As cold and angry as Rocco had been, she was excited to have more freedom on the ship. She was also relieved he did not ask about the feather. Why would Poussin tattle on her interest in Tempest, but not that?

That evening as she crawled into bed, she waited for Rocco to return, angry with herself for wanting to see him. With Eric, her only hope was to someday be fond of him. This pirate stirred her heart. She wished to see him again as she had that first day—a ruthless, horrid man to be hanged from the nearest yardarm. But it was impossible. When she awoke alone, she had to fight her disappointment.

Dressing, she tucked the back of her skirt between her legs to form pantaloons and placed the dagger in its sheath on her belt. There was no food on the table, but she had saved a piece of bread with dried meat from the night before. She ate as she brushed her hair, braided it, and tucked it into a tight bun under her hat.

Taking a deep breath, she climbed the stairs to a new day, slipping soft, white fingers into the coarse leather gloves.

The burly, ruddy-cheeked man she had seen talking to Rocco stood at the top of the stairs. "Name's Maurice Bouchard, but folks calls me Chunk. Cap'n ordered me teach you bout sailin'."

"You can call me Lizzie. I am eager to learn, Chunk."

What followed were grueling hours of the hardest

work she'd ever done. Granted, being a high-born lady in a fine house meant she didn't need to lift a finger, but she chose to groom her own horse and walk along the beach, and she did like to pick up a sword and spar with brother Jules.

All of those things combined did not in any way equal what was needed on the ship. Chunk directed her to hoist up a bucket of seawater, mop the deck, pull on this rope, and climb that one. Along the way, she learned a little about the masts and sails, and that everything onboard had a name. The ropes were called *lines*, or *sheets* or *halliards*, and she wasn't mopping, she was *swabbing* the deck with saltwater to help seal the planks.

The cool breeze of yesterday only came for brief visits and disappeared when her muscles were straining the hardest. Her hands were slick with sweat inside the gloves, but she dared not take them off. Even with them on, the lines were like sandpaper, and the rough wood splintered against the leather.

When the sun collapsed into the sea, Lisette longed to do the same.

Chunk rewarded her by slapping her shoulder, pitching her forward. "That was a good day's work, Lizzie."

"Thank you." She did her best to walk upright to the stern of the ship and then shuffled down the steps to the cabin. Once inside, she shut the door and stumbled to the bed, where she dropped her aching body. Staring at the ceiling, she listened to the whoosh of water as the ship cut a path southeast. The smell of her own sweat made her long for a hot scented bath, and Genevieve's stiff but loving fingers.

"How are your hands?" Rocco had entered at some point. She managed to turn her head in his direction. He was carrying a bowl of something steaming.

"I believe they survived." With some effort, she

raised her arms and pulled the gloves off. The palms were red but not roughened. She flexed her fingers and clenched her fists with varying degrees of success. "I do not believe I will be able to pick anything up for a while."

He sat on the bed next to her and gently raised her to a sitting position. She did her best to lift her uncooperative body. It was good to feel his arm around her shoulder supporting her.

"Drink." He held the bowl to her lips. "A good friend taught me to make this. It will wash away the aches."

She sipped a delicious combination of spice and richness. The broth was almost magical, the way it satisfied her hunger and soothed her pains. Her hands overlaid his on the bowl, steadying the flow of liquid down her throat. He flinched from the touch. "Thank you, Captain. Will this get me ready for tomorrow?"

"Ready for what?"

"To work again."

He chuckled. "I suppose if you can move, you can work."

She struggled to sit more upright without his help. "I doubt if you let Poussin sleep in if his back is sore."

Lisette watched his eyes search her face, displaying tenderness and longing as they settled on her lips. Her own eyes drifted to his mouth, lips parted, surrounded by dark bristles. He was leaning closer, and she did the same, instinctively.

As she prepared for their lips to at last meet, his face grew hard, and his eyes cold. He stood, wrenched the empty bowl from her hands and strode from the cabin. She sank down, angry at the tears rolling down her face. Tears of exhaustion and pain, in both her body and her heart.

She slid from the bed, and wiped her face, willing

her heart to harden. Stretching her sore body tall, she limped around the cabin. Her legs groaned with her own weight, from hip to heel. Tomorrow would come too soon, but she was determined to earn her place with Captain Rocco. If he did not desire her as a lover, he would respect her as a pirate.

Lisette stared up, squinting into the sun at the crow's nest, pitching back and forth with the roll of the ocean. Her stomach turned watching the top of the mast.

"Go on, Lizzie." Chunk's voice was encouraging but firm. "We're all a mite off the first time. Keep lookin' up to your goal, you'll be fine."

She removed her gloves long enough to wipe the sweat from her palms onto her breeches. After the first day of dealing with her skirts, Rocco found some small men's clothes for her.

She had spent the days learning to be a good sailor. What first looked like a tangle of lines hanging from every mast now had their own names, halliards to buntlines and they were not tangled but in specific knots for specific reasons. Every fiber in her body ached, her bruises had bruises, yet she refused to complain.

Still, she blanched at the order from Chunk, to climb the ratlines up the main mast and report what she observed from the top.

Dragging her feet to the ladder, she took the first step of her ascent toward what would certainly be a bad stomachache.

As Chunk instructed, she kept her eyes on the platform while she climbed. Her passage was slow and shaky. By the time she arrived at the top, she was lying against the lines, gripping with her arms, as well as her hands. The mast was swaying to and fro, taking her with it.

Grasping anything she could hold onto, Lisette edged out onto the platform and sat, adjusting her insides to match the swinging. She looked down at tiny Chunk, far below. He motioned for her to look out at the horizon. It was hotter up here, especially without the sea spraying her face. She swallowed down her rocking guts, praying she didn't throw up from this height.

"Lizzie," Chunk called. "What d'yer see on the starboard side?"

She shook her head, eyes squeezed shut. "I don't know. I can't look."

"Chin up, my girl." His booming voice comforted her. "Lift up yer noggin, then take a little peek."

Raising her chin, she allowed a shard of light into her view, enlarging the sliver slowly, blinkingly, until she could look at the horizon and pretend that she wasn't on a slender platform high above the ship. The sky was bright and clear, and where it met the sea, it sparkled merrily. The endless noise of the crew was lessened from up here, and she was amazed to be alone with the soothing quiet.

"Starboard side is open sea, Chunk," she called.

"And to port?" The pride in his voice was apparent.

"Port is clear as well." Without thinking, she

looked down. She ignored the distance and the height that had frightened her before. All she could see was the smile on his face. "Can I stay here long enough for a look around?"

"Aye, Lizzie. Enjoy the view."

The gray ocean she saw from down on deck looked nothing like the patterns of colors from this viewpoint. Dark blues and deep greens, velvety and rich, glistened as far as she could see. The ship glided over the water like a sea bird on the wind, and she was atop it all. She felt birdlike, soaring, and wished she could escape the ship and take wing wherever she pleased.

"Have you no work to do?" Rocco's voice interrupted her daydream. "Chunk, is she pulling her weight or not?"

"Ah, she's doin' fine, Cap'n." Chunk sounded calm and upbeat. "Lizzie, yer can climb down, now."

Climbing up seemed like the easy part, as Lisette looked over the platform at the lines. She grabbed the rope to steady her body, and carefully eased her foot down until it rested on a rung. As close as she hugged the lines on the way up, she fairly molded her body into them on the way down. Fingers squeezing and arms taut, she put one foot on a rung, tested it, before bearing her weight and reaching for the next one.

As she neared the deck, Chunk reached up to her waist and steered her. "Pretty good fer yer first time, I'd say."

"Thank you, Chunk. I like the view. I just don't like the climbing—yet."

"Chunk!" Rocco barked. "The helm needs swabbing."

"Aye, Cap'n, it does. I was sendin' Lizzie to do just that."

Rocco scowled at her. "Well, get to it."

He turned and walked toward his cabin, Lisette

scoffing as he left.

"Mon dieu." She stamped her heel. "What a blackheart."

"Ah, Lizzie, let it roll off ya. Water from a duck, treat it like the bluster it is."

She reached down to grab the handle of her bucket and stood, shrugging both shoulders to stretch her tension away. "Bluster or insolence, I shall scrub his precious helm."

"That's my girl." Chunk slapped her shoulder.

She looked back at him, and let her view rise, to the crow's nest she'd visited. "I think I'll be back there. Better than any bell tower."

*Maybe even at night to see where Rocco is, when he's not stumbling into the cabin.*

The top of the mast soon became Lisette's favorite getaway when Rocco was not finding extra work to tire her out. In the day, she could watch the foam churned by their ship's journey, and the sparkles of the ocean beyond, urging faster and faster. By night, the moonlight sprinkled stars across the path, and a pale, slim line revealed the edge of the sea. The view was never more stunning than during the full moon, when the bright orb cut through the dark of night to show the ocean at its most mysterious.

Two days' sail from their destination, she stepped on the deck after grabbing a hard biscuit to quiet her stomach. Her plan was to get her chores done early and spend some time on the platform aloft. Tomorrow, Rocco would task someone to be lookout for the island and she knew he would not ask her.

# 16

The morning was bright but strange, the sky a dark and uneasy blue. The wind was light and barely pushing the ship across the water. She walked to the starboard side to lower her bucket and gather water for the morning swabbing.

"You, Girl!" Rocco's voice boomed from the helm. He never called her anything but Girl on deck. "Help Chunk with the lines."

She dropped her bucket and ran to her new task, working the mainmast lines with her mentor. The air wrapped itself around her breath, trying to drag her to the deck. Her body wilted, but her skin prickled as if it might give off sparks.

"Squall's coming." Chunk pointed toward the starboard horizon.

"Uh-huh." She'd seen plenty of storms on her island. They were fearsome sights of lashing rain and wailing winds. Lightning sometimes burst from the clouds, announced by claps that rattled the walls. She never feared them, although she'd never been asea during one. "Will it catch us?"

"Mays be. Cap'n will be tacking west soon. We may outrun it."

She tugged extra hard on the line and tied it firm. The sail caught all the breeze to be had but it was still only half-full. She looked forward. All the sails were mostly slack.

Rocco stood tall behind the ship's wheel with no expression. He seemed unconcerned with the lack of speed, barking orders for the crew to prepare the ship to come about.

Chunk and Lisette left one side to adjust braces on the other, tightening some, and setting the mast up for the turn. On the port tack, the wind picked up, growing quicker and stronger. Soon all sails were bulging, and the ship was skipping across the whitecaps. The crew leaped from one line to the next, moving to keep the sail in the wind. Rocco strained at the wheel, forcing the rudder to turn.

As wild and fast as the wind came, it suddenly calmed to a manageable blow. Lisette leaned against the hull and took a breath.

"If you're a-thinkin' we've missed it, don't." Chunk was beside her, frowning. "We ain't gonna outrun it. This here's the calm afore."

She looked up at the sun, a dull yellow ball covered in haze. It was rising toward its zenith but there was no brightness to the gray sky. The air closed in, squeezing the breath from her body, and making perspiration flow like a river.

"You! At the mast!" Rocco's voice cut through the

gloom. "Ease that sail!"

Lisette jumped at his command and ran forward to grab the line, buoyed from behind by a strong gust. Before Chunk could back her up, she freed the line from the cleat.

As soon as the line came away from its mooring, the wind whooshed across the ship, sending the belly of the sail skyward. She clung to the flailing line, which took her across the deck, half-dragged, half-falling. Not daring to let go, she clutched tighter, grasping and folding rope, attempting to get back on her feet. The wind was now howling, and a few drops of rain drove upon her, followed by a burst of water from the churning waves.

The squall had arrived.

Lisette took flight, whipping back and forth, her right arm wrapped in the line. Water pounded her face and pain ripped through her. Her shoulder strained and pulled, like it would soon separate, allowing her body to float away in the storm. Grabbing the line with her free hand, she tried to take the pressure off but the wind spun her like a top. Unable to stop or free herself, she tucked her head and tried not to drown in the pummeling downpour.

She heard screaming and tried looking for Chunk, but the storm was blinding. Past all exhaustion, her head spinning, she spotted a large, dark object in front of her. *The mast.* She grabbed it, smashing her face against the wood.

Her arms could not encircle the width of the pole, but she dug her fingers into it, trying not to slip away. The ship was now nearly sideways, and she envisioned herself swinging on the line until she was over the edge. She commanded her weary arms to cling to the mast, no matter what.

Sheets of rain pounded, attempting to wash her

away. Her right arm was still tangled around the line, losing all feeling, and the corner of the sail whipped her upper torso with abandon.

Lisette peered down as the raindrops beat against her face and glimpsed the railing of the ship. It was angled enough—if she could drop backwards, she might be able to slide across the deck and be caught by the rail. Stretching her free hand down, she found the dagger still in her belt. She pulled it out and tried to hack at the tangle of line. The wind and rain made it impossible to see what she was doing, but it appeared each swing of the blade hit a different place, cutting a few strands of hemp in random spots.

She laid the dagger firmly against the line, sawing as fast as possible. The storm took a breath, easing its ferocity, and she bore down with the blade, cutting for her life. Her arm fell free, and she threw herself as hard as she could, backward and down.

The wind whisked her forward, but her back hit a hard, flat surface. She prayed it was deck. As she slid, the rain lightened enough to glimpse the railing, coming straight on. Skidding across, she had barely time to fold herself into a ball.

She took a couple of bounces away from the rail before settling against it. The impact knocked the wind from her chest, but she reached out with both hands and held on, turning from the rain, struggling to breathe.

She rested there, huddled against the wood, until she became aware of voices shouting. Captain Rocco was screaming orders through the pounding water. Chunk had grasped a line, what was left of the mainsail sheet.

Pushing from the corner, Lisette staggered over and took hold of the line's end with her left hand. Together, she and Chunk pulled it to its starboard cleat and fastened it. Now that the sail was stationary, they could ease up and secure it. Lisette looked up, hoping for Rocco's approval.

Rocco was at the helm, grappling with the wheel for control. His veined and bulging muscles held the course, his hair blowing, eyes focused ahead. The sun behind him glowed through the darkness, giving him the look of a god on fire.

Chunk grabbed her by the waist and pulled her to the gunwale. Poussin and one of the other sailors were lashed to the deck.

"You was the last one, Lizzie." Chunk had to scream above the storm and the creaking of the ship. "I couldn't leave ya up there, swingin'."

"The captain." Her voice was weak as she leaned into Chunk's ear. "Isn't anyone helping him?"

"Rocco's seen us through these afore. This ain't even the worst."

As if he'd said magic words, the rain ceased. The last of the wind pushed it and the clouds away from the ship, setting them upright and bringing the sun. This Lisette had also experienced at home. These tropical storms galloped through in a furious race to get somewhere, leaving everything drenched for the sun's heat to dry.

Freeing herself, she stood, still reeling from her experience. The rest of the crew was already hard at it, checking the ship for damage.

"Haul out that sail." Rocco was still shouting orders, and everyone was scrambling. "Chunk, you and the girl work the foresail."

Lisette ran to catch up, despite the pain in her shoulder, working with her partner to haul out the sail as ordered. Soon the ship was straightened out and flying across the whitecaps, heading away from the sunset. She paused, taking in the sight of it all, the calm to starboard, the blackness that swept away from the port side. As she looked around, she caught a view of Rocco at the helm. While his focus remained, the fierceness of his struggle against the wind was gone. He was just a man again.

Heavy hands patted her shoulders, and she turned to find Chunk beaming. His bushy gray hair was still dripping, and his clothes were streaked with dirt.

"That was a close 'un." He embraced her in a hearty bear hug. "I was a-scared to lose you."

She hugged him in return. "I was scared, too."

"By the gods—what happened?" Rocco barked at them. "We nearly lost that sail and overturned. Chunk, where were you?"

She glanced up at Chunk. He stood erect, terror in his eyes. Rocco was going to lay this at his feet unless she took ownership.

"It was my fault, Captain." She couldn't let her friend and mentor go under the lash. "I didn't realize how quickly the storm was coming. I should have waited for Chunk's help."

"Get below, you useless wench." His voice was a low growl.

Chunk stepped forward, his mouth opened to speak but Lisette pulled at his arm.

"I am fine," she mouthed to him, and scurried back toward the helm and down the steps.

In the cabin, she changed out of her soaked clothes and looked at her arm. Red welts wound like a snake from her wrist upward. She carefully checked the movement of each joint, bending and straightening. It hurt, but nothing felt broken or out of place. She regarded herself in the mirror. Her face was unmarred.

"Can't have bruises if I'm to be sold at port," she murmured.

Satisfied, she took a dry cloth to her dripping hair. She was reassembling her braid when the door opened and Poussin entered, carrying food. It was the first time he'd delivered food since that day he tattled on her.

"Poussin! How are you?" She tiptoed behind him and locked the door.

He dropped the platter of food on the table, upending the roast bird. "Now, see here, you let me out."

"Not until you tell me why you told the captain I was asking about his wife."

His eyes were as large as the platter. "I didn't mean to. Honest. I'm much too a-scared of the Cap'n. He seen me carryin' your tray and asked about you, and I started to fuss and fidget. After that, I told him everything."

"Not everything." She took the feather from her pocket and waved it about.

"Be careful wit' that." His voice rose two octaves.

"Why didn't you tell him about this? Is it yours?"

"No! It's—" He clamped both hands over his mouth.

"It's from a blood dragon, isn't it?"

He nodded.

"Is it the captain's?"

He shrugged. "Leave it alone, m'lady. Throw that thing away."

"I can't." She stroked the feather. "I have seen a dragon."

He collapsed in a chair and dropped his head into his hands. "So've I."

She rushed to his side. "What did you see? Where was it? Did it see you?"

"I can't." He jumped up and ran to the door. "Let me out."

"Not until you talk to me. Please, it sounds like we've been through the same thing. Let's share our experience."

"I don't want to share." He shook his head as he

backed away.

The latch turned in the door, stopped, and a fist pounded on the outside. Rocco roared, "Open up!"

Lisette hid the feather, and ran back to the door, unbolting it. Rocco burst in, scowling at her. He nodded to Poussin, who fled faster than a rabbit into thick brush, shutting the door behind him.

Picking up the pitcher, Lisette asked, "Rum?"

"Why was the door bolted?"

"It was a mistake. I was helping him with the food and the bar fell." She had not lied for some time and hoped this one held up to scrutiny.

"Or perhaps you used it to trap him into giving you more information."

"I said it was a mistake. What could he possibly tell me that would help me?"

"I told you to stop asking about Tempest."

"And I did not. All I wanted this night was food and drink." She swallowed a big gulp of liquid courage. "Today's storm was enough excitement for me."

"Good." He sat at the table and tore a leg from the roast bird. "How is your arm?"

"It's all right." Her left hand drifted up, rubbing her right shoulder. "Some redness, but it should pass quickly."

"Good. I don't want to sell a virgin with bruises. They don't bring as high a price."

The rest of the meal was eaten in silence, as usual. The captain was restless tonight, taking large bites of his food, pushing the leftovers around on the plate. He chugged his rum, refilled the goblet, and chugged again.

"Is all well, Captain?"

He stared at her, chewing on a piece of bread. "I'm aware of your nighttime wanderings."

"I'm not wandering. I like the crow's nest. It's a

beautiful view at night.”

“Tonight, you will not leave the cabin.” He was expressionless, although she detected irritation in his voice. “That is my order.”

“Is there something dangerous I should beware?”

“No.” His answer was clipped. “I don’t want you out on deck because I don’t want you out on deck. Because I’m the captain and my orders are obeyed.”

“Aye, Captain.”

As usual, he stormed out as the light dimmed. She ran to the door and listened to him disappear. His footsteps went along the corridor, not up the ladder to the deck. Her body was still pressed against the door when the latch turned. She jumped back as it opened.

It was Chunk. He had to bow his head to fit through the entrance. “Cap’n sent me to collect the dinner.”

“Poussin had enough of me again?”

“I couldn’t say.” He picked up the plates. “Why? Was you givin’ our little chick a rough time of it?”

“I’m a little more curious than he likes.” She poured another goblet of rum and offered one to her friend. “Chunk…what do you know about blood dragons?”

He stopped stacking plates and stared at her. Finally, he took the goblet, and sat. “I learnt the myth as a boy, thinkin’ it was all puffery.”

“And now you think differently?”

He spoke slowly, choosing his words more carefully than Lisette had ever heard. “There is a dragon, they say, what lives only to claim vengeance…so the story goes. When someone’s been wronged…awful wronged, they can…call on this dragon. It follows ’em, sort of, wherever they go, huntin’ for the ones what wronged ’em, killin’ ’em.”

“You’ve seen them?”

"Not on purpose. It's true, they are huntin' specific folks, but when they're in their blood lust, they don't always care if yer who they want. They're dragons. They cut the innocent down with the guilty." He rose, gathered the dishes, and left.

The last of the sun was dipping behind the water's edge. Tonight, the moon would be a crescent. The only time the dragon visited her, the moon was either a sliver, or darkly new. She remembered Rocco's map of the moon's phases. The waning to waxing drawings had a circle around them, with the words, "Dragon eyes." Perhaps there was a connection.

Rocco had not told her to stay away from the windows, only to stay in the cabin. What if Rocco had a dragon? She was not sure how he kept it during the day or where he hid it.

But she would find it.

# 17

Lisette leaned against the windows, looking out and up, until the sun had almost disappeared. Darkness crept forward from the east, devouring the sun's rays.

She had promised Rocco to stay here, but curiosity overcame her obedience, and she cracked the cabin door open. Her heart thumped in her ears as she took the first small step, and the next, until she was crawling, low, up the stairs. Any noise startled her, causing her to freeze until she heard quiet again.

At last, she could see the helm. Rocco was there, focusing on the sea, as usual. The golden light gave sharp angles to his features. He grasped a rope with a loop and set it over one of the pegs of the wheel, lashing it in place.

She tucked down flat as he stepped from the helm and disappeared. A low moan came from somewhere, followed by heavy panting. She held her breath, pressing her body harder into the wood. For a few moments, there was nothing except the sound of lapping water and shipboards creaking.

Lisette looked toward the sky—there was a dark form, lifting from the stern.

As it rose toward the moon's crescent, she made out the silhouette of the dragon, its wings reaching through the air. The blood-red feathers were dark in the moon's shard of light, although the occasional reflection caught the dark tips outlining the beast. It swept up until it was over the ship, turned and banked left, making no sound.

She raised up to see if Rocco was back at the helm. As if sensing her movement, the dragon whipped about, the sparkling silver of its eyes searching the ship.

Leaping down the stairs, she tripped, falling to the lower deck. She scrambled back into the cabin, half running, half crawling, anticipating the piercing stab of the dragon's talons at any minute. The door stuck and she shoved it closed with a screaming grunt. Clambering for her dagger, she stood and watched the door, her heart trying to escape from her chest.

She waited for several minutes, anticipating Rocco's angry return. He must have known she was spying on the dragon. When no one and nothing stormed in after her, she at last collapsed to the floor with a heavy sigh. She pulled the feather from her pocket and held it out, studying the soft plumes. Soft feathers for silent flight.

It was true. Rocco had a dragon.

She slunk into bed, thinking about tomorrow. There were so many questions but asking them would require finesse. He could not know that she had disobeyed him. He had threatened her with death, after all.

Or worse—he might lock her in the cabin again.

The covers felt cool to her skin, yet her body was heated. She kept tossing them off, pulling them back, repeating the cycle. Her chemise twisted around her waist and hips, constraining her. Between her fights with the bed and her clothing, she squeezed her eyes shut and attempted slumber.

"Argh," she groaned and sat up. Pulling the slip over her head, she tossed it to the side and pulled the covers around her. Rocco had not been sleeping in this cabin, and when he did, it did not seem to matter what she wore. Her body felt soothed immediately.

As she snuggled into the mattress, her hands ran across her curves, and she let them linger. She considered all of the different Roccos. He was cruel and harsh. He dropped her at the last port with coldhearted abandon and could have killed her in his drunken rage. He was also passionate and heartbroken, yearning for his Tempest. That part of him was only visible when he was half-asleep, but it existed.

In the end, her highest praise for him was he hadn't killed her—yet.

As her body and mind settled, she imagined the feel of his hands caressing her, and his lips melting her body with their touch. This was so different from anything she had been told.

Genevieve's description of her romantic nights with her husband did not sound like this. Mama's assessment of physical intimacy was that men and women coupled like animals, without much feeling. Both women claimed love for their husbands, although Mama's began as the duty of a lady. Neither of them described what Lisette felt. Was it love or desire? Did it matter?

Was it such a sin to crave a man's touch more than, say, to enjoy a delicious meal or hear a pleasant tune?

She said a brief—if blasphemous—prayer that Rocco would return and find her tempting enough to ravish, whether he was awake or asleep. God would have to forgive her lust. She relaxed into the covers and slept at last.

The creak of the door woke her. Rocco stumbled in and flopped onto the bed for the first time in two weeks. As usual, the light from the windows was muted and gray. She lay still, affecting sleep. He slid under the covers, groaning, and almost immediately fell to snoring.

Certain he was in deep slumber, she moved closer to him, nestling against his back. He did not stir. His body was warm, and she closed her eyes in relaxation.

A gentle fondling of her thigh awoke her. She felt his hand on her skin, soft yet firm, as if each fingertip was committing her form to memory.

"Tempest."

Tempest had never left his heart. Lisette was merely the vessel. An odd sort of jealousy soured in her stomach.

His fingers took the inside route this time, tickling and exciting her, until he brushed the hair where her thighs met. It was a delectable feeling, a tease promising something even better. By the time his hand embraced its goal, Lisette was forgotten, and she was happy to be his Tempest, yearning for more.

As he kissed her neck, his fingers continued their exploration. The warm but ambiguous sensations she had experienced before were now fully centered on a small but central piece of her body.

*If I'd known it felt this good, I would not have waited this long.*

Rocco's lips and tongue kept warming her neck as his fingers worked their wonders, giving her intense delight. Her gasp dissolved into shallow breaths that caught with each rub.

Pressure built within, an almost unbearable swelling and heat between her thighs. She felt her back arch and hips raise, trying to both relieve the tension and enjoy it more. Turning to him, she cradled his face with both hands and pressed her lips against his. His mouth parted and she melted, ready to accept anything else he might give.

Dark eyelashes fluttered open, revealing his sapphire eyes. As he awakened, his face revealed intense love, followed by brief confusion, ending in a coldness that drove into her like a stake. He pulled away, anger twisting his mouth. Leaping from the bed, he snatched clothes from the trunk and stomped from the cabin without giving her another glance.

"Rocco." She stared after him, clinging to the covers. "Please…?"

He was gone. She rose and dressed, alternately crying and stomping around the room.

The sun had climbed a bit higher when the door opened again, and Poussin brought a tray of food. "Cap'n says yer goin' out tonight, so no work above today. I'll be bringin' yer dress later—and he says make sure yer bathed proper."

He placed the tray on the table and left. She sat and picked up a piece of dried meat, pushing away her sadness at Rocco's rejection, and wondering what kind of danger she'd be getting herself out of tonight.

Hopefully, she wouldn't need to kill anyone.

Lisette didn't see Rocco the entire day. Instead, Chunk waited at the boats for her. He assisted her into the dinghy and waited for it to be lowered before climbing down the ladder and taking his own seat.

"Captain having a busy day?" she asked.

Chunk nodded. "Went ashore early to nose around, make in-quire-ies. Gave me marchin' orders an' disappeared."

They sat, quiet, while the crewmen's oars stroked the waters. Chunk patted her arm, smiling when she glanced at him. She could see the worry in his face.

"It's okay, Chunk. I know what I'm doing."

"Of course you do, Lizzie. I've all the faith." He nodded.

"Thank you." She was aware of the leather strap

hugging her thigh, and touched the bodice of her dress, where she had hidden the sleeping potion. The cold shaft of her lucky feather pressed against her chest as she patted the vial.

They passed the dock and went to a small inlet, away from the lights. Two of the crewmen leaped out and pulled the boat to shore. Chunk took her hand, guiding her onto the beach and up the cobbled street. He looked up and pointed. The road went uphill to a large castle. This was a different atmosphere from Isla de la Soledad. Richer, and happier. Even the castle looked like Lisette's home.

She looked up the path, patting Chunk's hand. "How long will the ship be here?"

"Cap'n says we'll be here a few days." He smiled at her. "Plenty o' time."

The sun still hovered above the horizon, yet the arch of waxing moon had appeared by the time they arrived at the hilltop castle. Chunk started toward the side entrance, but she stopped him.

"Don't let the ship leave without me." She held out her hand.

He took it and escorted her to the door. "I'll be waitin' fer ya."

When it opened, a man of enormous height and girth greeted Chunk. He rattled a leather bag before them, tinkling merrily with the sound of coin. "You have the girl?"

"You have the gold?" Chunk accepted the bag and pulled her into the light.

Lisette stumbled to the door, and the man yanked her inside by her wrist. Chunk held onto her arm. She saw the worry on his face as he released her, and the door closed.

They stood in a sort of pantry, and she studied the space that looked so much like her own kitchen. Her heart fluttered, thinking of her family. She hated being torn away from them. A horrible homesickness washed over her.

The large man whipped her about to face him. "I am the Duke de Martinmas, Girl, master of this house and lord of this land. The pirates tell me I've purchased the daughter of a carpenter from Isla de la Soledad. Might I enquire, what is your breeding?"

She knew this man, had seen him at her castle with her father. He did not appear to recognize her. "What does it matter, my lord?"

"I should get what I've paid for." He looked her over as if inspecting a broodmare's conformation. Rocco had found her a pretty, if simple, frock showing lots of cleavage, and she had taken time to wash her hair and braid it. At last, he nodded. "I've purchased you for my son. You have until dawn to service him. If you succeed and become pregnant, I will give you a home and immeasurable wealth. If you fail, I shall sell you to the town brothel. If you try to escape, my guards will kill you."

The duke steered her up the back stairs, holding a large ring of keys in his other hand. They wound through corridors and up more steps, stopping at a large, wooden door. He selected a key from the ring and unlocked it.

With a firm shove, he pushed her inside and closed the door. She stumbled into the room, struggling to keep upright. The sound of the key scraping metal meant she was locked in, with God only knows what or who.

A faint tapping sound made her turn. It was a cavernous room, decorated with a fine tapestry of what she assumed to be the family patriarch in battle. There was a bed, tables and chairs, and most impressively, a floor-to-ceiling wall of books. She had a library at home, but it didn't contain nearly so many volumes.

In a far corner, overlooking the balcony, there was

an outsized chair lit by candles. A man's legs extended from the seat, crossed at the ankles. His hand tapped on the arm, as if bored. This was no doubt the duke's son.

Lisette walked toward him. "Buenas nochas." She spoke Spanish, as his father had.

The hand stopped tapping and waved languidly. Whether he was inviting her over or dismissing her, she had no idea, but she walked around to face the chair. A young man slouched in the seat, holding a goblet. From the length of his legs, she guessed him to be tall, much like his father, although perhaps a quarter of his girth.

He had the most beautiful countenance she had ever seen. Unlike his father's wide, porcine face, his bone structure was strong and masculine, with a well-defined jaw and cheekbones, but his features had a delicacy to them, as if carved by an artist.

Large, dark eyes studied her, as his full lips pursed and pouted. "So you are my virgin du jour?" His soft voice mocked the words.

She could not tear her eyes away from his beauty. Losing her virginity to this god might not be so bad. "Yes, Sire."

"Have you a name?"

She hesitated. A real one, or a fake one? There was one name which might give her courage. "Tempest."

A sly grin played on his lips. "Tempest, eh? So your parents believed you would be a stormy child?"

"I was named for one of my ancestors. A family tradition."

"And I am the Marquess Constantine de Martinmas, also named for my ancestors. You may call me Connie." He extended his goblet. "Mead?"

She had not tasted mead since that night. Its sweetness used to call to her, but now it held memories of her betrayers' voices, her spinning head, and her current predicament.

"I'd love some."

He swung his hand to the right. "You'll find it on the tray."

She retrieved the pitcher and a goblet, remembering that night and the drugs. "May I refill your cup?"

He held his out, so she filled it, along with hers. She watched him take a long sip before raising her goblet, satisfied. He raised his in response, saluting.

"Now that I've proven there's no poison, please enjoy."

She smiled. "I thought I was being clever."

"There's nothing wrong with being clever." He raised himself from the chair, towering over her. "I consider it a shrewd move on your part."

She smiled and took a sip, letting the sweetness coat her senses. Eric's face entered her mind, Mercedes' laugh returned to her ears, but she gritted her teeth, banishing them. She would enjoy the wine.

"Too sweet for your taste?"

"No, it's good." She took another drink in defiance of her demons. "It brings back memories."

"We have plenty of time, if you'd like to tell me your life story." He gestured around the room. "Between the lock on the door and the guards outside, you'll have to stay the night, although I do apologize in advance."

"For what?"

"You will leave here in the same state you arrived, which means you'll go to the brothel."

"May I ask why?"

He raised his glass to an enormous painting over the fire of a stout man, astride a stout horse. "This is the game my father and I play. You see, women do not tempt me. I am attracted to men. Ordinarily, this is not a problem, except dear Papa wants me to produce an heir.

He is adamant. For some reason, he thinks it would be fine for me to copulate with a woman once, produce a child, and go on my merry way."

"And this is something you cannot do?"

"It's become a battle of wills between us. I find the thought of lying with a woman abhorrent. He believes if I can do it once, I'll realize it's not so bad." He sighed and took a long deep drink. "I've been locked in here until I come to my senses."

"So…if you lay with me, your father will free us both."

"Not exactly. I would be released, but you would be held captive until it was proven that you are pregnant. After the baby's birth, you would likely be tossed aside."

"And if I'm not pregnant?"

He shrugged. "I am guessing that my father would drag me back to perform again until we got it right. That is, of course, if he can find me."

"So that promise of a home and riches for the mother of his grandchild was not true?" She sipped her mead.

"True for the child. I cannot imagine my father letting his noble cronies discover his bastard grandson was born of a servant girl, bought with gold."

"Would I be treated better if I were the daughter of a duke?"

He grinned. "My father would die of giddiness."

## 19

Lisette let her gaze wander around the room, looking for escape. "How long have you been locked in this battle with your father?"

"A year so far." He waved his hand. "I admit, I am weary of my imprisonment, but I cannot yield."

"If I was able to free you, would you be able to free me?" Lisette strolled to a bench in front of the bookshelves, sipping from her goblet and thinking.

He regarded her, his eyes narrow. "How might this be possible, without the obvious solution?"

"I could help you escape if you would return the favor." She sat, gesturing for him to join her on the bench. "We give your father the proof he requires to believe you have done the deed. You are set free, and take me with you, at least to town. We can find some excuse. Anywhere that I can make my escape."

Connie sat, silent, for several minutes while draining his goblet. At last, he spoke. "You are a canny young woman, so different from the ones I've been dealing with. What kind of proof will you offer?"

"Where is the sheet that would capture the blood of my virginity?"

He gathered it from the bed and handed it to her. Keeping her eyes on him, she bit her lip, hard, until she drew blood, blotting it on the sheet. "There, m'lord. You have deflowered me."

His laughter filled the space, bouncing off the walls and ringing around the room. It took several moments for him to calm himself. "If you were a man, I should be in love."

"And man or woman, it would be easy to return the feelings." Lisette handed the sheet back to him. "How is it possible that no other woman offered to solve the problem like this?"

"Because the other women only saw the riches awaiting them if they could seduce me. Even the most virtuous maidens were lured by the idea of having a nobleman's heir. Especially if it was accompanied by a large sack of gold."

At that moment, someone shrieked beyond the balcony. Connie rushed out the arched door, and she followed but shrank away from what she saw.

The grounds below were a walking garden of pathways through beautiful exotic plants. A slender shaft of moonlight gave the edges of the flowers and leaves a soft glow.

An old man was running through them, in and out of the frangipani and jasmine, and across the stones. He screamed as he ran, and for good reason. Charging at his heels was a dragon.

The end came quickly. One false step, and the man

was down. He turned and half-begged, half-shrieked for mercy. The dragon's talons slashed, its fire roared. Within moments, the old man was reduced to charred bones.

"Philippe." Connie whispered the name.

The dragon flapped its large, feathered wings three times and was aloft. His crested neck and sculpted head reminded Lisette of her father's stud horse, rearing against the night sky. He looked at the balcony. His eyes found hers, and he roared again, a thunderous sound, accompanied by a flash of fire.

She backed to the doorway and collapsed, her hand covering her chest. Connie was in front of her, lifting her. He carried her into the room and laid her on a velvet chaise. Her body trembled and she kept her hand at her throat, still defending herself from the beast.

"He wants *me*," she mumbled.

Connie rose and looked carefully out the arch, stepping further outside, until he turned back to Lisette. "It's gone."

Calming herself, she asked, "Who was that unfortunate man?"

"My father's visitor. The Viscount de Thibault."

Her stomach dropped and she fell back into the lounge. Connie disappeared and reappeared with a goblet. Sitting her up in his arms, he held the drink to her lips. It was not mead, but rum, strong rum. She coughed from the burn of it, relaxed against him and said what she had never said aloud to a stranger.

"When I was six, I saw a dragon kill my uncle."

Connie surprised her again. "It's the blood dragon."

"You know?" She sat up and faced him. "You must tell me. What is a blood dragon? All I know is they live to avenge wrongs."

"True. There's not much more to the story."

"But where do they come from? Where do they live?"

He gave her a quizzical look. "They live among us, Tempest. They are us."

"I don't understand. How are *they* us?"

He went to his collection of books, and returned with a small, leather-bound journal. "I believe this will help you. It was written by my abuela and tells you everything."

"About blood dragons?"

Connie nodded. "I was ten when I saw the dragon kill another visitor to our court. My parents did all in their power to convince me otherwise, but mi abuelita believed me. She gave me this book, her journal of all she knew of blood dragons. She also told me that if I met anyone else who had seen them, I was to pass the book on to them."

He leaned forward and kissed her cheek. "You're the one who needs it now."

"I still don't understand, Connie. What do you mean 'they are us'?"

He pointed to the book. "It's all in here. There are people who turn into blood dragons."

She frowned. "People?"

"Well, I believe it's just one person at the moment in our corner of the world. As I've heard it, it all began 19 years ago, with the birth of a young noblewoman, my cousin Mercedes de Medina of Spain. I doubt you have heard of her."

Lisette blushed and held her tongue.

"The man who is a dragon is hunting every nobleman and woman who were on Isla del Lagarto the night of her birth," he continued. "The houses of Thibault, Medina, Bauchene, and de Lille. He has been hunting them for many years now. He will not stop until they are all destroyed."

"De Lille? That is—" Lisette stopped herself from saying more.

"That is—what?"

She became aware of her hands in his, as his beautiful face expressed kindness and concern. "That name is familiar to me."

"Ah, I'm guessing you're not from here?"

She hung her head. "Not exactly. But it doesn't matter. Why is he hunting them?"

"There is only one reason for a blood dragon to hunt. These people did something to him or his family, something unforgiveable, and he cannot avenge himself in any other way."

She imagined a man, twisting and turning, becoming this creature. She shook her head. "It is unimaginable."

"Perhaps so, but true nonetheless." Connie gathered her up from the chaise and helped her to stand. "Come along, now. With all the chaos in the courtyard, it's the perfect opportunity to get you out and safely to wherever you belong."

"What about you? Aren't you going to leave?"

"Yes, but I must prepare. Now that you've lost our virginities, I'll be free to go whenever I want." He winked. "I'm not certain Papa will afford you the same luxury, until he realizes you are not with child. When he finds you are not, I fear he might force us to try again."

"Yes, of course." She glanced out the window. Chunk awaited at the shore for her. Rocco had promised more ports and more coin.

A large group had gathered to attend to the dead man, including the few guards that had not chased after the dragon in an attempt to kill it. Connie led her to the far end of the balcony which wrapped around the corner.

"Can you climb?"

She nodded, so he motioned to a large vine crawling up the wall. Peering over the stone edge and seeing there were no guards, she removed her slippers and dropped them to the ground. She grasped the main stalk of the vine, swung her right leg across, found a foothold, and followed with her left.

"Wait." Connie removed something shiny from his hand and pressed it onto her index finger. In the dimness she could make out a ring with a crest upon it. "This is my private seal. It might give you some help along the way."

"Connie, I—"

"Go, quickly! Before they recall that we need guarding."

She clutched a branch of the vine, steadying herself to clamber down. "Connie, why didn't you climb down and escape when you had the chance?"

A broad smile revealed dimples to swoon for. "Tempest, my dear. I'm afraid of heights."

She couldn't help but laugh. "I shall always remember you."

Her careful descent was tempered by the plethora of leaves and blossoms. She tried not to knock too many of them off, lest the stripped vine betray her escape in the morning. When she was close enough to the ground, she jumped to the grass. She searched for her slippers, feeling around in the darkness.

"Looking for these?"

She straightened up and turned. The duke held her silk slippers in his wide, stubby hand.

"M'lord—" Lisette's usually-nimble mind was so preoccupied with dragons, she could not get it to concoct a lie.

"Little known fact." His voice had a frightening softness to it. "A distraction of any kind is useful when one is making an escape." He took her face in his hand and held it up so he could stare into it. "I knew, when I first laid eyes on you, you would run."

She wondered whether to tell him about her "success." He grabbed her arm and was dragging her back into the castle. *Perhaps not yet. There is no reason for him to believe me.*

They returned to Connie's room. The duke opened the door and tried to shove her in again, but she bounced against someone else. Connie was standing there, blocking the doorway.

"Father, what are you doing?"

"I am returning this wench. She has a job to do."

Connie sighed, a most indulgent, patronizing exhale that almost made her laugh. "Which she has done. I have given up. Come in and see for yourself."

The duke pushed her aside and strode into the room. Connie had pulled the covers off his bed and stirred the sheets about to look as if they'd been the scene of passionate activity. The sheet with the bloody proof was tossed casually to the side. Lisette looked at Connie. He gave her a quick wink as his father inspected the evidence.

"At last," the duke said. "That wasn't so bad, was it?"

She tried to work up a blush. It was difficult, but when she remembered last night with Rocco, the heat rose up her neck.

The duke turned his attentions to her. "If you were successful, why were you escaping?"

She lowered her eyes. "I confess, m'lord, the thing in the courtyard...I saw a man on fire. The horror of it—all I could think of was how to get away from this place. Your son tried to stop me, but I fought him. I'm sorry."

Connie picked up where she left off. "She was crazed with fright. She evaded me, slippery as a fish, and threw herself from the balcony, onto the vine."

The duke regarded the scene, his small, puffy eyes glancing left and right. Lisette prayed their lie would hold.

"Well, I'm sorry you were so frightened, miss—I should have your name, now that there is a chance you could be bearing my son's child."

"Tempest."

He grimaced, and she wondered if he had some knowledge of Rocco and his wife.

"Tempest." His voice choked. "You will be our guest for a little while."

He turned to Connie. "Now that you have done your duty to our family, you may be released from your quarters. Please believe me, there was no joy in what I did, only honor. We must keep our family line from dying." He paused and reached for Lisette's hand. "And you, dear girl will lack for nothing. If in time you prove to be with child, you will be treated like a queen until the babe's birth. At that time, you can leave with my blessing and a hefty sum of gold."

"Thank you, m'lord," she said through gritted teeth.

The duke escorted her to a new jail, a tower at the opposite end of the castle. The first thing she did was go to the balcony and look out. In the dim moonlight, she observed the outline of *L'Implacable* on the water. She strained, trying to determine if the small boat was still on the shoreline, but it wasn't visible. Chunk said she had a few days.

The moon's crescent had moved and was over the ship. In her imagination, a dragon hung in the sky and stared at the deck. Lisette let her mind drift to Rocco, staggering into the cabin at dawn. In that moment, she stopped fighting what she knew. Rocco didn't have a blood dragon—he *was* the blood dragon. It didn't matter how inconceivable the idea was. She had to believe it.

The door behind her creaked open. "M'lady, I brought you some dinner."

A young woman entered, possibly younger than Lisette, in a plain brown frock. Her hair was covered by a large cap, but ebony curls peeked from the edges. With large dark eyes and long lashes, she was a pretty girl, no matter how she tried to hide it.

"What's your name?"

"Pinar."

"Thank you for the meal, Pinar."

"M'lord says you must eat it all. He says you must be healthy."

Lisette grimaced. "M'lord thinks I might be carrying his son's child."

Her eyes widened. "Oh, that would be glorious. So, the young marquess is free again?"

"Yes." Lisette looked out to the ship once more. This time, small boats were nearing it. They were going back without her. She closed her eyes. "Yes, Constantine is free, and I am trapped."

"Oh, no, m'lady. Only until you have the baby."

Lisette gestured to the balcony. "Please set the tray out here."

Pinar put the tray of food on a small table outside and withdrew. Lisette picked at her meal, watching the sea. The moon was heading toward the horizon. Were the sails being unfurled? She could not tell in this dim light and leaned against the balustrade, so intent on what was happening, she nearly toppled over the edge.

"No, no, no," She kept repeating. A few days—Rocco promised a few days.

She knew which line should be touched next, which sail hoisted. But the ship remained. The sails remained secured. It was her imagination and fear painting the scene. She had time.

Sinking back into the chair, Lisette picked up the goblet and drank. She kept drinking until her mind grew soft and blurry. As she closed her eyes, the tip of the mast was the last thing in her view.

It was late morning when she rose and stretched. Spending a night in the sea air, curled at odd angles, had left her stiff. For some time, she walked the length of the balcony, to and fro, trying to come up with a plan for escape. *L'Implacable* still sat in the bay. Lisette could almost feel Chunk waiting for her.

The sun was sufficiently high to chase most shadows and leave nothing unseen. She watched people on the pier, walking in the sunlight like tiny bugs, their shadows reaching across the planks of the dock. A warm breeze blew her disheveled hair across her face. She brushed it away from her eyes and out of her mouth. As she did so, she looked back at the anchored ship.

The mainsail unfurled, undulating with the wind until taking shape and filling with air. Lisette gasped, watching the rest of the sails join in the work, and move the ship through the lapping water, toward the open horizon. Her mouth remained open as her escape plan collapsed with each puff of wind into the canvas. She could not believe that Chunk would leave her here on purpose.

Rocco must have ordered it so. The captain's orders are to be obeyed.

She watched the ship until it was swallowed by the sunlight's glare upon the sea, leaning over the balcony as if to fly to the deck. When it was gone, she sank into the chair. Her hopes sank with her.

# 21

Pinar brought food again, smiling and friendly. Lisette gestured to the table next to her but did not turn to look at it. Food had no appeal. The girl returned with fresh clothes. Glancing at the untouched plate, she made a disapproving, tsking sound.

"Eat, m'lady. The baby must grow strong."

Lisette turned to her and attempted a weak smile. "There is no baby, Pinar. The young lord and I pretended to complete the deed, to free him. He was supposed to free me to join my ship. Now it has left, bound no doubt for the next port, and I have been abandoned."

"My pardons." Pinar stopped at the doorway and gave her a sideways glance. "But do not despair, m'lady. Things have a way of working out to the best."

Lisette watched her leave, heard the door locking. Telling Pinar the truth was not on her agenda, but either weariness or courage loosened her tongue. The maid's response intrigued her. Perhaps she could think of a way out.

As she ate, she read Connie's book. "*My name is Countess Lenore de Triana. Let this serve as warning,*" it began. "*When I was a child, I beheld a great beast.*"

It was written by an old and trembling hand, inked in lines that wavered between fat and skipping. Crude drawings illustrated her story of witnessing a member of her family struck down. Her description of the event could have been Lisette's own. As the writings progressed, it was obvious her obsession with the dragon outdid Lisette's. She searched everywhere for the truth about blood dragons, distressing her family and distancing her from most of polite society.

A young villager was able to point the countess toward a hovel, deep in the inner jungle of a small island, Île des Anciens, where an old woman lived. This crone was a purveyor of healing and hexes. She could cure a fever, or curse a neighbor, and she had potions to make people beautiful, or smart—or a dragon.

The key jiggled in the door, so Lisette stashed the book under the chair cushions. Connie swept into the room.

"How are you this morning?" He gave her a quick bow. "I'm so sorry my father trapped you here."

"And I'm so sorry he's going to make us spend the night together again when he finds out I'm not with child."

"Yes, true. Forgive me, Tempest, I enjoy your company, but you're not quite right for my ideal evening's play." He beamed his dimpled grin.

She should have been cross, but he was both handsome and charming. She'd have gladly handed him her virginity. It was her bad fortune he wouldn't take it.

"And what about you? Now that you have been let out of your prison, you have a small window of time to be free, until my childless condition is discovered."

"I am scheduled to visit a friend of mine, Count Barragan on Isla de la Soledad. It may take a lengthy time to discuss our—arrangement, and I may be delayed in my return, depending upon what rumors I hear from the staff." He winked, and she guessed his meaning. "From there, Xavier—I mean, the count—and I are scheduled to travel to Isla del Lagarto to attend the wedding of my cousin, the Marquise Mercedes de Medina."

"Do you know your cousin well?" She looked away to hide the tears that threatened.

"No, but rumor has it, she's absolutely beautiful and completely untrustworthy."

Lisette collapsed into the chair, weeping. Connie knelt beside her, his arms in a warm embrace. His beauty and strength, the way he smelled of spice, it all made her cry more.

"I am going to be stuck here forever," she mumbled between sobs. "Stuck and a virgin. You don't want me because I'm Tempest and not a man, and Rocco doesn't want me because I'm Lisette and not Tempest. My home has been claimed for Spain, I don't know what has happened to my family, Mercedes and Eric have won, and I am in ruins. I should throw myself from the balcony."

He took her chin in his hand, wiping her tears with his fingers. "First, this balcony is not high enough to kill you. If you jumped, you would merely be crippled for the rest of your too-long life. Second, you are a beautiful young woman and if I did not prefer men, believe me, I would take you to my bed in a heartbeat. Third, I know of Mercedes and Eric, but who is Rocco, and who is

Lisette?"

She managed to slow the river running down her face and stared into his wide dark eyes. *Time for the truth.* "I might not have been honest last night. My proper name is Lady Lisette de Lille, but you may call me Lizzie."

And with that came the entire tale of who she was back on Île des Oiseaux, and who she was now, aligned with pirates. She left out the part about killing four Spaniards and sleeping next to a captain who was also a blood dragon, but she included the names of her betrayers. Connie nodded the entire time, his expression sympathetic, except for a raised eyebrow at certain points.

She ran out of words and tears and stopped. In the silence, she could hear the birds chattering in the trees, and the waves on the distant shore.

"I am sorry," Connie said at last. "My cousin's daughter has behaved most badly. In her defense, let us remember her family is under the thumb of El Rey. Do not fool yourself, Lizzie. Each country has its own interest in acquiring property and will do whatever it takes to secure more land. Even steal husbands."

Lisette stood, a bit of her stubbornness, and much of her anger, returning. "They may want more property, but I am not some 'thing' to be bought and sold. She ruined my *life,* not to mention my family. I'm so angry, I could hoist Mercedes' head on a stake."

He shrugged. "They are my cousins, but I am not overly attached to that branch of the family. I fear they are not long for this realm at any rate. Rumor is the Count de Medina is the dragon's main quarry and has evaded the beast these many years. But he cannot hide forever.

"So, here's what we shall do, Lizzie. Tomorrow, I set sail. If you can remain here one more day, I will arrange for your escape to the village. I confess, I cannot return you to your ship, but in town, you may be able to procure passage on the next ship to anchor here." He gave her a chaste kiss on the cheek.

"I would be most grateful," she said, managing a wan smile. "One more favor—at the moment could we keep my true name and my circumstances a secret? I fear my situation might become awkward if your father knew."

"True, if dear Papa discovered he actually did purchase a duke's daughter, and a French one at that, I'm not certain how he would react. Rest assured I will not divulge your story. Luckily, I never tell him anything important." He grinned and left.

Lisette fingered her emerald, which she had stowed in her pocket. Passage would take currency, of which she had none. She wondered how far the jewel would get her. His promise was not ideal, but she hoped he would keep his word. At least she had his signet ring. It might gain her access to someone or something useful.

In the two days that followed, she was caught between waiting patiently and pacing frantically, sure that she had been abandoned. She watched the port from her window. A Spanish ship arrived, stayed a day, and sailed. She could only assume Connie was on that ship. The port was empty after that.

Pinar became oddly distant. She delivered the meals without speaking and left the room as quickly as possible. After the second day, Lisette knew she had been fooled. The duke's son had never intended to help. In the end, he only helped himself.

She spent the next day studying the room, and the balcony, looking for any means of escape. The vine she had used at Connie's room did not extend to this wing of the castle. The stones here were smooth, unclimbable.

She still had her dagger, the feather, the vial of

sleeping potion, and her emerald. Of all these, only the emerald seemed useful. Servants never supped with their lords and ladies, so it would be difficult to slip the potion into something Pinar might drink. Threatening her with the dagger was harsh. If she refused, Lisette knew she did not have the heart to kill her.

She could bribe the maid with her jewel, but then she'd have nothing to pay for her passage. As she pondered, she pressed her hand to her chest, feeling the plumes of the feather against her skin. Walking around the room, she looked at the bed. She hadn't slept in it for three days, preferring to sleep on the balcony, and as little as possible.

The bed was stuffed to be as comfortable as nobility deserved, with plenty of covers to hide from the night's chill. Lisette regarded the covers and realized they could be sliced into strips. Strips that could be tied together to make a rope. She retrieved her dagger and picked up a sheet. Somehow, she would escape this place.

The key jingled in the door, giving her barely time to get the knife back into its sheath, strapped to her leg. She was fluffing her skirt when the duke entered the room.

The duke's harsh demeanor from their previous encounter had transformed into one of fatherly concern. "How are you feeling?"

"Well, m'lord." If Lisette could convince him of her good health and possible condition, he would leave and let her get back to business.

"I suppose it's too early for any sign of a child?"

"Much."

"Come. Let us speak." He sat in a massive chair near the open fireplace and invited Lisette to take the seat opposite, smiling in a way she did not care for. Still, she obeyed. He folded his hands across his expansive girth. "Little known fact. A few years ago, I was a visitor at the court of the Baron Luc de Thibault. The baroness was receiving her sister at the time, a Duchess Juliette de Lille, with her two children."

He stared at her, a wry look on his face like he was baiting her.

Lisette was determined not to bite. "I hope you had a nice visit."

"I'm struck by how much you resemble Juliette's daughter."

"Many people resemble many people."

"Don't misunderstand." His leer broadened. "It would be so much better to discover I truly bought a noblewoman, as opposed to a simple girl from a peasant family. And the daughter of the Duke de Lille would be heralded as a miracle."

She kept her voice level but curious. "Why is that, Sire?"

"Not only was she kidnapped by pirates, but shortly after, Île des Oiseaux was claimed for Spain." He shook his head. "Her poor parents."

"Yes, they must miss her."

"Ah, would that they could." The duke stared at her intently. "Sadly, they have both perished."

Lisette's hands, folded neatly in her lap, gripped each other to the point of drawing blood from her palms. She maintained an expressionless mask as the life drained from her. A response was expected, she knew. The duke was waiting for her to break down and reveal her identity.

She cleared her throat. "How unfortunate," she whispered.

"Yes, well, I assume you know the unfortunate soul who was struck down in our garden, Philippe de Thibault. His family is currently sailing here. They were planning to pick up poor Philippe on their way to Isla del Lagarto for a wedding celebration. Sadly, they'll have to make other arrangements. The baroness, Elena de Thibault will be joining us. She was the Duchess de Lille's older sister." He leaned forward. "It's a pity she won't be able to reunite with her niece."

Tatie Elena—the one family member she did not long to greet. Previously, she wanted to scold her wayward aunt. Now she wanted to run a sword through her.

She managed to find her voice once more. "I hope they find her, wherever she is."

The duke uncoupled his hands and lifted himself from the chair. "I shall leave you now. You must have rest and food. When the baroness arrives, I shall arrange for you to take walks in the garden. Her niece was about your age…I'm sure it will comfort her to spend time with a young woman so much like, what was her name?" He tapped his finger against his lip, his eyes focused on hers. "Lisette."

"Of truth, I do not know." She rose and gave him a small curtsy. "But I shall walk with this baroness if you insist, m'lord."

He left, and once again, the familiar key clicked in the lock. Before this, he had seemed almost benign, even if he did pay for her virginal services. Now she envisioned herself kicking him between the legs. The ruling class was becoming less appealing to her with every encounter. She returned to the bed and took out the dagger. Picking up a sheet, she nicked an edge, put the knife down and pulled the material apart.

While she worked, Lisette considered his offer. She could reveal herself, be taken into the de Martinmas house, and probably be married off to Connie, at least for appearances. There would be gold available, gold to find out what happened to her parents, gold to hunt down Eric and Mercedes, and Tatie, and power to get justice for what they'd done.

Tears fell on the strip of sheet in her hands. Her

parents, dead? She wished the duke was wrong, wanted to deny it, but in her soul, it had the ring of truth. And where was Jules? Dropping the strip, dropping the sheet, she fell onto the bed and sobbed. She remained there for some time, weeping silently, in case the duke kept his ear to the door.

Kidnapped, defiled, orphaned, all for a stupid political land grab.

"They will pay," she growled through gritted teeth. As she said these words, warmth grew against her chest. She put her hand up to discover the feather was hot, as if it agreed with her desire for revenge.

Perhaps she could also reclaim her island for France. She had never been politically inclined, but this would honor her parents, and spite Mercedes and Eric. The only question was whether to take the island back before or after she killed them.

The duke's offer might afford her riches and some influence, but it was attached to many strings. Surely, he would not approve when she killed his cousin and her betrothed. He might not even give her the chance to exact her revenge. And if he married her off to Connie but expected an heir, who would sire the child? Certainly not his son.

Rocco's sapphire eyes flashed in her memory and she shuddered. Kind to her one moment, cruel the next. As the dragon, he wanted to kill her—why hadn't he yet? He'd had many opportunities. It was a tale that needed an ending, and only Rocco could provide it. She pictured him, standing at the helm, strong, brave, handsome.

"I don't want to love you." She ripped the sheet violently. "I'm afraid of you. I don't want—any of this."

In the end, she distrusted the duke more than she trusted and feared a pirate. She still had her emerald, her dagger, and now Connie's signet ring. And the feather—

it had to be of some use, besides stopping daggers and fanning the flame of her anger.

"I'll make my own way, somehow."

She had three strips torn when the familiar noise at the door made her hide her handiwork. Pinar entered with the midday meal, took it to the balcony and set it at the table. Lisette was accustomed to her dashing from the room, but today she stood by the food, fidgeting from one foot to the other, and glancing at her.

"How are you today, Pinar?" She walked toward the table.

"It's a good day, m'lady." Pinar gestured toward the ocean, sounding happy and relaxed. "You'll have a pretty view today."

Lisette looked up. The sun glistened on the water, blurring the horizon. She recognized a white triangle heading toward port. "Looks like a ship is headed our way."

"Not any ship." Pinar moved closer and lowered her voice. "A ship that could take someone away, if that someone still wished to go."

Lisette's heart rose. "Tell me more."

"I know the ship and its captain. They're without country, so to say, although they've done a few missions for royalty." Her meaning was not lost—it was a pirate ship.

"How much would this ship demand to take me on?"

"Not a thing if you're willing to work. Of course, someone must vouch for anyone they take on." She looked Lisette over. "Would you be able to do a day's labor for food and board?"

"You can tell the captain I'm capable and willing. I previously sailed on…a similar ship, without country."

"Yes." A sly grin crossed her lips. "*L'Implacable*."

Lisette stepped back. "How do you know this?"

"Relax, m'lady. It is easier to fool nobility than the servants, and we have nothing to gain by telling our secrets. Plus, my captain is aware of you."

"Why aren't you on that ship?"

She put her finger to her lips. "I have been part of the captain's crew for a few years now. She placed me here, to keep track of the island's nobility, to take advantage of their absences and their intrigues. There are many of us, on all the islands. It's an easy way to keep the larder stocked, as well as to play the families against one another."

"You scheme against the nobility?"

"Spain, France, they have all bullied their way onto these islands," Pinar said. "They take the lion's share of everything the natives grow and have and do. Our captain does what she can to encourage them to leave."

"Wait...*she*? Your captain is a woman?"

"Yes." Pinar nodded. "The entire crew. We fly the flag of *Dişi Aslan*."

"Deeshee...?"

"It is Turkish for 'lioness.'"

"Your captain is from Turkey?"

"As am I." She shrugged. "But our crew is from everywhere. The ship will be in port for a small time, only two nights. I can get word to the captain to vouch for you, but you must show proof, a promise to join the crew."

"What kind of promise?"

She rolled up her sleeve and turned her palm up. On the pale underbelly of her forearm, a lioness' head had been tattooed in henna tones.

"A tattoo?" Lisette had never met a woman with tattoos and was taken aback.

"A partial tattoo." She pointed to the lioness' face.

"I would ink the eyes, nose, and fangs. That is your password, to get you onto the ship. Once there, if you are a hard worker and accepted by the crew, they will complete the design. You will be one of us—no matter where your travels take you, you can call on us for aid."

Lisette pulled up her sleeve and looked at her arm. Even though she was darker than Mama, her skin looked like alabaster next to Pinar. "But I am a noblewoman by birth."

Pinar smiled. "It is your choice, m'lady. Only you can decide which world will serve you best now—the one of titles and breeding or the one of piracy and freedom."

Nobles did not allow their skin to be branded. Such a permanent stain on her body made Lisette wince. Today she might be in the company of pirates, but she still hoped to someday resume her former life with all its privileges.

*Hoping is not the same as having, and my life will never be as it was.* She held her arm out. "If this is the price of freedom, do what you will. I declare my allegiance to the *Dişi Aslan.*"

Pinar pulled a silk bag from her pocket and led Lisette to a seat on the balcony. "Sit here and watch the water. It is easier if your mind is occupied. And I brought mead with your lunch. It will dull your senses."

Lisette raised the goblet and drained it, before handing her left arm to Pinar, who took out her supplies and lay everything on the table. After some moments,

Lisette felt the first hard scrape, and jerked her arm away.

Pinar held her hand firmly. "Yes, m'lady, it does hurt a little. Much like a cat scratching."

"If Connie had kept his promise, I should not be going through this." As soon as the words came out, Lisette regretted them. "My apologies, Pinar. That sounded like selfish privilege. I assure you I have been a hard worker on my previous ship and enjoyed it."

Pinar smiled. "I am not offended. I was not supposed to say but it was the marquess who instructed me to find a way for you to escape. When I contacted my captain, she already knew much about you."

Lisette took another drink of mead and handed over her arm again. With each scrape of the needle, she imagined freedom, and thanked Connie for keeping his promise. The scratching ebbed, and soon it felt like no more than an annoyance.

She had just poured a third round of wine when she felt something moist and soothing on her arm, followed by a fabric wrapping. Looking over for the first time, Lisette saw that Pinar had wrapped a strip of material around her handiwork.

Lisette gingerly patted at the bandage, feeling the permanence of Pinar's work. No matter what happened, she would always have this—eyes, nose, and fangs. *And whenever I look at this, I'll renew my vow to avenge my family.*

"Rest now, m'lady. Your arm might be sore. We will take the wrapping off before you board the ship, in two days."

"Pinar, when you said your captain already knew about me—"

"You can discuss that with the captain when you see her." Pinar slipped out of the room, as silent as her arrival, and left Lisette to finish her meal and her mead.

She tried to be heartened, but two days seemed an eternity.

Once again, Lisette found herself at the mercy of people who made her promises. Cradling her left arm, she could only hope Pinar was an agent of *Dişi Aslan* and not the Duke de Martinmas. That thought alone made her aware of how much she had changed from the naïve young woman who didn't know she was being kidnapped until she was on a pirate ship.

She passed the next day in restless wandering around the room, checking for any sign the ship was pulling out early, making alternate plans to escape if she had again been betrayed. At least the duke did not visit, but Pinar brought her food and withdrew without speaking.

As the sun crept further toward the horizon, she moved her pacing to the balcony. She slept in the chair outdoors, for the little sleep she got, trying not to take her eyes off the ship.

The following morning, Pinar arrived with a tray as usual. Lisette sat outside, staring at the ocean listlessly. Pinar's pirate ship still sat in her view but she was losing faith that she would ever be on it.

"Good news, m'lady." Pinar's voice was low yet excited. "The ship is expecting you and we will get you on board tonight when I return with the evening meal. Be ready."

Lisette smiled. "That is exactly what I needed to hear."

The day could not pass quickly enough. She searched the room and found a large velvet pouch to hold what few treasures she had. The feather, Mama's emerald, and Connie's ring went into the bag, and she tied it around her waist, under her gown. She kept the vial of sleeping potion out, hiding it in her cleavage for quick access. The dagger stayed in its sheath, tied around her thigh. Once prepared, she settled into a chair and revisited Countess de Triana's book.

Light was dimming when the door finally opened. She expected Pinar. Instead, a large shadow entered. The duke had returned.

"I decided I would make certain you are comfortable for the night. I did not want you to be lonely, my son having been gone these few days."

"You needn't worry, m'lord. I expect my evening meal to arrive shortly."

"Oh, do you spend much time in conversation with Pinar?"

She tried to read his face. "Only the most trifling of exchanges. Pinar has her duties and cannot spend much time in my company."

He stared at her, nodding. Her stomach knotted in distrust of him. As they stood in the tense silence, the door creaked open. Pinar entered with a tray of food.

The duke stepped aside to allow her entry.

She gave him a slight curtsy, a Madonna-calm expression on her face. "Good even, m'lord. I brought the young miss dinner."

"Put it on the table here." Lisette gestured to the table inside. If he found she was eating outside, he might realize how badly she wished to leave. "Thank you, Pinar."

"One moment." He stopped her to study the meal. "Only one meat? Don't we have venison, too? She should have the venison as well as the duck. And where are the potatoes? Oh, yes, here they are. Cider? No, rum is better for the child. Leave this and come back with what I've ordered."

The maid put the tray down, gave Lisette a knowing glance, and left.

"Tempest, come and sit with me again." He

motioned to the chairs. "I confess, I already miss my son. You are a comfort to this old man."

"As you wish." She sat and focused on remaining calm and unhurried.

"I can't help but think about that first night, when you and Connie met. The more I consider it, the more I wonder." He paused and stared at her. The silence was intimidating. "You completed the task in record time. How did you succeed where all those other girls failed?"

Lisette worked up a blush and stared at the ground. "He said he was tired of being locked up, m'lord. I appealed to his sense of logic."

"Yes, but, if you'll forgive my impropriety, it was all over so quickly."

Now she blushed in earnest. "I have no way of determining that. It was my first time."

"I suppose." He tugged at his chin and folded his hands. "The first time does tend to be a speedy event. And often doesn't result in a child."

She regarded him suspiciously.

"I would be happy to give nature a helpful push." His voice was oily, invasive, his expression leering. "Keep it in the family, you understand."

She fought to keep the blush from setting her face on fire. Putting her hand in her pocket, she dug through to the knife. If he tried to take her by force, she was prepared to fight back.

"When Pinar returns with the rum, we'll have a drink and relax," he said.

She remembered the vial, hidden in her cleavage. Finally, a nobleman who was in the position to be drugged.

Pinar returned with another tray. Lisette leapt to her feet and hurried over. "Let me serve you, m'lord."

She eased the vial from her dress, making certain

to keep her back to the duke. Opening the top and pouring the contents into his goblet was a quick motion. Pinar was quicker—she filled the goblets from the pitcher, brushing Lisette's hand in the process so she could take the empty vial. Lisette picked up both drinks and headed back to the chairs.

"That will be all, Pinar," he said, sending her from the room.

"Here you are, m'lord." Lisette handed him his drink. "Shall we toast?"

They raised their cups as he smiled at her. "To an enchanting and bountiful evening."

He brought his goblet to his lips and tipped back. She also tipped her drink, although she kept her lips tight to take in a mere sip.

"This rum is delightful." He took another swig. "Its sweetness prepares me for your charms."

"How long have you ruled this island?" She tried to steer the conversation away from what he intended to do with her. Some things were better left unsaid.

"My family has been on Isla de Pimienta since my great-great-grandfather was sent here by our King. There has always been a Martinmas here, for as long as this island has been civilized." He drained his goblet. "Mmmore."

She took his cup and refilled it, wondering how long the potion would take. As she returned to the chairs, he reached for his freshened drink, and his eyes rolled back. She stepped out of the way, and he kept reaching as he fell, face first, to the floor.

The potion worked quickly, but she had no idea how long it would keep him unconscious. She ran to the bed and gathered the three strips she had cut days ago. Digging out the knife, she held it in her teeth while she tied his hands and feet, ready to use it if he woke early. He was snoring by the time she had completed her task.

The door creaked open, and she jumped back, dagger ready.

It was Pinar again. "He is not—"

"Dead? No, merely sleeping. He will awake soon, with a bad headache."

Pinar was carrying a parcel, which she shoved at Lisette. "Here, put these on. They are servant's clothes. I will sneak you out through the kitchen."

Lisette began to untie her top.

"Quicker!" Pinar ripped the ribbons free, tearing her clothes. "We have to move now!"

Quickening her efforts, Lisette threw off the layers of silk and ribbons, and slipped into the brown sack-like garment of a housemaid. She placed the dagger back in its sheath along her leg. As she ran to the door, she tripped on a mat and looked down at her little silk slippers. They would give her away. Tossing them aside, Lisette followed Pinar out of the room in bare feet.

The stone floor was cold, but they were moving too quickly for her to care. The maid led her down the back stairs, through a series of narrow hallways, until she glimpsed a light through one of the arches. At this entrance, Pinar stopped and turned, putting her finger to her lips. Lisette stepped back against the wall.

Pinar disappeared into the light. Lisette could hear voices, Pinar's and what sounded like an older woman. They complained about the duke's demands for her meals and discussed his dinner needs.

"Is His Lordship still with the girl?" the old woman asked.

"When I left, yes," Pinar told her. "Where are you going?"

A shadow moved into the doorway. "To the girl's room. Ain't he takin' his meal with her?"

"No, he told me he'd be supping in his chamber as

usual," Pinar said.

A hand beckoned Lisette from the doorway and she went. Pinar grabbed her arm and pulled her across the kitchen, to the door, shoving her into the courtyard, checking all around for anyone who might stop them.

"Stay against the wall to the left and go toward the sea." She gestured directions. "There is a small boat, set against the cliff, where the rocks meet the sand. Tell the woman at the oars, 'I seek Begum Derya'. They will give you safe passage."

"What about you? Are you safe here?"

She nodded. "I have been here long enough to be trusted, and I have allies within. Go, and good fortune come to you."

The two young women hugged, and Lisette ran off, barefoot, into the night.

The new moon gave no help as Lisette stumbled toward the sound of the sea. Her feet were now unhappy with their nakedness, and she cringed at every sharp rock and thorny plant as she made her way. Still, she did not dare slow down. She needed to get on that ship.

The sound of waves lapping on land steered her in their direction. A large object blotted the stars—it must be the cliff. Her feet found blessed softness of sand, and she knew she had reached the shore. Now she needed to find a boat in the darkness.

A strong hand wrapped around her mouth, and her ribs were pressed with a sharpness she recognized as a knife. There was hot, foul breath at her ear.

"No shouting, dearie." The voice was female, but harsh as if it'd been soaked in hard rum. "What brings you out this dark night?"

The grip on Lisette's mouth loosened enough for her to whisper, "I seek Begum Derya."

The knife remained at her back, and she feared Pinar had steered her wrong. The hand that had been across Lisette's mouth pushed her shoulder and launched her forward. She stopped when her knees hit something hard. A dinghy.

"Let her go, Mar." This was a soft voice with a precise accent. "Put her in the boat."

Rum Voice, aka Mar, protested. "We don't know who she is."

"Pinar sent me," Lisette whispered.

Mar seized her arm to stop her from jumping into the boat. Lisette spied a lantern on the seat, dimmed between two women. She wrenched her arm away and pulled up her left sleeve. Shoving it toward the light, she was aware of several heads, straining to get a glimpse.

"I've come to work aboard the *Dişi Aslan*."

After their look at the unfinished tattoo, everyone agreed, and someone helped her into the boat, guiding her to a seat. There were some murmurs around, many voices, and more bodies in the darkness.

Mar grumbled, "All clear," and they shoved off.

"Who are you?" Soft Voice asked.

What name should she give? Lisette de Lille might give her respect, or it might mark her as a valuable hostage. "My name is Tempest."

The oars slipped in and out of the water with little splashes. Twinkles of light from the town and the ship revealed clearer shapes in the boat. Some of the women whispered and giggled as they traveled. Mar was at the oars, propelling the boat in brusque strokes. She was substantial, with a full neck and wide face.

They bumped to a stop against the ship. A rope ladder was lowered, along with lines for the dinghy.

Two women tied the rowboat to the lines as the others climbed up to the ship. Lisette waited for everyone to disembark before taking her turn to climb up, demonstrating her awareness of her low position on the ship.

As she reached the rail, a familiar strong hand grabbed the back of her dress with a fistful of her braid and yanked her up and onto the deck. Lisette was unprepared for this method of landing, and found herself face down on the planks, struggling to stand. A few women laughed.

"Ah, that one's too small, Mar. Throw it back."

Lisette managed to clear her skirt from under her feet and stand, wondering how to proceed with this crew. She dealt with Rocco's men by pulling her dagger on them. As she looked at the faces, she decided against trying to intimidate them.

"My name is Tempest." She held out her arm again revealing her brand. "I seek Begum Derya. Pinar sent me."

Expressions and stances relaxed, except for one. Mar demanded more convincing. "How do we know she wasn't sent by our enemies?"

Everyone stood and looked, from Mar to Lisette and back again.

Lisette stepped forward. "I have no proof of my intentions, but I tell you the truth. I was being held captive by the Duke de Martinmas. Pinar helped me escape. I want to be away from this place, and I have experience on a ship."

"As what?" Mar scoffed. "Serving wench?"

"As rigger—" Lisette spoke each word with emphasis, stretching up, regally. "Aboard *L'Implacable*."

Murmurs rose like a wave preparing to slap the shore and died as a figure parted the group. A small, lean woman approached Lisette, her features angular and her eyes green as jade.

"I am Begum Derya, captain of this ship. How is it you were a rigger on an all-male crew?" Her voice was deep, but sharp and commanding. She spoke French with an accent Lisette assumed was Turkish.

"It is a long story, but Captain Rocco and I had an arrangement that required my travel aboard his ship. I was too curious to stay below deck, so he set me to work atop, to keep me out of trouble."

Lisette could not read the woman's expression until her mouth spread open in a wide grin, revealing large teeth, one of them gold, protruding slightly over her bottom lip.

"Come to my cabin, *Tempest*. We have much to discuss."

Lisette stepped forward, but a hand on her arm held her to the spot.

"Cap'n, you don't know if this wench tells the truth. Shouldn't I at least come wit' you?"

The captain raised her hand in dismissal as she turned and walked aft. "Thank you, Mar, but I believe I shall be safe with this one. Release her."

Mar let go, but not before her nails gave a painful dig. Lisette kept herself from wincing and yanking her arm away. Instinct told her to remain neutral. She would pick her battles carefully with Rum Voice. If they couldn't be friends, they could at the least ignore one another.

The captain's cabin was as luxurious as Rocco's was sparse. Fine silks of jeweled colors draped every surface, even the walls and the ceiling. Large pillows invited lounging, and the candlelight was magnified by the mirrors and crystals hung everywhere. The bed hung from ropes and swung above the pillows. In the center of the room was an ornate table and chairs, carved from a dark wood.

The scent of the room was different as well. Incense and flowers were much preferable to Rocco's cabin with its wood, rum, and musky male aromas.

Lisette got a better look at her host. Captain Derya was a beautiful woman but hard, as though she might tear rocks apart with her bare hands. Her cheekbones were high and her eyes large with long eyelashes. Her clothing was unique, at least not like anything Lisette had ever seen. She wore a silky, brightly striped top and breeches, a dark corset of what looked like leather, and small black boots, which she removed and placed by the door.

Colorful designs ran down each of her arms. Lisette had never met a woman with tattoos. These were beautiful renderings of mermaids. The blue and green of the scales rippled across her muscles, ending at a gold cuff on each wrist.

"How is our friend Rocco?" she asked.

"Hale and hearty when I last saw him. He pulled out of this port a week ago."

"Sit, please." Begum nodded. "I would like to hear your story."

# 25

Lisette regarded her new captain. Or was she her new captor?

She sat at the table, aware of the cushions on the seat and at her back. "Captain Rocco and I had an arrangement. I am on a mission to raise gold—"

Begum held up her hand. "Before you continue, I should be honest. I am already aware of who you are and how you came here. I am interested in your side of the story, and to know what your plans are."

Lisette studied her hands quietly for a moment, before shrugging. "At the moment, I plan to survive. In time, I plan to avenge the wrongs done to myself and my family."

Begum grinned. "Spoken like a true noblewoman, of high spirits and low tolerance."

"May I ask how you know of me?" Lisette gave her a slight frown. "If you'll forgive my ignorance, I had not heard of you until Pinar told me."

The captain retrieved two small, delicate cups from the cabinet, placing one in front of her. A narrow copper pot with a long spout and equally long handle sat on the table. She picked it up and poured a dark liquid into both tiny cups.

"Coffee," she said. "From my empire. Try it."

Lisette sipped the bittersweet brew and marveled at its unusual taste. "Thank you. It's good."

The captain smiled and sat down across from her. "Some months ago, a request came for services that were, let's say unique, even to pirates. While a clumsy attempt at contact, we all understood what they wanted. It seems there was a scheming pair of nobility offering to execute a sale—one virgin of noble birth. I believe the name was Lisette de Lille. We warned Rocco not to take the bait. Nobility is fond of using pirates, then serving their heads to the fishes. But when he heard the name, he was transfixed." She stared at Lisette. "He had to have you."

Lisette glared at her, eyes wide and mouth open. "Did every pirate in the southern seas know of Mercedes' plans?"

"Quite likely. Now, would you like to tell me the rest of the story?"

With a slight bow, Lisette told her tale to the captain from her mundane beginning to the bitter present, leaving out the part about watching Rocco's dragon—Rocco himself—fly into the night. It was enough that she described Philippe's death truthfully. Lisette expected the captain to display some form of disbelief, but she said nothing.

At the end, Lisette took a long sip of the dark brew, wishing for sleep, and a close to this adventure.

160

"And so, your parents are dead?" Begum asked.

She nodded, brushing a tear that had escaped. "At least, that is what the duke told me. I can only assume he told the truth."

"It is all right to cry. Losing people you love is hard." Begum poured more coffee into her cup. "I believe I knew your father—Claude, yes? He spent some time in Turkey."

"You knew him?" Lisette smiled through her tears and took her emerald from her pouch, pushing past the red feather. "He gave me this. Said it was given to him in Turkey."

Begum smiled but did not reach for the jewel. "Yes, it is a lovely necklace. I knew the jeweler well. His gold work was the finest quality."

"I have kept it safe so far. I look forward to the day I can wear it again without fear of being robbed."

"You fear being robbed? By whom?"

Lisette gestured toward the windows. "By everyone. Did you not hear my story? I have been at the mercy of viscounts, dukes, pirates…"

"I was listening." Begum grinned and held her cup aloft. "And I salute you. You have done well."

"Done well? What have I done well? True, I had no strong desire to be married to Eric, but I was willing to do my duty. Kidnapping was not my second choice, or even third. I've killed four Spaniards and left another one bound and gagged—a duke, no less. I decided virginity is a ludicrous virtue, but I can't get a man to oblige me. Not only is my island now Spain's property, my parents are dead. My brother may also be." She wiped back the tears that were now sadness mixed with anger. "And now I am on a mission to kill the very man I was supposed to wed, along with his horrible paramour and my treacherous aunt. I am…lost and irredeemable." She broke at these words, burying her face, weeping.

"No, you are not." Begum reached her hand to Lisette's, giving it a kind squeeze. "My dear, you have survived. How many of your prissy titled friends could have done as you? Would that woman, that Mercedes, have thrown away her pedigree to stay alive? No. True, your course has not been straight. But I believe there is a spiritual life that has its own timeline. Your spirit must endure a little more, to learn something vital to your success. It will come."

"I have lost everything. Please don't tell me there's something else I have to endure."

Begum rose from her chair and came to Lisette, lifting her chin and studying her face. "Yes, I am sorry about your family. That is a hardship. If I can offer you any hope, it is that your loss will make you stronger, and more empathetic."

"At the moment, it's making me bitter and more vengeful."

"And that has its time, too. Take care that you do not stay there too long. Vengeance is a beast that feeds upon itself."

There was a knock and a young girl entered, carrying a tray of food. Lisette's stomach grumbled in response.

"Sit, eat," Begum said. "Tomorrow you will work with my crew. If we catch up with *L'Implacable*, I will return you to Rocco to continue your journey, if that is what you wish. Until then, we have some missions that should net us good profits. We all share in the success, which should put a few coins in your pocket."

Lisette pulled a leg from the roasted bird in front of her and ate. As she did, the captain disappeared behind a screen. She returned wearing a soft gown and robe.

"Once you have eaten, Ruhee will help you with proper clothing, and show you to your bunk." She sat across from Lisette and sliced a thick chunk of the meat, shoving it inside a thin round of bread.

"Captain," Lisette said between bites, "you do not seem surprised that I reported seeing a man killed by a dragon. Is it because you have encountered them?"

After Begum had downed a good sip of coffee, she spoke. "It is something we do not discuss, but yes, I am aware of him."

"Him? There is only one?"

"Perhaps I misspeak. Many have borne the curse of the blood dragon, but most have fulfilled their quests. There is only one who still hunts in these skies."

Rocco. Lisette stared at her, trying to figure out if she knew. Her eyes were too dark to read in this light, but the way she sat back and cocked an eyebrow told Lisette much. She opened her mouth to say his name, but Begum spoke first.

"You will have your own hammock in the crew's hold. I am afraid Mar has taken a dislike to you, but do not worry. She dislikes almost everyone but is intensely loyal to the ship and whoever is in command."

And with that, dragons were taken off the list of topics.

"Whoever is in command?" Lisette asked.

"Pirates are not like conscripted navies. Our captain is elected by popular vote. Usually, a captain holds his position by either giving favors or being so fearsome his crew is loath to vote against him. On our ship, we let everyone have a chance to control the helm. Everyone gets a year at their position, then they rotate. If one does not wish to be captain, they can pass it on to the next person in line, or the crew may vote to keep the current one."

"It sounds so civilized." Lisette did not add, *for pirates*.

"Yes, for pirates." Begum finished her statement. "But it is also practical. Every one of our crew learns every position on the ship. In battle, we do not have a weak link. Even if our captain is struck down, another can rise to command the ship."

"Has that ever happened?"

"Not yet—not exactly. But I have sworn an oath. I shall die if it means the ship is saved."

It was late and there was too much to take in. Lisette rose from the table, taking a piece of bread. "I should get some sleep, Captain. Tomorrow comes early, and I assume I am to start at the bottom, as a swabby."

"True, Lisette—or shall I call you Tempest? I need not divulge your secret."

"My only concern with being labeled a noblewoman is I may be seen as useless for labor, or worse, a bargaining chip."

"Once they understand your circumstance, they would realize you are not of great value to the ruling class."

"True enough." Lisette thought of her parents gone and her brother missing. She might be the last of the de Lille family. "You may call me Lizzie, Captain. I will say my goodnight and be ready to work in the morning."

26

Begum opened the door and clapped her hands. The same girl who brought the food appeared. "Ruhee, take Lizzie to the storage hold, and get her suitable clothes for working the ship. Oh, and take care of that tattoo." She pointed to Lisette's arm. "There is no point in testing you. You will be one of us now."

Lisette followed Ruhee down the steps from the captain's cabin. At the next level, they stopped at the door to a hold. The larder was filled with food, drink, and other supplies, including, to her surprise, clothing.

"My last ship did not have a stock of clothes."

Ruhee nodded. "We have found it is easier to keep the crew happy when we have spare shirts and breeches. It is nice, when you have torn or stained what you wear in work or in battle, to have a fresh change of clothes."

Lisette gathered a shirt, breeches, and leather slippers for her bare feet. Glancing at her still-soft hands, she wished for her fingerless gloves, but they were in Rocco's cabin.

"Perhaps you'd like to change here before we take care of your tattoo. Then, I will show you to your hammock."

Lisette agreed, and Ruhee stepped outside the door. She wasted no time in stripping out of her frock and into new attire. A small stack of leather pouches caught her eye. She had taken a pouch from the duke—soft, velvet, and inappropriate for swabbing decks and hauling lines. She took a leather one, and stuck her treasures within, belting the bag around her waist. Still in its sheath, she fastened her dagger to the belt as well.

She was ready, but a nagging at her gut stopped her from opening the door. Taking the feather from the pouch, she used a drawstring to fasten it to her body, the tip nestling between her breasts.

*I may need your protection.*

Gathering her old clothes, Lisette joined Ruhee outside, and followed her onto the deck. There was no moon, and the stars were hidden behind clouds, so Ruhee lit a lantern and put it between them, where she motioned for Lisette to sit.

"It is better in the night air," she said, and pulled out her kit of needle and dye.

Lisette sat and looked out to sea. The ocean was calm and dark, and the sea air was cool on her skin. Pinar had given her plenty of drink to take the sting away, but Ruhee did not offer, and she did not ask.

The process hurt again, perhaps even more than the first time. Each dig of the needle pierced Lisette's heart as well as her wrist. Every scratch into her raw skin wrote her story—betrayal, rejection, failure upon failure.

**166**

Nothing would ever be the same. She would never be the same.

After the tattoo was wrapped, Ruhee pointed to the stairs and they went below deck, before the mainmast. They came to an open area, filled with swinging canvases. From their outlines, most of them were occupied. There were low conversations whispering in the darkness, and a musky smell from the combination of many bodies and little fresh air.

Ruhee escorted Lisette to the foremost hammock. This was considered the worst berth on the ship, as the bow was less stable and in constant motion. For a new sailor, this meant a miserable time trying to adjust to sea life.

A familiar voice taunted her as Lisette threw her clothes into the swinging bed.

"Hope you ate lightly, Tempest." Mar's words held her scorn. "I don't want to be woken by your heaves."

"You need not worry. I have adequate sea legs." She turned and faced down the row, taking a breath and clearing her throat. Mar's pale, rheumy eyes and flushed cheeks peeked above her hammock. "And my name is not Tempest. I am Lisette de Lille."

She stared at Mar, watching her red face grow redder. Murmurs came from the other berths.

"I was noble born, but I am a pirate by trade. I look forward to earning my place in the crew." Turning away from them, she used the hammock's swing to lift herself into it and nestled her body deep within its folds. The movement was soothing, like a baby in a cradle.

The room soon fell silent, apart from a symphony of snores, deep growls to high whistles. A few portholes along the sides allowed gray shadows across the floor. For a moment, Lisette missed being in Rocco's spacious cabin, almost more than she missed his company. Above all, she missed her own bed, and allowed the tears for her family to trickle down once more.

She closed her eyes. Her ears tuned into the sounds of the darkness, creaking wood, and splashing waves. She heard a noise that made her eyes pop open.

Footsteps.

Perhaps someone was coming to bed or going on duty. It was most likely part of the ship's routine. But it might be someone, Mar came to mind, trying to haze the new swabby.

Lisette had witnessed razzing on Rocco's ship, one sailor bullying another. It never got out of control because Rocco managed to end it without judgment. The two men could both choose to leave the ship or to stay. But promising to stay meant they were not allowed to fight. If they were caught again, they'd both be kicked off—whether the ship was in port or not.

She hoped Captain Derya had such a policy but until she knew, she drew her dagger from its sheath and put it under the frock she was using as a pillow. The footsteps lightened, but her sense of caution didn't. She kept her eyes half-open and her breath quiet. Gripping the dagger tighter, she waited.

A shadow crossed the floor, coming her way, stopping two berths from her. She heard whispers, and the quiet pressings of lips upon lips. An extra swing of a hammock, and two bodies soon practiced the art of silent lovemaking.

Lisette sighed softly in relief, closing her eyes again, dagger still at the ready.

The sun brightened her quarters too soon, and she awoke grudgingly. Her eyes fought the light, and her head was mushy as a bowl of porridge. She swung from bed and looked around. Others were rising and stretching as well. They were all moving toward the steps and their morning duties.

She slipped her blade back into its sheath and made

her way to the deck. As she climbed upward, the morning light hit her face, along with a smooth, cool breeze. This was going to be a good day.

Mar stood over a wooden pail, looking at Lisette with a smirk. In the daylight, she looked even more robust with her white-blond hair cut short, rising in stray tufts with each gust of wind.

"Ah, Your Highness." Mar made a pretense of bowing. "Tis a shame to wake you, m'lady, but duty calls."

She launched a wad of soaked rags at Lisette, catching her full in the face. Lisette grasped at them on their way down. Her natural instinct was to stuff them down Mar's throat. She squinted, sizing up Mar's physical strength, and her options.

For her part, Mar stepped up, feet planted. She was ready for battle. The women around had stopped their work to look at them. Throwing rags was a small thing, barely a challenge. If they were friends, it would have been funny.

Lisette took a breath and managed the largest laugh she could from deep in her gut.

"My, how refreshing!" Walking to the bucket, she dropped the rags in, and smiled at Mar. "Thanks for the wake-up. I'd better get to work."

Mar twisted her features into an ugly, menacing grin. With one motion, she stepped forward and kicked the bucket over, attempting to elbow Lisette in the ribcage at the same time. Lisette threw her hip up to deflect Mar's strike. Off-balance from the kick, Mar went over backward.

Her rump hit the deck with a thud.

The crew burst into laughter, all except Mar, who scrambled to her feet, face crimson. She seized Lisette by the wrist and drew her hand back, spitting curses in a guttural tone. Lisette raised her free hand in defense and turned her head from the oncoming blow, but none came.

A lean, wiry woman with wild curls held Mar's outstretched fist. "She didn't do nuthin'. You slipped on yer own big feet."

Mar pushed Lisette away and turned to her defender. Lisette moved between them to keep Mar from flattening the woman, but a low voice rang through the chaos.

"What is this—fighting?" Captain Derya strode from the helm, fire in her green eyes.

The three women popped apart like a broken string of pearls. Lisette's defender slunk into the crowd that had gathered around them and disappeared from view. Mar stared at the captain, scowling in indignation. Lisette knew there were many ways this could go badly.

"Would someone explain what this is about?" Captain Derya demanded.

"She started it." Mar pointed to Lisette as she spurted the words.

All eyes shifted to Lisette, including the captain's.

"Is that true?"

Lisette looked at the captain and prepared to take a whipping. "I confess, Captain, it was my unfortunate doing. I am not accustomed to these shoes, so I slipped. In my attempt to right myself, I bumped into Mar, setting off the chain of events you witnessed." She lowered her head in submission, then turned to her large, huffing enemy. "I'm sorry, Mar. It happened so quickly I didn't get to apologize."

"Is that what happened?" The captain asked.

Mar's face still registered the anger she had tried to unleash upon Lisette. She opened her mouth, possibly to contradict her. As before, she was interrupted by a familiar voice.

"Yes'm." It belonged to the woman who had come to Lisette's defense. She shot a punishing glare at Mar. "The pail had slopped too much water and the new swabby took a bad step, bumped against Mar. Seemed like Mar thought the swabby had tripped her a'purpose."

The women around Lisette agreed. Mar scowled at them, her face hardening into a defeated pout.

"Mar?" The captain asked.

"I took offense," she replied through gritted teeth. "I believed her attitude to be unwilling to bend to such menial tasks as cleaning, being a lady and all."

The tact Lisette had been cultivating evaporated. "Unwilling? How dare you accuse me—you've not even seen me work! I did my share, same as any of the others on my last ship."

"Then why are your hands so white and soft?" Mar shot back.

"Because. I. Wore. Gloves." She spat each word as she leaned toward her. Hands on each of Lisette's shoulders held her back. If Mar wanted a fight, she was ready.

"Ha! Why would they—" Mar began, but the captain stepped between them, waving her hand, the mermaid on her arm swimming.

"Never mind, Mar. Her story is true." She regarded them both. "Can the two of you get along or not? If either one of you wants out of the other's company, say the word. I'll assign you to opposite ends of the ship. If that is not enough, we have other ways to make one of you go away."

Lisette glanced at the rest of the crew. "I have no wish to fight with Mar or anyone here."

The crew all glared at Mar, frowning.

"I'll not fight," Mar said at last.

"Good." The captain turned to the crew. "Back to your stations. Come on, then—harden up!"

Everyone dispersed and left Lisette to her tasks. She picked up the bucket and went to the rail, where she lowered it from its rope and held fast. It filled with seawater quickly, and she lifted it. She had done this task before on the other ship, but now the harshness of the rope scratched at her hands. If left bare, her palms would be bloody by noonday.

She quickly tore strips of the rags she was using to wash the deck and wrapped them around her palms before setting to work. Washing the deck with seawater was drudgery, but one she accepted. It was a good test to get a day's hard labor from a new jack.

The sun seared the deck where she worked. Fortunately, the steady breeze from the ship's speed kept her from overheating. The *Dişi Aslan* was slightly smaller than Rocco's ship and shot across the water like a flat rock over a smooth lake. Lisette scrubbed heartily, thankful for her long days on *L'Implacable*. She was no longer the frail lap dog with no skills other than to walk prettily in silks and brocades. The week she spent in the duke's tower had softened her only a trifle. At six bells, she was sore but not stiffened. She completed her day's work and joined the crew for the meal.

As Lisette entered the mess, Mar was at one end of the table and everyone else at the other. For a moment, she felt badly. As Mar pushed food into her gaping mouth, Lisette felt less charitable. The dogs in her kitchen ate more daintily.

She paused, considering where to sit—with the crew and seal Mar's anger toward her, or with Mar and invite derision from a dozen other women? She grabbed at the dried meat, hard rolls, and boiled potatoes, and split the difference, taking a place at the end of the group closest to Mar. Mar glared in her direction.

In return, Lisette smiled. "The meal agrees with you?"

"Shut up, wench."

"Don't pay her no mind," said the curly-haired woman who had helped her today. "She thinks she can throw her weight about, but we don't bow to her."

Mar tore a chunk of roll with her teeth and pushed it back in her mouth with her fingers. Her eyes were dull as she stared at the group and chewed.

Lisette turned her attention to her food, eating quietly and listening to the various conversations around her. Amazingly, there was talk of family, shopping, simple things she might have discussed with Genevieve, or Mama, or any of the women she used to talk to. Their soft, high voices gave her a melancholy she had not experienced since the day she awoke in the ship's hold.

Mar wiped her mouth with the back of her hand and left without a word. The woman next to Lisette had stopped talking to her friends and was having some cider. She was hefty, dark-skinned, and dark-haired.

"Why doesn't she have any friends on this ship?" Lisette asked, nodding toward Mar.

"She don't like us."

"All of you?"

"When Mar had her turn to be cap'n, she warnt a good 'un. Barkin' orders, givin' us half-rations and no rum. Worst was gettin' hit by a Spanish ship. She crumbled like a sandcastle. Lost two of our crew, almost lost the ship until Begum and Oleta took over." She pointed to the woman who had come to her defense earlier. "They led us to victory, and we voted Mar out of her position, after no more'n two moons."

"That's a pity." Lisette nodded and rose from the table. As she tried to pass the doorway, the cook held her arm.

"Where you think you're going?"

"To my berth, I suppose."

"No, you're not. Swabby cleans the mess."

At that pronouncement, the crew stood and walked out, leaving plates, cups, and food scattered everywhere. Mar may have been the biggest slob, but she wasn't the only one.

Lisette stifled a yawn. "Yes, ma'am."

Cook stayed behind to watch her gathering plates and taking them to the galley. As Lisette stacked them on the counter and prepared to scrape their debris, she told her, "Water's in a pot on the fire. Soap's in the cabinet above."

Lisette listened to her footsteps disappearing, sighed, and went to work. It would be a long night before she'd see her hammock again.

Lisette learned to pace herself in her duties, swabbing by day and cleaning by night. The other women proved to be friendly, but she soon abandoned any hope of winning Mar's favor, joining the rest of the crew at dinner and leaving the big woman to sulk alone.

By the end of the first week, Oleta asked her to help man the halliard. Lisette leaped at the chance to haul out the sail, adjust the braces and sweat the line.

"Good job," Oleta told her. "You weren't bragging about your experience."

Lisette smiled. "I had a good teacher on *L'Implacable*."

That evening at dinner, Oleta stood at the table and raised her mug of rum, clanking her dagger against it. Everyone stopped talking and turned to her.

"I have an announcement. Our new swabby done a good job riggin' today—such a good job, Cap'n decided this'll be the last night she cleans the deck—or mess." She turned to Lisette. "Tomorrow, Lizzie, you start handlin' the lines."

"Who's gonna swab?" Mar growled.

"We go back to the usual way—each of us takin' the turn." Oleta shot Mar a wicked grin. "You're up first, Mar."

Mar's face grew crimson, and Lisette believed she might explode. Pounding the table, the large woman opened her mouth to protest. A light appeared in her eyes, as if reconsidering. Her face relaxed into acceptance. "Aye, Oleta."

The crew toasted Lisette happily, finished their meals, and left her to do one last cleanup. Lisette noticed, with a small laugh, that they did not make it any easier for her last night, piling dishes everywhere as usual.

An hour later, she was wiping the broad, wooden table when unsteady footsteps pounded down the ladder. The heft of each step convinced her it was Mar. She took out her blade and rested it in her right hand while she scrubbed with her left.

Mar clomped into the mess and flopped down at the table. The breeze from her mass carried the distinct smell of rum.

"Can I get you something?" Lisette kept cleaning.

Mar put her finger on the wet wood and made circles on the surface while Lisette wiped the seats. When she had finished, she had to walk past Mar to the galley to throw the rag in the bin. She gripped her dagger a little tighter and moved forward, facing her at all times.

Pointing to the blade, Mar said, "You can put that away. I din't come to start nuthin.'"

"Why are you here?"

"Cause I don't understand why you keep tryin' to be nice to me." With each word, her face scrunched as if she was clipping the slur off before it rolled sloppily from her tongue.

"What?"

"I been nuthin but mean to you, but you still wish me good morn and all. You don' scoff or ignore me like everyones else."

Lisette shrugged. "I didn't want to give you more reasons to hate me. I'd prefer to get along."

Mar turned away and pounded the table. "I don't like nobody."

"Why do you stay on this ship?"

Mar's pale, red-rimmed eyes got redder, as did her cheeks. Tears streamed and she made guttural, sobbing sounds. Lisette could not ascribe beauty to her in any way. Crying made her look even worse.

With a sigh, Lisette sat and listened.

After wiping her eyes and nose on her sleeve, Mar said, "I stay here cause they ain't tossed me off yet. My family's gone. I wouldn't be good at nuthin women do—I mean, look at me. I'm an oaf, with a bad temper. I'm trying to get to Whale Island, but I may not last 'til the next port."

"Have you tried being nicer, instead of meaner?"

Mar scowled at her, pushing her idea away with a wave of her fist. "Ah, they don't wanna hear that. I'm a big, blustering lout. They expect me to talk loud, push around."

"Is that what they expected when you were captain?"

"Nobody ever let me be in charge before."

Lisette agreed. "It must have been even harder when the Spaniards attacked."

Mar teared up again. "I was so scared. I never been in that kind of a fight, not with men tryin' to kill me. B'lieve it or not, I was a proper lady afore this, with a ladies' maid."

"I'm sure it was rough."

They sat in silence. Mar wiped her face again and Lisette tried to come up with something helpful to say.

"I don't have a solution, Mar. I have never walked in your shoes. I have barely walked in my own. A few months ago, I was a noblewoman, preparing to marry and live a sheltered life. Now I am a pirate, desperate to make enough gold to return to my home and punish those who put me in this position. The one thing for certain is I could have stayed a noblewoman when I was kidnapped, but I chose to become a pirate." She looked down at her red hands, her gaze drifting to her new tattoo. "And know what? It saved my life. Maybe you should choose what you want to be, instead of letting life choose it for you."

Lisette rose and went into the galley, where she put away the rags and spent a few minutes making certain everything was clean. When she returned to the mess, Mar was gone. She climbed to the next deck and made her way back to her berth.

Mar was in her hammock. She was too busy snoring to acknowledge Lisette as she passed by. Lisette crawled into her own berth for some rest. As she floated into slumber, her neighbor again greeted her paramour with hushed kisses.

She woke to the dawn light through the porthole to her left. Rolling from bed, she headed toward the upper deck, anxious to begin a new day with a new job to do.

"Lizzie." A voice barked as she neared the steps. The cook was calling her down to the mess.

And it was a mess when she walked below. Dirty dishes piled everywhere on the table, which was smeared with grease. Her mouth hung open as she tried to make sense of what she set eyes on.

Cook was a pale woman with a round face. Her cheeks glowed with rage. "Is this the way you leave things on your last night?"

"I assure you, Ma'am, I cleaned both of these spaces, the galley and the mess. I—well, Mar can vouch for how clean everything was. She came down here and we talked."

Cook glared at Lisette and yelled for Mar.

Mar descended into the room with her usual lack of grace. Her expression was lax, her mouth hanging open, her eyes glazed and clueless.

"The new jack here says you saw her clean this place last night. Says you was chatting."

Lisette smiled at her. She could tell Cook the truth. Instead, her jowls quivered as her head shook. "I wasn't nowhere near here. Why would I be chattin' with this wench?"

Cook turned back to glare at Lisette again, her fist rubbing into an open hand. Mar shuffled a turn and pulled herself up the first step to leave. As she did, she looked over at Lisette and grinned, an evil bend to her mouth, and a wicked gleam in her eyes.

Sighing, Lisette faced Cook. "You may or may not believe me, but I did clean this space, and I shall clean it again."

She gathered all the dirty plates and carried them to the galley. Next came the rag, bucket, and soap. Cook still stood in the midst of the chaos, watching her every move.

Lisette held up the rag. "By the by, this was the rag I used to clean after dinner. You might notice it is still damp. So I must have done something."

They were silent for a long time, Lisette working and Cook watching. When the dishes were clean, Lisette scrubbed the table. Cook scrutinized the plates she had washed. Her annoyed expression relaxed as she checked each dish and did not find any smudge or crust.

"Mar and me started off as friends," she said at last, taking up a rag and helping. "She was always a bit spoiled, used to throwing her weight around to get her viewpoint across. Didn't take her long to wear out her welcome."

Lisette put the cleaning supplies back in the galley and put her hand on Cook's shoulder. "So why did you believe her today?"

"Because we was friends once, and I still want to believe."

She reminded Lisette of her home and her friends and how part of her didn't want to believe they would betray her, especially Tatie Elena. Lisette sighed and headed up to start her new assignment.

"Lizzie!" Captain Derya's voice stopped her in her tracks. Lisette turned to squint into the sun, looking for the captain at the helm. She couldn't find her, until she heard, "You're late."

Lisette whipped around to face her. "Sorry, Captain."

"Why were you late to your post?"

Mar stood by the mainsail, grinning.

"My apologies, Captain. My work last night in the mess was undone by *someone*…" Lisette paused here to stare pointedly at Mar. "And I had to clean everything *again*."

Captain Derya clenched the handle of her blade and scowled. "Who did this?"

The air was thick with her anger, but Lisette didn't flinch. "I am not certain, Captain, I can only assume there is someone on this ship who likes making my job difficult, instead of welcoming me into the crew."

The captain strode around the deck, glaring at the women. They all shrank from her, and Lisette wondered if speaking so boldly was wise. As the captain paced, she clutched the hilt of her dagger. The silence was suffocating.

After some time, Captain Derya spun on her heels and faced them. "This ship sails as a team. We are as weak as our weakest member. It is our duty, therefore, to strengthen one another, to help each other to complete our tasks, and to keep this ship running at its best. When we encounter another Spanish ship, we must be more prepared. I shouldn't have to remind you of what happens when we are not."

Everyone nodded except Mar, who stood quiet, her face crimson.

"I was going to issue you all a punishment until one of you confessed," the captain continued. "But I do not think that would serve our crew. Instead, I will interview each of you. The guilty will be dealt with privately."

She turned to Lisette. "You will go back to swabbing until I have finished my investigation."

Scurrying aft, Lisette retrieved supplies, and went to work. She dunked the rags in the bucket and pushed them across the deck in hard, fast swipes, anger driving her strokes. The sun was on its upward arc, and today's wind was a whisper, making the ship's progress slow and the deck sweltering.

Lisette was so drenched in sweat she was soppier than the rag she was using. She had an hour or more of work to do when the dinner bell rang. The sun was dipping itself into the western waters. It would be night soon. Sighing, she wettened her rag again, and worked on. *Perhaps Cook will save me some scraps.*

Galumphing footsteps shook the deck behind her. She straightened and turned around, ready to fight the only person who could be making such a ruckus.

Mar walked past her, carrying a sloshing bucket. Without a word, she sank down a few yards from her and scrubbed.

"I can't imagine you're helping me out of the

goodness of your heart," Lisette said.

Mar threw her rag into the bucket with such force, the water splashed up and over her face. This only made her look angrier. "Cap'n talked to three of us—three of us. Cook, wench in the berth next to mine, and me. Thanks to you, I'm swabbin' until I'm tossed at the next port, if Begum don't kill me and roll me to the fishes."

"I am sick of your stupid anger." Lisette glared at her. "Do not blame me for your problems. I picked no fight with you. You've been malicious to me from the start." Sinking down, she returned to her scrubbing, mumbling to herself. "Get drunk, cry like a lovesick mule, probably the only way she could ever open up to anyone is with too much rum. Crazy woman doesn't understand friendships. Stab her own—"

Mar charged at her, knocking Lisette backward. She straddled her, and punched at her face, landing a blow to her cheek. Lisette held up her hands at first, trying to block the onslaught. As Mar pulled her fist back again, Lisette sent her knuckles, right and upward, aiming for the soft spot under Mar's rib cage.

Her hit landed and Mar crumpled, holding her chest, and trying to regain her breath. Lisette pushed her away and stood, digging at her sheath to withdraw her dagger.

Mar looked at her blade and sneered, pulling one of her own. "Making this a fair fight?"

"That's a bold move for someone who doesn't like a battle," Lisette said.

"I don't, unless the odds is in my favor."

Mar dove in low, veering high in an attempt to stab up, into her ribs. Lisette pulled her torso away and plunged her dagger down toward Mar's shoulder. Mar blocked it with her arm as she twisted backward, and they jumped apart. The big woman was swaying, watching her opponent. Matching her movement,

Lisette stepped sideways, out of her range.

Someone in the distance yelled something, but the two women were locked in battle. Bodies ran past them, and Lisette wanted to stop and join them in whatever was happening, but the bloodlust in Mar's eyes kept her on the defensive.

"Break it up, you two!" Oleta jumped between them. "Spanish ship's attacking aft!"

The ship lurched hard to port, throwing them to the deck. Lisette rose and looked about, spotting a distant form on the starboard flank, and a puff of smoke from a cannon. There was a breath of time to recognize the Burgundy Cross before she ran to Mar and seized her by the arm. Mar swiped at her with her dagger, scraping a gash across her shoulder.

"You idiot!" Lisette screamed and pointed.

The shot caught the tip of the railing, sending splinters everywhere. The three women hit the deck together in a pile. They scuffled to standing as everyone around continued to work their positions. Captain Derya was at the helm, barking orders.

The ship swung about, trying to buy time while they loaded the cannons. The wind had awakened, giving the Spanish galleon speed as they closed the gap.

Lisette was surprised when the captain sped the ship toward the enemy instead of retreating. For a moment, she stood and watched the rest of the crew prepare the cannons for battle.

Someone screamed an order at her. "Swabby, bring up more powder!"

Lisette ran down to the hold, located a small keg, and carried it to the first gun crew she found at the top of the stairs. The woman at the gun scowled as she pried the top off and took out one of the sacks.

"Open it next time," she snapped.

This was no time to argue over whether she'd been trained to do this. Lisette felt lucky enough to have found the keg.

"Yes'm." She picked up the powder and ran to the next gun.

By the time Lisette had serviced the cannons on both sides, they were nearly upon the larger ship, still running at a speed that would ram them broadside. She was on her way to the hold for more powder when the ship changed directions, jerking to port. Being smaller than the galleon, they were more maneuverable. When they had exposed the starboard side, they let loose with all three guns.

They made one hit, taking out one of the enemy's cannons. Lisette was as impressed with their aim as she was the captain's brazenness. The ship kept moving, streaming past the Spanish to get out of their range.

Their answer came quickly. Lisette crouched, bracing for impact as the smoke spewed from their cannon. The shot should have been a direct hit, but the small ship made a difficult target. The cannon was high, rubbing the mizzenmast before it hit the water on the other side. The crew kept the ship coming about in order to fire with their port cannons.

Lisette fell into a quick rhythm, waiting for the

captain's command to "Fire" before running to refill the firing side. After a few passes, she understood her strategy. With each hit they delivered, they sailed further out to come about. The galleon could not match their speed or their ability to turn swiftly. By the time the enemy cannon fired, they were either close enough to shoot over, or far enough away to be in no danger.

There was no time to do anything except run powder to the cannons. Lisette handed the last sack to the port aft gun crew and turned to run back for more. As she did, the spotter in the crow's nest yelled a warning that made her stop and stare.

"Squall to starboard aft!"

A solid wall of black, punctuated by brilliant streaks of lightning, rolled toward the ship, carried by the ever-increasing wind.

The spotter in the crow's nest yelled something else about its approach and pointed toward the dark clouds that were intent on swallowing them within moments. The Spanish galleon turned south, and Lisette saw men leaving their cannons and running to the sails. The *Dişi Aslan* pulled past the cumbersome giant, racing to stay ahead of it and the storm.

Lisette ran aft to help with the lines. As the darkness descended upon the galleon, one final puff bellowed from their forward gun. Someone was throwing her sideways onto the deck as splinters exploded from the blast. The ship rolled starboard, and she slid with it, along with a heavy body atop, pinning her. They remained this way, the ship listing fully starboard, at times dipping the rail into the water and spraying up from below as the rain pelted down from above. It was impossible to get to her feet, even if Lisette could have removed her unresponsive burden.

At last, the ship leveled out, and Lisette was able to free herself. It was Mar who rolled onto her back and huffed a large, gurgling breath, groaning. Lisette sat up and looked at her. Her right side was soaked with blood, and there was a large chunk of railing embedded in her rib cage. They were at the edge of the storm now, with a steady but light rainfall.

"Let me get help." Lisette rose but Mar clung to her arm and pulled her down.

"Stay." Her voice was low and drawn with pain. "Come close."

"Mar, lie still. We'll help you." Lisette fought her grasp.

Mar squeezed her arm tighter. "I have to tell you."

Even injured, her strength was formidable. Lisette could not free her arm, so she sat. "Tell me quickly so I can get help."

Mar coughed hard, and Lisette held her to keep the woman's body from shaking.

"Secret..." She was barely whispering, blood mixed with spittle foaming at the corner of her mouth. Lisette leaned closer. "Take my locket...my neck."

Lisette opened the shirt collar, revealing a silver locket on a thick chain. "Mar, please—"

"Take it. For *Dişi*."

Mar was commanding her, but Lisette felt like a thief. Her stomach lurched as she undid the chain.

The woman's body shuddered, and her voice weakened. "Inside...follow it...treasure."

"Let me get help." Lisette's words choked in her throat. Raindrops hit her face, mixing with her tears.

"Least I could do...so mean. Sorry...so sorry." She groaned and winced, and Lisette held her tighter. Blood was now trickling down her chin. "Tell everyone...forgive me."

Mar looked up, and Lisette could feel the death rattling in her chest. She breathed once more as she stared at the sky. Her body relaxed. She continued to stare.

Lisette bowed her head, wishing she could recall her prayers, suddenly ashamed that she never carried her rosary and hadn't said as much as a Hail Mary since her kidnapping. Mar was still staring, her eyes turning milky, so Lisette gently closed them. There was nothing to cover her with, so she rushed to find the captain, sobbing, her fist squeezing the locket.

The ship ran at the tail of the squall now, under gray skies and a mist that swirled up from the sea and down from the heavens. Everyone worked their posts, making great speed. Captain Derya stood at the helm, strong arms on the wheel, giving orders.

"Captain." Lisette pointed behind her. "Mar is—dead."

The woman closest to her ran aft. As she passed, she gestured toward Lisette's shirt. "You've got blood all over you."

Lisette looked at her arm, to examine the scrape from Mar's blade, but the front of her shirt got her attention. It gleamed, thoroughly wet and dark red. It was odd, since she was holding Mar on the opposite side of her wound. Lisette pulled her collar out and looked inside. The sight made her knees weak.

The shaft of her lucky feather had punctured her skin, skimming upward against her ribs. In all the action and Mar's death, she had felt no pain. She touched the feather. The plump red plumes were about half their size, limp, and stained with her blood, which was seeping copiously.

Lisette lifted her head, to look at the captain. "I seem to be bleeding."

"We should get you below."

"No." She spurted the word, her eyes widening. "I mean, it isn't bad. Mar told me to give you this—"

She held the locket out, but her vision blurred, and her legs buckled as she fell, losing consciousness on her way to the deck.

When Lisette opened her eyes, bright colors whirled around her. She lay motionless, trying to focus on her surroundings.

It took a long moment to recognize that this was Begum Derya's cabin, and she was in Begum Derya's bed. Her arms were leaden, but she managed to lift her hands, with some effort. She raised the covers a bit and peered at her body. Someone had dressed her in silk pajamas. Her ribs and chest felt like they were being stabbed with a thousand little needles. She touched underneath her shirt and found she had been wrapped in bandages.

The door creaked and footsteps came into the room. The shadow of a figure approached the bed.

"Ah, you are awake at last." It was Begum. She smiled—a benevolent, perhaps thankful grin.

"Sorry for being away from my post, Captain."

Begum leaned over to the pillows, fluffing and stacking them. "Can you sit up?"

"I can try." Lisette pushed up from her elbows. A deep burning pierced her chest, almost to her heart. Wincing, she continued to push until, with Begum's help, she leaned, semi-comfortably, on the pillows.

Begum left her side briefly and returned with a bowl of some kind of broth. "Drink this. It has healing herbs and flowers."

It tasted like the broth Rocco had fed her after her first day of work. Both savory and sweet, it soothed the body with its warmth. Begum held the bowl, keeping it tipped at the proper angle for Lisette to drink comfortably. Lisette lifted her hands to the bowl, attempting to regain the use of her limbs.

"Patience," Begum said. "Your strength will return."

When Lisette finished, Begum set the bowl on the table and pulled something limp and rusty brown out of her pocket. "Would you like to explain this?"

Her lucky feather. The shaft looked as if it had been charred in a fire.

"I found it in Rocco's cabin." Lisette filled her in on finding the feather and its role in protecting her against the Viscount Barragan, whose death she now explained.

"So it was you who killed the domuz."

"The pig?"

"That is what we called Barragan. He was a little rutting boar. A few of my crew had unfortunate encounters with him." She grinned. "Did he squeal when you stuck him?"

"Like a piglet."

"I am glad he's dead, but I would not tell that tale

to anyone else. The island's Count Barragan was his brother, and he is offering a sack of gold on behalf of El Rey to anyone who can find his killer. Of course, I am told the count didn't like him any better than we did."

"A reward?" Lisette asked. "Enough gold to tempt a ship's captain?"

"Take money honestly from the royals? There are things even a pirate won't do."

Lisette tried to laugh, but her chest disagreed with her. She laid her hands gently on her ribs to stop the burning. Begum helped her to lie down again.

"We must talk about your wound. It is not a normal injury." Begum held up the feather again. "This is from a blood dragon. I will do what I can. In five days, we will pass a small island. A crone lives there who can help you."

Lisette recalled Connie's book. "Île des Anciens?"

Begum cocked her head. "You have heard of this place?"

"I read about it. It's where you get a potion to turn you into a blood dragon."

"It is more complicated than that." Her expression was serious, and a little sad, a heaviness to her words.

Dread stood upon Lisette's heart.

"In the meantime, we will not discuss your injury with the crew. Talk of blood dragons is the source of gossip and fear. I do not want to encourage any weakness in the women."

Lisette nodded and stifled a yawn.

"Sleep now. You will stay in my cabin until we are at Île des Anciens. We will drop you off there."

"It's such a small island, from what I have read. Will there be another ship stopping for me to find passage on?"

"Do not worry." Begum looked away. "You will be

able to leave the island."

For Lisette, the next five days churned in an endless cycle of sleep and broth, always served by the captain. The burning pain left within a day, but her body was sluggish. Moving her limbs was like dragging heavy, wet ropes. Her head ached beyond reason, and she could barely open her eyes, especially against any light.

The dreams, however, were the worst. Images of blood and fire. In one recurring vision, she was on Rocco's ship, on deck, looking at the night sky. The dragon swooped down from above. He landed before her and placed his claws upon her shoulders. They became hands, and he became Rocco. Embracing her, he kissed her with wild ferocity. She returned the intensity of his mouth with hers.

As they embraced, her hands grew into claws, and bumps emerged on her back that became wings, lifting her. Rocco returned to his dragon form, and they flew together, two dragons across the moon. She soared away from him, toward the shore, and a wall of stone. It rose from the sands, surrounding a castle.

A faceless figure screamed and ran. She chased it. One swipe of her claws, and the sting in her soul was released. As she pushed herself back into flight, she turned and opened her mouth, raining fire on the limp body. At that moment the face on the figure became clear. It was her own.

Sweat and terror jerked her awake with each bloody vision.

On the sixth day, she rose. Her body felt wonderful, light and rested and full of energy, as if her injury and the nightmares had never happened. Her mind was clear. And she was hungry.

Captain Derya entered the cabin, carrying a tray of meat, potatoes, and fruit. She set it on the table and invited Lisette to eat.

"You are feeling well this morning?" she asked.

"Yes, thank you." Lisette sat and reached for the food.

"Good." Begum strode to the door. "I must attend to the ship. We arrive at the island when the sun is high. I will return. Be ready to depart. There are clothes for you beside the bed."

She left, and Lisette continued to eat. The food tasted as if she had never eaten before. The texture of the potatoes, the savory quality of the meat, were all heightened. The apples were crisper, juicier, more delicious.

Once sated, she poured water into the wash basin and used a cloth to clean herself. Being in bed for five days left her in need of freshening. The water was cool and tingled where it touched her skin.

She looked at her arm as she rolled the cloth down it. Tiny pimples appeared, making her arm resemble a plucked chicken. She dropped the cloth, alarmed. There was a mirror in the corner. She ran to it and stared at her reflection.

Her eyes were still green, her hair still long and auburn. She had a less curvy figure, but not only had she been ill, working on ships had brought a sinewy quality to her body.

*Relax, Lizzie. You have been through a lot.*

She returned to her task. When she felt sufficiently cleansed, she retrieved the clothes from the side of the bed, a muslin shirt, trousers, and a pair of shoes. They fit nicely. She was only missing her pouch and her dagger. She searched carefully among the chests by the bed where the clothes had been.

Nothing.

It dawned on her that the ship had not been moving forward in some time. She looked out the windows. It was anchoring.

The door opened.

"Lizzie, are you ready?" Begum asked.

"I can't find my pouch, or my dagger."

"Do not worry about them. Come." It was less of a response and more of an order.

She obeyed.

Captain Derya headed the dinghy toward a small island. The entire coastline could be seen from the starboard side of the boat. It was covered in dense brush and appeared impenetrable. Thickets of mangrove lined the shore. Once they arrived at the island, Lisette had no idea how they'd disembark.

Begum rowed at a leisurely pace, speaking as if she was giving a tour. "Do not be deceived by the hostile appearance of this island. Past the shore, you will find it is lovely. Many lagoons and waterfalls. Beautiful flowers everywhere."

"How long must I be here?"

"A little more than two weeks." Begum continued to look toward the island, rowing.

"Two weeks? What am I to do for that long?"

Lisette pursed her lips. "I will not be able to find Rocco, or gather any gold, or even find my brother, if that's possible."

"Do not worry, there is time for everything. You will soon understand why you must be here for so long." Begum sighed. "I was not tasked with giving you this information, but I shall. The feather of a blood dragon is filled with magic, magic that can be siphoned and used in small amounts. Unfortunately, you managed to drain the entire feather into your own body. There is only one who can take care of you now. Her name is Lamya de Sang."

Lisette sat back, her hand touching her neck. "What has the feather done to me?"

"That is difficult to explain." Begum shook her head and fell silent. They were almost at the island before she spoke again. "You and the feather have a similar quest. You seek vengeance against those who betrayed you. The feather seeks someone who is filled with a demand for revenge. The feather has found its target. Now it will help you find yours."

She maneuvered the boat along the tangle of brush until they came to a rill hidden by the overgrowth. Slipping in between the cliffs, they followed the stream inland, to a lagoon surrounded by black sand. A waterfall splashed down from the far side and lush greenery with swaths of color surrounded them. The scent of jasmine wafted on the warm breeze.

Begum rowed the boat to the shoreline and Lisette jumped out to help her pull it up. As her feet hit the warm sand, her legs shook with a fear of the unknown, but she kept them moving to hide her weakness. With the captain's urging, they set off on a path leading inland.

The breeze did not follow where the two women went, pushing through the evergreen thickets that encroached on the path. Even their deep shade could not keep the sweat from pooling at the base of Lisette's throat, rivulets snaking around her breasts. The once-pleasant aromas from the flowers mixed with the smell of the earth to become an odor of decay. Birds called to each other, their voices harsh and cutting. The only other sounds were the buzzing of insects that insisted on torturing her, and her own ragged breath.

They traveled for at least an hour if not two, Lisette following Begum as she wound her way through the jungle. At several points, it did not appear they had a trail at all. Begum would stop and look around until she found a sign of some sort before continuing. She did not share this information aloud—she didn't speak at all.

Lisette had many questions but kept silent because she feared the responses.

The sun was touching the tip of the western hilltop when Begum stopped and turned to her. She put her fingers to her lips and indicated Lisette stay. Lifting a large branch that blocked her way, she stepped through and disappeared.

Lisette stood in one spot as quietly as possible, swatting at the bugs only when she could no longer stand them swarming her face. She fanned her shirt out, trying to capture a bit of air and cool her damp skin. Begum had not told her how long she would be gone.

Soon, she focused on the noises around her. Being alone in this strange place amplified each rustle of branch, each whisper of leaf. As the time stretched on, impatience became fear that she had been abandoned.

She was nearly in tears when Begum reappeared and told her, "Come with me."

They trudged down a narrow path to another lagoon, smaller than the one at the edge of the island, with a larger waterfall. The water here was bluer, the flowers brighter, and the greenery more vivid. Begum touched her shoulder.

"This is where I leave you. Good luck, Lisette de Lille, and God be with you." She held her hands out. "Here are your things."

She held Lisette's pouch, her dagger, and Mar's locket. Lisette took the pouch and the dagger but hesitated at the locket.

"Mar insisted I give it to you. Said it was for the *Dişi*." She lowered her hand.

Begum pressed the locket into her palm. "Mar had shown this locket to me. She claimed it held the secret to riches galore—Sandoval's treasure. It is an old story, and every pirate has searched for the gold. If it exists, call it my intuition, but I believe it was meant for you to discover."

"I will tell you if you were right." Lisette hugged her, wanting to beg her to stay, and not leave her here alone. Her lips trembled, but she managed to find her strength. "Thank you, Captain Derya. Godspeed to you and all aboard the *Dişi Aslan*."

The captain pointed to her wrist. "You have many sisters now. That is your calling card, wherever you go. And you are welcome to return to the *Dişi* once you have completed your journey."

With a final wave, she disappeared into the jungle. Lisette turned to face the waterfall, and her fate. She did not wait long. As she watched the stream of white curls flow from the cliff, making ripples in the aqua lagoon, a form appeared in the ribbons of water. So slow was its movement, she blinked to make certain her eyes were not lying.

A woman emerged, like no one she had ever seen. She was tall and muscled, her skin dark and smooth. Her hair, coppery and thick, draped her naked, glistening body. She stepped out of the water and over to a rock, where she retrieved a long, green robe, which she fastened about her. The robe covered and exposed her at the same time—tight at the waist, it opened wide at the top to display cleavage, and was slit high on the sides, revealing her long, dark legs as she strode toward Lisette.

Her eyes were the most curious part. They were gold, deep and burnished like an ancient coin. She offered Lisette her hand.

"I am Lamya de Sang." Her voice had a languid, purring quality.

"I am Lisette de Lille." She took the woman's hand to shake, but Lamya clutched hers and turned.

"Come." She pulled her toward the waterfall. "We have much to do, and you are hungry."

Lisette followed as the woman walked to the falls and turned toward a wall of vines, twisted together. Brushing them aside, Lamya revealed an entrance and indicated for her to walk ahead. A dim light shone in the distance, so Lisette moved toward it, winding through a rock tunnel that curved this way and that. A small stream of water trickled at her feet, evidence of how the tunnel had formed. Each time she believed they had arrived at the end, the dim light turned out to be sunshine peeping through a cenote. Another dim light, another distance, meant she kept moving until they stepped from the cave and into the sun.

"Come." Once again, Lamya took her hand and pulled her to a clearing. A fire burned steadily in a pit. She motioned for her to sit. "I will bring you food."

She returned with a bowl of fruit and cleaned cooked roots of some kind. Lisette had never seen any of these, even the fruits, but they were all delicious and filling. Lamya watched her eat without saying a word. Once she had finished, Lamya took the bowl from her hands and looked up at the sky.

Night was upon them.

"You have many questions," she said. "I have answers."

Lisette hardly knew where to start. "Begum told me the feather drained magic into me. What did it do?"

"Think, Lisette." Lamya stretched her hand out to place her palm upon Lisette's heart. "The feather came from a blood dragon. It emptied into you."

Lisette whispered the words. "It made me—a blood dragon?"

Lamya sat back, as if satisfied. "I will teach you. Tomorrow night will start the blood dragon's cycle. It lasts from the waning crescent, through the birth of the new moon, to its waxing crescent. Thirteen days, from the dragon's eye looking forward, to the dragon's eye looking back."

"I have heard stories, but I'm still unsure. What is a blood dragon?"

"It is the manifestation of vengeance, a physical answer to egregious wrong. When a person has experienced aching loss from the hands of another and cannot get satisfaction, becoming a blood dragon allows them to hunt their tormentors with impunity. Fire and talon are the dispensers of revenge. And it is difficult to capture a dragon, much less send them to the noose."

"But the feather—it was an accident."

Lamya shook her head. "The feather seeks a heart darkened by loss and anger. You would not have found it, it would not have released its magic, if you did not want revenge against Eric, Mercedes, and Elena. In that way, the feather found you."

Lisette sat up, her eyes wide. "How do you know their names?"

"I know much, Lisette. I know you traveled on Tristan de Rocco's ship. I know you still scarcely believe he is a blood dragon." She laid her hand atop Lisette's.

"You are right." Lisette looked into the fire. "I know I should, but it's just so difficult to imagine."

"You have not seen him change, but now you will know what he endures," she said. "The first few times, it will be hard. You will feel much pain. You will also be unable to control your rage, and I will help you learn to focus with your human brain. This first cycle, you will stay with me. When you leave, you will be able to live in the world as what you have become."

"Will I always be like this?" The question quivered in her voice.

"You will remain so until there is no need for the dragon in your life."

"You mean, when I complete my revenge?"

She smiled. "When there is no more need."

Lisette looked up at the night sky. "All I ever wanted was—I don't know. My life was planned for me. I suppose I wanted it to all be easy. Marry Eric, have the children, hold the parties."

"You did not want to love your husband, and be loved by him?"

"I was taught that it wasn't necessary. It was my duty, king and country, you know." She shook her head, thinking of Rocco. "Love is so complicated."

"True, it is a thing of greatness." Lamya drew circles in the dirt. "Big feelings that fill the heart. Without love, pain takes its place."

"I have plenty of that." Lisette frowned. "Now I only want vengeance."

"That is a goal to keep you a dragon forever." Lamya rose. "Perhaps one day you will examine your heart and make a new goal."

Gesturing to a pile of silky material on the other side of the fire, she said, "That is where you will sleep. You have only one thing to do before you can rest tonight."

"And that is?"

"Cry. Cry for your loss. Cry for your anger. Weep hard. They will be the last tears you shed, at least until you are no longer a blood dragon."

Lisette stood and walked toward the silks. Stopping, she faced Lamya. "By the way, how did Begum know about you, and where to find you. Is she a blood dragon?"

"She was, but her time was short. Her anger burns hot and quick, and she thought everyone else's did. That is why, many years ago, she brought your Captain Rocco to me. She did not think he would cling to his revenge like a man to a sinking ship."

"Why is he still a blood dragon?"

"We will discuss Rocco tomorrow." She turned and walked into the darkness. "Now, good night."

Lisette spread out the silks and sank into them, exhausted in body and soul. Taking her emerald from the pouch, she held it in her palm, rubbing it. Its weight and warmth kept her father close.

Mar's locket rattled in the bottom of the pouch. She brought it out and opened it for the first time. It was old silver, with many small dents and scratches. The locket was empty, but "whale's spout" had been etched on the inside. She closed it and put it away. Mar and her treasure. How big of a treasure would she need to go back home and make everything the way it was?

Lamya had told her to cry before she slept. Lisette believed she had already cried too much. Crying for her family, crying at Rocco's rejection, even crying for Mar.

But as she closed her eyes, a tear crept out and ran down her cheek, followed by another. She allowed herself to imagine and miss her father's embrace, her brother's teasing, even her mother's discipline. Genevieve came to mind, with her gentle, maternal care. Soon Lisette was weeping. As soon as she would catch her breath, her heart would break anew, and the sobs would begin again.

She even cried for Rocco, although it surprised her. At some point, she wrung every tear from her body, and passed into slumber.

The morning light had barely found the ridge of the valley when Lamya awakened her. She threw something at Lisette's feet. "Put these on and come eat. We have much to do before dusk."

Lisette rose and picked up what had been given her. It was a shirt and breeches, but they were small and short. She wondered if she could get into them but did not try to argue. The shirt was more like a cotton chemise, cut off at the waist. It molded itself around her chest, and the two thick straps over her shoulders gave her breasts support. The breeches stopped at the top of her thighs, exposing her legs. This was not an outfit for civilized society.

"Um, it's a little…baring," Lisette told Lamya as

she joined her by the fire.

Lamya was wearing something similar, although there appeared to be even less fabric involved. "It is necessary to free your arms and legs. We must work your body, tire it out for tonight."

Lisette shivered.

"Do no worrying." Lamya patted her bare arm. "I have done this many times. It will go well."

Lisette picked up her wooden bowl and took a bite. There was twice as much food as last night. "Why do you do this?"

"I do not understand the question."

"Who are you, why do you teach people to become these beasts?"

Lamya looked up, toward the sun, as if listening to another's voice. "I am one of the Ancient Ones. We are here for the protection of the world."

"Forgive me, you are who? Here to do what?"

"Mmm, how to explain…there is Magic in this world, Magic everywhere. People do not see it, are not supposed to see it, only in small pieces. Too many of them do not believe, would try to destroy it. They fear it. The churches and temples have convinced your people that the age of Magic is over. Miracles built their faith, yet they have pushed them aside. But Magic is strong, and left alone, it grows. The Ancient Ones were sent to keep it under control. Without us, it would overpower all life. We…mmm…prune it like a garden. Witches and dryads on land, mermaids and naiads in the sea, they must all be tempered."

"And blood dragons."

"Especially blood dragons." She looked at Lisette's bowl of half-finished food. "You must eat it all. You will not eat again for a few days."

Lisette was unaccustomed to eating large quantities

of food. Lamya goaded and cajoled and pushed until she had eaten every speck and was one step away from hurling it back up.

"Good. We begin." She stood and offered her hand.

They moved toward the waterfall, Lamya carrying two large machetes. At the edge of the tumbling roar, she motioned for Lisette to go ahead of her. Lisette crept along the rock, wishing Lamya would lead her, until she came to the falls and discovered a path between cliff and water. She passed through easily, the mist coating her skin and hair.

After a short walk through the cliffs to the other side, they emerged in a green valley that stretched from horizon to horizon. Lisette blinked in disbelief.

"I didn't think this island was so big," she said.

"It isn't."

"Then how—" She stopped herself. "Magic."

Lamya grinned, her broad lips stretching across her face. "You are quick to learn."

At the center of the immense valley stood a mountain, slender and tall, and so brilliant in red and yellow Lisette supposed at first it was on fire. Lamya pointed to it. "That is where we are going. It is the Dragon's Breath."

Again, she let Lisette go first, but handed her a machete.

"What do I do with this?"

"There is no trail. You must create it." Lamya pointed toward the mountain. "That way."

With a doubtful look, Lisette raised her machete and stroked forward, hacking at the dense brush and the heavy vines hanging from the trees that entangled them. After a short while, Lisette's back groaned with each swing of the blade. Bringing it down or sideways made her arms burn. Soon her entire body quivered from repeated hewing with the large, heavy implement. Still, Lamya did not relent, but pushed her onward until they reached the base of the Dragon's Breath.

Upon closer look, the red and yellow of the mountain consisted of many blooming plants, bird of paradise to hibiscus, to bougainvillea, to flowers Lisette did not recognize. She grimaced at the bougainvillea. Their vines were covered in long spikes.

*I hope we are not going to try to climb this mountain.*

"Up." Lamya pointed.

She looked at the mountain before her, at least two furlongs high, possibly three, and no gentle slopes. It was all straight uphill.

"I don't think I can."

"You must. Do not think, climb." Lamya put her foot on a rock and pulled herself upward on a vine. "I will be beside you."

Emulating her, Lisette found a foothold and a non-spiked vine, and followed suit. The sun had hit with its full strength, making the sweat pour from her body with each exertion. Several times, her foot slipped on a rock, and she hung from her arms until she could get her legs under her again. Her arms were already fatigued and burning from the machete.

"This is torture," she moaned.

"Yes." Lamya reached above for another vine. "But it is necessary."

They traveled this way until the sun was at its peak. As Lisette pulled herself up on the next vine, she spied a small ledge that had been hidden by the flowers.

Lamya read her mind. "Yes, we will rest there."

Lisette lifted her body up to the ledge and threw herself upon the rocks, not caring if they jabbed. Letting out a deep groan, she realized how thankful she was for the large meal earlier. She was even ready for something else if there was anything else to be had.

There was. Lamya produced two packets of what appeared to be cakes made with yams. They were chewy but good. Lisette tried not to wolf hers, savoring small bites.

"You said yesterday you would talk about Rocco today."

"Did I?" Lamya chewed a bite of her cake.

"He's been a blood dragon for a long time, hasn't he? Is he different?"

"Perhaps more stubborn. He has a problem with his thirst for revenge, one that may not have a solution."

"I thought you said, you kill your tormentor, you stop being a dragon. Seems easy."

Lamya laughed. "Nothing about this is easy. You already have a dilemma, about your aunt. Kill her because she wronged you, forgive her with all your soul because she is your family, or do not kill her and do not forgive her and remain a dragon forever."

"Rocco's problem is worse than that?"

"So much so." She paused, nibbling again, staring at the sky. "Rocco swore revenge on everyone in the castle the night his wife died. Everyone. There are two people left for him to kill. One is the man who took Tempest from him, the Count de Medina."

"And the other?"

Her golden eyes lowered to find Lisette's. "You."

"Me? I don't remember any Tempest, dying in any castle."

"You were but a baby, barely two years old. Your mother brought you with her to meet the count. She left the castle that evening, to bring Elena back from a, hmm, meeting with a gentleman. You were in the great room with your nurse."

Lamya stopped here, taking another bite of food while she drew circles in the dirt with her finger.

Lisette grew impatient. "Then what happened?"

As if awaking, Lamya blinked and looked about. "Hmm? Oh, your mother did not find Elena, but she found a young sailor searching for his wife. She realized that the count's courtesan was Tempest de Rocco and showed the young man a secret entrance to the castle."

Lisette pressed her fingers against her chest. "How sweet."

Lamya shook her head. "It did not go well. He burst into the great hall, sword in hand, crying out for his wife. Tempest was holding you when she stood to answer him. Before his name could leave her lips, the count stabbed her. She collapsed and the count set the guards upon Rocco. He escaped, swearing his eternal vengeance on everyone there. As she died, Tempest gave her last breath begging him to spare you, an innocent."

"Then why would he still have to kill me?"

"Because when you accept the spell of the blood dragon, it is based upon the original oath. Rocco swore vengeance on all, even you. But Tempest stays his hand."

"The way he looks at me." Lisette struggled for the words. "There is a hardness, as if he hates the sight of me. But sometimes, I see tenderness in his eyes. And pain."

"I believe Tempest has forged a bond between you and him. You are the one to open his heart, allow him to love again. But he is still torn—his human side cannot let Tempest go, and his dragon side demands your blood. It will be a difficult choice for him, to love you or kill you."

"If he doesn't kill me, though, he'll remain a dragon forever."

"I did not say that. His desire for revenge could be replaced by forgiveness. Or love." She stood. "Come, we must keep moving."

Once again, Lisette's feet searched for strong rocks to hold her, and her hands clung to vines, whether they had thorns or not. The sun was on the back side of the mountain, casting long shadows, and giving her some relief from the heat. Finally, almost at the summit of the Dragon's Breath, she hung back, panting in rough, painful breaths.

"Come along, Lisette. We are nearly there."

"I'm so tired. My arms, my legs."

"Yes, they are. They have to be. Trust me." She looked at her. "Count to five. Five more pulls. That is all."

Lisette took a deep breath and grasped. "One…this is so hard. Two…my body is shaking. Three…I'm going to fall to my death. Four…almost there. Five, ugh…no more."

Lamya's strong hands grabbed her forearms and pulled her over the edge, onto the mountain top. As before, Lisette lay motionless and sweating, trying to push her heart back into her chest and breathe again.

"It is good you are tired," Lamya said. "Come, we have much to do."

All Lisette could do was groan in response, but she managed to raise herself upright and follow her guide through the brush to a flat, rocky space with little greenery. Lamya started a small fire in a rock pit, pulled an animal-skin sack from her belt and held it over the flame. Handing it to Lisette, she said, "Drink all."

Lisette put the sack to her lips and squeezed it. A warm, savory liquid came out, much like the broth from a rich chicken stew. She drank it all without any problem, instantly sated and energized.

Lamya was not finished, however. "Hurry, come.

The sun will be gone soon."

Lisette followed her to a barren patch of ground surrounded by a ring of large boulders. From the center of the ring, four long cords of woven fibers pushed from the ground as if planted and growing.

"What is this place?" Lisette asked.

"It is your training ground. Go to the center. Now."

Lamya's commands were so forceful, Lisette did as she was told, with no questions. As soon as she was in the center, Lamya put Lisette's hands and feet in loops at the end of each cord. The loops were silken against her skin even as the cords weighed her limbs down.

Lisette looked up at Lamya. "I'm confused. What—"

"You must be restrained until you can control your dragon," Lamya said.

The last ray disappeared, folded into the night sky. Lamya was chanting. Her low, purring voice floated on the warm air.

*"Heated blood,*
*Blackened heart,*
*Love and mercy,*
*Torn apart."*

Lisette had read those words in Rocco's cabin and shook uncontrollably. She now knew what they meant.

Lisette's bones were on fire. She watched her arms stretch—was she hallucinating? Her skin pimpled, like a chicken's after plucking, all white and bumpy. The bumps kept growing, pushing out of her body. She screamed with the onslaught of searing pain.

"You are doing well, Lisette." Lamya's voice sounded distant. "You are almost there."

Lisette felt the arching of her back and the extension of her claws before losing consciousness. The rest of the night was a blur of rage. Flames were everywhere, heat rose from within and erupted in her screams, and anger ate her soul. There were brief moments when a shrill whistle interrupted her thrashing, but she knew nothing except to strike out, to slash and kill anything, anyone.

And then she was spent, lying in the dirt.

Something soft covered her, and two arms carried her away. She tried to pay attention, but her eyes were no less exhausted than her body. Soon the fire was in front of her, and she rested on a bed of fresh and fragrant greens. She let out an enormous sigh and slept.

When she awoke, Lamya was sitting and watching her.

"You did well for your first time," she said.

"Aren't you going to ask me how I feel?"

"It would not matter. You will change, whether you feel good or bad about it."

Lisette pushed herself to sitting. "True."

"Your dragon is clever. I haven't seen one this clever in many years." Like last night, Lamya handed her the sack, warm and filled with liquid. "Drink."

Lisette's mind believed she should be famished, but her stomach disagreed. The liquid breakfast was perfect. As she drank, she looked at her body, wrapped in a blanket. She had scratches and bruises everywhere.

"Will I always be this beaten up? It's most inconvenient."

"Humans." Lamya scowled. "So fragile. But no, your body will adjust." She rose. "Finish your nectar. I will return soon with work for you."

With a few long strides, she was across the mountain top and gone. Lisette returned to her drink, savoring its taste, and the way its warmth spread through her limbs.

When Lamya reappeared, she waved for Lisette to come to her. As she approached, Lamya was rocking a large boulder with her bare foot.

"This is your work for the day." Lamya stepped away from the rock and pointed. "You will push this to the grove of trees there."

"Then what?"

"You push it back here."

"All day?"

Lamya narrowed her golden eyes. "You must be tired tonight. It is necessary."

There was no use trying to argue with her. Lisette pushed the rock. It was heavy and required a little lift before each shove, straining her arms, back, and legs. Sometimes she could get it rolling for a turn or two, which would result in it getting stuck in an uneven patch of ground, jarring her shoulders. In this way, she pushed and hefted and shoved the irregular rock across the irregular land, until she got to the grove of slender trees. It took a long time, and she was hot, sweaty, and trying to catch her breath in the shade.

"No rest. Push it back."

Lisette tried to protest. "I cannot keep doing this. My body will not continue."

"Your body will thrive. Keep pushing."

Wiping sweat from her hairline, she put her shoulder down and began again. Today they didn't even stop for yam cakes. Straining all of her muscles seemed to take the hunger from her. When Lamya finally allowed her to stop, she had pushed the rock to the grove and back six times.

"It is enough," Lamya said. "Come to the fire."

Lisette stood and stretched. Yesterday, she believed her muscles were not going to carry her over the ridge. Today, the ache and burn amplified in her limbs. She wobbled to the fire and half-sat, half-fell onto her seat.

As always, Lamya handed her a skin full of liquid.

Lisette sipped her dinner, happy for its soothing effect on her mind and body. "Lamya, how is my—my dragon—clever?"

"She is angry, yes, and wishes retribution with claw

and fire, but she is much like Rocco, cautious and willing to wait for her prize. She is more calculating than he ever was and nearly escaped her bonds on the first night. I must be more vigilant." She took out a cake and nibbled at it. "Tonight, you will begin to hear me with your human brain, a small amount, a whisper. Try to listen to it. Accept your new form. The more you accept it, the less the pain."

Lisette scowled. *Even without the pain, I didn't ask to be a blood dragon.* She feared her capacity for violence, and her memory never strayed far from the horrific dream of her body bloodied and burned.

"Lamya, yesterday you said my vengeance against Mercedes makes everything worse instead of better for Rocco. How can that be?"

Lamya did not answer at first. Lisette thought she was sleeping.

"Rocco will soon find out." The Ancient One looked up at the sky, as if speaking to someone in the clouds, before addressing her. "Tempest was with child, a child by the count's brutality. When she died that night, they were able to save the baby—a girl, named Mercedes."

"Mercedes de Medina is Tempest's daughter?" Lisette frowned. "But she is not Rocco's child—and he does not know this?"

"This is true. However, she is the one thing, the last thing Tempest left on this world. She is half Tempest. I believe he will want to protect her, especially from you."

The sun began its descent too soon, and Lisette could not stop her body quivering with fright. The previous night's pain was unbearable. Lamya said it would get easier if she accepted her new form. Lisette looked to the heavens and prayed she was right.

"I am right, you will see," Lamya told her.

"You read my mind?"

"I am aware of all vibrations of this world." She glanced at the sun. "It is time."

Obedient, if begrudging, Lisette dragged herself to the chains and allowed Lamya to place her limbs in the cords. The cool air of darkness descended as the fire inside her rose up.

"Calm your mind, slow your breath, relax your body." Lamya's voice lulled her, helping her to do all three. Soon she began the chanting. "Heated blood, blackened heart…"

The fire in Lisette's chest spread outward, down her limbs, up her spine. She did her best to keep calm, to breathe, while the heat grew and pulsed. Fingers, toes, head were all radiating. She closed her eyes and a white burst of light exploded behind them, blinding, accompanied by a flash of the intense pain of last night. She screamed once and wrath filled her.

As before, she had no conscious knowledge of where she was or what she was doing, except that her body thrashed. This time, she lifted herself from the ground with an awkward flapping. A piercing cry caught her attention and Lamya's voice echoed through her head.

"Lisette, hear me. Remember. Who are you?"

She returned to the ground, still fighting for freedom. The night passed thus, each time her writhing became too violent, she heard a cry and Lamya again. When sunrise came, none too soon, the bright light signaled her pain, and she was human again.

Everything was as before. Arms carried her to the fire, she slept, and awoke to find Lamya standing guard.

"I heard you," Lisette told her.

Lamya handed her the broth-filled sack. "Good."

Ten more days, Lamya worked her until her body cried out to surrender, but she grew strong. Ten nights, Lisette corralled the beast in her until she was able to change into a dragon and retain her own mind. Each night, Lisette tried her wings, spit fire, and looked down to find Lamya, smiling and nodding, hands guiding the cords that held her captive.

On the final day, she awoke and awaited her task. "What do I do today? Roll two stones across the mountain? Climb every tree in the glade? Cut a new path to the other side?"

"Today we rest," Lamya told her, and laughed at her shocked expression.

"I don't understand."

"Tonight is your last night of changing—for this moon's cycle. I cannot help you when the new moon comes around again. You will be on your journey, and I will no longer be by your side. This is the night we discover if you can maintain your own soul within the dragon's anger."

Fear crawled up her neck. "What if I can't?"

"Don't be silly, Lisette." She echoed Lisette's own mother for a brief moment. "You have been a good student. For a few nights now, you have had complete control of yourself."

"How can that be? I am still at the mercy of my bonds."

A sly smile played at the corners of the woman's mouth. "I will reveal to you now, I have loosened the loops in the cords for three nights. You could have left the mountain, but you did not."

"But if I believed I was confined, what good did that do?"

"I told you, your dragon is clever. If you had not been in charge of her, she would have tried it, as she tried for the first six nights. And look at yourself. You are not as scratched and bruised as when you began." She stood and gestured. "Come with me."

35

Together, the women strolled past the grove of trees into a long, wide thicket made greener by the shade. There was a narrow path to follow, wide enough for one person.

"Lamya," Lisette whispered as they walked.

The Ancient One slowed, turning her head to hear. "Hmm?"

"Now that I am a dragon…am I still a woman?"

Lamya stopped and reached out to her, cupping her chin in her long, graceful hand. "You will find that you are very much still a woman."

"I feel as if I live in two worlds now. Which one is really mine?"

"When it is important, you will know."

They came to a lagoon, sparkling aqua in the

sunlight. Bubbles gushed up on the far side and large-leafed plants hung down from the edge.

"This water comes from an underground spring," Lamya said. "I think today you would like to bathe."

It had been weeks, perhaps months since Lisette had done anything more than wiping herself with a cloth. She walked into the cool water without another word, clothing and all. Lamya laughed and tossed a square block at her.

"Here is soap. Take off your clothes and give yourself a good scrub. I will return with something fresh for you to wear."

Lisette stripped and threw her meager outfit—torn and stained—onto shore. The lagoon was not deep, and for a time, she paddled and floated from one end to the other. Becoming a blood dragon had heightened her senses, so even when she was in human form, she could hear a bug drying its wings, smell the dank underbrush by the shore, and distinguish each shade of verdant growth around the lagoon, as well as the water's shifts from aqua to turquoise.

Unbraiding her hair, she let the long tangle of curls loose upon the water, feeling its weight as she submerged and came up again. She ran her nails through her scalp, rubbing the soap in and rinsing the grime away. Next, she turned to her body, running soap over her arms, and submerging to rinse herself clean.

She floated on her back, absorbing the sunlight on her chest, while enjoying the cool water beneath. The warmth on her breasts was delectable, and she closed her eyes in sheer delight. She let her hands glide over her entire body, noticing the way her soft curves had been exchanged for lean muscle. In the past, she would never have touched her naked flesh, not even in the privacy of her own room. A proper lady treated her body as if she was only slightly acquainted with it.

Now she ran her fingertips across her ribs and reveled in her own strength.

A woman shouldn't be this strong, at least according to Mama. Women were the weaker sex, meant for rounded flesh and a generous bosom, to entice a husband, and bear many children. But Lisette wasn't just a woman now. She was a dragon, a creature of destruction as well as a vessel for creation.

Her hands wandered to her thighs, and soon she was exploring their intersection. Rocco had done so, had put his palm here and his fingers there, rubbing. She found she could elicit the same excitement as he did, a sensual deliciousness that grew in such intensity, she was afraid it wouldn't end and sad that it would. She spent unmeasured time here, discovering what made the feeling grow and ebb, taking the sensations to the edge of unbearable ecstasy, then easing back to a manageable pleasure.

At the moment Lisette feared she might explode and leave pieces strewn about, her body instead bucked with gratifying convulsions, releasing all tension, and leaving her weak and relaxed, peaceful, floating across the water.

Lisette raised her left arm and stared at the tattoo. Pinar had warned her that she would have to choose which world suited her. The lioness head stared back, reminding her of the path she chose.

She floated awhile longer, regarding the sky and planning what she should do when she left the island. Her first goal should be killing Mercedes and Eric, but she wished to return as a lady with some wealth. She wanted to incite their jealousy before she destroyed them.

Gold was needed to fund her journey. Her choices were to find Rocco and collect her share, or search for Mar's treasure. It occurred to her that she and Rocco would be hunting the skies as dragons at the same time. Perhaps Mar's treasure would be her safest choice.

"Refreshed?" Lamya was on the shore again, holding something in her hands.

Lisette swam to her. "Much, thank you."

The Ancient One spread out the clothing she was holding. A chemise, a simple skirt, and a robe, much like the one Lamya wore at their first meeting. "This is for you."

Lisette stepped out of the water and into the clothes. They fit her as if tailored to her exact measurements. The robe was black and like Lamya's, was tight from her waist upward, supporting her breasts. Long sleeves were attached at her wrists, but split to her shoulders, exposing her arms. The neckline was low, and the slits on each side allowed her legs to swing through as she walked. She ran her hands down the fabric, enjoying its touch. Soft, yet strong.

"It is a special fabric, fashioned by the Ancient Ones."

"How is it special?"

"It will protect you against much in the world," Lamya told her. Pulling the front of the robe, she revealed large pockets sewn into the skirt, each one with a flap that tied shut. "And it has pockets to carry whatever you require."

"Thank you," Lisette said, opening a pocket to place her leather pouch. The robe felt as if nothing had been placed in it, so she opened the pocket again. There was her pouch. She looked at Lamya. "It's magic!"

"It's special." Lamya gestured toward camp. "Come, let us eat."

Real food awaited her at the fire, including some kind of fowl. Lisette sat and pulled a little of everything into her bowl. It all tasted as if she'd never had food before—luscious and exotic and filling. She'd never seen Lamya eat anything but flowers, fruits, and roots, but the Ancient One joined her, tearing a leg from the roasted bird.

"This meal is part of the ritual," Lamya said. "The hibiscus is red to represent the blood of those you seek. The fruit of the mango is soft, like the underbelly of your enemies, and the stone in the middle is your heart, which will be hardened against them. The bird's wings represent your own, in your dragon form. He sacrificed his life to lift you on the highest current."

Her words made Lisette slow her eating and be thankful for each morsel. She wished she could offer a prayer, but it had been so long. The church would never condone sorcery or dragons, or even pirating. Not only did Mercedes and Eric ruin her life, they ruined her afterlife.

They ate the rest of the meal without speaking, Lisette acutely aware of it being their last time together.

"Will we ever meet again?"

"After tonight, my task is complete. I cannot say where your path will lead. Tomorrow, you begin your quest for revenge."

Lisette nodded, with a wry grin. "Justice with her sword."

Lamya's face, already serious, turned to Lisette with a horrible scowl. "Do not be deceived. Justice and vengeance are not the same."

"I only meant—"

"Justice is a punishment that fits the crime. Do you think Mercedes and Eric deserve death?"

Lisette did not try to hide her shock. "Of course. They killed my parents. They ruined my life."

"Do you know this for certain?" Lamya leaned back, arms folded across her chest. "And ruined your life—did they? You did not want to marry Eric."

"Of course, I did!"

"No. Do not lie." Lamya's voice barked her disapproval.

"I would not lie to you."

"I do not care if you lie to me," Lamya said. "Do not lie to yourself. You do not love Eric. You did not want to marry him. You wanted to live an easy life."

"All I know is that if I had not been kidnapped, my island would not be under Spanish rule now. And if that had not happened, my parents would be alive, and I would not want to kill Eric and Mercedes with every breath in my body. And what is wrong with wanting an easy life?"

Lamya threw her hands in the air, huffing. "An easy life is a life without the living. If life is not difficult, then you do not appreciate it when it is beautiful. If it is all easy, you appreciate nothing."

"Well, what is there for me to appreciate now?"

"So much, Lisette." Lamya sat back and smiled. "Your resolve to honor your family by reclaiming your island. Your wits that allowed you to survive your kidnapping. Your strength—you are a dragon!"

Lisette felt a sudden burn on her wrist. She grabbed it, turned it over, rubbing. The lioness head tattoo glowed upon her skin. The past months came rushing back in visceral clarity. Lisette saw and felt it all within an instant—the sting of the squall, the sun on her face, the crass grab of the dead viscount's hands, the tender caress of the pirate-dragon Rocco.

"You are right. It's difficult to appreciate those things when they have come from such pain." Lisette lifted her eyes to gaze at the sky. "And yet, it has not all been miserable."

Lamya bowed her head, smiling. "I mean no judgment toward you, Lizzie. But you must understand. Yes, these people have harmed both your family and your island. They should be punished, and in this realm, dragons are the punishers, either with justice or with vengeance. Justice is without passion, which is almost impossible for the human heart. Humans experience pain and respond with deep anger. It is not your fault. All you have is retaliation, which is vengeance."

As always, the sun dipped too soon. This time, Lisette rose first. "It is time."

# 36

Lisette walked to the center of the cords, preparing to assume her normal position. Lamya shook her head.

"Not tonight, Lisette. Tonight, you stand outside the circle. Are you ready?"

"Yes, Lamya." She moved away from the boulders. The sun dipped and the fire was banking in her chest. "Thank you. I'll miss you."

"Goodbye, Lizzie." Lamya stood tall, smiling, but Lisette saw a moist sheen in her golden eyes.

By now, Lisette was no longer disgusted with her form. She watched her arms lengthen and her feathers growing, breathing slow and steady and absorbing the heat of the transformation. She waited for the bright light, ready for the final shock. The excruciating pain she'd experienced in the beginning was now a momentary discomfort.

Lisette spread her wings and pushed away from the mountain, taking flight over the island. Mar's locket had the words "whale's spout" etched in it. Isla de la Ballena, Whale Island was southeast of Île des Anciens. The words in Mar's locket could mean anything, but Whale Island seemed the best place to start.

But first, she had to fly over the lagoon for one reason only—to regard her own reflection. The sliver of moonlight did not illuminate her well, but she managed to glide to the shore. A black dragon looked back at her from the lagoon's stillness, turning to admire the line of golden spikes down her back.

Having seen enough, Lisette rose up into the cloud cover in case human eyes watched the sky this night.

Having a human mind in a dragon's body was like being in a dream. She could feel the wind on her face, smell the life of the ocean, hear a symphony of sounds. The desires of her dragon body were basic, if formidable. Pleasure, not pain. Satiation, not hunger. She had to concentrate on her human side in order to use the power her dragon possessed.

Aided by her memory of Rocco's maps, she looked up at the stars to find the constellations that would lead her to Isla de la Ballena. Setting her course, she turned toward her destination and used her dragon instincts to seek currents, spreading her wings and drifting with the wind.

After a few hours' flight she detected the scent of land. Hoping it was the right island, she descended. It had been named Whale Island because for many years, sailors avoided it, believing it was a pod of whales feeding, with humped backs and arching tails. Her approach from overhead revealed nothing but a normal island, hilly, but not approximating sea creatures.

Glancing down to her left she saw small, dark

structures. She assumed they were homes. To her right was the pier and a long row of well-lit buildings, an inn with its accompanying ale house.

Her dragon ears could detect bad music and loud talk from that end of town and her dragon nostrils sensed the blood of humans. For a moment her instincts focused on that odor and the desire to kill arose in her heart. She had to avert her eyes toward the mountains to stay on the path. Fortunately for the town's inhabitants, the blood she detected did not belong to any of her enemies although there was a familiar smell to it.

As she swooped past the outskirts of town, she observed what those early sailors reported. It was a magnificent deception, an unending roll of hills and mountains that looked like several whales come together. The arc of moonlight enhanced their shadows, and she could make out the head of one, the humped back of another, and several tails, rising and curving.

The moon was descending as was her strength. She would change soon and needed a place to do so unobserved. As she flew, she saw a tall, thin needle of land with an overgrowth of bushes and vines that spiked out. It gave the appearance of a whale's tail, high and arched. She was still almost a league away, but she dropped down a little lower, gliding toward the bottom of the formation.

Passing over a high ridge she heard a rumble and hiss. She slowed, curious, in time to get a face full of water rushing up from below. Rising she shook and flew, zigzagging to get away from the spray.

Light crept up the horizon and she could feel the burning desire to change. She angled her body down and raced toward land. The formation she had aimed for was now lost, so she looked for any kind of grove to hide in.

Spotting another whale's tail to the right she veered over and glided to a landing. This needle appeared shorter, but its flukes were fat and wide. Wayward plants fringed the top like the hair jutting from a monk's skullcap.

Lisette scanned the landscape. There were no homes, nothing but the chatter of waking monkeys and cries of birds. She did not smell any human presence nearby, nor for some time past. There was just enough time for her to hide in a nook between two large rock piles at the base of the tail before the sun and her human body appeared.

As before the change was quick and nearly painless—a pinching flash and she was Lisette again, dressed in the garments Lamya had given her. She checked the pocket of her robe and found her pouch. Withdrawing her dagger, she nestled into the soft moss between the rocks. Sleep was required before exploration. As her eyes fluttered into slumber, she recalled the gust of water that had shot at her from the arched ground.

*The whale's spout.*

The sun had barely reached midmorning when she awoke. She wanted to sleep longer but the whale spout had filled her dreams, fermenting in her mind, and begging her to investigate. Rising, she looked at the hill where the water had appeared and set out in that direction, hoping to happen across fruit or some other sustenance.

Her first discovery was a glade with a bubbling spring. She made a brief test of the water, before drinking. Surrounding the spring were trees with bright red fruit she didn't recognize. A few fruits were strewn on the ground with bite marks, having been nibbled on by some creature, then left to rot. If something else had tried these things, they must be safe for people.

At least, that was her hungry stomach's reasoning.

She spied a tree with lower hanging branches. With

a little jumping, and some tree-shaking, she got one of the fruit to drop into her hands. She rinsed it in the spring and took a bite.

The skin was fairly tough but sweet, as sweet as the meat inside. It tasted somewhat like a mango combined with an apple. It was also large and filling. She ate as she studied the terrain. There was no path, so she'd be pushing her way through rough and thorny brush all the way. She regretted not being able to change into a dragon and fly to the spout.

By late afternoon, she spotted another grove of trees and vowed to reach it by nightfall. Her hands bled from grabbing at the branches and pulling them to the side so she could pass. She wished for her gloves. Warmth rose from the ground to meet the sun's heat, drenching her in sweat. She prayed with each step for this grove to be like the morning, full of fresh water and some kind of sustenance.

"Go ahead and pray," she told herself. "It's not like God will hear you. You're a blood dragon, remember?"

The sun was nearly gone by the time she arrived at her destination. Smaller than the first glade, it still had a spring and plenty of red fruit trees edged the water. Lisette drank first before freshening herself with a swim. Her clothes came off quickly and she entered the cool water in her chemise, skin prickling at the shock.

She had no soap but rubbed at herself and rinsed her hair. Soon she was refreshed and searched for food. As she walked around the edge of the water in her chemise, a familiar bunch of leaves caught her eye. Dark green, large, and heart-shaped, she knew these—wild yams. Pulling on a stalk, she found her prize, a deep red root. She would require a fire for roasting, but the delicious satisfying meal was worth it.

Gathering branches and dried leaves, she used her dagger and Lamya's training to spark a small flame and tended it into something manageable. Her dinner of yams and red fruit meant a full belly to sleep on.

She arranged her nest of soft leaves, hoping she had been traveling in the right direction. She hadn't seen the spout since it sprayed. What if she was even slightly off-course? Slightly off-course would be as bad as completely wrong.

*Please, God, I am now a wretched infidel, but I ask for your help. Show me the way.* She spent the night in restless semi-slumber. By morning's dimness, she could not toss and turn anymore. She rose and dressed, turning to survey the land.

A hiss behind her made her spin. The sound turned into a gurgle and the gurgle turned into a great surge of water into the sky, not ten meters from where she stood. It gushed so high, with such force, droplets rained on her.

When the water receded, she hurried to its source. Looking down she saw a hole of maybe two meters wide, so deep and dark she could not see the bottom. What she could hear, however, was the sound of lapping water. The ocean had pushed underneath this part of the island, and over the years, the high tides had worn a cenote into the earth.

The first step was successful. She had found Mar's whale spout.

Lisette got the locket out and studied it again. Even the etching of "whale spout" was worn with age. She held it up to the sunlight, to determine if there were any other markings. Only one other—a faded arrow, pointing left.

Left was a relative direction, depending upon which way she approached the spout. Facing it put the arrow pointing to the ocean, as did facing left. To the right, it pointed the direction she had already traveled.

There seemed to be only one way to follow the

arrow—when she held the locket pointed north. The vines grew thicker on this side, crawling across and through the brush and impeding her progress. They covered what looked like a grove of small trees, so she pressed on.

When she got to them, she discovered it wasn't a grove, but a shelf that hung over the bushes. She pushed the vines aside. It wasn't a shelf, either. It was a cave.

After a few steps inside the ink-dark walls, she backed out. She had to find some way of lighting the way. If she waited long enough, she could use her dragon breath, but she had never been a patient woman.

Walking back toward the cenote, she glanced around, looking for something to use as a torch. Everything looked so green, and she had no experience in making useful objects from nature.

She plopped down at the edge of the spout. "What now, Lisette? Did you come all this way to give up?"

Staring past the cenote she observed the terrain rise again, giving the appearance of another whale, head up. Across the hill to the right, there was only ocean. At the dip between the hills, several palm trees teetered at the edge, looking into the tidal pool below. Like most palms, their new fronds sprouted into the air, while the brown, dead fronds hung down their sides.

Dead fronds might catch fire.

She scurried down the hill to the trees. Though dead, the fronds weren't easy to pull loose. Each one fought to remain, releasing scores of insects to crawl on her. After a few rounds of tugging, followed by shaking spiders from her hands while she squealed, she had nearly given up. She stood back, wiping her hands on her robe, and coming up with another plan.

The sound of the waves made her look over the cliff to the beach below. Sea water sounded heavenly for dipping hands and arms, but it looked like a long trek through more undergrowth. She noticed a dark ridge that wound back and forth.

A path.

It was narrow, to be sure, but negotiable. She moved down the sloping zigzag until her feet hit the sand. Walking to the tidal pool, she dipped her hands in the salty water. They stung at first from the scrapes, but the coolness felt delightful.

As she turned to go back, she found a messy pile of loose palm fronds that had fallen from the trees above and tumbled down. She gathered several and hurried up the path, stopping at the top only long enough to catch her breath. After making another small fire she braided each frond so the spikes would stay close.

When she had one sufficiently braided, she held it over the fire. The flames leapt up without much effort. She sank the thick stem into the sandy soil nearby and watched it burn while roasting a yam. It stayed alight until she had eaten supper, at which point the fire died to an ember.

Heartened, she took the other fronds and wove each to make a torch. Lighting one, she put a rock in her pocket to use as a flint and withdrew her dagger from its sheath. She returned to the cave.

*God keep me safe,* she prayed, and went inside.

Lisette headed into the darkness one small step at a time, her heart pounding. Her fear urged her to run quickly, find whatever Mar had left and flee to fresh air and freedom. Running, however, would not be good for her makeshift torch. She took a breath and gripped her dagger a little tighter.

With slow, deliberate steps, she proceeded, holding the torch ahead. The path led downhill, not steeply, and the soft dust was not slippery. Still, she hesitated, lighting the ground with every step, lest the path fall wholly away.

Between her dragon senses and the echoing quality of the cave, every sound was amplified from her own breathing to her footfalls on the floor and an occasional scratching noise she did not dare try to identify.

The walls were close, but she didn't touch them. To

put her fingers on crawling insects or vermin would send her screaming, treasure or not.

The air was cool and stale, like a room long closed and full of dust. After some time, there was a noxious odor. She put the back of her hand to her nose in a vain attempt to keep the smell at bay without letting go of her dagger. Turning the corner, her flame discovered the source.

A chamber to the right was filled with shadows, hanging from the ceiling. The floor below them looked like rich, dark mud. Bats.

She slipped past them as silently as she could. Small fluttering noises brought her to a stop until they settled again. Beyond the entryway, something skittered across her bare foot. She knew better than to scream, but could not contain a single, high-pitched gasp, loud enough to echo through the cave.

Flapping wings exploded from the chamber. Lisette crouched, more afraid of them than of whatever had run over her toes, and the sudden movement made her drop the frond in the soft dust of the cave floor, snuffing the flame. The bats did not acknowledge her, other than to avoid knocking into her as they flew toward the entrance.

Choking back shrieks of terror, she reached for the stem. When she looked up, she was surprised that the cave was already lit. She looked around for the source but could not find any. Was it possible that the night vision she enjoyed as a dragon had carried over to her human form?

She crouched again and placed the frond between her feet, using the flint and dagger to relight it, just in case. Holding her light aloft again, she continued.

"Let us proceed a little further," she whispered. "If we don't find anything soon, we will return." Talking to herself using "we" made her feel less alone.

The path bent to the left. As she moved around the corner, the wall shone as if it contained soft sunlight. She stepped to the side and studied the sparkle. The glittering was no doubt from quartz crystals embedded in the dark rock.

As she kept staring, she noticed a pattern in the sparkling. An arrow had been scratched into the cave wall, pointing to the right. Turning that direction, she spied another path. She entered the new passageway, praying she would not be confused on the way out.

This path emptied into a small chamber which produced a blindingly radiant light. She stood for a moment, shielding her eyes. The glow was coming from several piles of gold coins, each as tall as her waist and some taller. The mound in the back corner went to the ceiling.

"Mar, what did you do?" Her voice rang in the stillness. "And why were you still on that ship?"

She stuffed her pockets as full as possible and gathered more in the folds of her skirt. Tonight at camp, she would count them, hide what she could not carry, and go into the village to buy the means to take more.

As she turned to exit, her foot struck something along the wall—a small wooden box, the kind someone would keep their trinkets in. She picked it up and carried it outside.

Nothing in this world matched the freedom of stepping out of that cave and being under the sky once more. The moon was already growing fat with light, and clusters of stars wove paths through the darkness.

She huddled by the fire pit and rekindled the embers. Grabbing a red fruit, she ate while she counted. One hundred fifty coins, more than enough for supplies. She could also purchase a bit of clothing and a room at the inn, even a bath.

Setting the treasure aside, she picked up the box

and looked at it. It was carved from a rich, dark wood with an intricate engraving on top of a naked woman holding a spear and a shield. She opened it. Inside was a letter written in thick strokes by a bold hand.

*I, Viscount Sandoval de Guerrier, give this account of the gold in this chamber.*

Her eyes widened. The legend was true, then. Sandoval's Treasure existed and she had discovered it. She read on:

*I was a humble servant of the Count de Medina. He is an evil man in all things, gluttonous, greedy, and wanton in his desires. His own riches were not enough for him, so he stole gold from every merchant, every ship, even other duchys on islands not under his control. I helped him in all this, with the promise of a percentage of gold being mine.*

*I am not proud of what I did, however I wished to use the gold to move my family out of the count's influence, possibly to the New World. My wife, Lucia, and our daughter, Marvedre, deserve a better life than to be forever under the influence of such a treacherous man.*

*Fortunately, I overheard the count plotting my murder, to take all the treasure for himself. I paid my servants to carry as much gold away as possible and hide it here, on Isla de la Ballena.*

*If I do not return to reclaim this gold, may it be used to defeat the house of Medina, its evil count, and all of his family. My prayer is that at least Lucia and Mar can be saved.*

Lisette felt a sting of sadness. Mar's father—he wanted so much for his daughter, and she ended up with so little.

"Well, Sandoval, I promise to kill Mercedes with it," she told the letter. "Will that do?"

She put as much of the gold as would fit into the

wooden box and dug a shallow hole in the sand under a bush. Placing the box in the hole, she covered it, pushing a few vines across the area. Exhausted, she put out the small fire and nestled into her soft green bed.

Dawn and her own racing mind woke her. She began her hike to the village, snatching a piece of fruit to appease her growling stomach. There was no path, so she was soon pushing her way once again through the dense patches of undergrowth. All the time, she reflected on last night's full moon. She would be lucky to arrive at the village before the waning crescent. Somehow, she would have to manage her transformation in a public arena.

As she descended the second whale's head, she discovered a path. This allowed her to quicken her pace and she wasted no time striding down the sand toward the inhabited side. She contemplated getting a few more clothes although she could not imagine her dragon form carrying a valise.

Lisette patted her pockets and wondered. If the material was light enough, perhaps she could store it. The robe Lamya gave her was a wondrous thing. No matter that she had traipsed through rugged terrain and had climbed into a cave filled with bat guano—it looked as new as the first day she put it on.

Still, she realized the villagers would wonder why a stranger would appear from the jungle. This would take her best lies and hopefully a miracle.

# 38

Even with a path she spent two more days walking to the village and its port. Each night as she watched a slice of the moon disappear her stomach filled with anxiety, and each day she increased her pace until she could go no faster.

She had but a day of being human left when she arrived, so she went to work immediately. Along the wharf side of the village, she found the dry goods merchant. It was late morning. She had hoped to be the only customer, but she spied an older woman through the window, purchasing a hat and some ribbon.

Tugging her chemise and robe a little lower and saying a quick prayer, Lisette burst into the door, heaving as if she had run a furlong. "Please. Can you help me?"

The two turned, their eyes wide and mouths open.

She put her hand to her robe, pushing at it as if to cover her décolletage.

"A man kidnapped me, from the ship." Lisette hoped there had been a ship at port recently.

"*Le Courageux*?" the shopkeeper asked. He was a short balding man, whose dark mustache wiggled as he spoke.

"Yes. He dragged me into the jungle." She pointed in dramatic fashion.

"The French swine." The woman added her opinion. "You poor thing."

"He…he…took my things, but I managed to escape." Lisette looked at the shopkeeper and widened her eyes. "Could you perhaps sell me something more proper?"

She revealed a quick glimpse of cleavage before pulling her robe tighter. His eyes kept watch for another peek, so she took out a coin. "He tried to bribe me with this. Would it be worth a few pieces of clothing?"

The man's eyes nearly bulged from their sockets. He took the gold, turned it over and said, "Madre del diablo! Spanish gold—could it be Sandoval's treasure?"

The woman's head snapped up and she scowled at him. His voice lost its greediness as he stuttered, "I mean, it has been so long since I seen gold coin in my shop—"

"Miguel, it is not important." She turned to Lisette. "Did you witness where the Frenchman got this?"

"No. We were on the ship. He pulled it from his pocket and offered it to me. When I took it, he caught me and threw me into one of the dinghies. He gave more coins like that to the crew, and they lowered the boat." Lisette wondered if the gold's legend would cause trouble for her. "He seemed to be a very rich man. I did not question that he possessed so much."

The shopkeeper and the woman glanced at one

242

another, before the woman raised her shoulders in a dismissive shrug. "Everyone on the island dreams of finding the treasure, but I'm sure it's just a legend. Too bad the rich man did not visit your shop, eh, Miguel?"

"Where exactly did he take you in the jungle?" The shopkeeper's eyes shone bright as he leaned closer.

"Not far." She backed away from him, feigning fear which wasn't difficult. Too many more questions and she'd have to answer them with her dagger.

"Miguel." The sternness in the woman's voice snapped him to attention. "She is only a young woman, and it is only a story. Now, get the poor thing some clothes."

He smiled and nodded before rushing to select some items of clothing and handing them to Lisette with a bow. "Here, m'lady. Finely woven, worth every escudo."

"Thank you." She took the clothes and moved toward the door.

The woman stopped her. "One moment, Girl. Miguel, does she not get change? Surely these few items do not cost so much."

"Of course." This time he scowled. He dug into his apron and pulled out a few coins. "Ten maravedis and two reals."

"I think maybe ten reals and two maravedis." Her voice had a commanding quality.

He reached into his apron again and handed Lisette what the woman had suggested. Gritting his teeth he added, "Thank you for your business."

The woman touched Lisette's arm and gestured toward the door, giving the merchant one more disapproving look. "Come with me, dear. I will help you."

As the two exited the store, the woman turned right. "My house is at the end of this path. You can have a nice bath before you put on your new clothes."

"Thank you, Madame, but I am happy to stay at the inn."

"Oh, no, the inn will not do." She shook her head. "This is a port of bad repute. The guests at the inn are a wicked and unbridled bunch. Why, they would bundle you up and sell you to the pirates."

Lisette stifled a laugh at her warning. "I cannot inconvenience you, Madame."

The woman's hand was on Lisette's arm and each time Lisette turned left toward the inn, she maneuvered her to the right. "It is no inconvenience. I am happy to help young girls in need."

She was an elegant woman, well-dressed and soft spoken with white hair arranged on top of her head. Still, Lisette sensed something wrong. She was far too eager to get a strange girl to her house. Uncertain how to extricate herself, Lisette had no choice. Nodding and smiling, she joined her. They walked up the wide boardwalk toward a small home at the end of the lane.

A few people passed and gave the woman nervous smiles. The men touched the brims of their hats but did not lift them. She did not appear to notice and smiled at each person who walked by. Her smile was less of a warm greeting and more of a benevolent ruler who might grant them a request if they groveled enough.

The small house at the end of the boardwalk turned out to be the frontage to a large, sprawling compound with a courtyard and a larger dwelling that looked like an inn. Stone and adobe walls surrounded the buildings, all made from the dried mud and grasses common to the islands, white-washed to a soft glow.

They entered the larger dwelling and Lisette was impressed by the subtle elegance. The interior of the house was white, punctuated by bright paintings and vibrant furnishings. She noted the piano in the front sitting room along with three small divans, each large enough for two people. Except for the piano, most of the rooms she passed by were decorated the same. The house had four hallways radiating from the main structure, each with several closed doors.

At the entrance to the leftmost hall, the woman turned to her. "My name is Adelinde Marquez, and as you can see, I am the owner of the town brothel."

It all snapped into sense. Lisette nodded. "I have never been in a brothel. Are they all as opulent as this?"

"No. I take pride in my home, in my work, and in the women who work for me." She smiled. "And with a place like this, I can gouge the nobility for three times the price of a normal whore."

She led Lisette to the last door and opened it. "One of my girls had to leave recently. You may use this room to clean up. We will have lunch and you can be on your way."

Lisette opened her mouth to protest, but the woman stopped her, taking Lisette's chin in her hand, and lifting her face to the light.

"With your looks, if you'd like to stay and earn a little silver, I think you could attract many customers. I assume the Frenchman has already…indoctrinated you…in at least some of the things a man wants."

Lisette hesitated. A few weeks ago, she would have been aghast at the notion. Now, she nodded. "Yes, Madame. It is worth considering."

Adelinde clapped her hands and shouted, "Marisha!"

"Madame?" A young, stocky woman entered, dark-skinned with the wide hips and apple-cheeks of the native people of the islands.

Adelinde sent her off with orders for the bath, then turned her attentions to Lisette. "When you are properly refreshed, Marisha will show you to our tearoom."

She floated out, closing the door behind her.

Marisha soon reappeared with a large, heavy bucket of hot water which she proceeded to pour. As she slipped away to fetch more Lisette was reminded of Genevieve preparing the bath.

Opening her purchase, she spread out the clothes she had gotten—a top, and a skirt, and a petticoat. Not nearly enough by nobility's standards but semi-modest.

It took some time, but the bath was finally ready. Marisha stood at the door, looking Lisette up and down for the first time. Her eyes had a dullness to them, her mouth slack, as if she had seen Lisette's kind before.

Her voice was high and as sweet as a songbird and her island accent thick. "Does Mistress require help with undressing or her hair?"

Lisette smiled. Her robe was fastened by a few buttons, and she knew her hair looked like a thousand monkeys had braided it. "I can manage, thank you."

Marisha pointed to a bell beside the tub. "When you are ready to be rinsed, ring and I will bring fresh water."

The tub was smaller than the one at the castle and not as refreshing as the lagoon, but it served the purpose. The soap had a soft fragrance to it, something Lisette had not smelled since her kidnapping.

At last, it was time for a rinse, and she rang the bell. Marisha came in with a bucket of water which she dumped, quickly and unceremoniously on Lisette's head. The water was cold and Lisette put her hands up in surprise.

Marisha gasped and dropped the bucket.

She came around to look at Lisette's face, her brows knitted in confusion. Holding her left arm out, Marisha rolled her hand over to expose her wrist. She also wore the lioness tattoo of the *Dişi Aslan*.

Lisette held hers out to confirm her suspicion. "I worked for Captain Derya. My name is Lisette de Lille."

Marisha smiled. "When did you see her last?"

Lisette told her as much as she could about the attack of the Spanish ship and being dropped off to receive proper medical care. The exact type of medical care she left a little vague along with her method of transport to Isla de la Ballena. Marisha knew many of the crew, even Pinar, and was particularly upset by

Mar's death.

"Do you also serve the ship as Pinar did on the island?" Lisette asked.

She nodded. "We all have our jobs to serve the *Dişi Aslan*. I was to return to the ship soon, but with Mar's death, I may have to stay longer."

"Looking for Mar's treasure?"

Marisha put a finger to her lips and disappeared. Some moments later, she returned with more clean water for another rinse. This time it was warmer. She held a sheet out to wrap around Lisette for drying. Motioning for her to sit in a chair Marisha reached in her pocket and pulled out a hairbrush.

"You must be careful here." Her voice was low, and she leaned close to Lisette's ear to speak. "Madame is not what she appears. She is not Adelinde Marquez, but Adelinde Marchand, bastard daughter of one of King Louis' courtesans and the Archduke de Montenegro. She has been in the business of making gold ever since she was banished from the royal court. Nobility pays handsomely to feed their twisted appetites here. When they are sated, they pay again for Madame's blackmail."

"I confess I am not sympathetic to their plight. The nobility I have met in recent days are worse than beasts in the field."

"Oh, we do not care about the men." Her hands continued to work with the brush smoothing Lisette's wild locks. "We care about Mar's treasure. She spent most of her time on the ship talking about it. If it's what we think it is and we can locate it, we have no more use for spies here."

Lisette reached into her robe, pulling a gold piece from the pocket, and whispering, "Is this what you are looking for?"

The maid took the coin and examined it, her expression remaining neutral. "Where did you find this?"

Lisette told her of Mar's last moments on the ship and of her search although she did not mention the treasure's exact location. "I will do what I can to put it into the right hands."

At this, Marisha stopped braiding Lisette's hair and tiptoed to the door. She stood for a moment, her hand at her lips. Returning, she completed the braid, speaking now in a normal tone.

"If Mistress will get dressed, she can join Madame in the parlor for cakes and tea." As she said this, she made a pantomime motion of pretending to pick up a cup and drink. She pointed to the cup and shook her head.

Lisette raised an eyebrow and mouthed the word "poison." The maid nodded.

The door opened and Madame stood at the entrance. "Are you ready, Miss—you know, you haven't told me your name."

"I will be ready shortly, Madame." Lisette felt a pinch from Marisha. "My name is…Tempest d'Arturo."

Marisha's expression remained neutral, but Lisette felt a light pat on her back.

Madame closed the door, but neither of the women felt safe from her prying ears. Marisha helped Lisette dress in silence. The sleeves were a little long, as was the skirt, but they would do. Lisette put on her black robe and fastened it.

As Marisha led her to the door, the maid whispered. "Stay sharp. I will help you escape this evening."

Madame awaited them on the other side. She dismissed Marisha as she took Lisette's arm. "Attend to Florinda's suite. I will take Tempest to lunch."

Lisette touched her sleeve with light fingertips in case she had to run. Madame responded by wrapping her long, bony hands around her arm, strong as any animal trap. They entered a room lined with curtained alcoves around the walls. Each alcove held a tiny round table and two chairs.

"My ladies bring their clients here for a small meal, or drink. The curtains give them privacy." She gestured. "Sit."

Lisette obliged, wondering how many drinks were drugged so Madame could rob their bags and steal their secrets. A young girl, pale with dark brown braids, brought a tray with cakes and sat it on the table. She turned to go back to the kitchen, but Madame stopped her.

"Chloe, clean the piano room. I'll take care of the tea." Madame turned to Lisette. "I shall be right back."

She returned with a tray containing a small white pot and two cups, both steaming. Lisette detected a foul odor coming from one of the cups. It was, of course, the one Madame offered her. Lisette was certain there was no odor to a normal nose, but nothing about her was normal anymore.

"I hope you enjoy this. I brewed it myself." Madame oozed charm. "It should soothe you after your ordeal."

Lisette found it impossible to raise the cup toward her face. The stench was so strong, she could scarcely stay in the room with it. There was nothing to be done except be rid of it. She reached for the brew, looked up as if distracted and knocked her hand against the table, upsetting the cup and dumping the contents on the floor.

She leapt from the seat and clutched her napkin, offering a range of apologies. "I am so sorry…my hand must have slipped…overly tired, I think…please forgive me…"

Madame remained unruffled although her eyes narrowed. "Naturally, child, think nothing of it. A small spill, easily cleaned."

She clapped her hands to summon Chloe, who swept in and looked at the spill with wide eyes. Chloe whispered something in her mistress' ear. Madame scowled and nodded.

"Our guest has spilled her drink. Clean it." Turning to Lisette, she gestured toward the table. "Please eat. I'll have Chloe get you a new cup of tea. If you will excuse me, I have business to attend to."

Lisette, still watching Madame disappear, became aware of someone pawing at her clothing, probing with busy fingers as they wiped. Chloe was mumbling something about the stain on her robe and shouldn't she remove it and let her wash it. Lisette pulled away and examined her skirt.

"There is nothing spilled on my clothes."

Chloe looked up from her place on the floor, still grasping at the hem. "Oh, Mistress, there are spots, spots on such a clean overskirt."

Lisette stepped back and lifted her chin, scowling. "The only spots are on your eyes. You will not touch me again."

The maid rose, slowly, and Lisette felt her eyes burning as she glared. Shrinking away, Chloe dropped to the floor, scrubbing.

It was time to leave with or without Marisha's help. Lisette walked into the hallway and headed for the door, hoping to make it through the courtyard and past the iron gate. Madame stood in her path, a riding crop in her hand, raining blows on a young man who squatted before her shielding his head.

"Stupid. Boy." Each word was clipped in anger and accompanied by a sting from her weapon. "I'll. Not. Have. You. Drunk."

The figure at her feet blubbered for mercy. He was familiar to Lisette from his frame to his voice to the smell of his blood. Even with his head bowed she recognized her brother Jules.

Madame raised her hand to deliver another blow, but Lisette's came up to catch her by the wrist.

Lisette's declaration was simple. "You will not strike this boy."

"Because?"

"Because I will not have it." Lisette pointed to the house and gave her a sardonic grin. "After I attend to him, let us have a chat. I think we can come to an understanding."

Madame huffed. "Why would I take orders from a stranger?"

Lisette reached into her pocket and withdrew a handful of golden coins. "Is this a good enough reason?"

Madame's eyes widened. She looked from Lisette to the house, and back. Eventually, she smiled, walked to the door, and disappeared inside.

"Jules." Lisette knelt in front of him and held him by the shoulders. "It's me."

In the few months they had been apart her brother had aged years. His hair was long and unkempt, and his face wore the stray hairs of a juvenile beard. The effects of drink were easy to spot in his red-rimmed eyes.

She watched him, dizzy with drink, until at last his eyes rested on hers. He gasped aloud when he recognized her.

"Lizzie! We thought you were dead." His hands slapped at her shoulders, and he fell forward. She caught him and helped him to sit at a nearby bench.

"What are you doing here, and why are you drunk? I heard about Mama and Papa—what happened after I was kidnapped?"

He sat back, holding the bench as if it might buck him off. "Mother is dead. Father is dead. You are dead. That's why I am drunk. I do not know why I am here."

She hugged him to her. "Tell me everything."

"The night you died—well, the night you were kidnapped, it was horrible. Eric staggered in. Said he fought, but the pirates carried you away. Mercedes was so helpful, tending to Eric, taking care of Mama. No one suspected, until we got the invitation to the betrothal."

"Of course not." Her eyes were burning, and it was all she could do to keep from screaming with rage.

"Within a week, we were informed that Eric and Mercedes would be requiring our castle. The families in power were going to align themselves with Spain. They knew our parents would decline." He stopped with a bitter laugh. "Father protested. He wrote a letter to King Louis. The letter was intercepted, and Father had a 'hunting accident' a few days later. We weren't even allowed to bury him in the family graveyard."

Equal parts rage and sorrow pounded against her

chest. "And Mama?"

"She had lost you, so recently. To lose Father also was her undoing. There were many days of her not eating, followed by a brutal fever, and merciful release." His voice quavered and he dissolved into tears.

Lisette's eyes felt aflame, and the harder she tried to weep, the more her chest squeezed and pinched in pain. When Lamya told her she wouldn't cry again until the blood dragon curse had lifted, Lisette believed she would not have the urge to cry, not that she would rail against her body, trying to force tears that wouldn't come.

"Oh, Jules."

"I got out with the clothes on my back and a few coins. Genevieve got me passage on a ship. I made it this far, planning to find work, wage war on those Spanish bastards who did this to our family." He sniffled and wiped his eyes. "Guess I got a little off track. Turns out, money is important."

"Don't worry, little brother. I will do the avenging." She patted his shoulder. "But for now, you must listen to me. You must not tell anyone who I am. I am leaving this place soon and I shall take you with me. My name here is Tempest. Do you understand?"

He smiled and she recognized the little boy who played games in their castle. "Yes, *Tempest.*"

"Good. I must go in and deal with the Madame. Do you have something to eat and a place to sleep?"

"Shopkeep lets me sleep behind his store. I can find food."

She nodded. "Good. Go there now and get some rest, get sober. No more drinking. I will come for you. Marisha will tell you when to expect me."

She rose and walked back toward the house. Marisha caught her at the front door. "Madame is waiting in the piano room. She has a knife."

Lisette pulled her dagger from her robe. "Then it will be a fair fight."

The curtains had all been pulled in the room, and a few candles lit. Madame sat near the piano, on one of the small divans, but she did not lounge. Her back was ramrod straight, as was the tight line her pursed lips formed.

Even though she did not like Adelinde, Lisette understood her. Nobility had betrayed her, too. Making a deal with her would be a kindness and it would be better to have her as an ally than an enemy.

Besides, she needed time. Finding Jules changed everything. She couldn't just pop him on her dragon back and fly off to another island. They required passage on a ship. Payment would not be a problem, but when was the next ship? Her plan needed to keep Adelinde busy until Jules was safely gone.

"Let us be frank." Lisette stood tall, her dagger hidden in the folds of her skirt. "You desire Sandoval's gold. I have discovered it. For certain concessions I will deliver it to you."

Adelinde stood. "Why will you not simply tell me where it is?"

"Let us say I am doing you a favor. As you can imagine, it is hidden well and is not easy to extract. And there is so much, I daresay you can afford to let me skim a small percentage as a finder's fee. I, too, have a score to settle that demands gold, Adelinde Marchand."

Adelinde's eyes rounded at her mention of her real name and Lisette caught a glimmer of blade by candlelight as it came hissing toward her. Before the dagger had missed its mark and embedded in the wall, Lisette's blade had found its target, trapping Madame's sleeve against the arch of the door.

Lisette strode to her and pulled her dagger from the wood, freeing her arm. A thread of blood ran from

Adelinde's hand, soaking her sleeve.

"I do not wish to expose you," Lisette said. "Nor ask you for pay to keep your secret. I simply wanted you to understand that we are alike in many ways and have common goals. My offer is a fair one and will get you what you desire. Take it now and ask no questions."

Adelinde nodded. "What are your terms?"

"Very simple ones." Lisette gestured toward the door. "I will leave here tonight. When I come back in two days, I will have a bag of gold for you. I will do this for ten nights. Ten bags of gold, and I will leave forever. If you try to stop me, I will kill you and everyone in this place."

Madame laughed but stopped when she saw Lisette's expression. Chloe appeared at the door, took one look at Lisette, and ran, white-faced, from the room.

Adelinde touched her wounded arm and studied the red stain on her fingertips. "It is a deal."

"Good." Lisette pulled three gold coins from her pocket and handed them to her. "Here is an advance. Oh, and one more condition—the boy in the garden. He is not to be harmed."

Madame bowed her head in acceptance, and Lisette left the room. The sun was setting soon, and she needed to talk to Marisha.

Lisette found her Dişi Aslan sister in the laundry, scrubbing wet fabric against the tin board. "Do you know where the ship is now?"

Marisha nodded. "We received word a day ago, they will be here within a week's time."

"How can I get a message to Captain Derya?"

Marisha dried her hands on her apron and soon handed her a parchment, pen, and inkwell. Lisette dated the top, and wrote, *Meet me at the northwest lagoon as soon as you can. I will appear at night. Come alone. LdL*

She folded the note and gave it to Marisha, praying her words would find the captain in time. This plan had as much chance of going badly as it did of going well.

"Is there a place behind this house where one could hide, say, a horse in the underbrush?" Lisette asked.

Marisha gave her a sideways glance. "Yes, perhaps. Follow me."

Lisette took several large laundry bags as they walked out a back door into a well-trimmed walking garden, with a fountain in the middle and benches tucked in the bushes. The exterior gate was iron, like the front gate. A footpath ran between the trees and tangled brush.

Marisha pointed. "The island deer often hide with their babies in this brush. I suppose a horse isn't that much bigger."

Lisette walked about, examining the plants, and looking beyond at the terrain. It would take some finesse, but she could glide low enough to swoop into the thicket unobserved, especially under a new moon.

"This will do, thank you. If I could trouble you for one more thing. Do you think you could find me some food that isn't poisoned?"

Marisha took a napkin from her pocket with a johnnycake inside. "This is my dinner, take it."

"Oh, no, what would you eat?"

She laughed. "Don't you worry about me. I get by, no problem."

Lisette hugged her and said goodbye. "You may or may not see me for the next ten days. Be well and I hope to see you shipboard."

The sun was low, and she felt a familiar warmth inside. She strode to the glade where Marisha had directed and found a place where she could hide. Quickly stuffing the laundry bags into the pockets of her robe, she sat and waited.

It didn't take long for the sun to set. Lamps were lit in the brothel. A white flash of pain and her transformation was complete. No one spotted the black dragon gliding on silent wings over the ridge.

She found the cave again with little problem and

the crescent moon still high. There were still many hours until daylight, so she glided over the ocean, looking for signs of the *Dişi Aslan*. Or perhaps *L'Implacable*. There was little wind, making the ocean glassy and smooth. She swept out from the island in ever larger circles, but no ships were in sight. At last, she felt the sunrise before she saw it, and landed.

Under normal circumstances, she would have slept. Today there was too much to do. Grabbing the laundry bags, Lisette filled each one with as much gold as they could hold. It took all day to load ten bags and drag them to the edge of the cave. It grieved her to pay ransom for her brother but killing Adelinde would not alleviate her curse.

At the appointed hour, she changed from human form, and picked up a bag in her talons. Claws did not have the dexterity of fingers. The flight back to the brothel took longer than anticipated, because she kept dropping the bag and having to retrieve it. The sun was threatening to rise when she glided to the back gate, laid the bag against the wall, then rushed to her makeshift lair.

Within seconds, she had changed into human form. Exhausted, she wrapped up in her robe and slept. When she awoke, it was late afternoon, and she was ravenous. Something brown caught her eye. At the edge of the grove, sat a basket. She dragged it into the brush. Marisha had prepared a meal of cakes and fruit, with a small jug of cider.

Lisette ate them gratefully and placed the basket where she first found it. Once more, by the darkness of the new moon, she changed, flew to the gold, and brought another bag. There was no scent of her enemies on this island, and yet she fought against her dragon instincts which wanted nothing but to look for Mercedes.

The next evening, another basket of food had been placed near her. This time, Marisha had scrawled a note. *Your message has been delivered. Look for the captain two nights from now. Be careful. Madame will not be satisfied with 10 bags.*

If the older woman knew the legend of Sandoval, she had to realize ten bags barely dented the treasure he had amassed. Madame would try to discover her path and take all the gold for herself.

Before she left that evening, Lisette found another, deeper spot in the underbrush. She was not certain her dragon body could fit into it, but she had to take that chance.

Two more days passed, and two more bags of gold. She worried Captain Derya would not arrive before the last bag was delivered. Jules would not be safe until she could get him off the island.

On the evening of the fifth bag, Lisette finally spied a ship anchored off the northern lagoon. A dinghy had been launched and was making its way to the beach. She stood at the top of the ridge and observed. It was a single rower. The captain.

Lisette watched her disembark and pull her boat upon the sand. The captain wandered a little, surveying the beach. Lisette lifted herself and sailed, as gently as she could to land before her.

The captain's eyes grew wide, and she backed away. For a moment Lisette believed she would turn and run. Lisette sat, head down, quiet. Placing her hand on her breast, Begum took a deep breath and also stood still.

"Lisette?"

Dragon lips and tongue could not form human language, but Lisette bowed, hoping that would signal her acknowledgment.

"Are you well?"

Again, she bowed.

There were a lot of things to tell her, and Lisette realized she could not communicate until the sun brought back her human form. She looked up at the sky. The moon was on its way to the horizon, but it would still be some time before dawn. Lisette walked to the edge of the path upward and turned to Begum, who did not move. She took a few more steps, turned again.

Either Begum was not understanding, or she was not agreeable.

Lisette returned to her and used her head to push the captain toward the trail. Begum stumbled and fell forward, consuming Lisette with immediate guilt. The captain rose and dusted her clothes. Again, Lisette looked at her and took a few steps up the trail. Again, Begum did not follow her.

"You want me to go with you?" she asked.

The dragon bowed.

"Lizzie, I cannot traipse through the jungle with you." Her voice sounded irritated. "The ship must sail. We cannot stay safe in these waters for long."

Frustrated, Lisette pushed off and flew to the top of the bluff, returning with one of the bags meant for Adelinde.

"Sandoval's gold? Allah be praised!" Captain Derya pushed through the coins, letting them slide from her palms as she raised her hands. "Is there more?"

Lisette bowed.

"Show me! Oh, how I wish you could speak."

*So do I, Captain.* Lisette looked at the moon again. She didn't know what would happen if she did not deliver a bag and there was no way to get a note to Adelinde. But Begum must not leave until she knew where the gold was. If her crew did not take possession of it, Adelinde might find it—she would take it all.

Lisette moved toward the path one last time. This time, the captain followed, leaving the heavy bag on the beach near the boat, hidden behind some rocks.

They hiked up the path to camp and Begum made a fire for herself. Lisette settled onto some boughs within the nearby trees, to lie and wait until dawn.

With a thin film of light on the horizon, the heat was in her bones. The flash of pain was much worse, harsher, due to her impatience. She returned quickly to camp. Begum was roasting their breakfast.

Begum's eyes widened at the sight of her. "Lisette, you have changed."

Lisette looked down. "I'm more myself than I was last night."

"No." She shook her head. "You are darker in skin and lighter in hair color. And so muscled."

"Time spent with Lamya de Sang."

"Yes. Of course."

"We haven't much time." Lisette explained her arrangement with Adelinde. "I will show you where the treasure is, but you must use all your crew, all your boats, to retrieve it. I fear she will not be satisfied, and I would rather the *Dişi Aslan* collect Mar's legacy."

Together, the women went to the cave, where Lisette picked up one of the palm torches she had made and lit it. "I don't require light in here, but you will."

She led Begum into the cavern, past the bats and into the treasure room. As they entered the room still flush with mounds of gold, Begum laughed and threw her arms around Lisette.

"I cannot hug Mar, but I can hug you. This is a godsend."

"I wish you well with it but be careful. Many people here are aware of this treasure and are willing to do anything to get their hands on it."

Begum agreed. "Yes, I know. We will use great care."

"Good." Lisette moved back toward the entrance. "I have a few sacks, but you will need more."

As they left the cavern and made their way to the sunshine, Lisette told her about finding her brother, and about Marisha. They shared their experience of being blood dragons and being taught by Lamya. Begum was surprised at her reference to Lamya's gold eyes.

"I remember her eyes being cloudy," she said. "After all, she was such an old woman."

"Old? She was young and beautiful, bronze skinned with red hair."

"Of course." Begum laughed. "She appears to each one of us as who we require. For me, she was a crone. For you, she was a warrior goddess."

"Wonder how she appeared to Rocco." At the mention of his name, they both fell silent.

Begum gazed at her. "Are you in love with him?"

"No." Lisette felt a pinch in her chest. "Perhaps. Were you ever?"

She shook her head, looking sad. "Pirates learn quickly. We do not fall in love."

"Am I not a pirate?"

"Yes, Lizzie, but you are also a noblewoman. I do not think the same rules apply."

"I think nobles are less likely than pirates to find love." Lisette shrugged. "At least, we'd prefer not to."

"We'd all prefer not to," Begum said. "But we do anyway."

"You must hurry." Lisette shook her head, changing the subject. "I only ask that you leave the bags meant for Adelinde. They are my brother's ransom for leaving this island—on a ship. Might he find refuge on the *Dişi Aslan*, at least to the next port?"

Begum nodded. "We will be picking up Marisha. Tell her to bring him along." The captain gave her one last hug before rushing back down to her dinghy.

The crew had made several trips by dusk. Lisette stayed hidden although it hurt to stay silent. Perhaps after she had fulfilled her purpose, she could rejoin the *Dişi Aslan*—unless she was dead, or still a dragon, or had sailed away with Rocco.

She shook her head. Death or being a permanent dragon were a better bet than sailing away with that pirate.

They had loaded all the gold by the last trip. The ship unfurled her sails, a black outline against the orange sky. The captain had promised to stay close, but they sailed out of sight and into deeper waters, out of harm's way. Lisette would work with Marisha to get Jules to the ship tomorrow.

She felt the familiar burning and changed. Winged again, she made her way back to Adelinde's carrying two bags, to make up for the night she had missed.

Hopefully, that would make her happy.

The new moon had passed, and a waxing arc peeked from the edge, which gave the night an eerie glow. Although accustomed to holding one bag of gold, two bags were quite different. Lisette found, as she was flying, that she had not loaded them equally, causing her constantly to be off-balance.

She pushed her wings faster, to make delivery as soon as possible. Something felt wrong in the pit of her stomach. As she approached the brothel, she flew lower, trying to skim the underbrush unseen.

A lone figure stood on the path, close to her hiding place. Short, curvy, with a scarf about her head, she recognized Marisha. The maid was crying until she saw Lisette. Her eyes widened with terror as the dragon swooped and landed before her. Before Marisha could find her legs and run Lisette laid down, lowered her head, and folded her wings.

Marisha took a hesitant step toward her, hand over her mouth. Lisette remained quiet, waiting.

"Aw, sweet baby Abram." Marisha parted her hand and spoke through her fingers, her voice shaky with tears. "Lisette, is that you?"

The dragon bowed which made the young woman jump back and approach again more slowly.

"I thought the captain was the only one to mess around with this dragon foolishness. What is wrong with you gals? Ain't being a pirate enough?"

Lisette was in no position to argue with her, for or against her dragon foolishness. She couldn't even shrug her dragon shoulders.

"I come to warn you not to go to Madame's. Something awful has happened. Madame got mad…there is nothing for you there." Marisha was weeping now in giant, shuddering sobs. "I'm catching the ship tonight. You need to leave."

Lisette pushed straight up into the air. Marisha was still calling after her, begging her to stay away which made her pick up speed.

The brush blocked her flight, so she landed heavily and galloped the path to the back gate. Outside, there was a devil's ear tree, old, with a thick trunk and branches that stretched out to embrace the sun. Something was swaying gently from the branch nearest the gate.

The smell of him was the first thing to reach her, a combination of familiarity and death. Jules, a noose around his neck, swung in the night breeze, too thin to resist the slightest wind. There was a large note on his shirt.

*You're late.*

The tears in her fought to rise up and burst forth but they were denied, replaced by a burning in her chest. A tiny wail of pain was all that could escape, like the mewling of a kitten. The latch lifted on the gate, and she folded herself into the shadows.

"Tempest? Tempest, is that you?" Adelinde stepped out and looked around. "Did you see my little surprise? That's what happens when you are late with a payment." Pushing at the young boy's body, making it twirl as it swung, she added, "Pity other people have to pay for your mistakes."

Lisette stepped from the shadows. She sat back on her hindquarters, stretching out her wings and raising her front legs to display her talons. Her mouth opened slowly to reveal gleaming, sharp teeth.

Adelinde's smirk opened into a wide-mouthed grimace, her eyes bulging from her head. She opened her mouth to scream but could only flap her lips, making little yipping noises. Then she spun and ran back in the gate.

Lisette extended her talons and swooped across the courtyard, seizing the older woman by the midsection. Her claws gripped Adelinde's ribs and she felt them crack, like crushing twigs to make fire. The woman screamed in agony, her hands pushing at Lisette, attempting to free herself.

The dragon shook her in violent jerks. She howled and her arms flapped like a ragdoll's.

Another scream made Lisette look down. Chloe was in the courtyard. Soon, Lisette imagined there would be others. It was time to end this.

With one broad swipe she sliced Madame's throat open. She had not tried her weapons before and in her anger nearly decapitated her victim. Throwing the body to the ground she opened her mouth and exhaled flames, setting Adelinde ablaze while Chloe hopped around shrieking.

Fanning her wings Lisette rose far above the scene

of death, lifted her head, and roared before swooping around back. As she left, she could hear the shouts of men and women filling the courtyard.

She spied the bags of gold lying where she left them, so she dove in and retrieved them. The *Dişi Aslan* was supposed to be coming in to pick Marisha up. She flew away from the town and toward the sea, searching for the flag with the lioness.

A shadow passed over the moon and Lisette looked to her left in time to spot a flash of crimson barreling toward her. Rocco rammed her shoulder, knocking her back and sideways. She nearly fell from the sky but managed to keep her wings moving.

He came at her again, growling, his claws extended. She turned and flew the opposite direction, wings pumping hard, zigzagging through the night sky. Dropping the bags, she faced him. He was coming at her, his talons high, so she flew straight into him, dipping at the last second to dig her own claws into his side.

As she suspected, dragon feathers did not protect one dragon from another, and her talons sunk into him as his pierced her shoulder. Both dragons screamed at that point and separated. This time, he flew away, and she chased after.

He circled and she kept up with him, looking for any signal he would attack. As he dove low, she stretched above him and bit one of his wings. He snarled and wheeled, his tail thudding across her side, his yellow spikes ripping furrows.

Lisette spit fire at him to keep him at bay, but he answered with his own. They ascended as they fought, past the clouds, bellowing flames at one another. The night air turned thick with smoke and the smell of burning feathers.

He dipped below her, twisting himself upside-down, extending his back legs, and making a straight line for her underbelly. At that moment, a shard of light hit her eyes.

Sunrise.

Lisette put her back legs out to defend herself and her claws connected with his. Tangled, she flailed her wings and shook her legs to try to free them. At the same time, she could feel the heat in her body warning of her transformation. A human would not survive the fall.

She grabbed his front legs with her talons and rotated toward the ground, attempting to slow the descent with outspread wings. Two bodies raced downward, one black and one crimson, twirling like a child's top until they hit the underbrush with a thud. The crash separated them, and Lisette crawled out of the thistles and onto soft, sandy dirt.

Her change happened immediately with a quick but intense burst of pain. She could not move, and lay on her stomach, trying to catch her breath. After a few moments, she managed to sit, and stripped her clothing off as she examined her wounds. Her arms, sides, and legs were scratched and bruised, tender, but superficial. She glanced to the left, and realized she wasn't alone.

Rocco had crept out next to her—he did not like thorn bushes, either. He had removed his shirt and breeches, and was busy examining his own wounds, using his clothes to dab at the scrapes and cuts. His hair was a little longer than when she'd seen him last, making him appear a little wilder, more dangerous, and even more handsome.

She recalled her denial that she did not want to love him and laughed. Love had nothing to do with it. She was a dragon and took what she pleased.

They were together, they were naked, and they had just tried to kill each other. The next step was obvious.

Taking his face in her hands, Lisette kissed him.

She'd always pictured her first kiss as being tender and a little timid. Nothing about this first time was either. Rocco kissed back, pushing past her lips with his tongue. She met him with her own and they rolled together until his body was atop hers. They could not explore each other fast enough. She ran her hands over his shoulders, down his back, caressing and kneading, as she licked, suckled, and bit his mouth.

His hands were searching, too, wandering down her curves and across her breasts. He tore his mouth from hers, tracing her neck with his tongue, pausing to nibble and suck her skin, as she arched her body toward him. When he kissed her shoulder, she sighed. When his tongue circled her nipple, she moaned. As he continued to tease and tickle and suck, her body writhed with delight, and she pressed her fingernails into his shoulders in an agony of desire.

His hand moved down, between her legs, where his fingers caressed and teased, increasing her pleasure to an almost unbearable edge. She wasn't certain whether she was going to explode or bite him.

And in a heart's second, he was inside her, holding her hips up, sliding back and forth. There was no pain, no pinch, only a ravenous ache. With each thrust forward, she yearned for more, and soon her legs were around him, pulling him in a hungry rhythm.

They rolled again and now she was atop him, rocking, her back arched in delight. He reached down and rubbed her again, firm against her wetness. The pressure built up even more now, and her hips were grinding against his.

The sweet release came, too soon, too late, too powerful, too everything. Her body convulsed, and, as she did, he stiffened, moaned, and shuddered. She collapsed against him, and he kissed her softly on the forehead.

"Lisette," he whispered.

In her weakened state—sated, too bruised and sore and content to move, she closed her eyes, swooning at hearing her name. The dragon-woman with the fierce appetite was gone. She was fully Lisette again and breathlessly in love.

The sun was high when she awoke. She was covered by her robe, lying by the side of a small lagoon. It was a place she had camped near the spout. Donning the rest of her clothes, she looked for Rocco.

There was no sign of him. She called his name, studying the sand for footprints. A set of large prints was near the smooth depression where she had lain. She followed them northwest until she lost them in the brush. He was gone.

This morning's bravado had fled. She was no invincible woman, no blood dragon queen prepared to take what she desired. She was a lovesick girl with a broken heart. Collapsing onto the sand, she sat with her head in her hands, her body convulsing with tears that couldn't come.

*Stupid pirate. Stupid love. Stupid me.*

Rubbing her burning eyes, she walked back to the lagoon, discarded her clothes, and dove into the water. Her body was stiff, and her skin was on fire from the numerous scrapes and cuts. This was the price she paid for fighting with another dragon.

A desire for tears squeezed at her heart again. She wanted to sob but physically could do no more than howl, the high-pitched wail of a wounded animal. Soon she was propelling her body across the water with kicking legs and punching arms. When her limbs could not sustain her tantrum any longer, she rolled over on her back, and floated until she had regained control of her emotions.

The water felt good even if she didn't. She had no

soap, but rinsed her hair and rubbed her skin, taking care to avoid her injuries. There was no one around, nor was there likely to be, so she crawled up on a rock and dried in the sun.

Dressing again and fastening her robe, Lisette walked to the spout and dug out the wooden box that she had filled with gold coins. She slipped them in her pockets and set off to town. Her chest still burned with the unfinished pain of loving someone who could not love her.

*At least, I'm no longer a virgin.*

## 43

Lisette hurried back to town, unsure what she might face. As she strode, she reflected on Rocco, their fight, and the aftermath. Would they forever battle, dragon to dragon, until they achieved the vengeance they sought and broke this enchantment? Would it be a fight to the death? Whose death? She shuddered. Last night's combat was short but fierce—she did not want a repeat.

Although she would not mind a repeat of their lovemaking afterward. She wondered if the pleasure she experienced was real or if her heightened senses amplified everything about it. In the end it didn't matter. She wanted more.

As she stopped by a small spring to drink and rest, she found a familiar object beside the bushes. One of Adelinde's bags of gold had landed here. It was heavy but not impossible to hoist. Lisette decided to carry it further and hide it where she could easily retrieve it.

Once at the edge of town, she found a perfect spot in the underbrush to hide the bag. She proceeded to the inn where Madame had assured her, she'd find "wicked and unbridled" folk. What she hoped to find was a ship to take her to Isla del Lagarto.

The inn was on the westernmost point of the shore, a sturdy structure of wood-and-clay at the end of a long wooden pier, white-washed by sea air. Rough, overgrown land cradled the village to the north. The curve of the peninsula created monstrous waves that continuously shot up the beach and into the trees, making small rills in the vegetation.

Striding to the inn, she pushed the creaking door open and stepped inside. She studied the room. It would be several days before she could defend herself again with talons and fire. At the moment she was a typical woman, alone and vulnerable—except for the dagger in her pocket. She patted it and felt more secure.

The innkeeper scurried to her side. He was a thin man, almost skeletal, with a few dark hairs on his head and a sparse mustache to match. His eyes were black and sparkled, no doubt with the anticipation of coin.

"Hello, Mistress, come in, come in." He gestured to a table in the center of the room. "Sit down, rest yourself. What can I bring you? We have a tasty meat pie today or a fresh stew. How about some ale? Cider? What is m'lady's pleasure?"

Lisette took a long look around. The room had many windows, letting in the afternoon light and allowing the breeze to carry off the smell of stale drink and sour customers. There were perhaps ten people in the place, mostly men. The women were underdressed and over-rouged. They would not have been up to Madame's standards for her brothel, so they made their money off the sailors who came through.

"I would prefer that table, Sire." She pointed to an empty table in the far corner, holding a gold coin in her fingers as she did. "Cider will do nicely. Have you bread and cheese?"

"Yes, Mistress, we can fulfill that request." He took the coin, his eyes lustrous with greed. Half-leading, half-following, bowing all the way, he pointed her to the table, gesturing with enthusiasm. "Sit, please, rest. I will bring food and drink to you, right immediate."

She took a seat against the wall and watched him hurry away. While he fussed around with a cup and plate, bringing her meal in staggered courses, she studied the crowd. Beside the women, the men looked older, greying, and bearded, in clothes that were not much above the station of serfs in the field. She doubted if any of them were going to catch the next ship.

The innkeeper brought a pitcher of cider. "In case you wants a refill."

"Would you know when the next ship is due to arrive?"

"We expect *El Gallo Blanco* next. She may be one or two days out, depending upon the weather."

"Where is she bound?"

"Isla del Lagarto." He hopped away to another table.

Sinking back on the hard wooden chair, she picked at the food, slicing a bit of cheese, and nibbling at it, along with a hard roll. He also brought a round of cured meat. Ordinarily, she would have pounced on it, but now, it did not appeal. Ever since her last meal with Lamya, she kept seeing the bird who sacrificed his life to feed her.

The sun lowered and more people entered. These were townspeople from their appearances—not too shabby, no dirt or sweat from heavy labor. No one glanced in her direction. She finished her meal and got the attention of the innkeeper.

Pressing one more coin into his hand, she asked, "Would you have a room available for two nights? Something at the back, where a woman would not be disturbed?"

If he was happy to have the first gold coin, he nearly jumped from his skin with the second. Lisette gave him a stern look and he quieted himself.

"Yes, m'lady," he whispered and reached into his pocket. He handed her a key. "Room 5, top o' the stairs and left, all the way t' the end."

"Thank you." She put the key in her pocket and sat for a few more moments until she was certain no one had observed, or cared, about their conversation.

Someone on the far side of the room had a squeezebox and was cranking out a hideous melody, singing along in an even worse voice. Everyone had enough rum and ale to bray along with the musician and soon the room was a cacophonous echo chamber.

She slipped out the back, climbed the stairs to the second floor and found Room 5. Her key fit the lock and she let herself in, locking the door behind.

Moonlight through the window allowed her to find the lamp on the dresser. She lit it and surveyed the room. It was small and dingy but clean. It also wasn't empty.

A small figure stood in the corner. Lisette held out the lantern toward her. Chloe, Madame's maid, stepped forward.

"Good evening, Mistress." She smiled, a cat's grin when it has a mouse in its teeth.

Lisette did not like this. "What do you want, Chloe?"

"I want what's mine."

"And that would be?"

She gestured toward Lisette, holding a small blade

in her hand. "That gold what's in your pockets. Liam told me you got plenty."

"Liam?"

"The innkeep." Her smile grew. "Didn't anyone tell you? He's my pappy."

"You don't want to do this." Lisette scowled. She did not have the time or energy for Chloe's attempt at robbery. "Madame's death was frightening, wasn't it? Did you see who killed her? Or should I say what?"

Chloe paled to the color of chalk.

"I wouldn't want to anger anyone or anything who could rip through a person's neck and set fire to them like that." Lisette let her annoyance turn to anger and felt it burning in her eyes. "Would you?"

Chloe trembled and pointed her finger at Lisette. "You-you-you are a…beast."

Lisette gave her a wry smile. "What are you talking about?"

"Your-your—eyes."

"Because they reflect the moonlight?" She sighed. "I have no argument with you, Chloe. All I want to do is get on the ship that is arriving soon. What happened to the bags of gold Madame received each night?"

"When Madame was killed, everyone went mad. The men, the women, they all ran through the house, trying to escape the—the monster. One of the girls knew where the gold was. She took as much as she could carry. The others followed her and scooped up the remainder." Chloe hung her head. "I stayed with Madame. There was nothing left for me."

"I suppose you made certain she had a proper burial?"

She wiped a tear. "Yes."

"And the boy? The one hanging from the tree?"

"Oh, yes, the shopkeeper came the next day. He cut

him down and took him to the cemetery himself. Buried him under a tree, in the back."

"That was good of him." Lisette crossed herself, an old habit. "What if I told you there were still two bags of gold on the island?"

"Where?"

"Bring me paper and pen and I will draw you a map. You and your pappy will be rich." Lisette was betting on three things: one, the second bag had landed close to the one she had found; two, they would waste time looking for both bags; and three, in any case, she would be long gone.

Chloe hurried out the door in hopping steps much like her papa. Lisette lit the second lamp, if only to prove to herself no one else was in any of the corners. Gripping her dagger, she even looked under the bed. Empty and dark like little Chloe's heart.

Upon her return, Chloe was good enough to knock. Lisette let her in and took the supplies. Dipping the pen in ink, she drew the path from the whale's spout to the town, explaining as she drew.

"The bags were thrown down around here." She made a circle around the general area where she'd found the first one. "It would be about a three-day walk from the edge of town."

Chloe's eyes sparkled as she studied the map. "Are you sure?"

Lisette glared at her until she flinched. "I know where I threw them."

Chloe nodded and took the paper. "If you're lying, Pappy will know what to do."

It was such a small act of bravado Lisette might have let it go but she couldn't afford to have this opportunist ruin her plans. She let her eyes glow in anger again and her voice drop to a growl. "And so will I."

Chloe fairly tripped on herself running for the door.

Lisette hoped she had put enough fear in her to keep her and Pappy at bay until she could leave this place. It would be impossible to sleep here with one eye toward the door and one ear to the window. She longed for a bed, but this one wasn't worth the risk.

After blowing out the lanterns Lisette left the room, locking the door. She returned to the place where she had hidden the bag of gold and nestled into the underbrush. It was not as comfortable, but at least she could relax enough to sleep.

The birds awoke her, announcing the dawn before its first light could stretch across the hills. She rose in the dark and returned to the inn. No one was stirring so she took a walk down the pier, sat at the end and gazed outward.

It felt like years since she had been rocked to sleep by ocean waves or let out a mainsail or climbed into the crow's nest. She was anxious to be aboard a ship again.

The jingle of keys made her turn. The shopkeeper was opening his store. Lisette rose and strolled over to him. He gestured at the door, and they entered the store together.

"Ah, Mistress, good morning. I have not seen you since the day you escaped from that French brigand." He remembered her story and she had to scramble to recall what she had told him. "Wasn't it horrible about Madame?"

"Yes, awful." Lisette brought a hand up to her face as if to prepare for tears. "And the young boy—I heard that you made arrangements for him."

"I had a soft spot for him, I confess." He bowed his head. "He was a nice young lad in a bad way."

"You are a kind man." Lisette's heart pinched and burned from wanting to cry. "I am eager to leave. The innkeeper tells me there is a ship arriving soon. I plan to buy passage, but I would like a change of clothes, and perhaps a bag to carry them."

She held out a coin. "Madame gave me this for the little work I did around her home, cleaning and cooking."

As before, his face lit up at the sight of gold and he came around the counter to show her several options. She selected a dark velvety skirt and bodice, along with a large tapestry bag, a smaller purse, and a few sundries.

"Thank you," she told him as she left, but he was still admiring his coin.

By the time *El Gallo Blanco* arrived that afternoon Lisette was at the dock and ready to travel. She had secured her coins in the tapestry bag making certain they did not clink together as the bag was carried and pocketing a few for her immediate use.

It was time to go to Isla del Lagarto.

The first small boat arrived, rowed by men in uniform. In the middle sat a little man, overly upright as if to stretch himself taller. He wore an over-decorated jacket and an absurdly huge hat. Lisette would have laughed at the sight of him, but he was no doubt the captain and she needed his permission to board.

The ship was large, much larger than *L'Implacable*. Cannons peeked from the starboard side, but this was not a war ship. It was much too cumbersome to maneuver for a fight. More boats were launching, dangling from its sides like chimes.

The captain strutted past her with a simple bow and touch of his cap. She turned and followed him to the inn. Chloe was there, sweeping the floor.

"Ale, Girl." The captain barked the order as he pulled out a chair.

Lisette waited until he had his drink in front of him and had taken a hearty gulp before she approached. Her first instinct was to be straightforward, but she recalled her past life as a genteel lady.

"Good morning, Captain." She curtsied, keeping her head bowed. "My name is Tempest d'Arturo. I am interested in procuring passage on your ship. I am trying to rejoin my family on Isla del Lagarto."

She let her eyelashes flutter as her green eyes slowly rose to meet his. He looked her up and down like something in a shop window, poured another draught, licked his lips, and smiled.

"I don't know, Mistress—d'Arturo, is it? Passage on a ship as fine as *El Gallo Blanco* requires a little coin. How much do you have?"

"I have a little." Fumbling about in her small purse she made certain he heard the jingle. Finally, she pulled out two gold pieces, looked at him, and pulled out two more. As she handed them to him, she let her bare fingers brush his palm. "Would this get me anywhere?"

He flinched at her touch, the blush shooting from his neck to the tips of his ears. She let him study the coins, keeping her expression demure and innocent.

"I suppose we could find room—"

Lisette felt the strong pull of someone's hands on her arm. She looked left to see Chloe dragging her away from her conversation and yanked her arm out of the girl's clutches.

Chloe was persistent and grabbed her arm again. "We need to talk." Her whisper was loud enough for everyone to hear.

Lisette stood her ground, softly telling her, "This is not a good time."

"It's important." Chloe paled but continued in a lower tone. "It's about the gold. Please don't tell Pappy about it. I want to surprise him."

Lisette shrugged and whispered back. "Not a word from me, but do toss Pappy a couple of coins, yes?"

Chloe scowled and pushed away. Lisette turned back to the captain. "My apologies, captain. I believe I was procuring passage on your ship."

The captain frowned. "Who is that servant girl and what did she want with you?"

She curtsied again. "She was asking me about my bill, how long I intended to rent a room. They are not a friendly lot, always wanting more and more of my coins."

"How did you come to be staying at this inn?" He sat back, scrutinizing her.

"It is a woeful tale." She lowered her chin, glancing at the captain through her lashes. "I was on the *Le Courageux* when a horrible man kidnapped me and dragged me onto this island. I managed to break free, but it was too late. The ship had sailed. I've been waiting for another ship to arrive."

He regarded her suspiciously. "How do I know you are not some putain? I cannot have my crew distracted by some wanton slut who earns her living on her back."

She put her hand to her breast, shrinking away. "Captain, I assure you, I am a woman of the highest moral standing."

"Can anyone vouch for you?" He shook the coins at her. "Vouch for how you got this money?"

Lisette blushed, stammering indignantly, and trying to think of how to get back in this man's good graces. Putting her hand in her pocket she felt an answer and slipped on Connie's signet ring. She straightened herself and thrust her hand to his face. "The Marquess de Martinmas would not appreciate you treating me so poorly."

A familiar voice came from behind. "She is correct. I can vouch for this woman."

Lisette turned to look into the face of the Duke de Martinmas.

He was larger than she remembered, or perhaps it was because he was standing almost on top of her, smiling.

She took a step back. "Good morning, Sire. It is a pleasure to see you again."

"Yes, we've missed you. I'm sorry I was indisposed during your last visit. I would have liked to have said farewell." The duke grinned wider, keeping his eyes upon hers. "Captain, this young woman wears my son's signet ring. She is like family to me. Surely we can find a spot for her on the ship."

The captain apologized, groveling. "I'm sorry, Sire, ordinarily, your wish is my command. In truth, I have too many guests and not enough beds."

The duke scowled. "And you have too many feathers in that hat and not enough brains in the head beneath it. May I remind you, your commission is the direct result of my influence, *Cousin?*"

Lisette hid her grin behind her hand.

"Yes, Sire." The captain sat a little straighter, adjusting his many ribbons. "I suppose I can give her one of the rooms in my cabin."

Sharing the captain's quarters meant she would be fighting his advances for the entire trip, but she knew she could handle him either with coin or her blade.

Her old captor intervened. "Since Tempest and I are old friends, you will change accommodations with me. She can stay with me in the captain's cabin."

"But—I am the captain," he sputtered.

The duke stared at him. "And I am the duke. And your benefactor."

"How long is the trip to Lagarto?" she asked.

"A week," the captain replied.

The waning crescent would be here in six days at most. She'd have to rely on her dagger to keep him at bay.

She smiled at the duke and held out her hand. "Sharing a cabin with you sounds delightful. I do hope we can talk about Constantine. I've missed him so."

His eye twitched, but he kept grinning and closed his massive paw upon hers.

"We sail at sunset," the captain said, his voice annoyed but resigned. "Do not be late."

She picked up her bag and withdrew her hand from Martinmas' clutches. "I will be there."

*El Gallo Blanco* had several masts with large sails to propel the behemoth forward. There were many sailors, all rushing around their posts, running out lines, using the tide to come about and harden up. The sails were spectacular, taut with air as they set out to sea, although they would not send the ship ripping through the waves as the *Dişi Aslan* would have.

Lisette looked up the mainmast, yearning to climb up to the crow's nest and view the path of blue before them. On this trip, sadly, she was expected to act like a lady.

The duke reminded her of the situation as she stood, dreaming of being part of a pirate crew again. "Mistress d'Arturo, our cabin is aft."

She followed him below deck, one level. This ship's quarters for the captain were immense. A large round table stood in the middle of the room, piled with charts and papers. To the right was a door, and to the left, a large bed.

On the near wall, the captain displayed his swords and daggers, no doubt gifts from dignitaries. They reminded Lisette of the display in Rocco's cabin, which were probably not gifts, but bounty from plundered galleons like this one.

The duke gestured to the right-side door, so she opened it and found a small hammock.

"Normally, the cabin boy would sleep there," he said. "It is not as comfortable as a bed, but I hope you will indulge me. I doubt if I could get my girth into that sling."

She doubted if he could get his girth through the door. Spying a hook and a block of wood, used as a makeshift lock, she smiled. She could at least sleep without worry.

"These accommodations will do nicely." She stowed her bag in the back corner.

He offered his arm. "Shall we go to dinner?"

His hand was on the door, but he turned to face her. "By the way, Tempest—or is it time to call you Lisette? Are we truly going to keep up this farce? All aboard this ship are bound for the Medina celebration. Elena de Thibault is waiting there."

"Elena who?" She kept her voice level but curious.

The duke patted her hand. "If Eric and Mercedes do not recognize you, Lisette, without question, your aunt will."

She was surprised to feel no fear of this pompous slab of puffery and kept her expression neutral. "I have no idea what you're on about. My name is Tempest d'Arturo. I am from Isla de Pimienta. My father is a carpenter, my mother a seamstress."

"We shall see." He opened the door and she passed

288

through.

Dinner was at a long table with other passengers. It was a meal fit for royalty. Roasted birds were served with exotic sauces, fruits, and vegetables. Lisette wondered what the crew ate and hoped they at least got leftovers.

After the meal, she walked about the deck, restless. Others were taking strolls as well. There were three groups of women, young girls with either their mothers or their chaperones. They steered clear of Lisette, a woman traveling alone, their noses held high. Several of the men tried to get her attention either by walking past with a smile or offering their protection from the crew. Lisette maintained a disagreeable expression and turned her back on them whenever possible.

She spent a lot of time watching the stars as well as the moon. It was full but she could make out the shadow on its right edge. At least it gave good light to the deck. It didn't take long for the excess of people to annoy her. She headed down the steps to the captain's cabin, stopping to palm the hilt of her dagger before entering.

As expected, the duke was waiting. He grabbed her by the waist as she turned to close the door. She brought her foot up between his legs, connecting with his tender parts. As he doubled over, she drew her dagger and laid it against his ear, outlining his throat with the point, hard enough to be felt without cutting flesh. He stood as she rounded his chin, pulling his head away from her, a grimace on his face.

"We will have an understanding, m'lord." She kept the point at his neck, pressing it when he raised his hands. "You will not touch me, and I will not kill you."

"You would not dare, upon this ship, with all these passengers."

"And when I go screaming through the ship that I found you lying in your own blood, they will look for someone strong enough to do the job. Not me, a mere woman."

"But-but-but…" He spluttered for a moment. "I am a duke."

"Yes, you are. A duke who will respect my wishes." She studied him in the lamplight. He was not the worst noble she had encountered. A memory of Viscount Barragan, his throat pumping scarlet life onto the floor, crossed her mind. "Sit down, m'lord and we shall have a truce. I'd rather have a friend than an enemy."

They each took a seat at the round table, and Lisette folded her hands in her lap. "I confess, I am who you believe me to be. I have reason to stay unknown."

She told him her story—at least, the first half. The parts about blood dragons and tattoos were better left to secrecy. Her acquisition of gold coin also was scrubbed to leave Sandoval's legend out of it. He listened without comment.

"So, you can see there is a score I must settle, and I will not be deterred."

He nodded and grinned. "You are a most determined young woman. Little known fact—the Count de Medina has dipped his fingers in every island intrigue from Aruba to Tortuga. To keep my own island, I have to pay him a yearly tribute, and every year, the tribute grows larger."

"So, if I deal harshly with his daughter, it will not weigh on your conscience."

His grin blossomed into a smile. "If you accidentally kill *him*, I shall give you a reward."

They shook hands. "I believe that can be arranged."

Lisette went into her room and locked the door, cautious but hopeful for their agreement. There was the smallest of portholes. She stripped to her slip, climbed into the hammock, and watched the light dance in and out of view. Gripping the dagger under her pillow, she fell asleep.

The next few days they enjoyed morning mist, followed by afternoon sun and cool evenings. The wind was with them and sped the ship toward its destination as fast as such a large ship could travel. Lisette spent as much time as possible on deck, walking laps around the rails and pausing to look for any sign of land.

The duke was polite, even protective of her, although she suspected he was merely guarding what he believed was his hired assassin. The other passengers had come to the understanding that if they left her alone, she would treat them with courtesy. On the other hand, she enjoyed chatting with the crew about the weather, the ship, and its course.

On the evening of the sixth day, she observed the moon's shape shrinking, its middle sucking in to make an arc. *Surely, tomorrow night, I will be breathing fire and flying through the clouds.* She hadn't figured out how to handle her strange affliction in the middle of such a large, populated ship.

It was after breakfast when the scout in the crow's nest called out, "Captain! Unknown ship, port side, approaching fast!"

She ran to the railing and peered into the morning fog. A ship approaching so quickly without calling out its identification could only be one kind of vessel. Did this one fly the flag of the lioness, or the skull and crossbones?

# 46

The pirate ship cut across *El Gallo Blanco's* bow and pulled to starboard, firing all four cannons. Sailors ran back and forth, shouting, while the captain screamed nonsensical commands. This seemed to be his first time under attack, and he wasn't handling it well.

Lisette turned and ran for the opposite side, arriving in time to be knocked off her feet by the explosion. She was pulled upright by the first mate.

"Have you ever been in a battle?" she asked him.

He looked at his captain, his face stern, and gave a short nod. "I have."

"Then I suggest you 'interpret' the captain's commands, to give your crew a fighting chance."

He stared at the enemy now visible in the morning light. Clutching her arm, he steered her toward the steps.

"Get to your cabin."

She paused before descending. The pirate flag was high and visible, and her heart leapt. *L'Implacable*. Another hand yanked her down the steps. The duke, pulling her into the cabin.

"Pirates!" He barricaded the door and dragged her behind his bed. "Maybe we'll sink them!"

She looked out the window and shook her head. The large ship changed positions and tried to come about but the movement was lumbering and clumsy. There was an explosion and the cabin jerked. They had been hit again.

The duke wiped his brow, panting, yet still clinging to Lisette's forearm. She patted his shoulder. "It's all right. We'll be fine."

She knew it would not be all right, and not everyone would be fine. *L'Implacable* would overtake *El Gallo Blanco*, the crew would be killed, and she knew how Rocco felt about taking prisoners.

Voices were shouting now on the deck. She fought free of the duke's iron grip on her arm. Reaching up, she pulled the swords from the wall and checked the blades. None had been honed to the degree she was used to, but they'd have to do. She tossed one toward the duke. He recoiled.

"You have one chance, Sire." Lisette pointed toward the sword. "Come up and give a sporting show of fighting. I know this pirate and he will take no prisoners. I plan to fight for my life."

She shoved the table aside and opened the door. The fighting was loud, riotous. A body came crashing down in front of her, leaping up to rejoin the battle. She recognized him.

"Chunk!"

"Lizzie!" He hugged her and picked up his sword. "Cap'n's up top. I gotta clear the decks."

"Chunk, don't let Rocco kill the passengers." She wasn't certain if he heard her as he bounded back up into the smoke and screaming.

She took a big breath and forced herself up the stairs. Fighting did not bother her. Being with Rocco again did. She steeled herself to not be distracted by him and just fight.

There was not much to do when she arrived on deck. For all the smoke and shouting, the fighting had been minimal. This crew was spectacularly ill-trained for fighting anyone, much less pirates. A line of sailors stood against the rail, held captive by Rocco's men.

There were five lifeless bodies, all in uniforms. The captain had died at the helm, his body draped across the wheel, clothes soaked in blood and urine. The first mate was missing, an apparent victim of cannon shot.

Lisette could not find Chunk and looked frantically about. The tops of heads appeared, coming up the bow steps, and revealing themselves to be passengers. The women shrieked and wept, collapsing at every other step. The male passengers, who had approached her with such bravado on previous nights were not so gallant nor confident now and slunk behind the women.

Chunk was the last one up, much to her relief.

"Anyone else below?"

Lisette recognized Rocco's voice. Turning, she met his gaze and her temperature rose, the blush rushing up her chest to her neck. Standing aft, he appeared tall and arrogant with that familiar bloodlust in his eyes. She nodded as she stared at him, entranced, wanting to rush to him and not daring to budge.

"The Duke de Martinmas," she said.

He sent one of the men down. The duke emerged muttering about promises of wealth and power if he was allowed to live. Martinmas looked at her standing in the midst of the wreckage, still holding her sword.

"You—" He shoved a finger at her. "You're *with* these dogs."

"She is not," Rocco said.

Lisette snapped at him. "Don't presume to speak for me."

Rocco leaped from the helm to the deck and raised his hand to strike her. She stuck her face up, defiant, and dared him.

"Coward." Her eyes glowed with anger.

His eyes remained dark and calm, but he did not spare the back of his hand. She recoiled from the sting on her cheek, threw her sword down and jumped at him, knocking him backward. Her hands alternated between pounding his chest and clawing at his face, trying to hurt him more than he had hurt her.

Strong, beefy arms pulled her off and turned her around, holding her wrists. It was Chunk. She tried to free herself, but he was far too strong. A blur caught her attention. One of Rocco's men was holding the bags from the cabin—including hers, where she'd hidden the gold.

"Now, Lizzie, get hold o'yerself," Chunk said.

Rocco nodded at Chunk. "Throw her with the rest."

She dragged her feet as Chunk tried to lead her away. Rocco pointed to one of his men. "Clean out the cabins." To another, "Lower the boats."

The smaller of the two men disappeared below deck while the larger one loosened the lines on one of the dinghies.

Rocco turned his attentions to the captives. "Ladies and gentlemen, forgive my manners, but this is a first for me. I usually leave no prisoners, as I'm rather fond of the sight of dead Spaniards. Today I am feeling generous, so you will all be put into boats and cast off. You are not far from Lagarto, if you can set the right course. I wish you luck in your journey."

The pirates used their swords to push everyone into the dinghies. They worked fast and without pity. One sailor stopped to argue about getting into a boat. Rocco's man sliced his throat and dumped him overboard. There were no more refusals.

Lisette was in the dinghy with Martinmas, and four other women. They were lowered in a jerking, unbalanced fashion. With each drop the women screamed. She looked up to see who was manning the lines and recognized the large sailor who had rowed her to Isla de la Soledad, all those months ago.

She shouted at him. "Look sharp, you dog. You man a dinghy like a landlubber."

Rocco's face appeared at the rail. He took the line from the sailor and glowered at her as he released it completely. The boat hit the water with a thudding splash, bouncing all from their seats, and nearly capsizing. This began a new round of wailing from the women.

One of the girls pointed to Lisette. "That was your fault!"

A second girl whined, "Why did you have to say anything?"

Lisette glanced at the duke.

"I was wrong," he said. "You weren't with those dogs."

The other boats had sailors in them, strong young men who rowed past them in short order. None of them were willing to help a dinghy full of mere passengers.

Everyone in Lisette's boat sat expectantly, waiting for someone to come along and pick up an oar. She glared at the group, grabbed the sculls, and swung them across, unconcerned for her shipmates' ducking heads. Pushing away from the hull, she dug the oars deep and broad, trying to put as much distance as possible between *El Gallo Blanco* and their little dinghy.

"Of all the boats why did I get shoved into one filled with useless people?" She rowed with all the strength and speed she had. "I understand you women, you haven't stopped wailing since the first cannon hit, but Monsieur le Grand Duke, big as a house and you can't pick up an oar?"

"I do not understand what you're on about, Girl." Martinmas sounded surprised more than offended. "You are well aware I have servants who do the work for me. And you are doing a splendid job. Though I don't understand why you must work so hard at it."

"Because." She gritted her teeth as she swept through the churning water, her arms burning with each stroke. "Rocco will soon set fire to our fine ship, and the further away we are, the less likely we shall be roasted alive."

The women wailed louder now and one of the younger girls fainted.

"Stop your bawling. You behave like lambs going to slaughter." Lisette glowered at them, spitting her words. "Do you want to die? Or would you rather survive this and return to your loved ones?"

They lowered their cries to whimpers which at least let her concentrate. They were a furlong from the ship when she recognized the familiar smoke. Rocco had lit a line to the powder. Within moments the inside of the galleon exploded, collapsing it in the middle. What didn't sink erupted into flames.

The women screamed and sobbed. Lisette stopped rowing briefly. The dinghy was out of danger, and she had to stretch her exhausted arms and aching shoulders for a moment before continuing. She had bowed her head and arched her back when one of the older women began clucking. It took her a moment to realize who she was addressing.

"Girl, what are you doing? Get back to rowing this

instant." A rigid, brocade-suited woman scowled as she chastised Lisette. "We must get to Lagarto, and this boat will not row itself."

Over her shoulder Lisette could see *L'Implacable* picking her way through the refugees at half-sail, crawling until she got free of them. Rocco was at the helm, looking back at the damage he'd done, no doubt enjoying the show.

Rowing to Lagarto was not in Lisette's plans. And once the sun set, she would not be able to row at all. Her gold was on Rocco's ship along with her emerald and Connie's ring in the pockets of Lamya's robe. She was wearing the new outfit she bought on Isla de la Ballena. All she had was her dagger still strapped to her leg.

She put the sculls back on the side of the boat and unbuttoned her bodice and skirt, tossing them overboard. The women gasped. Even Martinmas blustered a few choice words in protest. When she was down to her slip, Lisette stood.

"Ladies, and good Sire, I must take my leave. That pirate has stolen from me, and I intend to recover my losses. In the meantime, I suggest that one of you pick up an oar and use it."

Before they could protest, she jumped into the water and swam toward *L'Implacable*.

Her arms still burned from rowing, but Lisette kicked vigorously, swimming a straight line for the ship. She wasn't certain how she would get up the hull and onto the deck but if nothing else, she could find a way to hold on until nightfall and fly up.

It'd be quite a surprise for the crew.

She was almost within arm's reach aft when Rocco called out the order to unfurl the mainsail. There was no indication he had spotted her in the water. She hoped he was too busy picking his way through the debris.

Her biggest, hardest kick brought her alongside and she clutched at the chain holding the anchor. She managed to wrap one leg around the chain to hoist herself up. Crawling to the hull, she grabbed the wood and pulled herself to a standing position. Splinters drove into her fingers, but she held on, finding a handhold in the planking, and dragging herself up the ship.

Her feet fumbled about, searching for a toehold as she kept stretching upward, inching her way up the corner of the bow. Her arms shook, reminding her of that first day's climb up the mountain with Lamya.

This isn't nearly so high, she reminded herself. *You can do this.*

The ship picked up speed, plastering her body against the hull and making her pull her body away in order to inch upward. The bowsprit was within reach but angled upward. If she could get her hands on that, she could easily grab the rail and get on deck. Unfortunately, she was too short to reach out to it and the hull jutted out, making it impossible to climb upside-down.

She would have to jump.

Even considering it was late afternoon and she wouldn't have to remain in the water long, she didn't dare miss.

She stared at the pole, stretching her right hand toward it. God might not hear her prayer, so she called upon whatever saint was the guardian of slim chances and sea birds. Bending her knees and pushing, she launched her body upward.

Her right wrist hit the bowsprit first, knocking her hand away but her left hand clasped the wood, tight, until her right hand could join it. The impact of leaping and stopping at the pole pulled her arms nearly out of her shoulders. She stifled a cry and swung her legs up, once, twice, thrice, until they crossed around the pole.

She wasn't safe yet, but Lisette released a little sigh of thanks. Edging along, she reached the hull and grabbed the rail above. From there, it was an easier pull, sideways, until she slid over the railing and onto the deck, right behind the helm. She felt like a fish dragged in on a hook and flopping about. If she hadn't been so sore and tired, she should have laughed at Rocco's expression. She struggled to her feet and faced him.

He scowled. "What are you doing here?"

"You took my bag. I must have my clothes." She straightened her back and lifted her chin. "Could you please point me toward your spoils?"

There was no sound but the whisper of the wind and creaking of the ship. Each mate's eyes were on her. Rocco might throw her overboard where one of the dinghies could pick her up. Or he might run her through first so no one would have to bother. Either way the sun was dipping lower toward the western sea.

"Captain, you might want to decide what to do with me," she said. "We haven't much time."

He let a few more awkward moments tick by before shouting, "Chunk!" Keeping his eyes on her he gave the older man orders. "Let her find her bag, then lock her in my cabin."

On her way from the helm, she turned back. "Thank you, Captain."

Chunk led her to the hold where she had first been stored as a captive.

"Here ya go, Lizzie." He pointed to the large pile of bags that littered the floor.

She waded in and dug through the stolen goods. It was warm in the hold even in her mere cotton slip and drops of sweat rolled down her back. Several bags jingled as she lifted them. At last, in the corner under what looked like the duke's valise she found her tapestry bag, squashed but still intact. She dragged it out and showed Chunk.

"My clothes."

They strolled to the captain's cabin, sharing what happened after separating on Isla de Pimienta.

"I was worried about you, Lizzie, but Cap'n says yer a big girl and can work it out yerself. We had to weigh anchor and move on." He opened the door to Rocco's cabin. "Sure is good to see you agin."

"Good to see you, too." She put her arms around his neck. He hugged her back and left, locking the door.

Her first act was to touch the lining of the bag and assure herself the gold was still inside. Next on the list was to change into her robe. Mama's emerald was safe, as well as Connie's ring, and there were still coins scattered about the robe.

All she had to do was figure out how to get it all to Isla del Lagarto, procure lodging, and hunt down Eric and Mercedes.

The door opened and Rocco walked inside, closing the door behind him. She stood still, chin up, trying not to let her weakness for him show.

He frowned. "What happened on Ballena—"

"When you tried to kill me, or when we lay together?"

"You must understand. When my wife died, I swore an oath."

Lisette put her hand up to stop him. "Lamya told me. Doesn't Tempest's dying wish come before your blood oath?"

He looked her in the eyes for the first time since entering. She walked toward him without hesitation until her body stood a hair's breadth from his. She could sense his strength, his breath, his heart beating. He raised his hand to her face and caressed her cheek. His other hand grasped her waist, pulling her in.

In one firm motion, he clasped her hands behind her back and held her tight. She felt rope around her wrists.

"What are you doing?"

He went to his trunk and dragged out something heavy. It looked like the top of a suit of armor, which he fastened around her chest and back. She had to sit from the weight of it.

"Years ago, I had someone make this for me, in case I grew tired of my quest. When I began to change into a dragon, this iron would hold fast, crushing my ribcage. To keep from suffering, I placed a tiny dagger in the armor, to pierce my heart as my body is broken."

"What? Me?" She stared up at him, her mouth agape. "How could you—?"

"I have been a blood dragon for a very long time." His voice was low and weighted with sadness. "I am close to killing the Count de Medina, but I have not been able to kill you. You are my weakness, and as long as you live, I shall always look at you and think of Tempest and feel my blood lusting for revenge. You called me a coward. You are correct. I cannot slay you openly and honestly. What I can do is imprison you in this armor and let sunset do the rest."

He touched her face, staring into her eyes. She opened her mouth to dissuade him from killing her and he brought his lips to hers, kissing her with a fierceness that reminded her of their morning together. Her body rose to meet his until the point of the dagger stopped her. She craned her neck up instead, to respond with her own passion.

He pulled away from her and strode toward the door.

"No-no-no, wait, we can work—" Her protests were ignored as he left. The door shut with a heavy thud.

She tugged against the rope around her wrists. It seemed immovable, but she kept struggling with it. The plates on her chest bland back were unwieldy, bound up the sides with leather cords and trapping her arms underneath. She could get her fingers out of the plates, to the side, poking them through the lacings.

Her dagger was still on her thigh, in its sheath. She

could not get hold of it with her fingers, but if she raised her leg the hilt knocked against the breastplate. If she could snag the armor on the hilt, she could perhaps pull her blade from the leather.

She raised her shoulders, lifting the armor up, then pushed forward. The dagger inside the breastplate scraped her breast and the bottom of the plate passed over the hilt without hooking it.

Again, she raised her shoulders and repeated the motion, pushing harder this time, while attempting to keep her chest from contacting the blade inside. Another near miss. With each move her body screamed for a break, but time was running away.

More attempts, each a little closer until finally the edge of the armor found its target. She raised her leg to allow the dagger to fall out of its sheath and in slow, gentle movements, raked the armor down her thigh, pulling the blade away as it went.

She stood and let the dagger fall to the floor. Dropping to her knees was difficult without toppling forward with the weight of the armor. Still, she lowered herself, wobbled, felt another scratch of the dagger inside, and finally knelt beside the blade.

The sun was on its final strip of light in the western sky, and she had to be quicker. She sat back and sideways, stretching her fingers down to get some kind of hold on her weapon.

The movement unbalanced her, and she fell on her side. She raised her shoulders and sank her breasts back toward her spine. The sting of the blade scratched across skin, hooking itself on her collarbone. It pierced into her shoulder, but she could not stop to ease the pain. All she could do was scream.

Reaching down and slightly right rewarded her with sharp metal. She was never so happy to prick her finger and quickly located the hilt. Grasping it with both hands, she turned it inward and sawed with as much speed and power as she could.

It took seconds to work through the rope, the sweat pouring down face, body, and hands. At last, the binding was weak enough to pull her hands apart. As she freed them, the dagger flew across the room.

The first star appeared in the window to the east. She had to hurry. Pulling the inner blade from her shoulder using one hand, she recovered the dagger, and hacked at the right side of the armor. Within seconds, she sawed through the right side, and thrust the dagger into her pocket. As she slipped from the armor, she felt the white-hot flash of change.

Having had no time to prepare and with elevated panic, this change was almost as brutal as the first. She choked back a scream and lost consciousness for several moments. When she regained her own mind, she was shocked at what she saw.

Rocco's cabin had been destroyed. The chairs and table were splintered hunks of wood, the swords and maps torn from the walls. His bed was ripped apart, leaving nothing but straw, feathers, and tiny strips of material. Broken bottles and broken blades were everywhere. The smell of alcohol was overwhelming.

Now lucid, she looked down at herself. She was still in dragon form. A trickle of blood glistened on her black, feathered shoulder, a reminder of the piercing she got from Rocco's contraption. She grasped her bag with her talons and smashed one of the large windows in the back. Crawling out, she extended her wings and lifted high enough to escape detection before catching an air current to carry her toward Isla del Lagarto.

# 48

Aloft, Lisette scanned the ocean, looking for an island. Far below her, *L'Implacable* was heading southeast. The small boats with the survivors of *El Gallo Blanco* followed, clumped together and quite a bit slower.

She could not keep the slow pace of these boats. Even *L'Implacable*, although the ship traveled fast, would not be in Lagarto for another day. Lisette had precious few hours to fly.

Lifting off another current, she sailed ahead, gliding to preserve her strength. When the wind speed lessened, she beat her wings to gain as much distance as possible. The entire time, her eyes were scanning the horizon, her ears attuned for any sound of civilization, nose seeking the smell of land.

The waning crescent was descending more rapidly than she desired, and she flew faster, though her body ached with the long hours of work. Her wings burned. A dim light crept from the east and her heart flinched. Sunrise meant changing and changing now meant spending at least a day trying to stay alive and afloat.

She kept propelling forward but dropped to a height that would be more manageable once she changed. That's when she spied salvation. A flat, broad shoreline, invisible from above due to the lack of mountains, trees, or buildings. The sand stretched back from the water to a slow rise of green brush.

When the sun's first ray hit, she was not quite over the island. A brief flash, a splash, and Lisette was in the surf. She washed in with the tide, finding her footing and wrestling with her clothes which were heavy with sea water. Her bag had fallen from her talons as they turned to hands, but it was easily located in the shallows.

She dug her clothes from her bag and dressed in the wet things. Fastening her robe at her neck like a cape, she hoped that the layers of fabric would dry while keeping her looking presentable. In the dawn, she could not discern any buildings, and wondered if she'd come to the wrong island. The wind was strong here. She walked along the beach, alone except for the sand crabs and sea birds. The breeze dried her clothes as she followed the shore, and she soon was able to fasten her robe about her waist and feel completely dressed.

By mid-morning, she was on the westward side of the island. The air was calmer here but carried scents that were familiar, some soothing and some agitating. Mercedes was here—she could smell the cloying sweetness. Eric's musky scent assailed her as well.

There was a gentle, friendly smell she could not name. Could it be Tatie Elena?

Lisette rested, wishing for food. This island was different from the others. More sand, less underbrush, more palm trees, less fruit. She was glad that her last meal on the ship had been a hearty one.

The sun was on its way down when she discovered a low overhang that encircled a beach. The wind here was quieter, the waves gentle. Wooden steps rose from the sea to the cliff, and several buildings appeared along the precipice.

She was desperately hungry but didn't dare try to climb the steps to find food. There was no harbor here, no ships on the horizon. How was she to convince anyone that she came in from the sinking *El Gallo Blanco*? Instead, she found a place of deep brush, uninhabited, and settled there, awaiting the darkness.

Night came and she flew again, gliding silent over the island to discover where she was, and what was on this place. The steps she had found led to a small shoreline village, a row of buildings. There were no lights on, and no movement. Still, she detected soft footsteps and voices within.

Of one point she was mistaken—there was a port here, on the other side of the shore, where the land made a slight crescent shape. The ocean was calmer here, as opposed to the side that had no barriers to the wind and weather.

She continued her reconnaissance, noticing the rolling hills, dotted with small, thatched-roof homes and what appeared to be fields of crops. At the topmost hill stood a castle, larger than the one she grew up in. To its left and right were two smaller castles, not so grand. The tall castle was fully lit from within, and she could hear music and lively voices coming from its halls. The smallest castle to her left had torches over the door, no doubt awaiting the lord's return.

The place to her right was dark. She ventured lower, to discover if it was occupied. There was no evidence of ownership, no carriage or animals, not even any torches over the door to be lit. Lifting back up into the clouds, she wondered who she would have to bribe in order to secure this place for herself.

As she rose, the smell of her enemies became stronger. They were in the large castle, Lisette was certain, and she felt drawn to them. She fought to keep herself from hunting tonight. It would spoil her plans to simply pluck them from the balcony—at least, not yet.

She spied a familiar face on the grounds, walking across a courtyard to a row of servants' huts. Genevieve, her former maid, was the source of the friendly scent. Lisette's heart leapt with joy at the sight, and she nearly swooped down to greet her.

*Genevieve would not enjoy meeting me at the moment.*

Lisette flew back toward the village and beheld a fortunate scene. The dinghies from *El Gallo Blanco* neared the shoreline and would probably arrive by morning. The boat containing the Duke de Martinmas and the four hapless women lurched along at the tail of the group. It appeared the two younger women were rowing. She almost felt badly for them.

Beyond the dinghies, *L'Implacable* made its way south, following the edge of the island, but clearly not interested in dropping anchor. She wondered which port they were bound for, to sell their loot.

Keeping the foliage between her and the boats, she made her way back to her temporary den. Morning was coming soon, and she had to preserve her strength. If she expected to be included as one of the castaways, she had to "come ashore" shortly after they did.

As she lit upon the grass, intending to walk to the underbrush, wings flapped above her, and she turned to spot Rocco, coming fast, his talons spread and pointed toward her. She reared and twisted, clamping his claws with her own. He drew her along the grass, into the thicket, where he snaked his neck around in an attempt to tear her flesh with his teeth. She met his fangs with hers, dove underneath and seized him by the throat. His fangs pierced her shoulder and she screamed but did not release her hold.

His thrashing grew more chaotic, and it was all Lisette could do to keep her grip on his neck. She bore down harder, until he weakened. At last, he collapsed, and she let go. Dawn was upon the land, so she awkwardly dragged him into the underbrush. The sun had not yet hit this side of the island, but she felt the familiar pinch of pain, and soon they were side by side and quite human.

Rocco came to consciousness with a start, pushing up from his prone position, gasping. She sat beside him, admiring his body's chiseled beauty. He looked over at her and scowled.

"You are supposed to be dead."

"And yet, I survived."

"You destroyed my cabin."

"My apologies, I have no memory of it. When I transformed, my dragon side was angry."

Pushing her to the ground, he knelt over her. "I swore an oath. You should understand."

Lisette grabbed his shirt and pulled him toward her until her nose nearly touched his. "Lamya said you can leave this life behind if you could only lose your thirst for my blood. What does it gain you to kill me? I couldn't have stopped Tempest's death."

He stared at her for some time, while she committed to memory the color of his eyes, the straight line of his eyebrows, even the ringlets in his hair.

Grasping her in his arms, he kissed her, and they fell together into the underbrush. This time he was the aggressor, and she was a willing participant. They explored each other's mouth with lips and tongue as their hands traveled across each other's body. He fed her

310

craving for him with an exquisite touch.

A part of her yearned to whisper her love for him. A part of her railed that he didn't love her in return. Those parts were overruled, as she was too busy moaning to do either.

As before, she woke alone. This time, she didn't bother to search for him. Her body still sang with the pleasure it had felt. Perhaps he felt it, too, in his own way. She pushed away all ideas of love and pining, locking them far from her heart.

After adjusting her clothes, Lisette trekked back to the beach and up the steps toward the town, carrying her treasure-filled luggage. It was necessary to appear that she'd come ashore with the other castaways. At the top, a boardwalk led to a dry goods store, a blacksmith, several houses, and an inn.

She headed to the inn for some information and, hopefully, a meal.

The outside of the building was whitewashed board, with the large windows typical of the islands, allowing light and breezes inside, lined by substantial shutters to close when the storms grew fierce. Lisette opened the heavy door and walked into a room full of familiar, shipwrecked faces. The crew and passengers of the *Gallo* sat around tables, sullen and demanding service.

"I am one woman with two hands." A woman's voice wearing an islander's accent came around the corner near the bar and the woman herself followed close behind. Tall and curvy, she wore a bright yellow sarong with a matching headwrap. The color popped against her dark skin, as did the many beaded necklaces and bracelets adorning her neck and arms.

She walked to the middle of the room and put her hands on her hips. "You will all listen to Trina. We have a fish stew and coconut rum. It is *all* we have. *We* is me, and I will put food and drink on your table when I get it there."

The whimpering passengers complained louder, which made Lisette rub the pain in her temples. They should be happy to be alive. Rocco could have left their charred bodies on the burning galleon.

Wishing to quiet the ingrates, she stepped forward. "I can help you shut these spoiled brats up if you would like an extra pair of hands."

Trina studied her from head to hem. "Chile, what you want to t'row in wit' an island woman for?"

"Because I am weary of these wastrels and want them as far away from me as possible. The quicker they're fed, the quicker they leave."

"Uh-huh. Wanting favors, then?" She pursed her lips. "Well, awright. Jes' know that, no matter how much you help me, I kin still say no to you."

"Naturally." Lisette followed her to the back and lined up bowls for soup, mugs for rum. The women worked this way, as a team, for a goodly fifteen minutes, until the only sound in the inn was the slurping of drink and stew. Once they were satisfied, Lisette went back to the kitchen and ladled her own meal.

She sat at a small table in the corner, away from the crowd. As she picked up her first spoonful, Trina placed a loaf of bread on her plate. Lisette gladly tore a piece and dipped it into the stew. It tasted strange and exotic, but filling. Trina sat across from her, with a mug of her own.

"Where you from?"

Lisette told her the official story, about traveling to Isla del Lagarto, being attacked, and having to make their way to this shore.

"Well, at least you come to the right island. But why you want to come here?"

She took a chance with her lie. "I was invited by the Count de Medina."

"Ah, yes. All the rich folk has gone to the tailor for new clothes. I am left here, to watch the inn while everyone sashayin' round town."

"Oh, who owns this inn?"

Trina chuckled. "The count own this inn. The count own everyt'ing. Samule, the innkeeper jes' run it for him. If Samule make him mad, the count t'row him into jail and hire someone new."

Lisette tried to remember this count the few times he visited her home. At the time he seemed boring yet agreeable. She had been completely wrong about him. If Rocco didn't kill him, perhaps she should. The Duke de Martinmas had requested it, after all.

"Trina, I need help and I am willing to pay for it." Lisette pulled several gold coins from her pocket and laid them on the table. "I can pay well."

Apart from Marisha, Trina was the first person who did not go into a greedy trance when she saw the gold. She didn't even pick it up. Instead, she looked at Lisette, her eyes tapered in suspicion. "I ain't killin' no one."

"There's no need for that. I simply ought to buy some finer clothes. I must present a polished image to the court and my things were lost at sea."

Trina smiled, full lips parting to reveal beautiful

white teeth. She picked up the gold. "What does m'lady wish?"

After their talk, Lisette stopped by the Duke de Martinmas' table. He was having another bowl of stew, and possibly his third or fourth tanker of rum.

"I see you were able to secure your belongings." He raised his tanker in greeting.

"Yes and was nearly killed for it. You once called me a determined young woman. Does it surprise you I would risk my life in order to complete my plans?"

"Not at all." He grinned and sat back, taking a swig of rum. "You also remind me of why I thought to help you in the first place."

"I do not want much."

"But what you want will require my help."

She gave him a slight bow. "I have the gold, but you have the connections."

"Little known fact. A title is not like a secret password. It does not open every door."

"True." She sat down and leaned toward him. "All I require is a place to stay, temporarily."

"I'm staying at the Castle de Medina."

"No, that would not do." Lisette shook her head. "And I think you understand why."

He smiled and drank.

"I spotted a smaller castle up the road," she said. "It appears to be vacant."

"Ah, yes." He leaned toward her, smiling. "Remember poor Philippe de Thibault? Brutally murdered at my own estate?"

"Of course. Did he have no family?"

"Oh, yes, seven children and one on the way, if you can believe it." The duke tsked. "Apparently, he could not leave his wife alone. With his death, they all hopped on a ship back to France. The widow desires a more civilized upbringing for her brood."

"You are so knowledgeable, m'lord." A little flattery never hurt a cause. "What do you think it would take for me to occupy their castle for, say, a fortnight?"

He folded his hands across his chest, the model of a dealmaker. "I do happen to know that the count now owns the property. He might agree to let it to you for a price."

"Would I have a snooping landlord?"

"Ah, perhaps. He does prefer a pretty face. If he sees you, I daresay he'll invite himself over, quite often and at the most inconvenient times."

"Then what would it take to purchase the property from him?"

"Hmm, that may prove difficult." He tapped his finger.

"What if you purchased it? Say, for your niece?" She gave him a wry grin. "You nobles all have your 'nieces.'"

He held out his hand. "One bag of gold should be sufficient. Let Uncle Oscar help you."

"The Lady Tempest d'Arturo thanks you." She rose and gave him a small curtsy.

Within hours, Lisette had access to the uninhabited stone mansion down the hill from the Medina castle. As it turned out, the count was more than willing to part with the property.

"Even though Philippe did not die there," the duke told her, "The manner of his death made his castle undesirable. The count is allergic to blood dragons."

Trina helped her find staff to run it and Lisette was happy to give her a finder's fee with each post filled. While the castle was being decorated, Lisette stayed in a room at the inn. There, she introduced herself and her significant coinage to the seamstress recommended. She chose cotton for everyday dresses and a golden silk brocade for her ball gown, as close as possible to the one she wore when she was kidnapped.

*They will recognize who I was before I destroy them.*

# 50

It took barely a week to get her new castle comfortable enough for Lisette to move into, but she could not wait longer. The moon was still in its new phase, and she was turning into a dragon at night. The inn became busiest when the sunset drew close and she could not afford prying eyes to see her transform.

She could smell her prey as she flew across the island but resisted the urge to hunt them. Killing them now would not fulfill her fantasy and she needed that, as much as she needed their deaths to quench her thirst for revenge. Controlling her dragon lust made her irritable and she spent most nights circling the Medina castle, watching the activities inside.

These flights were always halted by Rocco's attacks. This infuriated Lisette as a dragon but left her aggressive as a lover. By sunrise, she was feverish with desire, taking him in a frenzy. Her yearning was followed by sweet release, over and over, until they were both sated—physically.

On the last evening of the waxing crescent, she spotted Mercedes on the balcony. Mercedes was looking into the castle, her hand upon the stone arch. She was tapping. Lisette descended upon the roof unseen and unheard, landing above the balcony as softly as a sparrow.

Tap. Tap-tap-tap. Tap. Tap-tap-tap. Mercedes' nail beat a steady and distinct rhythm. Within moments, Eric joined her on the balcony.

"I thought you were never going to come." Mercedes sounded petulant. "We need to talk about Elena."

Lisette could see the top of Eric's head passing in and out of her view as he paced the length of the balcony. "I still don't see why we have to kill her."

"You are as big a buffoon as the day we met," Mercedes said. "While Elena lives, we cannot have our money."

"But she is already so old and frail. We have enough to get by, until she dies naturally."

Mercedes straightened herself to her full height and crossed her arms. "I am a Medina. I do not 'get by.'"

Eric persisted. "Anyway, are we certain the de Lille fortune still exists? Or that I am still named as Lisette's betrothed?"

"Elena shared a few secrets with me. The Duke de Lille did not have time to change his papers." Mercedes pressed her body close to his. "Don't worry about Elena, my love. She will go peacefully, in her sleep. She has been so sad, so sorrowful. I have already been helping her, with a little something extra in her nightly port. We will bring her joy, to be with her family again."

Her dragon wings made soft whispers as Lisette

lifted herself back into the clouds, still watching Eric and Mercedes on the balcony. She could grab them both tonight and kill them. If she acted now, she could keep them from killing Tatie Elena. She considered her heart's desire, to reveal herself before killing them.

Were her fantasies part of the blood dragon spell, or would their killing be enough? What about Tatie Elena—would Lisette have to be the one to kill her, and could she do it? Lisette wished she could ask Lamya a few more questions.

Rocco hit her like a battering ram, knocking her out of the sky and into the brush, where he dragged her far from the castle. She struggled mightily against him, gnashing, and clawing at him. This time, he did not attack her with talons or teeth, but pinioned her to the ground.

He held her there for several minutes before releasing her. She took one last swipe at his head, leaving a gash across his jaw, before flying away.

She swept past the Medina castle again, but Eric and Mercedes had retired for the night. They were perhaps murdering Tatie Elena already. She could not stop them.

Gliding back to the ground she returned to the hidden bed of brush outside her new home. She took deep breaths, closed her eyes, and reveled in the pain of changing. Without the ability to shed tears, only physical pain soothed her sorrows. Human again, she walked inside, climbing the stairs to her bedchamber to sleep off the night's disappointment.

Rocco awaited in her bed.

Lisette stood in the doorway. "I should kill you right now for interfering with me."

"It is hardly my fault if you squandered your chance."

Rocco stood and padded over to her, naked and

barefoot. Lisette took his chin in her hand, turned his face, and ran her fingers down a long red scratch, letting her fingers drift down to the charm at his neck.

"I'll try to avoid the face next time. I'd hate to scar you for life." She gave his cheek a stiff smack.

"You already have."

"Those people—" Her mind went blank for a moment as he unfastened her robe, letting it fall open. "They're going to kill my aunt. They may be killing her now. You stopped me."

"True." He pushed the robe from her shoulders and led her toward the bed.

She followed him, trancelike, halfway across the room before pulling away. "No. I don't want this anymore. I don't want to be a dragon. I don't want to want vengeance. I don't want to want—you."

He leaned down, his beard tickling her cheek as his lips brushed her ear. "I don't want to want you, either, Lisette, but I do."

Soft kisses traveled up and down her neck as he continued to whisper. "I've fought against you, fought loving you. I thought if I took you, laid with you, I'd satisfy my lust and move on." His hands cradled her head as he studied her face, kissed her, studied again. "It didn't work. The more I have you, the more I want you. I just can't fight you anymore. I love you, Lizzie."

She draped her hands on his shoulders and he wrapped a hand around her waist. They kissed deeply and tenderly like lovers reunited.

A knocking sound interrupted them.

"Mistress?" It was her new maid, Nan. "You have a visitor."

Lisette grabbed her robe and went to the door while Rocco stepped behind the bed curtains.

"Who is it?" She cracked the door a bit to hear the

maid better.

"The Duke de Martinmas."

She mouthed a curse. "This is not convenient. Can you tell him to come back later?"

"He's most insistent, Mistress. Says he has important news."

In addition to procuring her home the duke delighted in reporting any gossip from the Medina court. He was also quick to remind her of what an enormous help he had been in order to capitalize on her gratitude.

"Very well. Tell him I'll be down shortly."

She shut the door and took out her simplest dress. Rocco stepped from the curtains.

"What kind of information would that toad have for you?"

Changing her clothes, she tried to explain. "Killing Eric and Mercedes will free me from this dragon spell, but I want the chance to show them I survived. They did not break me. They betrayed me, they murdered my family, and they cannot pay enough, do enough, say enough to earn my pardon."

His grin was made rueful by his expressionless eyes. "How many times will they have to die to earn your forgiveness?"

The question drove into her heart. "When I kill them…when they are dead…it will be over. I will be finished."

She remembered Begum Derya's words. *Vengeance is a beast that feeds upon itself.*

He was right. Killing them once might not be enough.

She smoothed her dress and shook her head, trying to clear her mind. "I have to see Martinmas."

"Very well." Rocco embraced her once more. "You have to finish what you've started. As do I."

With slow and reluctant motions, she tore herself from his arms and went downstairs to meet the duke.

"I do apologize for the inconvenience, but this was most important." The duke dabbed at his temples with a silk square, his forehead beaded with sweat.

She nodded for the maid to bring him drink. "Please go on, *Uncle Oscar*. What news is there?"

"First, I must tell you, the court is most curious about you. They have discovered that you have taken residence here, that you are hiring many workers, seamstresses, and maids. Rumor has it, you are searching for an artist to paint your portrait."

She laughed. "No, but I suppose I could."

"Since I mentioned our traveling together, the count and his wife are wondering if you could accompany me to dinner tomorrow."

Dinner was not what Lisette was after and not tomorrow. Her betrayers' wedding would coincide with her dragon cycle. Anything earlier would not do. "I was rather hoping to be invited to the wedding celebration."

"Yes, of course." He nodded. "I suggested dinner in order that you might ingratiate yourself and secure an invitation. The count has particular tastes. I suspect he will not be able to resist you."

He launched into an account of the Count de Medina's sexual peccadillos, which was unfit for mixed company. She was sickened, and tried not to listen, although she was no longer surprised at what pigs noblemen were.

"I've also learned some interesting gossip." He leaned forward. "There was a woman he kidnapped many years ago—"

"Sire." Lisette put her hand up. Rocco had never expressed knowledge of Mercedes' parentage—what would happen if he knew? "We need not discuss—"

"Wife of a common sailor." The duke ignored her.

"They say she became pregnant with the count's child and the count killed her. But the child lived—Mercedes!"

The door upstairs slammed shut. Rocco had heard it all. If he had not known before, he knew now. A cold weight hit Lisette's stomach. Now he had two reasons to kill her. The worst case was that he blocked her from killing Mercedes then killed her before she could exact her revenge.

If she could have cried, she would have sobbed. There would be no hope for her eternal soul if she died as a blood dragon.

Lisette folded her hands across her dress. "Thank you, Sire, that is most helpful."

"May I tell the count that you and I will dine with them evening next?"

"Yes. That will be fine." If she refused, she might not be invited to the wedding. Of course, showing up for dinner might expose her true identity. Either option was bad.

After prattling a little more about town news and gossip the duke finally departed. She ran upstairs to find Rocco, but he was gone. She picked up the closest object, a metal bowl, and threw it against the wall. Nan came running into the room.

"Oh, m'lady, I was afraid something bad happened." The maid's full cheeks were flushed from scurrying up the stairs.

"No, it was me. I am…unhappy. Nan, do you know any of the servants at the Medina court? A woman named Genevieve?"

"Yes. They do not treat her well, because she is French, but the young count Eric protects her when he can."

Lisette was surprised, but glad. "Could you take me to see her now? Secretly?"

"I s'pose I could." She pushed her hair away from her face and wiped her hands on her apron. "I know a back way into their castle. Only servants use it."

The two women left the house and traveled northeast, up the hill to the Medina castle. Nan huffed and puffed her way to the wall surrounding the rear of the property, stopping at last to lean on the stones and let her breath catch up with her. She pointed up at the sky.

"Sun's overhead. Means they've finished their meals and will be having a nap."

Lisette nodded as Nan looked around carefully. She led Lisette to a small crack in the stone wall, tucked her skirt into her waistband, and found a foothold. Halfway up, she looked back and cocked her head. Lisette tucked her skirt and followed.

They both scaled the wall easily and lay flat on its width, resting. No one was watching so they hopped down and walked between two of the servants' cottages. Nan led her to the back of the castle. The cottages here were older, in bad condition.

Nan gestured to the cottage at the far west corner. "There's where Genevieve lives."

Lisette knocked at the door—a weathered collection of wooden planks held together by decaying strips of leather. It rattled at her touch as if it might tumble inward. A slender woman with hunched shoulders and sad eyes answered the door.

Genevieve. She looked so much older, sadder, almost frail. Her clothes were clean but old and mended—patches atop patches. Lisette held back a gasp.

The maid squinted up at her. "May I help you?"

## 51

"Genevieve, do you not recognize me?"

Genevieve studied her for some moments. At long last her mouth parted and her eyes widened. Her voice dropped to a whisper. "Lisette?"

Lisette nodded. Genevieve looked around at the grounds, her eyes furtive, before gesturing. "Come in, quickly."

Lisette and Nan entered the small hut. One room served as everything from kitchen to bedroom. It was a far cry from the servants' quarters on Île des Oiseaux. Once they were inside, Genevieve shut the door. The two women fell into each other's arms, laughing and crying.

"We were told you were dead," she said. "Before the Count de Medina—"

Lisette cut her off. "I know what he did."

In alternating tales of sorrow, each filled the other in with what had happened since that night. Lisette hated to stop but she had pressing business.

"Genevieve, have you seen my Tatie Elena? Is she well?"

She shook her head. "She is very ill. I do not understand what is wrong with her, but she can barely walk."

Lisette looked at Nan. "Mercedes has been poisoning my aunt. I must find a way to get her out of this castle."

Genevieve did not appear surprised. "I see the servants at night, carrying her to a chair outside."

"At night?"

"Yes, the sunlight hurts her, but she enjoys the air."

Lisette tapped her fingers, thinking. "If she can hang on until tomorrow, there might be a way."

"You would save her?" Genevieve frowned. "I do not enjoy giving bad news, but…"

"Do you know something about her that I should know?"

She placed both hands over her mouth then reached her arms toward Lisette. "I swear if I had known, I would not have let it happen. When the Baroness de Thibault came to stay here, she drank and cried for days. I overheard her drunken mutterings one day, all about how she betrayed you and deserved to die."

"Did she say why she did it?"

Genevieve shook her head. "Mercedes gave her the promise of safety from some kind of beast. It sounded fantastical."

Lisette snorted. So, Tatie Elena believed the same dragon who killed her husband was looking for her.

Nan leaned over and touched Lisette's sleeve. "The

household rest is almost over. We should go before we are discovered."

Lisette rose and turned to Genevieve. "Thank you."

The maid hugged her, her bony arms grabbing at Lisette's heart. She could not leave her in this squalor. "Genevieve, how hard would it be for you to come and work for me again?"

"It would be difficult." She lowered her head. "The count and his family treat me poorly, but they refuse to let me to leave this place. They enjoy having your parents' former servants in their employ. I believe they feel they are still abusing your family by abusing us."

"This is unacceptable." Lisette's wrath increased to include the count and his wife. "I shall get you out of here, I promise."

They said their goodbyes and Lisette and Nan snuck away, over the wall again.

Lisette strode back to the house, leaving poor Nan to run in order to keep up.

"Miss." Nan's voice wheezed from lack of breath. "Miss—am I understanding right? You are not Lady d'Arturo?"

Lisette slowed her pace. "I'm sorry to make you run, Nan. No, I am not, although I trust this information stays with us."

They walked at a more leisurely rate while Lisette told her story to the maid. As usual, she left out the part about the dragons.

"They'll get nothing outta me," Nan said at last. "I'll protect you and your secret."

As they arrived at the castle, Lisette was still restless. "I'm going to walk on, Nan. There are puzzles I need to work out and a good walk sometimes awakens my mind."

She headed down the road toward the pier. The sun

was bright, but there was a cool breeze and a few rainclouds threatening. She needed a plan to rescue her dear maid. One option was to wait for her dragon form and kill the count's family, thus freeing Genevieve and all the servants. Another possibility would be to find someone she could trust, who could remove her friends from their tormentors.

In the meantime, she had to choose what to wear to dinner tomorrow. She would need luck and extra prayers to ensure Eric and Mercedes didn't recognize her. Soon she arrived at the shore and strolled to the inn in search of Trina.

Today, Trina wore a pale peach sarong, which accentuated her curves. She motioned Lisette to one of the empty tables. There were few people in the place, mostly men. A quartet of blowsy women were half-heartedly plying their wares, sitting at a table, drinking, while they exchanged raunchy banter.

"Cider," Lisette told Trina. "And maybe a little information."

Trina poured them each a cup and sat. "What is it you are wanting?"

"There are people who require my help, people being hurt by the Count de Medina and his family."

"Sistah, we is all bein' hurt by that family." Trina stirred her drink with her finger.

"One of them—my aunt—is at the castle. I am not certain if I can save her. She's very ill already, but I have to try. She is being poisoned."

This made Trina look up.

"I must be the Duke de Martinmas' companion tomorrow night when we go to dinner at the castle. I will require a carriage. Do you suppose I could find a driver and a footman, both with particular skills?"

"Mebbe a pair who can cause a distraction, help a frail woman make her escape?"

"Maybe."

"When do you want them at your house?"

"Let us say at dusk."

"Do I get a finder's fee?"

"At least you're direct." Lisette smiled and paid her for the drink, adding a fat gold coin to the stack for her help. "Now I only have to get through the evening without being recognized."

"Oh, you got to hide in plain sight? Trina can help you wit' that." She rose and walked toward the kitchen. "Come wit' me."

Lisette followed her to the back room, beyond the food and drink, to a tiny alcove with a table, chair, and mirror. Trina motioned for her to sit, reached up to a shelf and brought several small clay pots down, along with small brushes.

"Wait." Lisette recognized the pots. "I cannot go to a count's castle all rouged up like a putain."

Trina stepped back, scowling. "Rouged up? Do I look rouged up?"

She shook her head. "You don't have anything on."

"Don't I?" Trina lowered her face. "Look closer."

What Lisette assumed was her natural beauty was a clever application of dark coloring around her eyes, and a soft pink stain on her lips. Her mouth opened a bit in wonder. "At court, we didn't use such delicacy in our makeup."

Trina chuckled. "Long time ago, the women of my island get tired of the sun. It hurt their eyes, dry their skin, make their lips chap. They weave hats but hats too hot. So, they find a plant that leave a dark stain and put it round their eyes. It protect eyes from the sun *and* make them look bigger. Then they t'ink how dry their lips, and again they look to the plants. They find one that stain light and make lips feel soft, like a baby bottom."

She took Lisette's chin in her hand and turned her face left and right. "Now, close your eyes and let's see what Trina can do here."

The brush fluttered across her left eye, making small strokes. The barmaid stopped a few times and made Lisette look at her, then had her close her eyes again so she could continue.

At last, she turned her face toward the mirror and said, "Look."

Only one of Lisette's eyes had the dark color on it. The other was still bare. Although they both belonged to her, she had two wholly different eyes. The one Trina had decorated was exotic and emphasized an almond shape, giving her the appearance of a high-cheeked, foreign woman. A woman who was not Lisette de Lille.

"Oh, my," was all she could say, before closing her eyes and turning her face back.

"This is how tis done." Trina showed her how to apply everything, until Lisette did not recognize herself. Her cheekbones were sharper, her eyes less rounded, her lips full. The stains she applied looked natural, not painted.

"Oh, Trina, this is magical." Lisette threw her arms around her for a hug.

Trina caught her left arm and turned it over. "What is this?"

"Nothing." She pulled away. "Just a tattoo. They're…they're all the style at court."

"I only meet two kinds o'women wit' tattoos." Trina was scowling now. "Women who been to prison, or worse."

She turned her arm over, unclasping her wide cuff bracelet and smiling. Hidden underneath her jewelry was a lioness head. "Crew of the *Dişi Aslan*."

Lisette hugged her a second time. "Can you contact Captain Derya?"

"Sure, it take some time, but it can be done."

Lisette pulled out one more gold coin. "I need another favor."

"Chile, you put that gold away. We are sistahs."

"Could you help me rescue another woman? If the

*Dişi Aslan* could take her away from here, it would ease my mind. Until it arrives, this coin could help hide her, feed her, give her hope."

Trina nodded and pocketed the gold. "I understand. Will my driver and footman be assisting wit' this task, or do we need more help?"

The two discussed several ideas until they arrived at a plan.

"If you don't mind me asking," Trina looked at her. "What kind o' woman lives in a castle, has a duke for an uncle, and wears the tattoo of a pirate band?"

"It's a long story." Lisette shrugged and told her tale, leaving out the dragons as usual.

Trina listened without comment. At last, she said. "And once you have your revenge, then what?"

"I haven't thought much about it. I suppose I must go back to Île des Oiseaux and reclaim the island for France."

"Mm-hmm." Trina reached for several small tins, putting dabs of her makeup in each and bundling them for Lisette. "Too bad you cannot reclaim the island for the people who live there."

As Lisette stared at her, the realization of the island's prejudiced and patriarchal hierarchy slapped her in the face. The spoiled French and Spanish nobles, living off the hard work of the natives. "Too bad I can't, Trina. I fear anything I could do would not be enough. If I cleared all the nobility off this island, the kings would both send more."

Trina smiled and stroked Lisette's hair. "I know, chile. They never stop comin'."

As Lisette returned to the front of the inn, she spotted a familiar face in the corner. The Duke de Martinmas was eating an enormous bowl a pungent fish stew. What had been so delicious a few days ago now assaulted her nose as smelling too much of the sea. A tankard sat beside him with a jug to keep it filled.

"Uncle Oscar, how nice to see you." She sat beside him and watched him take large bites, pausing to lift his napkin to his mouth. For all his good manners, he was dispatching his food with great haste. "Have you arranged for a coach tomorrow eve?"

He stared at her suspiciously, until a light suddenly appeared in his eyes. "Lisette! Why, no, I am already staying at the castle. But I suppose you cannot walk all the way, especially in the dark."

"I cannot." She narrowed her eyes. "I can arrange the coach, but you will have to arrange something else for me. All you have to do, apart from being my uncle is to arrange for me to be alone with Elena de Thibault."

"Might she give you away?"

"I am hoping that we do not have company and if we do, that she is too weak, and it is too dark to see me clearly."

He stared at her. "You may be right. Even now, you look much different from the girl I remember. If I did not recognize you, she shouldn't, either—or perhaps I've had too much rum."

"Simply keep in mind, Uncle, my name is Tempest d'Arturo. *Lady* Tempest d'Arturo."

The duke's mouth twisted into a little lopsided grin. He was correct. He'd had too much rum. She was counting on him to keep her secret—at least for a few days.

It was getting late, so she made her way back to the stone mansion. Nan met her at the door, taking her robe and clucking over her like a protective mother.

"I was worried, Mistress. You shouldn't go off by your own self."

"I'm safe, Nan, thank you. Could you take something to Genevieve?" Lisette went to the desk and pulled out paper, pen, and ink. After some hasty scribbling, she handed the note to Nan. "Can you get this to her tonight? I can send one of the men to accompany you."

"I can do all right." Slipping the paper in her pocket, she pulled her dark shawl around her and left.

Lisette headed upstairs to find a suitable dress for tomorrow night. It had to be fit for a dinner party. At last, she settled on a simple gown of wine-colored brocade. There was a bit of lacing up the front, a few ruffles on the long sleeves and the deep, square neckline was obscured by an insert of sheer material.

She strolled to the kitchen for dinner, but the food did not appeal. This morning, she had asked for a chicken in wine sauce, which the cook had prepared nicely. It smelled rich and hearty. Still, she was unmotivated to put even a taste on her tongue.

When she was a child, the family cook was native to Île des Oiseaux. She had taught Lisette to prepare certain plant leaves and spices in hot water to relieve her upset stomach. Lisette went outside and looked for the familiar leaves. Soon, she was steeping a pot of memories. With the pot and cup on a tray, she returned to her room.

She took her cup to the balcony and sat, looking at the stars. The drink soothed her as nothing else had recently. There was much to do, and it all fell upon her shoulders. A heaviness of heart and body settled upon her.

A small girl appeared next to Lisette and tugged at her sleeve, startling her.

"Where did you come from?"

She was a sturdy little thing of perhaps four, dressed in a green frock. Her dark hair hung in curls around her face and down her shoulders. She looked familiar.

"Mama, I am your daughter, Alara. I know you are

tired, but you must keep fighting. Look!" She flung her arms open, toward the sky and sparks flew from her fingertips.

Lisette's focus followed the sparks, and she watched her life play out across the night as little Alara narrated the scenes.

"This is when you were five. You wanted a new dress, so your mama had one made. It was green, like mine. And now you are twelve and are riding your horse on the beach. Mama is angry. She says sitting astride a horse will make you wanton."

As time advanced, the images became short and blurry. Genevieve was smiling. Tatie Elena was crying. Eric dissolved into ashes and Mercedes was screaming. Naïve Lisette became shrewd Tempest and then transformed into the fierce blood dragon.

The child's words were as fuzzy as the visions. "I'm not certain what happens here, except you get some of what you seek but not all of it."

At last, there was nothing but Rocco's face, looking into Lisette's eyes and smiling.

"And there's my daddy," the little girl said. "Isn't he handsome?"

The vision ended with a brilliant light, accompanied by bangs like firecrackers, and Lisette jumped from the chair. She looked around for the little girl, but she was gone.

*If she was ever there.*

Her heart pounded against her chest. She stood, taking deep breaths, trying to calm herself. The air was still and stifling. At the rail, she knelt and laid her face against the cool stone. Sweat rolled from her. After several minutes, she rose, still shaking.

*My daughter, Alara? That makes no sense—where would I get such a name?* Rocco's child. What a dream. *Or was it?* She slipped on her nightgown, recalling the

336

mornings spent with Rocco. They had not done anything to prevent a child. This was pure folly, on both their parts. Lisette's poor excuse was that as a dragon, invincibility lingered with her long after her form had changed. After all, dragons did not bear children.

*Or do we?*

Her hands trembled and ran across her stomach. In her journeys, she had grown lean and muscled. Her stomach was flat, hard, as was the rest of her body. She had not had a monthly blood flow since Rocco's feather pierced her.

It seemed impossible. She had lain with Rocco less than a week past. She could not be able to tell whether she carried a child within. Then she remembered the first night they fought as dragons, the first time they made up as humans, on Isla de la Ballena.

That was a month ago.

Lisette climbed into bed and lay atop the covers. Whether she was with child or no, the girl in her dream was correct. She must keep fighting. Tomorrow would be the first of many battles.

Morning's light was no surprise. Lisette had been staring at the darkness, waiting for the sun. She rose, washed her face, and went downstairs. There were leftover leaves and spices in a bowl, so she boiled more water and made another sachet. She took her cup outside and walked around the garden. The sweet fragrance of frangipani seeped into her head, too strong for her dragon senses—or was it the sickness that came with childbearing? She had to walk away, back toward the house.

"Mistress, what are you doing up so early?" Nan asked. Her cheeks were as red as if she'd run a race, though she was not out of breath. Her face was the only thing of color on her, ever. Her dress was brown, her hair was brown, even her eyes were the color of dust.

"I have much to think about," Lisette said. "I am going to dinner at the Medina castle tonight."

"No." Nan's barking command startled her before her voice softened. "I mean, I wouldn't. They are not nice people."

"It's all well, Nan. I will be safe." That wasn't true, but Lisette would act as if it was.

"It's only…they…" The maid stumbled so for words that Lisette grew suspicious.

"What aren't you telling me, Nan?"

Nan shook her head, lips pursed.

Lisette went to her, took her hand, and cradled her face. "You will tell me. It is safe here."

Her face burned bright, but Lisette held firm. Nan finally opened her mouth and blurted, "I overheard the delivery man talking to the cook. There is a rumor, coming from the Medina castle about who you are."

Lisette dropped her hand and stepped back. "Who do they believe me to be?"

"A servant girl who is carrying Constantine de Martinmas' child." She cocked her head. "Who am I to believe?"

Lisette smiled. "You may believe me. How did this rumor get started?"

"There was a sailor at the inn who was drinking too much. He was crying about his niece, who he sold to the duke for his son," she said. "Then one night in the tavern, there was a duke talking about a girl named Tempest. It was two plus two, m'lady."

"Ah, yes, the duke. I'm certain he was happy to throw more wood on the fire. Thank you for telling me." Lisette dismissed her and continued her pacing. What old man could have sold his daughter to the duke? She stopped mid-stride—Chunk. *L'Implacable* had docked here, and he still felt badly for handing her over to Martinmas.

She was a little more relaxed about her dinner tonight. Instead of wondering if she might be Lisette de Lille, her betrayers would be anxious to discover if she was actually the Lady Tempest d'Arturo or a mere common street girl. The Count de Medina would be the most interesting, finding out how he handled having another Tempest in his castle.

Lisette took her time preparing for the visit, first applying the kohl shadows to her eyes as Trina taught. Although she was still paler than the island women, her mirror showed a suntanned face that was no longer creamy white, but more the color of wet sand. The subtle kohl around her eyes enhanced their shape and gave a smoky quality to their green hue.

As dark as her skin had gotten, her hair had lightened. Blonde streaks ran through her auburn curls, which were now like strands of copper. Nan helped her to style it in a sleek bun with braided accents.

She put on a corset, though she barely needed one. Stepping into the gown, she looked in the mirror as Nan laced the front.

In her heart, she pictured herself as Lisette, the impulsive girl with an open, friendly face and naïve dreams. Instead, here stood a stranger—a grown woman, somber, beautiful, and possibly wicked. A woman who had taken life. Who had purposefully rid herself of her virginity. How could Eric and Mercedes recognize her?

*I don't even recognize myself.*

At the sound of hooves, Nan looked out the window.

"The coach is here." She looked out again and

turned to Lisette with wide eyes. "Mistress, I know them men that's with the carriage. They're thieves and worse."

"Yes, they are in my employ tonight. We must take care of a little business."

Lisette had prepared this gown the same as her other dresses, with a slit to allow easy access to the dagger at her thigh. She slipped Connie's ring on her finger but left her mother's emerald in its velvet bag. The ring would be her little joke on the Medinas—with luck, it would throw them off any scent about who she really was. Tonight, she would be Tempest. Going down the stairs, she greeted her drivers.

The men at the coach had done their best to clean up. They had found white breeches and dark blue coats and were somewhat bathed. The heat from the uniforms gave their faces a sheen of perspiration, but at least it helped slick their long hair back.

As she approached, they leapt to an overly upright salute. She could tell, by their missing teeth and their awkward movements, they were not used to serving the upper class.

"Trina sends her regards, m'lady," the tallest one said. "She says we're to do you a little favor."

"Yes, gentlemen." Lisette got into the carriage. "I'll explain on the way."

Two chestnut horses pulled them onto the road toward the Castle de Medina. She glanced back. Nan stood at the gate, wringing her hands. It occurred to Lisette she should be wringing hers, too, but she'd prefer to wring them around Mercedes' neck, where they could be useful.

The sun was almost in the sea when they arrived. Jack and Clay, the carriage men, had understood what she requested of them and were agreeable. They pulled up to the entrance, where Clay helped her exit the carriage before Jack drove the horses around to the side to await the signal.

Lisette stepped to the opened door. The Duke de Martinmas was there to greet her.

"Uncle, always a pleasure." She curtsied and took his arm. "Been spreading a few rumors?"

He patted her hand. "Rumors? I never."

"I've been told our hosts think I'm a servant girl." She shot a look at him. "Pregnant with Connie's child."

He blushed a glorious crimson.

"Don't worry. You did me a favor. They will not be thinking of Lisette de Lille at all." She held out her hand to him, revealing the ring. "This will certainly help confuse them."

"Yes, I saw that at the inn on Isla de la Ballena." The duke smiled. "I confess, I was troubled at first, but my boy must trust you, indeed, to give you such a present."

The pair were at the door to the great dining hall, when a low, clear voice announced them. Lisette softened her expression and steeled her heart and mind.

Smiling, she entered the snake pit.

The Duke de Martinmas had been the largest man Lisette had ever seen, until she met the Count de Medina. He was not as tall, but his girth approached incredulity. Tempest's letters told of his insatiable appetite for all things. It would seem gluttony had overtaken all other desires.

"Sire, is this your lovely niece?" The count held his hand out to her. Swallowing back her revulsion, Lisette took it.

"Yes," Martinmas said, handing her off as one would pass a roast on the table. "This is the Lady Tempest d'Arturo."

"Lady d'Arturo. Enchanted." He kissed her hand. "You must call me Juan. Please come, meet my daughter and her betrothed."

At the end of the room stood the two people she most despised. Mercedes approached first. She had not changed from that night. Her gown was blue, her dark hair pulled high, and her lips in a perpetual sneer. She examined Lisette as she walked forward, her eyes beginning at the gown and casually rising. When they reached Lisette's face, she stared for a long time. At last, she extended a limp hand.

"Lady d'Arturo, how lovely to meet you."

Afraid she or Eric would recognize her voice, Lisette lowered it to a soft rasp and prayed her choice of words would not betray her.

"Mercedes, was it?" She extended her fingers to touch hers, affecting a condescending ennui. "How delightful. Please call me Tempest."

Eric hovered in the background. He was still handsome with that same vapid smile. Lisette looked past her to him. "And you are Mercedes' betrothed?"

He took her hand and gave it a thin-lipped kiss.

"I was led to believe you two had already married. Uncle Oscar, are you telling stories again?" She patted the duke's arm, adding, "Sometimes his gossip turns into a little fib. Once, at a party, he told everyone I was a serving wench and pregnant with Connie's child. Isn't he impish?"

The group shared a polite, social laugh, but she noted Mercedes' stare. Her father was behind Eric, choking on his drink.

"When is the happy day?" Martinmas asked.

"Well—" Eric began.

Mercedes cut him off. "In less than two weeks. We are so looking forward to it. I do hope you are able to attend—and bring your lovely niece."

"It sounds most amusing," Lisette said, cocking her head and lowering her eyes like the Baroness de Thibault used to do when bored. It had the desired effect of making Mercedes' face cloud over in a brief pout.

A woman appeared in the doorway, short, robust, and over-powdered. The Count de Medina was at Lisette's side again. "Lady d'Arturo—I mean, Tempest, this is my wife, the countess."

Lisette curtsied to her. "Countess, it is my pleasure to meet you."

The countess cast a cold expression toward Lisette. "Charmed."

A bell rang and a servant walked in. "Dinner is served."

The count took Lisette's arm. "Will you do me the honor and sit by me?"

"Of course, Sire." She pasted on a genteel smile and moved toward the table.

As she took her seat, she could see the count studying her cleavage. He was openly ogling and for a moment, indignation bested Lisette's restraint. She swept her hand out to adjust her skirt and caught the tip of his goblet.

"Oh, Sire, forgive me!" She stood, gushing apologies as he mopped the red wine from his lap, a scowl on his face.

Angered at her mistake, Lisette quickly decided to beguile him for her own use. She took her napkin and dabbed at his coat, continuing to murmur regrets. Her dabbing took on a stroking quality, down his chest, to the edge of his girth, before beginning at the top again. "I am so sorry."

He went from incensed to aroused within seconds. As she dabbed, she pushed away her fear, and let her eyes draw his attention. He sat down with a small grin, fully conquered.

"I am most clumsy tonight." She sat back down and turned to her companions. "It's a good thing I'm not Tempest the serving girl, isn't it?"

The count's face went red, white, and settled on a mottled combination with an uncertain smile. The countess seemed unaffected, although her right eye twitched once.

Lisette's dear "uncle" sat back and took a hearty draught of his wine, as if waiting for the next act in the evening's entertainment. Eric leaned forward with his lips parted in a look of desire. His betrothed was rubbing the hilt on her carving knife as it lay on the table, studying Lisette's throat as she did.

Lisette wrapped her fingers around her goblet, raising it, making certain Connie's ring was visible on her finger, and fawned compliments on her two enemies. "Allow me to toast the happy couple. I wish you both the life and happiness you so richly deserve."

The hatred and suspicion on Mercedes' face turned to an interested smirk as she spied the ring. They all gave her gracious nods, Eric smiling like a large oaf.

The dinner was far richer than Lisette was used to, and the spices assailed her in a troubling way. Her stomach asked if she could leave the table and go out into the night air, but she had to refuse. Instead, she pushed the food around her plate and ate as few bites as she could manage while maintaining a lively conversation.

"Lady d'Arturo, you do not approve of our fine meal?" Mercedes asked.

Lisette narrowed her eyes in annoyance. A lady did not inquire about the appetites of her dinner companions. She smiled wanly at the count before slowly turning toward Mercedes.

"Please call me Tempest. The food is exquisite. I fear I have been too lost in conversation to worry over my meal." She returned to her plate and forced a forkful of meat between her lips.

"I hope you are not in fragile health." Mercedes

pressed on. "If you are, we have some excellent healers on this island. Unless, of course, your condition is a temporary one."

Lisette sipped her wine, deciding that no comment was best.

"Daughter, pay attention to your own plate," the count scolded. "Our delightful guest does not wish to stuff herself." He patted and rubbed Lisette's arm with his sweaty paw while she gritted her teeth. "She might have other plans."

She turned her grimace into a smile. "Perhaps."

The meal at last ended and they all rose together. Lisette pointed to the large open windows that exposed the balcony. "The breeze is so refreshing tonight. I wonder, Sire, if I might have your permission to walk in the gardens?"

She assumed he would volunteer to accompany her and that she'd have to insist on the duke's presence. To her surprise, Eric spoke first.

"I would be honored to escort you. We have many scented flowers that bloom only at night."

The count pushed his lower lip out in a pout and daggers shot from Mercedes' eyes.

"That sounds lovely." Turning to the duke, Lisette attempted to save the situation. "Uncle, would you like to come with us? As I recall, your gardens might benefit from night-blooming vines. Especially the north side."

She slipped her hand around his arm and gave him a teasing grin, offering her other hand to Eric. "Shall we?"

The night was warm, but the ocean breeze brought her the scent of fish and seaweed and freedom, aromas that leavened the cloying sweetness of night jasmine. As the path veered, she dropped both men's arms, giving the duke a small squeeze as she did.

"Uncle, do look at the way the jasmine clings to the

stone. Don't you think it would grow on the north side, where the guests' rooms are?"

His smiled glistened in the full moon. "Yes, but it might give them the idea of escaping my hospitality. I'd hate to have them leave early."

As he strolled down the path to the left, Lisette took the one that led right, close to the castle. She could hear Eric shuffling behind her, no doubt trying to decide whether to herd them in the same direction. Glancing over her shoulder, she saw him standing at the fork, his head bobbing left and right. She gestured in the direction of her own path, fanned her eyelashes at him and continued to saunter away from the duke.

Eric was by her side in two steps.

She turned to study him, letting her eyes roam from his head to his shoes. In the moonlight, she was surprised to see the blush on his neck growing up his jawline. As the golden boy, he was used to being desired.

He did attract her desire—to ruin him, humiliate him, pull his organs from his body, one at a time, and roast them on a spit before feeding them to Mercedes. She stood close, touching the outline of her dagger through the layers of petticoats. It would be possible to finish him in one stroke. Ideas for the story she'd tell played out as she stared at him—a description of the madman who leapt from the bushes and attacked, Eric's valiant struggle to save her.

A rustle in the bushes made both turn toward the sound. Lisette spied a small hand, so she clutched Eric's jacket, pulling his lips to hers. She kissed him, hard, and ran her hands down his chest, almost to his breeches. He gave a little moan. Over his shoulder, she saw Genevieve smiling and pointing to her right.

Lisette pushed Eric away and walked down the path where Genevieve had gestured. He followed, his fingers brushing at her shoulder, trying to stop her.

"I don't understand."

"I am sorry. It is something I should not do, must not do. You are engaged to Mercedes. And yet, I have felt the attraction all evening. Do you not feel it?" It took enormous effort to keep the disgust from her voice.

"Yes." He wrapped his arms around her. "You remind me of a girl I knew."

Embers of banked rage rose up and she fought to keep her voice calm. "What happened to her?"

He shrugged. "She is dead."

It was not the words, it was the way they were said, as a fact with no feeling. They had not been in love, to be sure, but it was clear to her that it didn't matter to Eric whether she lived or died. He was so near, they were alone, and she was so heated, it was nearly impossible to stay her hand. She reminded herself of her plan and vowed to stay on course.

"Eric? Tempest?" Mercedes' voice pierced the air.

"We're here." Lisette looked past Eric to answer.

"Oh, there you are. I was out for my evening walk and thought I heard you." The sweat on Mercedes' temples belied her claim to be strolling.

"Eric has been showing me your lovely gardens." Lisette took his hand and patted it. "It must look spectacular in the daylight."

Mercedes' jaw tightened. "Yes, we do love the gardens here. It will be hard to leave and live in the new castle. The de Lille family did nothing to cultivate beautiful things."

Lisette looked up at the moon, begging it to hurry and wane so she could swoop down and annihilate both of these horrid people.

"Uncle Oscar must be wondering where I am." Lisette reached out to Mercedes first, touching her shoulders lightly while she air-kissed her. Turning her attention to Eric, she gave him a longing gaze before placing a soft, lingering kiss on his cheek. "I look forward to the celebration of your nuptials."

Lisette walked further down the path, looking around for Genevieve, and hearing them argue behind her. They would still hold the wedding, still serve the mead, but the next week would be hell for poor, stupid Eric.

Genevieve stepped out, motioning toward a path. "Come with me."

Lisette nodded and followed as the maid trotted ahead, glancing left and right. They were at the east-most side of the castle when she stopped and pointed. "There she is."

A few steps above her on a balcony, a small figure slumped in a chair. Lisette tiptoed up to her, looking about for servants. There was no one else around. Tatie Elena, stricken and weak, had grown years older in the few months since she'd seen her. She had helped Lisette's enemies, had conspired against her own family, her own sister, and yet Lisette was overcome with pity.

She knelt at Elena's feet, laying her hand upon the older woman's. Elena lifted her head, wobbling upon her neck, and her eyes attempted to focus.

"Tatie, I am going to get you out of here."

The old woman's eyes grew bigger at the sound of her voice. "Lisette? Could it be? Child, I can't leave. I am so ill."

"Mercedes is poisoning you, putting it in your port.

I am here to sneak you away."

She heard voices drawing closer. The count was on the path below, while her "uncle" regaled him with useless information in a pronounced voice. True to their agreement, Uncle Oscar was attempting to distract the host from her mission. She stayed in a crouch, looking for her helpers.

A movement caught her eye—Clay, the shorter of the coachmen, being led by Genevieve. He had taken off the blue coat, wisely, to avoid detection, but there was no way for him to get her aunt out of danger while the count was below. She peeked above the railing, caught Martinmas' attention, and motioned for him to turn the count's back to her.

"Come clean, old man," Count de Medina said. "This Lady d'Arturo is not your niece."

"They are all my nieces." Martinmas chuckled, pointing to something on the other side of the path. "Little known fact. The average garden spider hangs a new web every evening. If they have not caught anything by the following dusk, they eat their own web and set a trap elsewhere."

The count had turned away from her, so she slipped down the stairs, turning toward the two men.

"Uncle, there you are. And Sire, let me say, your gardens are most fetching, even at night." She walked past the balcony steps. "Let me show you the vines that Eric pointed out. They are in this direction, I believe."

She took the count's arm and nudged him down the path and away from Tatie Elena. At the same time, her left hand signaled for Clay to get to his task. All she could do now was pray and hope God listened to a blood dragon when saving a life was on the line.

The trio examined flowers in the moonlight, the count trying to get rid of the duke, and Lisette trying to herd them both back into the castle. It took much longer than she had planned. By the time they crossed back inside, Mercedes had gone to her room with a sick headache and Eric was in the hall, drinking.

Her mission being completed, Lisette gave the two men a smile. "And now, sires, if you will excuse me, I must take my leave."

"But it is early." The count sounded disappointed. "The night is not yet done."

She squeezed the duke's arm as he helped her into her carriage. "But I'm afraid I am. I have promised to go to Mass in the morning. When you run your own household, there is always so much to do. Thank you again for your generosity this evening, Count de Medina. I look forward to seeing you again."

"Do make certain your uncle brings you to the wedding," the count said. "And call me Juan."

"It would be an honor, Juan." She flashed one more smile at him before signaling her driver.

The carriage was out of their gates, down the lane and onto the main road before the blankets in the coach stirred. Genevieve was the first to raise her head.

"M'lady, I am worried," she said. "The count will surely discover it was you who stole us away."

"He might suspect, but he will not know." Lisette turned to Jack, who was driving. "We go to Trina's."

"Trina?" Genevieve asked.

"She is a friend on this island, a friend who knows a ship to take you home. You will hide at her place until the ship comes to port."

Genevieve protested. "No, m'lady, all ships must report their passengers to the count."

Lisette shook her head. "Not all ships."

The maid looked alarmed.

"Genevieve, I would not put you in harm's way. Trust me, these sailors will take good care of you."

Lisette pushed aside the last blanket, next to her in the seat. Tatie Elena looked even more frail, half-sleeping and half-mumbling. She wrapped her arm around her. "And you, Tatie, will spend some time with me, away from those horrible people."

Elena sighed and relaxed. Lisette could feel each bone in her aunt's slender body, which worried her. Perhaps she was too late, but she had to try.

# 56

After dropping Genevieve at Trina's place, Jack and Clay drove Lisette and her new guest home. Clay was kind enough to carry the bundle of blankets containing her aunt into the castle and up to her room.

"Put her in the bed and wait here." She disappeared into her dressing area and returned with a small sack of gold coin. "This is for you and Jack."

Clay took it, felt the weight, opened the drawstrings, and peered inside. His eyes grew round and shiny.

"Ah, m'lady, this is too much. Even a thief's got his standards."

She smiled. "You and Jack risked much. I appreciate your work. And I'll appreciate it even more if no one ever hears of what you've done."

He gave a semi-toothless grin in return. "Jack'n me, we're sure grateful. You call us, anytime."

Nan skittered in as he left, giving him a sideways glance. "Are you all right? They didn't do nothing to you, did they?"

Lisette glanced up from tending to her aunt, slipped her hand into her pocket, and held out a sachet Trina had given her. "I'm unharmed, Nan. Take this and steep it in boiling water. Bring it to me, with a mug."

Nan looked past Lisette, to Tatie Elena. "Mistress! Who is that—why is she here?"

"Nan, this is my Tatie Elena. I've brought her here to save her if I can."

Nan's face showed no emotion. She curtsied and ran from the room. Lisette went back to tending her aunt, who was awake and wondering aloud where she was.

"Tatie, it's me." She stroked her hand. "Lisette."

"Lisette?" Elena opened her eyes, wide, and studied her face. "You are not my Lizzie."

"It is me. I am disguised." Lisette wrapped her arm around her. "Remember when I was five and you gave me the little red dragon to keep my coins? Remember the last time we were together at my birthday? You said to always remember you loved me."

As she said this last, her chest and neck burned with the desire to weep. Tatie had no problem—her eyes filled as she sobbed.

"Oh, Lizzie, I never meant our family harm. They told me they could save me if I did this one little thing. I was so frightened. What happened to Luc…" She trailed off and Lisette thought she had fallen asleep again, but Tatie gripped her shoulder and pulled her close, whispering with hot pungent breath, "The dragon."

She blubbered and mumbled more, but Lisette held

her to her breast and shushed her. "No more, Tatie, dear. All is forgiven."

Nan brought the broth, so Lisette propped her aunt up against several pillows. "Here, drink. This will soften the poison, I hope."

"Why were they poisoning her?" Nan was still behind Lisette, watching.

Lisette told Nan of her betrayal and kidnapping. "Eric believes he is still in line to receive the de Lille fortune. Tatie Elena is his last obstacle. Or so he thinks."

A loud banging at the front door interrupted them. Nan's face paled. "Who—?"

"That would be Count de Medina's guards," Lisette said. "Go downstairs and let them in."

Nan gave her the kind of look that said she should be locked in a madhouse, but Lisette pushed her from the room and rushed back to Tatie, working quickly to arrange her in the fine feather bed so she was entirely covered by blankets and pillows. Lisette stripped down to her silk chemise, laying her robe on the chair, before climbing in bed next to her.

A handsome young officer burst through the door, striding forward until he saw Lisette in bed. She had never seen anyone stop with such force. He nearly fell backward, catching himself on the chair. The medals on his deep red jacket clinked as he sat.

"Why, Captain, to what do I owe this surprise?" She sat up, holding the covers with a dainty motion of her hand, exposing far too much of her shoulders, with a hint of more.

"Mistress, with all due—"

"My title is Lady d'Arturo. Would you mind handing me my robe? If I'm going to receive visitors, I'd like to be more dressed."

"M'lady, the Count de Medina sent us to find someone." He stood frozen, looking at the chair.

"Yes, Captain. My robe if you please? Who is the count looking for?"

She watched him pick up the robe and turn toward her, holding it out like a hissing snake, his eyes studying the floor. When his gaze lifted to look at her, she dropped the covers and stood, hand out, waiting for him to come closer.

"Um, the count." His voice jumped an octave. "The count is looking for Elena de Thibault."

She brushed his hand as she took the robe and fastened it about herself, button by button, in slow motion. "Elena? Was I introduced to her this evening?"

"I do not know, m'lady. She was staying with the count. After you left, she was missing."

"I'm sorry. Was she a guest at the Medina Castle?"

He blushed. "Yes."

"Are guests not permitted to leave?"

His blush turned burgundy. "Of course, they are, m'lady."

"Perhaps she took a walk. I often walk at night." Lisette moved closer to him. He was lovely—tall and dark-haired, with a trim mustache.

"I do not think this lady was capable."

She knit her brows in worry and gazed up at his face, leaning into him, touching his uniform sleeve lightly. "Oh, dear. Is she ill? Should we send men to search through the brush?"

"The count thought perhaps she had left in your carriage." His blush brightened and his voice deepened.

"What would I be doing with a stranger in my carriage? Did he send you here to look for her?" She beamed. "You are a handsome man, Captain. I would gladly send my thanks to the count if he sent you here to search me."

His posture was still rigid, but his hands were on

hers. He whispered, "I don't need to look any further."

She raised her hand to touch his face when the sound of boots clomped up the stone steps. The officer jumped away as if she'd bitten him.

"Captain Dantes, we've searched the rooms." A short, swarthy guard appeared at the door. "Every room except this one."

Captain Dantes gave her one last, longing gaze. "This room is clean as well."

Lisette curtsied.

"Farewell, m'lady. Sorry to have intruded." He turned on his heel, sharp, and left the room, along with his compatriot.

She collapsed into the chair and sighed. The sounds of women yelling, cursing, came from downstairs. Nan and Babette, the cook, were arguing, either with themselves or with someone else. Lisette grabbed her dagger and ran down.

Clay and Jack were in the kitchen, sampling Babs' fine cooking. When Lisette entered, they pulled their fingers out of the pots and stood at their version of attention.

"What are you gentlemen doing?"

"Pardon, m'lady," Jack said. "We thought we'd give them fopdoodles a chance to look through the carriage. Meantimes, we're a mite hungry."

"Yes, of course." She smiled at the cook. "Please, Babs, can you get them a plate of something? They did a grand job for me."

The scowl remained on her face, but she shrugged. "For you, m'lady."

Lisette returned upstairs, to find her aunt sitting up, supported by many pillows. Rocco sat at the edge of the bed, holding her hand.

"Quite the performance for the count's errand boy," he said.

"Exactly how long have you been here?"

"As long as you." He stood and wandered about the bedroom. "I followed you here."

"From the castle?"

"Well…from Trina's. But yes, first, from the castle."

She picked up Tatie's cup of grog and warmed it with more from the kettle. "So, you followed me, all evening. Why?"

"To keep you from doing anything foolish." He strode over, stopping when they were toe to toe. She refused to step back. "Be warned, Lisette. You will keep your hands off—and dagger out—of Count de Medina.

He is mine."

Her mouth fell open a bit. "Don't be foolish. Why would I want to off that rutting goat? Unless, of course, he tries what he should not with me."

"Even then. He is not for you to slaughter."

She sat the grog on the table. "And Mercedes?"

"She must be dealt with according to your curse." Angry crescents glowed in his eyes. "If you survive to accomplish your goal."

"If I survive?" The rage in her own eyes shone in response. "You still plan to kill me?"

Their bodies were close without touching, a wall of heat building around the two. She took the dagger from her pocket and held it out to him, hilt first.

"Here," she whispered. "My blade is sharp. One slice and I will be out of your life."

He wrapped his hand around hers, eased the dagger from her grip and held it aloft. She prepared for her last breath, hoping it would not be so. His lips parted and the blade in his hand glimmered as he brought it to her neck. She tilted her head, exposing bare flesh, a throbbing pulse to pierce. He blinked once and sighed.

She heard the clank of metal on the table. Arms embraced her. His mouth found hers, pushed past her lips. Mouths, lips, tongues searched one another's again and again, always wanting more.

Her robe and chemise were so thin, she sensed every nuance of his body's desire. Her own body was in complete agreement. The fog of her lust parted enough to remember Tatie Elena lying in her bed.

Not only in her bed but possibly dying from whatever Mercedes had been using to poison her. Placing her hands on his chest Lisette managed to break the spell.

"I have to attend to my aunt—"

He placed his fingers on her lips. "Let her die, after what she did to you."

She shook her head. "At the end of all my hatred, the fact remains she is my family, my mother's sister. My mother is dead. Tatie Elena is my connection to her."

"If you cannot break the curse…" He pointed to the frail figure. "That is why."

"Surely you understand. You, too, have a connection to someone you loved. Someone you still love."

"True, Mercedes has made it all…complicated." He pulled away from her and moved to the window. "The wedding is next week. The first night of the waning. I will see you then and we will decide what is important to us."

She watched him crawl through the window and disappear. A groan from the bed brought her back to the moment.

"I'm sorry, Tatie." She gathered the cup and returned to her duties. Wrapping her arm around Elena's shoulders, she steadied her frail body while holding the cup to her lips. Elena held her hands up but could not raise them enough to cradle the cup while she drank. Tiny sips were all she could manage.

"This doesn't taste good." She made a face in between sips. "Where's my port?"

"Port cannot help you." Lisette tried to reason with her. "You have poison in your body. This is your best chance for getting it out."

"Poison? How would I be poisoned?" She pushed at the mug, to get it away from her mouth, but she was too weak.

"Mercedes. She believes I am dead, and you are the last person to stand between her and my father's money."

"That horrid wench." She sipped a little more, grimacing. "This tastes awful. Can't you hide it in some port?"

She kept complaining, kept asking for port. Lisette tried to understand although it grew tiresome.

"Tatie, just drink this down and I promise, I'll get you port." There were two sips left in her cup, so Lisette called for Nan. "Could you bring my aunt a glass of port?"

Turning away from Tatie, she motioned with her fingers to indicate a small amount. She turned back to help her with the last of the elixir when Elena grabbed her shoulders, sinking her yellow nails into Lisette's skin.

"You must believe me, Lizzie, I didn't want any harm to come to you." Her voice was an attempted shout although Lisette still had to lean in to hear her. "But they promised money and I've had none since Luc died. It's not my fault. My sister always got the best of everything."

"Mama loved you. Mama made certain we all loved you."

"Love. Pfft. She could afford to love me. She had a handsome husband, a duke no less, with a lot of riches. She had children." Her face twisted from a pinched, painful look to a sneer. "I had an ugly little baron who could not give me babies and spent all his gold on that awful mother of his."

Lisette tried to ignore her ramblings. "Let's just get you well."

"I'm sorry I helped them sell you, Lizzie, but I always knew you would survive. You've always been the chosen one, so adored." Jealousy oozed through her words.

"How much did they pay you for your help?"

"Fifty ducats."

"Pity, when Mercedes and Eric made five hundred."

"Yes, and I told them, too!" She missed the scorn in Lisette's voice. "They had to give me much more when I hid the letter."

"The letter?"

"Your father was a stupid man. Wrote to King Louis to warn him of what was happening on the island." She looked out the window and smirked. "I promised to take it to the ship."

Lisette's heart hardened. "What was never sent could never arrive."

"Precisely."

"Leaving my father open to a hunting accident."

Tatie shrugged. "Accidents do happen."

"And my mother to die from heartbreak."

She touched Lisette's cheek. "Oh, Child, don't be angry. Your mother was so sad. I made certain she didn't suffer."

"What?" Lisette stood, pushing her aunt away. "You—killed—my mother? Your own sister?"

Tatie at last became aware of the fire and ash in Lisette's voice. Her eyes widened, mouth gaped. "You—your eyes look like the dragon did that night."

"You saw him, when he killed Uncle Luc?"

She nodded.

"You saw him come to me?"

Another nod.

"Why didn't you try to save me?"

She scowled at her. "What was the use? I was too weak and afraid. Besides, your mother was expecting again—she would have another child to take your place."

Lisette launched the mug, smashing it into rubble against the wall. There was not much else to toss from her place on the bed, so she picked up a pillow to hurl. She could hear her aunt, crying and whining her excuses for being weak and petty and jealous and greedy. The pillow found a much better use as Lisette closed it over her aunt's mouth and nose and pressed.

Footsteps at the door brought Lisette to her senses and she pulled the pillow away. Elena gasped, gulping air like a fish on the shore, large eyes staring at Lisette in terror. Lisette staggered across the room away from her and what she had almost done. The dragon could kill with impunity but not Lisette de Lille. She was very human when she was smothering her mother's sister.

Nan entered with the drink. Lisette did not turn around but gestured to the bedside table. "Thank you. Leave it."

"I'm sorry, m'lady. I guess the poison done its work."

Lisette turned and rushed to where Nan was standing, focused on the figure in the bed. Tatie Elena lay motionless. She was smiling and her face looked carefree.

"No—she was breathing!" Lisette stared at her aunt, shaking her head. "She was coughing, gasping, but she was breathing!"

"I'm sure, m'lady," Nan said. "You tried, but it was already too late."

Lisette continued to stare and shake her head in denial until she became aware of the silence and Nan's presence. Taking a deep breath, she closed her eyes and calmed herself.

"You're right, Nan." Lisette picked the port from the table, her hands shaking, and pointed it toward her aunt. "Godspeed to you, Elena de Thibault on behalf of a woman whose soul is departing and who cannot speak."

"Amen." Nan bowed her head and crossed herself.

Swallowing the drink, Lisette turned to Nan. "I suppose the count also controls the priest on this island."

"Sadly, yes."

"My aunt requires a proper and sacred burial, but if the Medina family discovers she is dead, they will help themselves to my fortune." Lisette paced around the room. "Have any ideas?"

"One, m'lady. I noticed, in my daily walks, at the back of this land is a family plot. It is not a sin for a noble family to hold their own services. Back in my homeland of France, a priest was not always available. The master of the house often had to bury the dead."

"And if there was no master?"

She shrugged. "The mistress of the house, of course."

Lisette bowed her head. Burial in the family plot was fine, but she worried about the rituals. There had been no one to administer the last rites. At this point, would it hurt Elena's immortal soul to be buried in an intimate cemetery by a close family member?

Even if that member was doomed to the fires of Hell and had possibly hastened her death?

# 58

"Are Jack and Clay still here?" Lisette asked. "I need one more job done."

The building of a casket and the digging of a grave could not be done overnight. In the meantime, she laid her aunt in the adjacent room, surrounded by candles, flowers, and incense, with a cross on her chest. Lisette prayed no one detected what they were doing.

She also prayed Tatie would forgive her for trying to smother her.

While Jack and Clay worked, she walked to the port village, stopping for a meal at the inn. As she exchanged pleasantries with Trina, she observed a new woman serving tables. Her eyes were dark, her skin tawny, and she wore a wrapped outfit in a bright color, like Trina. There was no way anyone on this island would recognize her as Genevieve.

One of Trina's customers bellowed about ale and why he didn't have any.

"You sit yourself down." Trina wagged her finger at him. "You know there was no ale on the ship what just come in. It will come wit' the next ship and the next ship comes wit'in two days, I hear. *All* the ships come wit'in two days, for the wedding."

She shot Lisette a look of intention and Lisette understood. The *Dişi Aslan* was on its way and would be here within a couple of days. Lisette was relieved, although she would not relax until Genevieve was on that ship, safe.

The weight on her heart wouldn't lift, however. When the gravesite was ready, she would be expected to deliver Tatie to her final rest. Even if she hadn't done the final deed, she had hastened it, if only by wishing it so.

"Lady Tempest, please join me." The Duke de Martinmas called across the room, so Lisette strolled to his table. There was a familiar face sitting next to him.

"It's good to see you again, Connie." She curtsied and smiled before sitting. "I thought your friend the count was coming with you?"

"Unfortunately, he had things to attend to at home. His brother was murdered." Connie shrugged. "It was quite lurid, and he has had to work to keep the village from holding him somehow accountable."

"Constantine." The duke shushed him. "We do not speak of such things. Not here."

"What brings you to Isla del Largarto?" Connie asked. "I am so glad you are no longer locked in Father's tower."

"Uncle Oscar has been showing me around to all of the desirable people on this island." Lisette touched the duke's arm. "I have been most grateful for my uncle's help."

A few beads of sweat rose on the duke's brow so she leaned in and lowered her voice. "Do not worry, Uncle. I will swear you never did anything unlawful."

Connie patted his father's back. "I'm proud of you."

Genevieve served their food and drink. Lisette did her best to treat her as another island worker. The duke did not find her interesting and Lisette was glad. Two more days.

"Should I arrange for a carriage to the wedding, m'lady?" The duke asked.

"Thank you, but I've procured a beautiful team of chestnut mares recently." She remembered what Nan had told her about the local priest. "Uncle, you've been staying with the count. Is his family involved with the Church?"

"If by 'Church' you mean 'the only altar and confessional on the island,' and by 'involved' you mean 'order the priest to your house and make him give you a cut of his tithes,' yes, they are."

"Then, if you will excuse me, good sirs." She rose and curtsied again. "I have the urge to pray."

The church sat at the end of the village, on the highest bluff, a picturesque safe haven for the residents when hurricanes blew through. Pulling her shawl over her hair, she walked up the steps and into the sanctuary, trying to ignore the cold shadow that crossed her shoulders as she did so. She knew what she was—a demon entering hallowed ground.

A figure in white stood at the altar, his back to her. He was hunched over, as an old man would stand. She looked down the aisle and hesitated. Approaching the cross directly seemed blasphemous, so she moved along the right wall, stopping twice on the way to genuflect in case one of them didn't take.

The priest did not acknowledge her until she was

almost at the altar beside him. He stood up straight and faced her. That's when she discovered he had been bent over to tend to the many candles in front. He was tall and quite a young man.

"Can I help you?" he asked. "I am Father Felix."

Her words stuck in her throat. Lying to a priest was almost as bad as being a dragon. "Hello, Father, my name is Tempest d'Arturo and I am—temporarily—on this island."

"Yes, I have heard of you." He gave her a faint smile. "I've been waiting for you to visit us."

She blushed, realizing her mistake. It would be awkward, at the least, and presumptuous at the most, to ask for a favor without explaining and atoning for her absence from the church. Asking him to hear her confession was out of the question. There was entirely too much to confess.

"My apologies, Father. I have no excuse, except that I…" Anything she told him might get back to the count. She sighed. "I knew if I came to church, I would have to go to confession and my sins are so complicated, I am afraid to speak their names, even to myself."

She turned to go. This would not be possible.

"Wait," he said. "I would like to talk to you. It is a brave soul who confesses their fear. Come, sit. We will simply talk."

She sat in the front pew, and he sat beside her, legs crossed, body leaning forward, encouraging.

"I believe there is a burden on your heart. Tell me what is troubling you." His words made her want to blurt out everything she had ever done and possibly a few things she'd only dreamed of doing. She contained herself.

"The Count de Medina is a powerful man." She began with caution. "I have observed that nothing happens on this island without his knowledge."

370

"It is true."

"But he does not seem to me to be a kind or benevolent ruler." She watched his face. "I do not perceive God in his heart."

Father Felix sat for a moment, staring at the tile floor. "I would like to tell you that you are wrong, but I cannot."

"I have heard a rumor, Father. A bad rumor, that the count takes the Church's tithes, takes God's money for himself."

He shifted in his seat, looking uncomfortable. "Well, Child, he says that as he provides the land and the building, he is entitled to the profits."

"Do you believe that?"

More shifting, more staring down at the tile. "No. God's house is not meant to make money for its landlord."

"So, if I gave you this—" She held out a gold coin. "You would have to give a large percentage of it to the count?"

He took it and examined it, turning it over and over, the sunlight catching and mirroring its warmth. Sighing, he handed it back. "It would do so much good. So much. But, yes, the count would require at least half of its value."

"And if I requested the services of the island priest to perform a sacred ritual, the count would have to know about it."

He shook his head. "Sadly, yes."

She could sense a ray of light, more than the one reflecting from the coin. "What do you need, Father, more than anything?"

He stared at her for a long moment before rising and pointing toward a door. "Come with me."

She followed him outside to a walled area behind

the church. They entered the gate and stood among the remnants of a large garden with a simple barn in the corner.

"This was our garden. We grew vegetables. We had chickens to supply us with eggs. My housekeeper and I could live all year on the food from this plot of land without burdening the parish. We had extra to share with the community."

"What happened?"

"The count happened. When he moved here, he demanded things. First, he took the horse I used to plow this ground. Next, my chickens. Last, my cow. Soon, I had nothing to grow, which didn't matter, because there was nothing to grow it with." He gestured. "So now, this land lies useless, and we buy from the count. Sometimes I believe we are buying our own eggs back."

"If I gave you coins, you'd have to give them to the count. But if I gave you a horse, and a cow and some chickens…?"

He beamed. "You would see the most grateful priest on any island."

"Until the count took them away again." She stared at him.

"God has bade me to be good, but He has not bade me to be stupid. At least, not stupid twice. The count would have to find out about them first."

"Does he not come to Mass?"

The priest smiled. "We do not have the pleasure of his company. It seems the hill we are on is simply too much effort for him to walk up and there is no path wide enough for his carriage."

The following morning, a tall, quiet man came to Lisette's home. She met him in the back of the castle in front of a large hole and a wooden box. There was a small conversation, although he did most of the talking.

As Jack and Clay lowered Tatie Elena into the

ground, Lisette wondered how her aunt's death would affect her blood dragon curse. Elena was by far not the worst of her quarry, but she had helped Mercedes and Eric out of a small and petty heart. As everyone walked from the gravesite, Lisette decided it was too soon to tell.

As for Father Felix, she offered him lunch and by the time he left, he had a sturdy horse pulling a cart full of chickens, and a cow following behind. It was a fair exchange for her aunt's Catholic burial.

# 59

Lisette awoke late with a sour stomach, her normal pattern since the night she dreamed of having a daughter. Each morning, she ran her hand over her abdomen, wondering if it was her dread, or if it felt bigger. Most days, she laughed it off and made herself a hot drink with an herbal sachet.

Today, she took off her clothes and looked at herself in the mirror. She was still muscular, still slender. Her stomach was taut, no detectable bump. At least her breasts were still large enough to fill a dress. It was not the rounded body she grew up with, nor had she taken on her mother's curves. It was a body meant for working, for fighting, for turning itself inside out as woman, then dragon, then back again.

She had not dreamed of the young girl in several nights. Shaking her head, she put her clothes back on.

"You have become a silly woman," she told herself as she went downstairs.

Nan had fixed her herbal drink, plus bread with some dried meat. The maid fluttered and fussed around where she sat at the table, looking over her shoulder and clucking like a mother hen.

"Why are you so worried?" Lisette asked her. "Stop fussing."

"I don't mean to be, m'lady—one more, small bite of the meat, please? You've been so out of sorts these past days, and you toss and moan so in your sleep. You're not rested. You're not happy."

"Don't be a goose, Nan. I'm sleeping quite well. If I am out of sorts, it is because I am anxious to make a good impression at the wedding." Lisette regarded her maid, whose face wore a map of worries in its lines. "I toss and moan, do I?"

"Yes, m'lady." Nan bowed her head.

"Do I moan anything understandable?"

"You keep asking Alara where her father is."

Lisette's stomach rolled over and she pushed away from the table. She had been dreaming of the child. She simply hadn't been remembering it.

"Nan, come here and sit down. There are a few things for you to know." She gestured to the chair beside hers. "You know that my name is Lisette de Lille, and that Eric and Mercedes are my enemies. Tonight, I avenge my family."

Lisette held her hands, gently. "I do not know what happens to me after tonight if I even survive. In any case, I may not be on this island tomorrow. I have set aside plenty of gold for you and Babs, enough to last your lifetimes. Share it with Jack and Clay if you can be generous. And understand how grateful I am for everything you've done for me."

Tears rose in Nan's eyes, so Lisette stood. "No

tears. Let's get ready for a wedding, shall we?"

As Nan drew her bath, Lisette looked out the window. Clay was hard at work, washing the horses. A few feet from him, Jack polished the tack and wiped the mud from the carriage wheels. At least she would arrive in style.

She entered the bath water, scented with flower petals, and sank down for a few moments, enjoying the lightness of her body. She recalled that afternoon on Île des Anciens and considered trying to pleasure herself for relaxation but knew she would not be at ease until her task was complete. The soap was within reach, so she scrubbed herself clean. Nan returned and scrubbed her back.

Next, the maid helped to wash her hair, pouring the water over while Lisette rubbed the soap through, until it was clean. Nan brought the sheet to dry her, and Lisette stepped from the tub. The maid's eyes widened.

"Is there something wrong?" Lisette asked.

"No, m'lady, I just—" She bundled Lisette up and stood back. "It's nothing. When you rose from the tub, you looked much like my former mistress did when she was newly with child. But that is of course untrue."

Lisette looked down at the sheet covering her body. "Of course."

As Lisette prepared for the evening Nan stayed close to her, tidying her chambers, and shouting at the cook to bring more tea. At one point, Lisette worried that her maid would snap in two. She distracted Nan by having her braid and arrange her hair in its old intricate style.

"Another curl, to the right," Lisette directed. "The tiny braid above it and the comb."

Nan fastened a small pearl-encrusted comb Trina had procured. Lisette wasn't able to duplicate the exact brocade on her gold gown, but she got close. She slipped into her chemise and strapped her dagger to her thigh.

"M'lady?" Nan walked in, holding the many yards of golden brocade.

Lisette stepped into the gown and stretched tall while Nan hooked the tiny buttons up the back. The gown fit loosely, unlike the last time she tried it on. Nan looked at her, tears forming.

"Now, none of that." Lisette turned away to undress again. "Here, I shall wear my robe underneath. What more can you do with a needle and thread?"

It took a little time, but Nan was able to alter the waist, and Lisette stepped back into her gown, now padded with her robe, and refastened it. There was one last thing to do. She held up the chain with her emerald and watched it twirl in the light. The jewel shone as deep and brilliant as that night—the last night she saw her family.

Tonight, there would be no island stains on her eyes or lips to disguise who she was. She regarded herself in the mirror, trying to get accustomed to who she had become. Eric and Mercedes had brought death to her family, but it was the woman in the mirror who had killed Lisette.

Putting the emerald in her pocket, she swallowed down the pain in her chest from the tears she couldn't cry before turning to hug Nan.

"Stay well, Nan. If I can ever help you, I shall." Lisette gave her a slip of paper. "These are instructions for where to find the gold."

Nan stood tall, her eyes red and glassy, as she opened the door. Once Lisette had stepped into the carriage, the maid put her hands to her face, sobbing.

The party had begun much earlier in the day, but any lady worth her title arrived late and it would not have suited Lisette's plans to be there too much before dusk. That's when the real excitement would begin.

Clay helped her out of the carriage one last time.

"Jack, you and Clay may take the horses home. I will be finding my own way back tonight."

Jack gave her a curious look. "Yer certain, m'lady?"

She gave him her most regal smile. "You and Clay have performed most excellently in whatever task I assigned."

The door to the castle was open so she stepped inside, attempting her mother's stately glide.

"Lady Tempest d'Arturo," the servant announced.

She smiled. Lady Tempest d'Arturo was invited to the party, but Lisette de Lille would be attending in her place.

# 60

The Duke de Martinmas approached her, held out his hand, and escorted her to the party.

"You look wonderful, m'lady," he whispered. "As a matter of fact, you look like a young woman I once knew."

"Thank you," she replied. "But that woman is no more."

The pair entered the great hall, which nearly made Lisette swoon at its resemblance to her castle on her own celebratory evening. Candles, crystal beads, and mirrors whirled sparkles of light everywhere while guests danced and drank, and music played. Someone handed her a goblet. Mead.

It was almost too much to bear, and she leaned on the duke's arm for a moment.

"M'lady, is something wrong?"

"Not at all, Uncle. I am overcome by the spectacle."

His lips were suddenly at her ear. "How can I help you, Lisette?"

She took a breath and steeled her heart. "Take me to Eric and Mercedes. I must congratulate the happy couple."

He gave her a tiny bow and led her to the dancers. As if reliving a memory, Eric stepped toward her from the group, his face flushed and smiling. His expression moved from happiness, to confusion, to surprise, to fear.

She curtsied and extended her hand. "M'lord, I am pleased to be here."

"Eric, you remember Tempest?" the duke asked.

"Y-y-yes." With a ridiculous grin splitting his face, he touched her fingers before pulling back as if burned. "Forgive me, but you look so different this evening. You look like—you look familiar."

"Do I?" she said. "This late season mead is delightful. Have you had some?"

"No, I'm afraid I've been too busy dancing. The music…" His voice rang and he ended with a hysterical laugh.

Mercedes appeared out of the crowd, her body swaying to the music, her alabaster gown sparkling in the waning daylight. Her face, much like Eric's, went through a litany of emotions before settling on her usual haughty stare.

"Lady Mercedes, you look lovely." Lisette hugged Mercedes and felt her shiver. "Getting married agrees with you. That gown is stunning."

"Thank you." Mercedes kept her refrain short, her eyes narrow.

"I should like very much to have one dance with

the groom," Lisette said, holding her hand to Eric. She lifted her goblet. "Mercedes, would you watch my mead for me?"

The duke intercepted the goblet and set it upon a nearby table. "M'lady, before Eric has the pleasure, would you grant your old uncle one brief turn around the dance floor?"

"Of course." Lisette hid her petulance and smiled at Eric. "Afterward, then?"

Eric nodded, still grinning like a fool. As she strolled away with the duke, she glanced back at the pair who were in frantic conversation as they stared at her. When their eyes met hers, they stopped talking and smiled. She smiled in return.

The duke bowed and Lisette curtsied before stepping to the music. He gave her a doting grin.

"What are you doing?" His voice was low as they passed one another.

"I am dancing with you, Uncle, dear. And after, I shall dance with the groom. It is good manners."

After one more circle and return, he said. "Little known fact—I was one of the guests at your last birthday party when you were supposed to be betrothed to Eric. Has it been over a year since?"

She scowled. "And you're telling me now?"

The pair bowed again and stepped forward. "I like my little secrets. They come in handy."

"Well, this one will do you no good." She considered what kind of interference he could be. "I suppose you think you will stop me from making a public display."

They circled, their backs to each other. "I do have a reputation to protect."

"Do not fear. I do not intend to—embarrass— anyone."

"I wish I could be sure." He stepped ahead of her and turned. "You have spent time among pirates. Are you planning violence?"

She looked up at him, coldness in her eyes. "The path I am on leads to a single end. I cannot change it."

"Lizzie," he whispered. "Don't—"

The music stopped and they bowed again. She stepped up, lifting her face toward his. "One more thing, Uncle. When the sun goes down, leave this place, and take Connie with you. I fear it will not be safe."

He stared at her for a long breath before his eyes widened with understanding. When he spoke, his voice quivered. "Little known fact—blood dragons generally do not hunt at large gatherings."

She stared back. "This one does."

His hand trembled as he took hers and they strolled toward Eric who stood waiting. Lisette wondered if the duke might try to stop her from what she was about to do. She was not exactly fond of the man, but she'd grown quite used to his presence and his occasional bursts of helpfulness. It would be a shame to have to kill him.

"I believe you will find m'lady an excellent dancer," he told her ex-fiancé before turning to her with a slight nod. "I serve at your pleasure."

A calmer Eric led Lisette onto the dance floor. As on that night long ago, they began with a formal bow and curtsy, pacing along with the music, back and forth, shoulder to shoulder, around one another. He was a bolder dancer than she recalled, taking a firm lead as they moved together. His ridiculous grin had subsided to a wry smile.

"This is a wonderful wedding party, Eric," she said as they danced.

"Thank you, Lady *d'Arturo*." He emphasized her name.

She let her voice purr. "I so enjoyed our evening in the garden. Are you and Mercedes still planning to live in the de Lille castle?"

"Yes, I—we will be ruling Île des Oiseaux. I will be Count d'Auguste." His chest puffed out as he said the words, his nose tipped up.

"Île des Oiseaux is such a sleepy little island. Do you and Lady Mercedes plan to be benevolent, or will your peasants take an iron hand to rule?"

"We do not intend to be unkind, but the island has so much to offer. I should like to utilize all of its wealth."

Lisette's father and Eric's had ruled jointly and gently, taking a small percentage of what the people earned, and paying for things like maintaining the pier. It sounded as if Eric was going to take a bigger piece of the pie and give less to the people of the village.

"Île des Oiseaux...was it not ruled by two other nobles?" She kept her voice curious and innocent. "Your father was one, I believe?"

"Yes, my father will still share the rule with me. The duke was killed. Hunting accident. Sadly, none of his family survived."

"None of his family? Not even the daughter—what was her name?" She stared at him, daring him to say it.

His face paled and he looked away. "Lisette."

The song ended and Lisette was glad. It had been a long journey to this point, and she was ready to complete her task. He led her away, toward the table laden with food and drink. As before, Mercedes was there, holding a goblet. She thrust it at Lisette, a little too greedily this time.

"Dancing can be so tiring. I thought you might refresh yourself."

The poison stunk like something putrid, but Lisette took it, holding it from her nose.

"Shall we take a walk?" She turned to Eric. "On the balcony? In the cool evening air?"

His hand at Lisette's back shook as he escorted her outside. She made a show of putting the goblet to her lips a few times to observe Mercedes' reaction. Each time she brought it down without drinking, a small pout formed on the bride's face.

They walked to a stone bench as before, but Lisette was not the one wobbling this time. If anything, Eric was swaying erratically as if drunk. Or a man giddy with fear and excitement.

She put the goblet to her lips one last time, holding her breath so she would not have to smell it. Eric and Mercedes leaned forward, smiling, waiting. She lowered the cup and strolled toward Mercedes. As Mercedes had done that night, Lisette picked up the stone hanging at Mercedes' throat and examined it.

"A diamond. How exquisite." She reached into her

own pocket. "Although, I do prefer my emerald. It's a gift from my father, you know."

Opening her fist, she revealed her necklace. "I fear I didn't have time to put it on before I arrived."

"It is you," Mercedes said. "Eric didn't want to believe it."

"By the way, Mercedes, Viscount Barragan sends his regards." She looked down at her necklace and back at her. "Or he would, if I had left him alive."

That's when Mercedes' face paled, and her body trembled. Eric still appeared to be in a daze, so Lisette turned her attentions to him.

"Sorry, Eric, but it appears you will not be getting the de Lille fortune any time soon. At least, not while there's breath in my body." She tossed the goblet and its contents into the shrubs beyond the balcony.

At last, he found his lost voice. "Lisette?"

"Surprised?"

Soft steps were sneaking up behind her.

"You should have had that drink," Mercedes said as Lisette turned. She had a small dagger in her hand and was lunging toward her.

Lisette scrambled out of her way and brought her skirt up, extracting her own blade. "Funny, that's what I told Barragan after I slit his throat."

Mercedes lunged again and again as Lisette feinted, fell back, and circled her. The sun was sinking but not fast enough. Lisette would have to engage her in battle, at least for a while. As Mercedes circled, Lisette slit the front of her gown and dropped it to the stone floor, stepping away in her black robe.

"I like to be unencumbered when in a knife fight," she said.

Mercedes looked confused but came in swinging. Lisette blocked her arm and swept her dagger underneath, giving her a deep scratch across her ribs. Mercedes fell back, a trickle of blood seeping from her gown.

Lisette worried that she would have to dispose of Mercedes while she was still human. Mercedes spent a moment touching her wound and whining, then glowered at Lisette, pointed her weapon, and charged.

Lisette easily stepped out of her way, raised a foot, and kicked her to the ground. Mercedes sprawled on the stone of the balcony, groaning. Lisette leaned forward and grabbed her hair, planning to pull her head back and score her throat with the blade.

Instead, a strong hand seized her arm and spun her about. Lisette's eyes met Rocco's and she froze. She felt a sting under her rib cage and a fire in her side.

"You cannot kill her, Lizzie." His voice was a snarl, but his tormented soul shone through his eyes.

Lisette looked down, to where his dagger was buried in her. A small droplet of blood was easing down her robe, followed by another, and another.

"No." It was a whisper from her lips, a prayer begging denial, asking that this not be happening. Her knees weakened and her body surrendered to the ground as she watched Eric and Mercedes run back toward the castle. They turned at the arch to stare at her.

Rocco cradled Lisette in his arms. "She may not be my blood, but she is Tempest's daughter."

Over his shoulder, the last rays of the sun were hitting the crest of the hilltop. A familiar burning settled in her chest, and she hoped her dragon form was less fragile than her human one. She moved his hand to her stomach.

"Here is your daughter. Her name is Alara."

His open-mouthed, wide-eyed expression was the last thing Lisette saw before she felt her body shifting, and the popping pain of change. She had never been with him during their change into dragons. It felt intimate—more intimate than their lovemaking.

Changed, she remained prone, watching the red dragon leap into the great room.

The sounds of chaos were immediate. There were screams from the people and furniture being tossed. The large windows framed flashes of the flames he spit as he flew about the hall.

Glancing down, she studied her wound. Rocco had left the dagger in her side. She reached with her claws to remove it, but they were too large to grasp the hilt and pull.

The pain was manageable, so she got to her feet. The wound had not bled much, because of the dagger still in it. She could still hunt down Mercedes and Eric. Spreading her wings, she sailed into the castle to end this.

Rocco had sent most of the guests screaming away. A few remained, curled into balls and weeping. Some were praying, begging for their lives. Some were motionless, perhaps dead. The obese count was running amok, zigzagging around, and shrieking like a girl. Rocco chased after him, grabbing at his girth and missing. He scooped up a young man by mistake and dashed him to the ground. The man groaned and lay still.

Lisette spied the duke and Connie crouching behind the staircase. An open door was behind them, so she wasn't certain why they were still there. If the count ran near them, Rocco might accidentally pick them up instead.

She flew to the two men, realizing there was no possible way to reveal herself. They crouched down further, flattening themselves against the stone floor. She had to make them run outside to safety. Landing, she placed her talon on the duke's back. He squealed and tried to shift away from her, so she wrapped her claw around his arm and pulled him to an upright position.

Staring up at her, he opened his mouth to scream, but stopped when she cocked her head and looked at him.

"Lisette?" he asked.

She bowed.

"What?" Connie had crawled to his father and sat up. "That's Lisette?"

"What can we do for you?" the duke asked.

Turning toward the door's arch, she spit fire, and turned back to them. They stood and ran toward the door, stopping to look at her. She bowed again, so they ran on. At the door, the duke stopped and wavered.

"I don't know—" He shook his head.

"Come, Father, show the courage that you exhibit in all your portraits." Connie bowed and dragged his father away. "We shall distract the guard, m'lady."

# 62

Whipping back to the scene of the commotion, she spotted Rocco still trying to get his talons around the count. She was impressed with the fat man's speed and agility. He was also using his guests as shields. He had dragged a young woman to her feet and was holding her out in front of Rocco. Her cries were shrill, heartbreaking, and she held her hands to her face. Tears were running through her fingers.

Lisette was behind the pair, watching Rocco parry with the count, attempting to grab him and leave the girl.

"You can't have me," the count was saying. "I've evaded you for too long, I'm too smart by far."

He stopped speaking when her talons closed around his legs. She lifted him as she rose toward the ceiling, turning him toward her so he could see her more clearly. His terrified shriek had become a yip, like someone stepped upon a small dog. A stain spread across the front of his jacket—he appeared to be wetting himself, an awkward thing to do when upside-down.

Rocco roared at her, charging, his claws out. Lisette held the count toward him—a peace offering among dragons. His talons reached around the count's girth but couldn't hold him without piercing his sides. The count now howled with pain, clutching at where the claws were embedded, attempting to remove them.

She released the punctured count and turned her head. The familiar scent of her former fiancé led up the stairs. The hallways would be crowded, leaving no room for flight. She decided to try the outdoor route and flew back out to the balcony and up to the next story.

The night was already black as tar, with scatterings of stars and a slim arc of moon. Her wings were slow and silent as she looked in each window, pausing to let the air carry the scents to her nose. The small amount of light from downstairs aided her night vision and helped her discern any shapes in the rooms.

She found Eric inside the fourth arch. He appeared to be alone and kept peering out the door, then pacing back and forth. She hovered over the small balcony outside the arch, wondering how to get into the room with him. The doorway looked small, and it would be an awkward entrance from the round, stone-walled terrace. He could easily run into the hallway, and escape down the stairs.

Lisette perched upon the wall outside and raised one of her talons. Tapping on the stone, she mimicked what she had heard Mercedes do that night on the balcony.

Tap. Tap-tap-tap. Eric turned and looked but stood still.

Tap. Tap-tap-tap. He moved toward the archway.

Tap. Tap-tap-tap. He moved closer.

"Mercedes?" he whispered, venturing a few steps outside.

It was an awkward position, but she reached down and wrapped her talons around his head. The intensity of his cry pierced her ears. Still, she held on and lifted him.

As she flew into the great hall, two women were screaming and wailing. One of them was Mercedes. Lisette flew toward her, Eric still dangling and screeching from her grip. His hands were around her claws, trying to avoid having his head separated from his shoulders.

The smell of ashes and death and burning bodies assaulted her. It was an acrid scene of carnage, lit now only by the fire in the open fireplace in one corner and the count's flaming corpse in another.

Rocco was still in the room, hovering above it all. She could only guess he was waiting for her. Mercedes knelt at the edge of her father's burning body, screaming. Eric was getting too awkward, so she landed and placed him on the floor in order to impale him properly with her claws. As she did, she was aware of a clanging and thumping on her front leg.

Eric had reached his dagger and was attempting to strike her. Her feathers puffed against each hew of the blade, knocking off bits and pieces of it as he struck. He looked at his mangled weapon, aghast, and hit his knees.

"Lisette, I'm so sorry—don't kill me, I'm so sorry." His voice was an octave higher than normal and accompanied by much slobbering and tears.

As she reached for him, a man ran between them, holding a shield and a sword. It was Eric's father. Lisette had no quarrel with him and reared back to keep from destroying him instantly. It was gallant for him to try to save his son. Gallant, but in typical d'Auguste fashion, not smart. He charged at her with his broadsword.

Before he could strike, she brushed him aside with one swipe of her foot.

He slid across the floor and banged into the wall. She turned her attention to Eric, who was still groveling for her forgiveness. Her paw wrapped around his chest, while her talons sank through his middle. The scream that had begun when she reached for him cut off in mid-strength and he twitched his last breaths as she pushed him from her claws. With one belch of fire, he was gone.

Mercedes shrieked and ran toward his burning body but stopped short when Lisette turned to look at her. Backing slowly, Mercedes screamed something unintelligible before turning and running. Before Lisette could give chase, but someone else had stopped the hysterical bride. The Countess de Medina, her own stepmother was pushing her into Lisette's path.

"Take her, Satan!" Her voice was the screech of a mad priestess. The powder on her face streaked down her neck to her stained gown, and her hair stood out, bristling and wild. "She's the one you want! She's the daughter of that wretched wench!"

Lisette rose up and flew toward her, only to be knocked sideways. Rocco had come to battle for Tempest's daughter. From the screams of the countess and Mercedes to the wails of the senior d'Augustes, a cacophony echoed around the room.

Bouncing off the wall, Lisette backed around Rocco, and slipped from his grasp. Mercedes was again trying to escape the room, but as she got to the door, Lisette managed to grip one of her legs and throw her across the floor. Her claws tore at the girl, and she squealed, causing Rocco to fly to Lisette and sink his teeth into her shoulder.

She roared and batted him with her talons, shaking him loose. He flew to the countess again, claws out, grasping at the mad woman. Mercedes ran behind her stepmother, and they fought, each attempting to shove the other into Rocco's jaws.

Rocco bore down on them with such intense focus, he didn't see Lisette until she swooped underneath and pulled the countess down in order to get to Mercedes. He pushed Lisette to the floor and grabbed at the countess who somehow escaped his talons.

Staggering up, Lisette found Mercedes racing to the balcony. She flew across the room, tracking her, single-minded in her bloodlust. She was almost to the door, but Lisette reached it first, blocking her way and pushing her into a corner.

A searing pain shot through Lisette's side. Eric's father had grabbed the hilt of the dagger still embedded in her flesh, and was turning it, digging it as far as it might reach. Blood was running freely from the wound. Lisette curled away from him, bumping Mercedes into the wall, pushing against her as she tried to rid herself of this persecutor. He was at her flank, out of range of her legs.

"Kill it!" Mercedes had maneuvered around Lisette's legs and joined Eric's father. She took his broadsword and slashed at the dragon. When contact with Lisette's body broke the sword in half, she threw it aside and reached for the dagger's hilt, to help her father-in-law twist the knife further.

Lisette roared in pain and thrashed, attempting to free herself from this pair of demons. Her wings could not unfold so close to the wall, and she had nowhere to go if she could not go up. Anger boiled into red-hot fury, and she swung her tail and belched fire. Still, they dug into her.

A pair of dark red claws reached around her enemies' legs and lifted them away. Rocco tossed Mercedes to the side while he dragged d'Auguste off. Their dragon eyes met, and he bowed his head. There was no dragon-speak between them, but she understood. Mercedes was hers.

Ignoring her pain, Lisette leaped from the corner, reaching to grab her nemesis, but Mercedes was gone. Lisette found her running across the balcony toward the stairs. Taking flight, she managed to turn Mercedes back inside.

Rocco greeted Mercedes at the door. She spurted left, running from both dragons. Lisette was desperate to be done with this task. She had dreamed of catching Mercedes, holding her, crushing the life from her bones. Now, as long as she was dead, Lisette didn't care how. Arching upward, she built the fire in her chest, and dove at her prey.

Opening her mouth, Lisette rained hellfire upon her. The flames caught the edge of Mercedes' alabaster gown, and spread upward in a stunning pattern, red and yellow feathers on a white skirt, outlined in charcoal and smoke. Mercedes' screams of terror turned quickly into howls of pain as the fire grabbed at her ankles and crawled up her legs. She ran across the balcony and leapt.

Amid the sound of sizzling fabric and skin, a body thumped, hitting dirt. The screaming died down to moans, and then silence.

A loud pop startled Lisette and she turned. Rocco rose from the floor, a man again. Lisette didn't understand. He looked up at her, still aloft in her dragon body.

"It is over." He held out his hand to her.

She lowered herself to the floor. Folding her dragon wings, she bowed to him.

"Come to me, Lizzie. I'll wait for you—and our child."

He grabbed his side, wincing, and his legs folded, taking him to the ground. A tiny red ribbon ran from his back. The Countess de Medina stood behind him, a bloodied dagger in her hand. She gazed at Lisette, expressionless.

"There now." Her voice was monotone. "That's better."

# 63

In a single movement, Lisette rose, seized the countess, and twisted her head until it was backward before throwing her on the pyre that had once been her husband. Returning to Rocco, she stood over him, unable to cradle him in her arms, or kiss his lips, or beg him to wake. She lay next to him, curling her tail over his body.

There were noises all around, shouting and clanging. The duke had kept the guards at bay this long, but they had now broken down the door and were running toward her. Arrows bounced against her feathers and fell to the floor. There were less than a dozen guards and she rose and spat fire at them.

They kept advancing, breaking their longswords on her. She was impervious to their weapons, but she was tired, and her wound hurt. She swiped at their shields, knocking several of them backward into their compatriots. They sprawled to the floor, and she reached out with her tail to knock a banquet table on its side,

It slid in front of them, where she breathed flames until it blazed. Knotholes from the wood popped up like tiny explosives. Some of them landed on the men, tar making them stick. There were screams coming from behind the curtain of fire she'd built.

She picked Rocco up, gently, in a cradle of her claws, opened her wings, and flew from the castle, keeping her back to the count's men to protect Rocco from further harm. On her way out, she noted Mercedes' path was charred and a pile of alabaster silk lay at the end, still smoking.

As she flew, Lisette searched the port for a ship, but there were none. *L'Implacable* had to be here. The moon was on its way down to the sea and she hunted for a place to land. A handful of guards had escaped the fire storm and, although they could not follow her into the air, were attempting to track her from the ground.

Her strength was waning. She was flying sideways, to keep from using her left wing as much as her right. She managed to reach the shore of a small inlet, surrounded by thicket. It would take some time for the men to break through—if they were even able to follow her across the black sky. She wobbled down to a landing.

Gently, she laid Rocco onto the sand. There was much more blood on him now. Looking down, she discovered that it was coming from her. She stood over him and turned toward the brush, awaiting the guards, preparing to make her final stand.

A rustle in the bushes made her look up. She sat back on her haunches, ready to strike out with talon and fire. A lone figure walked onto the beach—Begum Derya.

In her weakness, her dragon instinct was strong. She growled at her, wrapping her tail around Rocco to protect him. Begum knelt.

"Lisette, it is me, Begum. I want to help Rocco. His men are coming for him. You and I must leave him."

Lisette shook her head and lay down next to him.

Begum circled around her. "You are wounded. If you stay here, Rocco's men will kill you. Do you want Chunk to kill you, then find out who he has killed?"

Lisette looked out to sea. *L'Implacable* had appeared. She was dropping anchor and boats were being lowered.

Begum was beside her, stroking her neck. "Come, Lisette. Let them take care of their Captain. Come back to the *Dişi* with me."

Lisette's side felt like someone had ripped the skin from her ribs and exposed the bone. Bowing to Begum, she growled again, but pushed her body up to semi-standing. The captain motioned toward a thick grove to their right. Lisette crawled away to a hiding place, turning to look at Rocco several times.

It took no time for the boats to reach the shore—and for the remaining guards to reach the boats. Begum stood by her left side, steadying her. They watched the crew of *L'Implacable* take on the count's guards.

It was not much of a battle. Only five of the count's men were there and from the moment Chunk shouted, "No prisoners," they lost their nerve. Two fell to pirate swords and the rest went running.

While most of the pirates were dispatching the guards, Chunk gathered Rocco in his arms and laid him in one of the boats, Poussin helping to staunch the wound. A large sailor joined them, pushing the boat to deeper water, and leaping in, rowing back to the ship. Chunk leaned over Rocco, tending to him. He looked up at Poussin and said something, but Lisette could not hear.

Poussin nodded and smiled.

Lisette watched them until every boat had returned to the ship. Begum remained at her side, examining her wound, and the dagger still lodged in it.

"This is most inconvenient," she said at last. "How are we to get you to my ship, let alone on it?"

Lisette craned her neck, to find the horizon. How much longer until sunrise?

The pain was getting worse and her dragon mind craved rest, even if it was forever. Her human side fought to survive for Rocco and their child. Prayers to the God of her church seemed blasphemous. There was one power who would hear and understand although she didn't know if they ranked high enough to help her.

*Oh, Ancient Ones, Lamya says you control all Magic. I am in need. My task is done, my vengeance is spent. Can you not change me back now? I ask for the child I am carrying. Please.*

Her dragon body could not stand any longer and Lisette collapsed in the brush. Begum was pleading with her to stay alive. She was so tired. The pain increased until the brilliant white light flashed, and she was in Begum's arms, human again.

"They answered me," Lisette told her.

"The sunrise?"

Lisette turned her head. Soft pink light reflected off the morning's low clouds. Smiling, she said, "Never mind."

"What happened?"

"Rocco. He didn't want me to kill Mercedes."

"But your feathers—"

"Only work when I am a dragon. He did this before we had changed." She tried to sit up, winced, and fell back against Begum. "Good thing his aim was poor."

"Rocco knows where to put a blade if he wants you dead. He left the dagger in, to slow the blood flow." Begum tore a section of fabric from her shirt. "Hold onto me and bite on something. This will hurt."

The blood around the wound had dried just enough to make the dagger stick to her robe, which Rocco had stabbed through. Begum yanked the blade from her ribs. Lisette's scream was muffled by her sleeve, which she had pushed into her mouth. Begum pressed fabric into the wound and bound it with her belt.

"Can you walk a little?" she asked.

"If you help me. How far?"

"To the pier."

"That may take a while," Lisette said, her teeth clamped in pain.

Begum stood, helping Lisette up and wrapping her robe around her. She placed her arm around Lisette's back for support. Lisette put her arm across Begum's shoulder, and they staggered out of the brush to the road.

"This is a long walk, even for you," Lisette said. "How did you get here?"

"Trina had a horse waiting for me. As soon as I dismounted, the horse turned and trotted home."

Lisette chuckled and quickly stopped, her side burning. "I guess you should have tied it to something."

They found the road and walked in the brush beside it, preparing at any moment to hide. Her wound was making Lisette weaker, and she leaned on Begum more. They couldn't stop until they were in the dinghy. Lisette was in no mood for talk. If Begum was, she did not say.

The ground rumbled and horses' hooves clopped down the road. They were not moving quickly, but they would overtake the women. Lisette touched Begum's shoulder and she nodded. They walked further into the brush, maintaining their forward movement, and watching for trouble.

Lisette soon detected the creak of a carriage, and a shadow came up behind them. They dropped down, out of sight. Two horses, dark in the dim morning, but familiar to Lisette walked along, their harness jingling. A lone driver was on the seat, looking on both sides of the road, whispering, "M'lady? Mistress Tempest?"

Lisette held up her hand as Begum braced her to standing. "I'm here, Jack."

He smiled. "Ah, there you are. Me 'n' Clay was worried, so we figured we'd stick round, if you needed help. Then all hell broke loose. We been looking for you since."

"Thank you, Jack." Her eyes were glassy with tears. "Could my friend and I get a ride to the pier?"

"Right away. Hop in."

As Begum helped her into the carriage, Clay saw the blood, now drenching the side of her robe. "You been hurt!"

This aroused Jack's concern and they both left their positions to fuss over her. Lisette waved her hands at them.

"It will be fine. Just get me to the pier. That's where the doctor is."

The men returned to their posts and Jack snapped the horses to a healthy trot. The sun had barely cleared the horizon when they arrived at the dock. Clay insisted on helping Begum out of the carriage while Jack carried Lisette to the dinghy.

"Thank you, gentlemen. You have more than fulfilled your contract with me."

"It's been a pleasure," Jack said, while Clay grinned and bowed. "Take care, now, m'lady. Good health to you. If you'll excuse us, Nan's invited us to the house. Says she's got business to discuss."

Lisette smiled, confident that Nan would do right by these men.

Begum hopped in the dinghy, took the oars, and rowed. Lisette sat and looked back at the island. Eric and Mercedes were dead and yet she was not at ease. Her thirst for revenge was sated. Why didn't she feel free? She felt worse than when she was filled with hate and anger.

"Did Genevieve get on board?"

"Yes. We will find her passage to France. Her husband is there."

"Good." Lisette rolled to her right side, holding her left.

"You will wonder what to do now." Begum's voice was soft, her accent lulling. "You may even be sad, depressed that it is over and so quick after such a long time of searching and planning."

Lisette nodded.

"The first thing I suggest is that you cry. Not being able to cry was the most difficult for me. Crying will relieve the residual anger. After you cry, you should sleep. You have not truly slept at night for a long time."

They reached the ship and the crew dropped lines, lifting the dinghy. Begum patted her hand. "You will have my quarters for a little while. Oleta will tend to your wound. As before, you must mend."

Grateful and speechless, Lisette smiled, her face wet with tears.

## 64

Familiar faces, including Genevieve, greeted Lisette once she boarded the ship. Her heart lightened at the maid's affections, but she was glad when Captain Derya gave the orders to raise the anchor and let out the sails.

"Ruhee," the captain called out to the young girl who had helped Lisette long ago. "Please escort Lizzie to my cabin and make her comfortable."

Ruhee helped her down the steps to the cabin. Oleta waited for them with plenty of orders once they opened the door.

"Help her to the bed. Now, spread these sheets around her. Lizzie, stay on your right side. I must have access to the wound. Ruhee, get me plenty of rum and clean rags." She leaned over Lisette. "This is going to hurt, but I have to stitch you back together."

Soon, Ruhee was sitting by Lisette's head, pouring spoons full of rum into her while Oleta used the liquor to clean the wound. When she wasn't drinking, Lisette bit down on the sheets while Oleta cleaned and stitched.

Once she had completed her task, Oleta leaned over Lisette, stroking the hair away from her face. "You should sleep now. It will all be well."

Ruhee helped her into the silk pajamas the captain had left, then made certain she was comfortably bedded down. Before leaving, she told her, "Whenever you need something, I will be outside."

Lisette reached across to the table and dragged her robe into bed. Clutching it as a baby might cling to a blanket, she dug her emerald from the pocket. She fastened it around her neck and collapsed back into the pillows, weeping for everything she had lost.

Each memory of Mama instructing her on ladylike behavior, each image of Papa sitting at the table looking strong and handsome, each remembrance of Jules and their pretend-dueling, brought on a new wave of sobs. She cried over Tatie Elena's death, accepting the extent of her own guilt. She even shed tears for the old Lisette, a good little girl who had never killed anyone, or had raucous sex with a pirate.

Rocco. The tears Lisette shed for him were a mixture of love and loss and anger and yearning.

Her hand drifted to her stomach again, questioning. Was she really with child, or had it all been a dream? What kind of child would result from two blood dragons? Fortunately, the rhythmic sway of the *Dişi Aslan* under sail was a powerful sedative. Soon she was asleep and contemplating nothing but dreaming of everything.

First, she dreamed of little Alara, who led her through the rooms of her old home on Île des Oiseaux. She disappeared and Lisette was back on *L'Implacable,* in Rocco's cabin. She looked all around the room, but she couldn't find him. She was feverish and thrashed about on his bed. Chunk was there, as was Poussin. She awoke with a start.

Her wound turned out to look and feel worse than it was. By the second day, she was able to walk about the ship, although she used a cane for support.

It was late afternoon on the seventh day at sea when Lisette strolled the deck without her cane for the first time. Captain Derya was at the helm, so she made her way up to her.

Begum smiled. "You look almost as good as new."

"I feel…better. It's time to resume my life."

"And where will this life take you?"

"I made a promise to reclaim my island for France," she said at last. "But now I'm not certain. I'm no ruler. I'd rather give the island to the natives who lived there first. What I really long for is a life at sea."

"The sea will always welcome you back." Begum smiled and attended to the wheel.

Lisette remained beside her, watching the sun dip into the ocean, rings of sunshine splaying outward like ripples in a pool. It was hypnotic.

Once again, a small girl tugged at Lisette's sleeve. "Mama! Mama!"

She looked down. "What, Alara?"

"You must prepare. You fly again. Right now."

Startled, Lisette looked around. Captain Derya was steering, looking at the horizon. Clearly, she had not seen Lisette's daughter or overheard the conversation. Still, Lisette could sense the familiar burning. She quickly took off her emerald and handed it to the captain.

"Take this and keep it for me. I'm going to change, but I don't understand why."

Begum turned to the few crewmembers on deck. "Do not be alarmed. This is a drill from our old days. Everyone below deck *right now*."

The crew obeyed although a few faces were questioning. The last woman had disappeared when Lisette felt the familiar flash. She glanced at her dragon body wondering why the curse was not broken and to her surprise she was no longer a black dragon.

Her feathers were now white with blue tips.

She looked at Begum, wishing she could ask what was happening. Begum's face showed her own confusion. Lisette bowed and pushed off, heading toward the clouds.

There was no island close enough to land on before morning, but she could fly all night and return to the ship before dawn. She flapped her wings gently, found an air current, and glided along, listening to the sounds of the night.

This was always the best part of being a dragon. Flying 'tween earth and sky, letting her mind travel where it would, enjoying the breeze combing through her feathers.

She sailed upon the current for some time before she decided to circle back and make certain she could find the ship. Lowering her right wing, she banked, to leave the airstream. The wind fought her attempt and kept her where she was, not allowing her to steer. She sat back and flapped her wings, trying to at least stop going forward, but to no avail.

She had heard of riptides that can trap a swimmer and pull them out to sea, but she had no idea there were air currents that could do the same. How long would she be caught here?

There was no choice but to let it take her where it would. She traveled for an endless amount of time and covered many leagues. Her body was exhausted from remaining balanced in the wind as well as fighting the current and losing. At the point of collapsing, she spied something that filled her with terror—the sunrise. When she changed, she would fall to her death.

*After all my fighting to survive. A sad end to a tragic story.*

Still, she fought. She had to survive for Rocco and for their child.

She folded her wings and sat back, intending to drop into the sea, hoping it did not kill her. Instead, the current carried her downward, lowering her to a more manageable height. She would not die from the fall although she wasn't certain of long-term survival in the middle of the ocean.

Until she saw the sailboat. All alone, a small boat with a single sail, floating as if moored at the end of this wind, waiting for her. The sunrise burst over the horizon, and she popped into human form, dropping gently into the water. The boat maneuvered beside her, and an oar reached out.

Lisette pulled herself up and flopped into the boat. Her savior was an old fat-cheeked woman who sat at the tiller, wearing a cotton dress and a multi-colored scarf tied around her hair. Her dark skin was ashy and wrinkled.

"Good morning, Lisette," her familiar voice purred.

Lisette could hardly believe her ears. "You sound like…Lamya?"

The woman tossed her head and cackled. "Yes, it is me."

"Forgive me, but you don't look quite like yourself."

"Don't be silly. I always look like what is needed." She adjusted the small sail to head northwest. "When you saw me before, you needed a warrior, to teach you to be strong."

"What do I need now?"

She grinned. "A special Mamha for a special mother-to-be and her even more special daughter."

"Why am I still turning into a dragon? Why do I have white feathers now? What will be so special about my daughter?"

"So many questions. Let us take this more slowly. We have seven months, after all."

She shifted the tiller, and the sail came through to the port side. The morning sun struck Lisette's eyes with such intensity, she had to shield her face. It was warm and wonderful on her skin.

"I believed my task was finished. My foes were vanquished, were they not?"

"Hmm, finishing the task of vengeance can be an ambiguous chore. But yes, I do think your heart has been cleansed of its desire for revenge."

"So, why—"

"It is enough for you to know that you are no longer a blood dragon, you are a moon dragon. You will serve a different purpose now, one that includes being mother to the child of two blood dragons. Does that feed your curiosity enough to calm you?"

"Not enough." Lisette reclined against the bow. "But I know you will give me more answers when it is time."

Lamya threw a piece of cloth at her, a sack-like cotton dress, unlike the more form-fitting bodice and skirt she wore. "You might want to change clothes. This is more appropriate to where we are going and what we are doing."

She took off her wet clothes, quietly happy for the extra fabric that did not bind her. "Lamya, did the Ancient Ones hear my prayer?"

"Ancient Ones do not usually attend to the wishes of humans." She gave her a cross look and turned her attention to the rudder. "But yes," she whispered. "I heard."

Lisette listened to the lap of water against the boat. With the cool wind blowing across her and the warm sun shining down, she ran her fingers through her wet hair, spreading and fluffing it to dry. She soon relaxed and closed her eyes. Rocco's countenance appeared in her mind, his blue eyes searching hers, his arms enfolding her. She wanted Alara to know her father. She needed him to know his daughter.

"I saw Chunk put Rocco in the boat," Lisette said. "I thought he looked…Chunk smiled…Is Rocco alive?"

Lamya stood and fluffed her pillow, her once-muscular arms now wrinkled and flaccid. She propped it against the back of her seat, where she scooted and rolled her hips around, trying to find a comfortable spot.

"We will discuss Rocco tomorrow. But yes, he lives. Now, good night."

Lisette closed her eyes. As impatient as she was, Lamya's dulcet voice gave her hope that she would be with Rocco again. She let the water lull her into slumber. This time, she would welcome her daughter into her dreams. There were adventures to plan.

# THE END...for now

# But what happens next?

*Lisette's story continues in Book 2 of Dragon Shadows, MOON DRAGON FALLING.*

*Here is a brief excerpt:*

"You must finish the coconut milk," Lamya said. "You will need it for your journey."

"What journey? Are we climbing the Dragon's Breath again?"

Lamya laughed. "No, you have already been on the journey of being a dragon. I speak of your journey to motherhood."

"Oh, that." Lisette shrugged. "Women have been having babies for a long time. It happens whether you are ready or not."

"It is true, the physical act is the same as of old, but your path to motherhood is different. One is your transformation to moon dragon. Unlike your blood dragon curse, being a moon dragon is a gift, one that you can call upon. I must teach you how to ask."

Lisette frowned. "If I only change when I ask, why did I change on Begum's ship?"

"Hmm…" Lamya drew circles in the sand. "Let us say, I required your presence on the island, and Alara helped me in this manner."

"I don't know that I like having my child in control of my body."

Lamya gazed at her drawings. "It was necessary."

"I'm still not happy about it," Lisette said. "So, what do you want of me now?"

"You must be prepared for your child. She has already shown herself to be a force."

"What kind of child—or dragon—will she be?"

Lamya was silent for some time. At last, she

muttered, "I do not know. We have never encountered a child born of two blood dragons. Alara will be a surprise to all."

"But I thought…" Lisette searched for the words. "You are an Ancient One. I assumed that means all knowing."

"We know much, but we are not gods." Lamya brushed at the sand on her toes. "Do no worrying. Even not knowing what she is, I have the wisdom to help you."

Lisette's shoulders slumped. "I should have been more careful. I was such an arrogant child, so full of myself. This is the price I pay, to tread this unwanted road."

"It may not be the path you planned, but it is the path you chose."

"If I hadn't been kidnapped, none of this would have happened." Lisette hurled her empty bowl at the sand. "Before that, I wanted—what? Nothing, except to live the life I was born to."

Lamya's face remained calm, her eyes soft. "Every day of your life, you have chosen what you wanted. That you do not admit your own desires does not make them go away."

"How did I desire this?" She pointed to her stomach.

The Ancient One stood, her lips pursed and her eyes boring icily into Lisette's. Straightening, she stretched to a height her unbent crone-body should never reach. As she continued to grow taller, Lisette's eyes widened. Lamya kept rising, expanding until she assumed her true form as an Ancient One. Gnarled as a tree, gray as granite, with hair of wild grasses and large eyes of sea foam, she was wondrous but terrifying. All of earth and sky were revealed in her being.

Lisette trembled, bowing her head in reverence.

"Lift your head and look," Lamya commanded.

Lisette obeyed. The Ancient One splayed her fingers, shooting sparks that formed an image. It was a kind of a map, with a large river that turned this way and that, leaving rills at the turns that fed tributaries, which in turn fed other bodies of water.

"This is your life, Lisette de Lille. It is a river, and each choice you make turns you toward another. You chose your nature from childhood." She pointed to an early winding. "Whether to find happiness in obedience or turn away in rebellion. You chose obedience because it was easy and cost you nothing. The feigning of a good girl, presenting a calm surface, so that underneath the water could rush and whirl, and you could be free to think as you wish."

She went through the map, highlighting Lisette's choices, until she got to Rocco. "Here are several places where you could have stayed on an island and perhaps gotten help to return to your family. Instead, you found your way back to Rocco. And here—did people tell you to get rid of the feather?"

"Just Poussin."

"How many people did you show it to?"

Lisette's eyes lowered. "Only him."

"Yes, because you knew everyone would tell you the same thing. Why did you keep it?"

She had no answer.

Lamya continued. "You chose to lie with Rocco. You chose to believe that you were invincible. Impregnable. The path was there all along. You chose it."

*Want more? You can have it on December 9, 2022 when Book 2 is released in print and ebook.*

# Acknowledgments

I should possibly start by thanking an old boyfriend who introduced me to the fabulousness of used bookstores, where I found a beautiful edition of The Count of Monte Cristo and fell in love. It was that general story that led me to Lisette de Lille's kidnapping, and her pursuit of vengeance. The dragons showed up when I realized I was writing fantasy—one should never squander a fantasy on humans, even if they are pirates.

And I must thank my friend Jeff Michaels for reminding me that the dragons must be there for a reason.

I had TONS of beta readers who gave me great advice—when you have friends willing to read your very large body of work and tell you what works and what doesn't, you listen very closely. Thanks especially to Megan, DeAnna, Claudia, Kat, and of course, Jeff, who helped me strengthen the narrative!

As usual, I owe mountains of gratitude to my editor and friend Jennifer Silva Redmond, who stuck with the story through its iterations and kept encouraging me because she couldn't get the characters out of her head.

And I'll always thank my husband for his patience with my incessant writing and my son for being a sounding board to bounce magical ideas off of. These guys are the air I breathe.

# ABOUT THE AUTHOR

G.S. Carline did not plan on writing a fantasy, but one morning in the shower it occurred to her that there weren't enough girl pirates in literature. She thought she would write a single story, perhaps a novella, about a young woman who has Important Life Goals and instead becomes the terror of the seas…and then the dragons came. The whole thing ended up as a trilogy and here we are.

At the time of this bio, G.S. is living happily with her husband and a Corgi. She also has a son and two horses, all of whom she thoroughly enjoys even if they don't live with her. You can find out more about her by visiting https://gaylecarline.com/

# Did you enjoy the story?

In all honesty, authors are a needy group. We shout our stories into the world, then lean forward and wait for readers to say, "Wow, that was fun-sad-scary-all-the-feels!" When we don't get that, our response depends upon our mettle. If we are insecure and easily dissuaded, we give up on writing and learn to play the ukulele.

If we are stubborn as mules, we will return to our pen and paper, insecurity notwithstanding.

Being stubborn, I shall continue to tell stories whether I have an audience or not, but if you like the tales I weave, this is where I beg you to leave a review.

It does not have to be a big, blathering paragraph of goodness. All you need is a title and a sentence (and throw a few stars at it). For example:

> ★★★★★ **Couldn't put it down**
> I love dragons and pirates and this book had both!

You may leave it on Amazon, or Goodreads, or wherever my books are sold.

Thank you so much. I appreciate you.